CURSE THE FAE

CURSE THE FAE

VICIOUS FAERIES
DARK FABLES WORLD

 3

NATALIA JASTER

Books by Natalia Jaster

VICIOUS FAERIES SERIES

Kiss the Fae (Book 1)

Hunt the Fae (Book 2)

Curse the Fae (Book 3)

Defy the Fae (Book 4)

SELFISH MYTHS SERIES

Touch (Book 1)

Torn (Book 2)

Tempt (Book 3)

Transcend (Book 4)

FOOLISH KINGDOMS SERIES

Trick (Book 1)

Ruin (Book 2)

Burn (Book 3)

Dare (Book 4)

Lie (Book 5)

Dream (Book 6)

Copyright © 2021 Natalia Jaster

All rights reserved
ISBN: 9781957824222

Cover design by Maria Spada
Map design by Noverantale
Typesetting by Roman Jaster
Body text set in Arno Pro by Robert Slimbach

For every book with an enemies-to-lovers trope—
thank you for the obsession

THE SOLITARY DEEP

THE MER CASCADES

THE DRIFT OF SWANS

THE SHIVER OF SHARKS

THE CREEP OF TORTOISES

THE FEVER OF STINGRAYS

THE FAUNA TIDES

N
W   E
S

ELIXIR'S DEN

THE PIT OF VIPERS

Dim the light. Feel the dark. Hold your breath.

DARK FABLES WORLD

THE BASK OF CROCODILES

THE TWISTED CANALS

COVE'S CHAMBER

THE SUNKEN ISLE

THE FOUNTAIN OF TEARS

THE GROTTO THAT WHISPERS

THE KELPIE RAPIDS

THE LILY POND

Drown your soul. Break the spell. Curse your fate.

From the Book of Fables

Deep beneath the water, a Snake bewitched a Viper…

Prologue

It's safe to fall for the hero. But it's deadly to fall for a villain.

Submerged within the space between dreams and nightmares, the division is as clear as water. As a girl, I'd known this. Truly, I heeded this.

If the stars come out, a knight will rescue a maiden, protect her virtue, and bow for a kiss. Yet on darker nights, a serpent will emerge from the depths, a reclusive monster who lurks beneath a rippling surface, his voice penetrating the marrow of her bones.

In dreams, the hero saves the girl.

In nightmares, the villain hisses in her ear, "Fight me."

While one vies for her affection, the other demands her courage. And while one longs to take her hand, the other wants to unravel her mind.

But which choice will she make?

It's forgivable to desire the hero. But it's forbidden to desire the villain.

Swept into fantasies under the cover of night, the differences become warnings, the sum of cautionary tales urging you to *behold* and *beware*. As I grew a little older, I'd also grown to believe this. Obediently, I relied on this.

If the midnight hour is kind, a noble will draw sighs from a virgin's lips. Yet in darker hours, the enemy will twist those sighs into fractured moans, the noises slick on her tongue.

In dreams, the hero coaxes her.

In nightmares, the villain rasps against her mouth, "Stop me."

While one is a refuge from sin, the other is a curse to the body. And while one will caress a female's cheek, the other will thrust and strike her heart.

But what price is she willing to pay?

It's harmless to choose the hero. But it's vicious to choose the villain.

Caught in the midst of slumber, the natures of good and evil are separate, the dividing line a shield against immoral magic. While maturing from a child to a woman, I'd still understood this. Eternally, I trusted this.

If the moon glistens like a white pool in the sky, a prince will light a candle for his lady. Yet from darker corners, a viper will slither into view, his golden eyes cutting through the blackened distance and stoking a fire in her blood.

In dreams, the hero spares the female from drowning in darkness.

In nightmares, the villain sinks with her and murmurs, "Trust me."

While one guards his lady from the murk, the other knows that in darkness, the light must be stronger. And while one will brighten her path, the other will flood the world in shadows for her. And within those depths, he will illuminate her soul.

But how deep is she willing to go?

1

Tonight, I'm being fed to a monster. Humans like me call them Faeries.

But my sisters and I call them many names including abominations, seducers, tormentors, tricksters, villains, and, yes, monsters.

Truthfully, I've forgotten one more: captors.

Midnight bleeds dark teal across this forsaken wild. I stand on a shadowed path beyond The Faerie Triad—the dividing line between my world and theirs, the boundary between my haven and this prison. My arms hang at my sides, listless yet warm from having clasped my siblings in a tight hug only moments ago.

I turn and manage one heavy step in the direction I've been ordered to go, then change my mind. "No," I sob. Whipping around, I leap toward the place where I'd last seen my family. "No, wait!" I beg. "Wait, please!"

Just one more hug. Just one more touch.

Please, please, please!

My prayers echo through the welkin, with no one there to catch them. Desperate, I scan the knots of ash trees for a pair of spruce green eyes or a cloud of white hair, but my sisters are nowhere in sight. Juniper and Lark have vanished into other parts of this terrible place, having passed through my hands like water—brief and preciously irretrievable.

One false step, one accidental trespass into this dark realm, has marked our fates. These monsters have separated us. The ruler of the mountain has claimed Lark, the ruler of the woodland has stolen Juniper, and soon I'll be...

I close my eyes, my wet lashes shuttering.

We belong to *them* now.

I belong to *him*.

I still taste the panicked slipperiness of my words, the salt of my cries just before they were taken from me: *I don't understand. We did nothing wrong. We did nothing wrong!*

But I do understand, and I have done something wrong. I've done something so very wrong, and it's not what my sisters think, and that's why I'm here. Yes, my sisters and I had trespassed into Faerie—forbidden territory to humans. It had been an accident, and now we're paying the price, but it's not the whole story. It's not the real reason he's punishing me.

My eyelids flap open. Tears are nothing to be ashamed of. Some might call it a weakness, but I think it's a sign of bravery. It takes courage to weep publicly, to expose oneself like an open wound, raw and overflowing. I'm not ashamed of crying. I'm strong enough to feel hurt, and I'm courageous enough to feel scared. It reminds me I'm human and alive.

And while I may cry, I won't yield.

"Curse you," I say, in case he hears me.

Ash trees cluster the forest. The boughs shiver, their leaves whispering secrets in the breeze.

Ahead, a spring cleaves across the ground, the water churning like liquid glass. Glowing lanterns flank the eddies, flames licking the air from inside the vessels, their light pulsating through the darkness and stroking the water. Flat rocks tread down the spring's center, marking a path along the serpentine current, which gushes into a tunnel.

Rather than wipe them away, I let the tears dry on their own. I imagine saltwater cutting across my cheeks like old ravines, the grief trailing down my face. Since it's the last emotion I had felt after saying goodbye to my sisters, I'm not about to erase them like some castaway emotion, unexpected and useless.

I'm not Juniper, who's as unyielding as an oak tree. Nor am I Lark, who can smirk or flirt away her demons.

Aside from our father, I'm the only one whom my sisters have ever shed tears in front of.

Who will take care of them now? Who will soothe their wounds? Who will be their haven?

I clutch the gold chain draped across my throat and dangling down my back, the waterdrop pendant resting against my spine. Visions of Juniper and Lark swim through my head. I keep those memories tucked like pearls in the clamshell of my heart.

Within the tunnel, the spring broadens and slides down a precipice. I've received no instructions about where to go from here, but I suppose this is my trajectory. I step one wobbly foot in front of me—just as something slithers through the grass from behind. I pause to register the sound of a figure disturbing the shrubbery, pushing through the underbrush, and prowling in my wake.

My pulse races, pounding like a gong in my temples. I grip the expandable spear buckled at my hip. My thumb pops open the closure that secures the weapon in place. I whirl, jerk the spear's handle to elongate its length, spin the weapon, and impale the ground between me and—nothing.

There's nothing there. I blink at the setting, which is ripe with midnight colors and dense vegetation. Had the noise been real or glamoured?

Hyperawareness bristles the hair along my arms. No, it wasn't glamour. Something is here, and it's close.

A predator? A monster?

One of *them*?

I walk backward for several paces, then pivot on my booted heel and flee toward the tunnel. The flat rocks protruding from the spring are stepping-stones. With the spear armed in my hands, I pad from one rock to the next while yards of shell-white cotton cascade and swish around my limbs, my dress loose and flowing. It's a free-floating garment, if one ignores the billowing sleeves that cuff at the wrists like manacles.

A pair of interlocking serpents is carved above the tunnel's entryway. Below that, tendrils of fog rise from the deluge. I hover at the landing and peer over the side where the current tumbles into a steaming void.

My intakes become shallow. They pump from my lungs and into the mouth of the abyss, the noise magnifying until it clashes it with the torrent.

The pack hanging over my shoulder grows weighty, reminding me of the two leaflets festering inside. My sisters and I had each received the same sets of missives. One had been an order to come here, the other a cruel welcome message upon arriving at The Triad. The inked writing had seeped into my blood, chilling it like a poison.

For your trespass, be our sacrifice—to surrender, to serve, and to satisfy. Under the vicious stars, three sisters must play three games.

Gentle Cove, your task is venomously lethal. Dim the light. Feel the dark. Hold your breath. Drown your soul. Break the spell. Curse your fate.

Welcome to The Solitary Deep.

The Solitary Deep. Home to the water Fae.

The Book of Fables says the underground river lurks far below the earth, but on second thought, something must be amiss. This can't be the main entrance.

Or do they expect me to jump?

Cautiously, I condense and harness the spear to my hip, then bat away shawls of mist. Beyond the vapors, a ramp of steps descends into a black chasm. Fables forgive me, but I shouldn't have worn a frock. Not that I own a pair of practical leggings like Juniper does, but that would have protected my skin from the sharp rocks. And I'm a swimmer, not a skilled climber like Lark, who can scale or descend from any edifice in a skirt.

I lift the dress's hem to mid-thigh, twist the material into a knot, and step into the tunnel. The water surges around my heels and spritzes my boots. I totter down the stairs, where a vessel bobs in a narrow channel.

The boat is slender and long, with a prow and hull that jut upward. I've never seen a transport this shape before, almost like a peapod. I suppose the Folk expect me to guess my way through everything.

Nevertheless, I waver. This arrangement is too easy, too convenient to be trustworthy.

My transport lacks an oar, yet the vessel jolts ahead the instant I settle in with my pack and spear. The boat cruises into a tapered artery enclosed by walls of jagged rocks, the cacophony of the spring fading behind.

That's when true darkness swallows me whole.

A hollow silence follows, broken only by my shallow outtakes and the wet surface lapping at the boat. Perspiration dampens the nape of my neck, beading under the intricate twists of my updo. An errant tendril of hair flutters in my face.

The flow steers me through a series of cramped conduits. I grasp the spear, unable to tell if the water is pulling the boat, or if the boat itself is riding the water.

The crevices of walls glitter in the darkness, the foundations glazed and providing flashes of incandescence. Small recesses appear on the fringes, the niches littered with fish scales and chalky ligaments.

Human bones.

A brittle, horrified sound rips from me as I reel from the sight, my palm shooting to my mouth. The sudden, unhinged movement causes the boat to rock just as it passes once more into in full darkness. I wave a hand in front of my face but can't see anything. My fingers fumble for my spear, but the panicked movements induce the water to move faster.

Or no, it's not me. The current is speeding up on its own.

While the boat rounds a corner, the echo of surging water fills my ears. My vessel skates toward a dripping archway illuminated by a mounted symbol—a glowing viper's head. It brims with faint light, as if marking a point of no return. Beneath it, the channel pours over the edge of an unknown threshold. And wherever it leads, it's deep.

Very deep.

I scream as the boat plunges. Liquid sprays my face and splatters my chest. The flux spills into a vertical dive, dropping like a stone into a bottomless well. Turbulent water floods my ears, drowning out the sounds tearing from my throat.

My left fingers balance the spear while my other hand grips the transport's rim. I fall into nothingness, then the boat slides horizontally and skids across the surface of a new pool, the crash producing a wave that douses me from head to toe. My body's waterlogged, and my joints quake from the impact.

Then I capsize. The nothingness around me whirls, my body flopping upside down like a fish, weightlessness catching me. I clutch the spear while my free limbs pump and kick.

It's as murky as the bottom of an ocean. I have no clue which way is up or down. Fear constricts my lungs, but I can hold my breath.

I can always hold my breath while submerged.

Remembering that, I fight to calm myself and feel the water holding me, supporting me, flowing around me. And I gauge the current, and I grasp where it's going, and I know in which direction to swim. I work myself upward and crash through, my mouth hacking up fluid.

Overhead, a crater digs into the ceiling, starlight poking through to offer a pinch of light. I beat my limbs in place, swimming in the heart of a pool that splits into ducts. Walkways line each tunnel route, the low ceilings encrusted with lichen.

My boat teeters upside down, propped against a wall, where the current zips around the corner. I whip my head toward the decline from which the vessel had tumbled, the bedrock tipped at an angle that reminds me of a chute or waterslide. It had been a long descent, as if I had fallen off the edge of a cliff.

How far down have I gone? How far have I yet to go?

The violent cascade and overturned vessel ensure the pack I'd brought with me is gone, including the supplies Juniper and I had amassed, items for survival and bargaining with the Fae, should the need have arisen. Either the objects have sunk or they're drifting somewhere through these channels.

A blast of light hits my eyes. The blazes flare, lanterns bursting to life around the pool and down the passages. The containers writhe with flames as if announcing—and spotlighting—my presence.

Or the presence of another.

From around the bend, the wet slap of footfalls resounds. I fist my weapon and barely have time to paddle to the boat, where I hide behind its girth. Dunking myself beneath the frame would be better, but no sooner do I reach the vessel than a large body fills the adjacent tunnel to capacity. I peek around the boat.

And I see him.

A water Fae.

The figure is tall, dark, and male. There's no mistaking the shape and size of that chiseled, masculine body. With his back to me, he strides into the vaporous corridor, his gait fluid yet aggressive, like a predator moving effortlessly through liquid. The Fae walks as though he would sooner step on anything that obstructs his path, rather than slip around it.

I hold my breath. Since I know how to do that well, it's my only source of protection, the only way to keep myself from being noticed. Because Faeries possess heightened senses, I can only pray to Fables this creature won't smell me, if not hear me.

An ebony hooded robe hangs off the brackets of his shoulders. As far as I can tell, the front panels are open rather than discreetly cinched. The thin garment puddles to the ground and drags like smoke across the floor, the material as black as eventide. Despite the lanterns, he carries darkness with him, his physique swathed in an utter absence of light.

Another male with hair the color of algae materializes from the sidelines, his form as thin as an eel's. Above the silken pants, his torso is bare, and he balances a halberd in his grip.

Like a guard, he bows to the larger, hooded figure. "Sire."

But the dark Fae doesn't stop, merely stalks past the guard without a response other than a dismissive sweep of fingers, the tips flashing like metallic jewels. For some reason, those digits extend to sketch the nearest wall as he moves.

Sire.

My heartbeat had been slamming into my chest at a rapid tempo, but now it stops. I cling like a barnacle to the boat. From within me, a tsunami breaks loose, blood ravaging my insides.

If he's called *Sire*…and if that means…what I think it means…

Too soon, I expel the breath I'd been holding. Too late, I realize this mistake.

It happens just after the guard vanishes, leaving the cavern empty but for the two of us, which provides more space for sounds to travel, for my mistake to be heard. In spite of the distance, my exhalation takes on greater volume, at least to the preying ears of a villain.

The figure halts midstep.

Although he stops walking, nothing about him signals hesitation. Because the instant he registers the noise, the water Fae moves again. With his hand still extended toward the wall, his knuckles curl as though catching the released breath and then suffocating it. Instead of turning, he lashes his arm toward a trickle of water leaking from the ceiling and dices his fingers through the fluid, his gesture intentional. Then he drops his arm and continues slithering down the cavern while etching the wall, as if he hadn't been interrupted.

That's when the water reacts, the surface agitating around me. And that's when I feel the tug. And that's when the water yanks me back under.

My mouth opens, liquid clogging my throat. The pool becomes a riptide, seizing my limbs and hurling my weight in an unknown direction. With a force of a rapid, it pulls me like detritus and throws me over another unseen precipice.

I fall into a second drop, careening down a slide flanked by rocks. The slide veers into sudden curves, this way and that, so sharp I nearly catapult into the rocks and lose my hold on the spear. The chute barrels into several dips and more twists, my body lashed by the sting of water.

I plow through a curtain of wet plants. At which point, the slide ends, and I soar into the air.

The freefall is quick, my limbs scissoring before I crash. I'm under for only a second before the momentum propels me back up. I've landed in the liquid basin of a modest-sized cavern.

Anxious, I pat around my throat, searching, praying. Relief washes through me when my fingers land on the dainty gold links draped across my neck. By a stroke of fortune, I hadn't lost the necklace.

My spear rides the water several feet away. Desperate, I breaststroke across the distance to catch it, but a ravenous thrust of water gets there first, suctioning the weapon beneath the surface.

"No!" I shout, then dunk myself under.

In contrast to the humidity and tepid water thus far, this pool is so chilled, it leeches every drop of warmth from my bones. My eyes open to scan the depth. The visibility is better here, revealing aquamarine water and rocky projections embroidered in vermillion moss.

My intricate bun has unraveled, the layers plastered to my cheeks. However, the hem of my dress is still knotted, enabling my legs to move freely. I swish about, hunting for a weapon inlaid with iron.

The subterranean colors are as brilliant as gems. They saturate the atmosphere, from the richest green to the brightest blue. I swim into a beam of light piercing from above, which enhances my vision further.

Something slick grazes my heel, a fin passing across my flesh in one clean swoop. I reel backward, dread creeping along my skin. In my world,

I would be excited by such a moment. But in this world, my muscles tense, thoughts of sea creatures from the Book of Fables manifesting in my head.

Fish and mammals with fangs and razor teeth. Fauna that can shift sizes, from diminutive to unearthly.

The current swirls, hinting that whatever's lurking down here isn't alone. There are many of them. And they're circling me, their rotation muddying the otherwise vibrant water.

My gaze jumps from one rock projection to the next, then stalls on a silhouette with a triangular dorsal fin protruding from its spine. From illustrations and oral tales, I recognize the pits of the creature's eyes, the pectoral fins, the gills slitting into its flesh, and the row of carnivorous teeth.

A river shark.

Terror claws through me. Where I'm from, sharks are not of my region, which makes them rare. So very rare.

But in Faerie, what is rare?

What I don't recognize from the Fables is the animal's jade skin and how it glistens with every stroke. That's not a characteristic of a mortal shark. Nor is the way one of them shudders into a larger form, thus doubling its size.

One shark becomes two, two become three, three become four, until a fleet of them ring around me: a shiver of sharks.

The lack of oxygen causes my lungs to singe. I can endure quite a while, but not this long. Nor can I outswim sharks. If I try, they'll cast me as prey.

A Fable floats through my head, one that Juniper had pointed out to me years ago, a tale in which the quarry didn't flee. Instead, it did something outrageous and reckless—and it survived.

This could be the end of me, but what choice do I have?

I paddle gingerly and unlace my boots. They're a hindrance to speed and will prevent me from gliding seamlessly. The shoes plummet, the laces trembling out of sight.

I flex my toes. Then I swim toward the sharks.

Immediately, one of them maneuvers backward, then another follows suit, then another, their ring dissembling. Wonder sparks in my blood. If I don't act like a target, they won't attack!

As the muddied water settles, my eyes stumble across the spear resting on the river floor several leagues away. I swim carefully past the sharks. Once I break through that barrier, hope flares.

Then it dies.

It dies because I've put my back to the sharks.

Dread curdles in my stomach. I vault toward the weapon, snatch it off the floor, and whirl to block the first incoming set of teeth. My spear batters the creature away, though it fails to discourage the rest. I can't move as quickly underwater, and my throat is scalding, and my mind is growing hazy.

A pair of sharks charges. I rotate and jab the spear in their direction, clipping each of them in the sides. And when the spear becomes too heavy to wield, I make a Lark-worthy fist and punch the next predator in the nose.

The shark lurches away, but it's not enough. They keep coming, forming that circle once more and fencing me in.

I clasp the spear, and my limbs beat in place. My head lashes from side to side, searching for an outlet. But then the faintest ripple skids across the water, alerting the sharks to an incoming threat. All at once, they scatter like a school of fish, the largest member quivering to its normal size before disappearing.

Only one thing would cause them to retreat like that. Something stronger and faster.

The water whisks into a frenzy, spiraling like a vortex. The force catches my ankles and thrusts me around. I maintain a death grip on the spear while my free hand gropes for purchase, seeking any stable foundation that will lug me out of the undertow.

This spiral isn't what had alarmed the sharks. No, it's the male figure that swoops past me.

A montage of olive arms and chest shoots across my vision, a whipcord mass of skin and sinew that vanishes before I have a chance to process more. As he loops into the depth, something long and glinting slinks behind him.

I swivel in place, seeing and hearing nothing. Then I feel it. The water convulses in a furious agitation of movement, akin to an incoming wave.

Following the motion, I turn. Just then, an arm thrusts out of nowhere. It happens too quickly, a hand striking the weapon from my grasp. The single backhanded blow catapults the spear from my fingers.

Warmth puddles around me, my bladder emptying. On instinct, I duck to evade my attacker's second strike and barrel toward the sinking weapon. Fables forgive me. I'm terrified of so many things right now, above and below the depth. But if I stop, I'll be paralyzed, and I'll never move another inch again.

My lungs heave, the lack of air charring my insides to cinders. I catch the spear in time—and I shriek as a force yanks me sideways. As though I've been lashed, pain sears across my flesh where the figure had struck. I hit a sandy surface and roll across the river floor. Bubbles spurt from my lips, and my forearm throbs from the assault.

Whatever he'd used, it hadn't been honed enough to pierce my skin. Yet it possesses the velocity and strength to snap bones if I'm not vigilant.

I tumble upright as the monster streaks toward me, shoving the current out of his way. A mane of onyx-black hair dashes around his head, though I can't see his face. I can't distinguish anything beyond those locks, that naked chest tapering arrow-like to an obscure place, and the forked daggers glittering in both of his hands.

I dive to the right. His arm swings, one of the blades shaving the water and narrowly missing my throat. Stabbing the spear into the ground, I use it to propel me in a full circle. After one rotation, my heels ram into his chest, which accomplishes nothing. He might as well be welded from steel. Instead of knocking him off balance, the impact throws me off.

His blades rotate and slice, executing a series of rapid-fire strikes, as if brandished through air rather than water. I thrust the spear, which mercifully blocks his attempts. My arms jellify, my movements slowing as every jab and parry scorches my muscles. The power of his weapon crashing against mine threatens to shatter my joints. Wildly, I envision battling an anaconda of The Southern Seas and fixate on how this moment compares.

Water ruptures around us. The fight continues across the river floor. With each collision, the tips of his fingers spark with a bronze sheen.

At last, the temperature rises, balmy enough to signal shallower ground. Overhead, the surface winks, liquid skimming my scalp.

Not only that, but the monster's movements begin to lag, if only marginally. And I realize why once my eyes leap toward the spear inlaid with iron scrolls.

The iron! Of course!

I catch an opening—a weak spot—and put my very soul into the motion. I ram the spear in his direction, the edge slicing his torso and sketching a red line across the grid of flesh. Thin tendrils of blood spurt into the water. Despite being submerged, I hear a furious hiss reverberate from his tongue.

Before he can retaliate, I launch upward and crash through, emerging in a spot where several retreating steps enable me to stand, the surface licking my ribcage. At the same time, he breaks from the gulf.

A geyser of water spews everywhere. In unison, his daggers and my spear arch, then collide above our heads. The position shoves me into him, our chests dripping. And that's when my gaze collides with a pair of vicious eyes.

2

Gold. So much gold.

The molten color sparks with hatred, penetrating me to the core. It's the color of heat and power. It's the sort of hue that will stop at nothing to disarm a viewer, impossible not to notice and equally impossible to resist.

I've beheld eyes like this before.

It's him. I know it even before glimpsing the rest of his face, with its ruthless inclines. Faint scales trickle from his temples, then loop to his cheekbones and meld into unblemished skin, his bone structure neither refined nor rugged. Rather, his visage is as honed as a blade. It's a venomous, unforgiving face—lethally beautiful, as I'd known he would be.

The Fae's countenance is the sort capable of reflecting only a handful of expressions in totality, including vitriol and disgust. On that score, I'd wager his face exhibits only one of those emotions at a time. Therefore, it does so fully.

My attention stumbles across the furious pulse point at his throat, then to the plate of his chest—slick and hairless—and then below that, under the surface. His abdomen narrows into a V, twin hipbones slicing into his lower half. But where there should be limbs, a tail flits about restlessly, its banded scales glistening like black and gold armor.

It's the appendage of a merman, though it lacks a fin. Instead, the tail embodies the likeness of a viper.

He's more than just a water Fae. He's the monster from my past.

Lord of the Water Faeries. Ruler of the River.

Brows as black as his hair slash at dangerous angles above the Fae's eyes, which burn like one of the underground lanterns. The viper's golden irises skewer my face. Yet he's not looking at me at all. Not directly. Rather, his gaze jumps from one end of me to the next, as if searching or sensing his way through.

He's blind.

Shock courses through me. His blades grate against my spear, and my arms quaver to stave off his weight, our bodies drenched and straining against one another. In my world, tales overflow about this ruler blinding others at close range, but it's not just that. He can't see any more than his victims can.

Confusion loosens my defensive stance. For a moment, I second-guess my memory. Either that, or I've misidentified him.

It can't be. He *cannot* be blind.

Either way, awareness and loathing flash in his pupils. "You," he says.

His baritone is raspy, a voice spawned from fathomless depths—dark, gritty, and suffocating. The word hits like a physical blow, accusatory and punishing. Somehow, he knows it's me. Despite his condition, he knows who I am.

Among my sisters, I'm the sweet one. But I wasn't always like that.

And he knows that, too.

Less than an hour ago, I had cried in my sisters' arms, my voice taking a vulnerable shape, as delicate as porcelain. I was a victim then, but in this moment, something new wrenches free from dormancy, an impulse I haven't felt or expressed in years. That old part of me unleashes, the part that hasn't shown itself since the last time I saw him, the part I've fought so hard to keep buried.

Nonetheless, I let that part rise from the pit of my stomach. I may be his captive, but I won't be his prey.

"Me," I confirm, proudly and defiantly.

The Fae's stifling breath coasts across my skin, leaving a trail of goosebumps in its wake. He had expected my arrival, since he's the one that summoned me here. What he hadn't anticipated was to feel me like this, wet and plastered to him, brandishing a weapon against him, and talking back to him. He may not see my rebellious expression, but he hears it.

In one vengeful swoop, the Fae arches his daggers, trapping my spear within the prongs. I give a cry as he uses the momentum to hurtle me so far backward, my spine smacks into a dirt wall padded in foliage. We'd emerged near a rim without me realizing it. Only a miracle spares me from hitting the edifice and cracking my head open like an oyster.

The serpent lurches forward. His daggers cross over my throat and pin me to the facade. My breasts heave through the drenched fabric of my dress, the swells mashing into his pectorals. I wheeze as he leans into me, cutting off my air supply and rousing angry tears to my eyes.

Tears this monster can't see. Tears he can smell instead.

A malevolent sneer dabs at the corners of his mouth but doesn't fully extend into more. Grinning would mean he's satisfied, which he isn't. He's nowhere near done with me.

Those irises sizzle. Instantly, I understand what he's about to do.

I flail and attempt to puncture him with my spear, but he jerks me in place, crushing me beneath his weapons so that I can't look away. If it were as easy as squeezing one's eyes shut, none of his targets would have suffered this fate. But he's too swift for that, his gaze too fast to dodge. His keen eyes somehow locate mine, then flash like a pair of suns, the gilded rings seeping in like venom. They probe my vision, trying to leach something from it.

Panic churns in my womb. I squint, but it's no use once the light sneaks through the cracks.

Please. Please, don't let him take my sight.

Will I remember the faces of my family? Will I forget the likenesses of water and the animals I've saved?

Whimpers froth up my throat but fail to reach my tongue. A spasm of movement follows. Without warning, the daggers loosen and jolt away. I cough, flooded by relief when the pool swirls back into view, in addition to a set of mercenary eyes.

The water lord glowers in confusion, his errant gaze brewing with menace. I should be sightless like him, but I'm not.

It hadn't worked.

His power doesn't affect me.

3

I register this truth at the same time my captor senses it. Yet my relief is short-lived. His grip on the daggers tightens once more, reinforced by a scorn as deep as an abyss.

He slams me back into the wall. Under the foliage, rocks bite into my shoulder blades, and the waterdrop pendant burrows into my spine. My dress is rucked high as the Fae's vast body sweeps between my legs, splitting them like a trench. The place where his pelvic bones dissolve into a tail grazes my parted thighs.

My right leg bends, and my foot plants on the surface behind me. I feel every feverish inch of him, from the humanlike chest to the slick, unearthly appendage below. He has the toned physique of a swimmer, and his scales are as smooth as the rest of his frame. Nonetheless, I recoil.

Beneath the water, his viper tail bludgeons the pool, whisking up a small maelstrom that travels over the ripples. It reminds me of a distress signal, though no one is around, meaning no one is coming to help me.

Despite his inability to see, the Fae gauges the location of my face. His eyes seize on my features, his pupils reflecting my petrified gaze. His breath is a vapor—misted and likely toxic. "Drop the fucking weapon."

Instead of obeying, I clench the spear in my grip. "No."

That onyx mane slides across the Fae's shoulders as he tilts his head, visibly picking apart my answer. Pointed ears peek from his hair, as tapered as pikes. Then in a single, seamless motion, he drives the crisscrossed dagger handles harder against my throat.

I gag, oxygen and circulation leaching from me, tingles prickling my toes and fingers. The water lord waits for me to expire, his orbs dicing me apart. His visage is equal parts unflappable and invested, detached and savage. For all the gold of him, and for the heat emitting from his body, his soul is as cold as the bottom of the sea.

Either that, or he does see me in a way I can't fathom.

I do my utmost to resist, to the point where his eyes glint with intrigued malice. He must be unaccustomed to humans lasting this long without air. I impress him for a second before my captor's expression turns inconvenienced, and he nudges the daggers even harder against me.

The spear rolls from my digits and splashes beside us. While keeping his vacant irises directed toward me, the Fae frees one of the daggers from my neck and uses it to flick the water, as if he's dealing with a pest.

My spear should be sinking. However, the ripples keep it afloat and ferry the weapon into one of the many nooks digging into the cavern walls, where a thin stream of water leaks through.

Grief and outrage sting my eyes. He might have my throat braced, but he hasn't shackled my voice. "Monster," I spew.

"Mortal," he grates, as if both words are equivalently contemptible.

Maybe this is as close as we'll get to acknowledging who we are to each other.

We pause, our bodies soaking one another. When the serpent leans in, I inhale zestful notes of bergamot and black pepper.

Water swabs my knees, which are still hefted around his waist. "Why am I here?" I ask. "Why did you force me to this place? What do you want from me?"

"Silence," he draws out while grazing his second dagger across my mouth.

My lips tingle, and I quiver at the sensation. He means if I don't hold my tongue, this heartless Fae will take it from me, the way he took my spear, the way he and his brethren took my sisters, and the way he stole my breath moments ago. He will do it expediently and without a shred of remorse.

Truly, I should comply. However, with his body crushed to mine, and with the water lashing around us, I recall the last time we'd been submerged like this—back when his gaze was more lucid but his hatred no less penetrating. Back when I was still capable of doing harsh things just like him.

The very thought unhinges me, causing a reply to vault from my lips. "You haven't changed."

It's the wrong thing to say.

His gaze slits. Some type of private rancor charges across his face and makes the gold flare.

Swiftly, he frees the other dagger. I go as limp as a string, plonking into the water a moment before he snatches my wrist and hauls me across the pool. His tail swats, surging us toward a bank fringed in bulrushes. Kicking him or battling against his grasp is futile. His vicelike grip drags me along, so that I flop about like a netted trout.

Even if I get away, what purpose will it serve? His sinuous bottom half proves I can't outswim this water Fae any more than I could have the sharks.

Something nips at my skin. Several somethings, in fact.

Belatedly, I notice bronze caps covering the tips of his fingers. Ornamented with intricate cut-outs, the tips narrow into spikes that resemble claws. They must be the source of that metallic radiance I'd seen during our skirmish. If I hadn't been busy fighting for my life within minutes of entering this realm, I might have had the sense to perceive them.

The caps pinch my flesh without breaking it. Be that as it may, this ruler could snip my tendons if he so wished. He could exert pressure there, should I give him a reason to do so.

The depth vanishes. As it does, my captor rises from the water, rivulets racing down his arms…and his hips…and his legs. As the air hits his body, fluid drizzles from his skin, and humanlike pair of nude limbs materializes beneath him. They shudder into being with every inch that emerges from the pool.

I have no time to gawk because, at the same time, the sandy floor scrapes my knees. The Fae hoists me to my feet. I stagger atop the embankment, as wobbly as a sailor on dry land, with wet grains sinking like sponges beneath my soles.

The Fae keeps going, striding ahead without preamble. For some peculiar reason, his fingers sweep the air as though he's tracing it. With his free hand, he tows me like a beast of burden and heads into an adjoining passage. Stones replace the sand, flat compared to the crusty ceiling and walls, though still precarious for me. I slip several times, whereas the fiend attached to me stalks forward like a shadow, his form exercising the stealth and grace of someone used to prowling these halls.

I catch a glimpse of naked skin, taut muscles, and the crescent of a sculpted backside. Then I avert my gaze, my cheeks scorching.

I stumble, a mini oath threatening to pop like a bubble from my mouth, although I've never uttered a curse in my life. "I can't walk like this." My lisp echoes through the atmosphere. "I have no shoes. Not anymore, as I've lost them to The Deep, though I wouldn't have taken them off to begin with, except there were sharks, and then you appeared, so I needed the ability to swim. Not that you've asked about my bare feet or that you tend to say much at all, but my point is, whatever I'm here for, whatever you expect of me, I can't do it if I break a bone."

He doesn't answer, nor does he feel obligated to stop. Of course, I hadn't expected a monster to behave like a gentleman, but I'd hoped for a reaction, or at least for him to slow down.

While I've never screamed or raged, I want to yell. Or not yell, precisely. I want to…raise my voice.

I open my mouth. That's when he stops and whips his drenched head over his shoulder. His eyes manage to land on my face, clicking there without having to guess. Although his pupils aren't directly affixed to mine, their affect is the same, producing a lurch in my stomach.

A mute warning contorts his features. I close my mouth, then grunt as he pulls me ahead. On the way, I keep my head high, even while my eyes stray to the rail of his spine and the athletic muscles bunching along his arms. He's not bulky, nor is he remotely thin. Instead, the Fae is sculpted like a statue, like some demonic king of the sea. Also, he's tall like me, though he still towers several inches above my height.

Additional scales protrude from certain joints, including his elbows and ankles. Other than the eyebrows, eyelashes, and hair—which plunges to the base of his spine—the rest of him is as sleek as a swordfish.

At least, from this angle. Since I can't tell what graphic details his front would reveal, my gaze trips to his narrow waist and the contracting swells of his…

I blink away. However unintentional and unseemly, the prospect of viewing the most private areas of his nudity burns my cheeks anew. This has nothing to do with interest. Fae or not, he's a loathsome specimen. He always has been.

Yes, our history is brief. No, we never knew one another's names.

But when I'd said he hadn't changed, I must have hit a nerve.

The thoroughfare multiplies into numerous corridors. For the first time, I notice golden lights radiating naturally from the ground. The floor illuminates conical masts that sprout from the earth and end in points, reminiscent of inverted stalactites. Verdant tufts of grass bloom from the floor and splay from cracks in the walls, the otherworldly greenery requiring no sunlight.

Without halting, the Fae releases me to snatch a pair of leggings off the ground and drive his legs into them, a visibly graphic process that I certainly, absolutely, definitely do *not* peek at. Afterward, he plucks a long, thin swatch of material hanging from one of the inverted stalactites. He maneuvers into the robe but leaves it gaping, then he grabs me and strides ahead. As we continue, the garment's hem slithers around his limbs and slaps his calves, and an equally long hood loops down his back. It's the same mantel I'd seen this villain wearing earlier, when I spied on him crossing into a passage.

He had heard me and known I was there.

For once in my life, I feel the urge to misbehave. The desire to burden him with noise replenishes my voice. "You commanded that water to attack me, didn't you? You knew I was there watching you, but instead of lugging me from the depth like a proper villain, you had the current throw me down that chute, where the sharks waited at the bottom. What other penalties do you have in store? Where are you taking me?"

The viper thrusts the hood over his head and ventures forth. As my limbs skitter around a bush, I struggle to pacify my voice, to mellow it as I do whenever striving to understand someone, to empathize with them, or to placate them.

Always, it has worked. Always, I've cared enough for it to work.

"Please," I hazard. "I don't understand what we've done to you, but it wasn't on purpose. My sisters and I trespassed on your lands to save ourselves, not to defy or insult your kind. Why are you punishing us for that? Have you Faeries no souls? No hearts?"

Again, nothing. He makes not a single, solitary reply.

The Fae stalks around the shrubbery, his open robe sweeping the floor and billowing behind him like a specter's costume. My own frock adheres to my hips and breasts, exhibiting them to the point of obscenity. As a muggy breeze strokes my limbs, I conclude nothing about my disheveled appearance has been left to discretion or the imagination. Without my pack, weapon, and shoes, the only thing separating me from being utterly stripped is my necklace and a filmy layer of cloth.

The passage condenses into a low tunnel, the muffled sounds of activity and rushing water resounding from the opposite side. We cross into darkness, my enemy's head scant inches from reaching the ceiling.

Then we emerge into light. I stumble in place. My mouth hangs ajar, and I feel my eyes widening at the sight before me. An underground water colony materializes, with buildings carved like masonry into the cave walls and more waterways than actual streets.

This must be the hub of The Solitary Deep—its beating heart.

Canals pass under short bridges and in between walkways, the ducts connecting stony lanes or splashing up against the buildings' facades. Seemingly, the only way to access these edifices is with the fleet of long boats coasting across the canals and moored to piers.

The lanky vessels are replicas of the one that had brought me here. Some of them cruise on their own, while others are controlled by Faeries standing at the backs and rowing with upright oars.

Water Faeries. I gulp at the quiet spectacle they make. Without uttering sounds, they coil out of windows, lean across the bridge railings, or bob their heads from the water to observe me. Despite the communal silence, their expressions cut to the quick. In contrast to their flowing tresses and liquid eyes, these Folk appear flinty and as razor sharp as sabers.

Humanlike features mingle with aquatic ones, such as the gills slitting across their necks like incisions, scales glittering around their eyelids, and glorious waterfall curls of cyan and ultramarine. Some have webbed fingers or fanged teeth. Others flaunt the tails and fins of merfolk.

I assume the swimmers are naked. On dry land, the Fae wear diaphanous silks that drizzle from their shoulders and hips or exotic, strappy pieces I've never seen before. The materials stretch and conform to their figures while leaving their limbs bare.

The garments are fluid and elastic. They're easy to remove or swim in. Other than that, I glimpse few accessories apart from my captor's fingercaps.

Aside from the residents with cascading curls, many keep their hair tied up or woven into complex twists and spirals, also practical for the water.

A great hush sweeps through The Deep. Hundreds of faces bank in our direction as their ruler tugs me behind him. They bow their heads in reverence, then scroll their eyes over to me.

I'd read the mountain Fae are lofty and elegant in their craftiness, whereas the forest Fae are rowdy, lusty, and mischievous. Both cultures favor amusement.

As for the river Fae, nothing could be further from that impression. Their spiteful attention bores into me. It's a visceral reception, with little patience for ceremony or diversion.

If not for the ruler clasping me in his grip, they might have leaped on me like piranhas and torn my ligaments to shreds. Their heads turn, following our trajectory over a bridge. They look resentful, confounded, and livid, leveling me with the same scrutiny as the villagers back home whenever receiving offensive news.

It brings to mind the ripple effect emanating from their ruler when he'd realized he couldn't blind me. In response, his tail had thrust about, and the resulting eddies had ridden the pool like a current…like a signal…like a message. This water lord is so mercurial, it's hard to know whether he'd intended it or not. Either way, that's why the Faeries are staring with ravenous fury.

They know. Already, they've learned I'm immune to their ruler's magic, which means I've just made myself into a greater enemy.

My palms perspire. If the hooded Fae carting me off notices, he shows no indication of it.

Impassively, he strides past his subjects. One male with hair the color of a swamp and a torso inked in tar-black markings steps forward with a trident in his hand. "Sire, we heard—"

The ruler strikes out his wrist, issuing a backhanded sweep through the air. At which point, a nearby waterfall takes flight and lashes the male in the face. It's the approximation of a dismissive blow, the water blasting the Fae off his feet. He twists at a severe angle and crashes to the ground.

The Faeries show no adverse reactions. Instead, they gaze at their leader with esteemed admiration and approval, the way followers idolize a paragon.

What vile creatures! I gawk a second before we leave the crumpled male behind, then I swing forward to glare at the ruler's back. "Was that necessary?" I demand, for all the good it does.

The buildings appear to be homes, forges, and merchant establishments with signs peddling opulently carved oars, complex netting, and aquatic weaponry. The edifices are interspersed among cattail ponds and small cascades tumbling down brackets of rock, all presumably originating from the river.

The Solitary Deep is a condensed yet sprawling vignette. The river proper runs through the colony, then splits like veins into outlying caverns and water tunnels. Splashes resound from below, where of long, bottlelike forms hurtle under the surface. I try to make out what sort of fish they are, but they flit by too quickly.

The river glistens the same aquamarine as that shark pool, as though a bucket of paint had spilled and dyed the abyss. Above, teal orbs glow from the ceiling. The river's hue, the rocky domes, and the lanterns hanging from boat prows and lining the walkways converge to set this place alight.

We charge from one lane to the next. With the colony ebbing behind us, the Fae continues to sketch the air with his fingers and tromps across a stone jetty that slopes downward. A guard stands sentinel at the walkway's end—a female armed with a harpoon-shaped lance. She nods sinuously to her leader, not anticipating or needing a response. That's all I have time to notice about her.

Bushels of giant reeds flank an archway behind the guard, then spread and curve on either side like a fence, shrouding whatever lurks beyond. The threshold leads to a massive cave filled with a lake and a grassy isle propped in the center. Stepping-stones rise out of nowhere, enabling us to cross. As we do, the stones sink one by one, as though they were never there.

A rotund dwelling hewn from scabrous rock stands upon the miniature island. Plants resembling wild celery burgeon atop the roof and crawl down the circular foundation.

With a flat palm, my captor punches the front door open and hauls me into the chamber. But instead of locking me in and throwing away the key, he stalks through the entrance. Then he twists, closes the door, and seals us both inside.

4

The door shudders in its frame. Although I don't see a bolt or any other locking mechanism, the partition makes enough of an impact, the great clap of noise resounding in my ears.

My eyes are granted precious seconds to stray. More wild celery-like plants lace the rounded walls, stems germinating from the ceiling and dangling like corded curtains. Several windows cleave through the dwelling, offering a view of the surrounding lake, while small lanterns glow on the sills. A woven rug of seagrass rings around the floor and encompasses a central crater of water, large enough for a person to sink into. The well gargles, as if choking, and tosses erratic strands of light across the chamber.

Although I glimpse a bed, the remaining details escape me due to the masculine figure taking up considerable space. The instant the door stops quavering, the Fae's shoulders flex like the planks of a ship. Then he whips around and stalks toward me.

His robe scrapes the floor, and his hood thrashes around his head, the garment dimming the margins of his face. The split panels reveal his burnished torso and those leggings adhering to his limbs. The closer he gets, the more savage my heart behaves. It slams into my chest like a caged thing, the only part of me that's alive and moving. The rest of me tenses.

He moves like a serpent—one moment bracing, the next striking. There's nothing hesitant about him.

Yet how does he know where I'm standing?

He stops shy of my breasts. That intimidating face slants down, and two rings of gold quest my features, the irises hot enough to cremate someone.

When his attention dips lower, my flesh burns with mortification. I'd been too distracted by the canals, too frazzled by the Faeries, and too repulsed by his fingers around my wrist that I'd forgotten my state of undress. I'd been lugged through the masses while publicly exposed and drenched to the bones, with every swell and curve of my body visible.

But now, with him in this room, it's a hundred times more distressing. I don't have to peek to know my nipples are poking through the dress's fabric, or that my undergarments are discernible down to the ruffled trim, or that the juncture of my thighs is likewise indecently evident. Coupled with my wet hair and unshod toes, I'm an explicit sight.

He shouldn't be able to tell, shouldn't be able to imagine. Yet those eyes kindle with awareness.

I swallow, and his pointed ears tick in the barest of movements. Then he steps forward once more, eviscerating what little distance had remained between us. The prow of his chest bumps into mine, my wet garments rub against his dry ones, and the tips of my breasts toughen.

He must feel them.

I edge backward, and he advances, inch for inch. His slitted features search for mine, his expression hardly amorous or enticed. He's maneuvering me into a corner, but this isn't about touching me or violating my virtue. Too much scorn brims in his pupils for anything else to fit.

How can one's demeanor be both deliberate and mysterious?

I sense myself getting closer to a wall, which can't happen. Before my sisters and I were separated, Juniper had whispered the moral of a Fable to me.

To be still doesn't mean to submit. Therefore, stand your ground amongst them.

I spasm in place. I'm not his property, no matter what he thinks. If I behave otherwise, he'll pounce all the quicker, because that's what Faeries do, Fables forgive them.

He stalls with a displeased gleam. So that's it: He likes to dominate.

We stand a hair's breadth apart while the bubbling basin fills the room with wet noises.

The Fae's voice shreds the air, his intonation low and accented. "Tell me."

"Tell you what?" I blurt out.

"Tell me how you did it."

"Tell you how I did *what*?"

"Tell me how you resisted." His head dips. "And let it be the truth." His orbs trail near my lips. "For if you lie, I will know." Then his gaze lifts. "And I will punish you for it."

From this angle, the scales tracking over his cheekbones appear sharper. His threat resurrects the memory of him attempting to blind me. "I have no idea," I trill. "It just happened. Truly, I had no control. Not that I would have prevented it if I could, as I have no wish to lose my sight, as I'm sure you understand. Otherwise, you wouldn't use that vile magic against innocent mortals who—"

With deadly calm, he sets a finger on my lips. I clam up momentarily as the intricate fingercap presses against me like a talon. His digit is a hot poker sizzling my flesh.

My eyebrows slam together, and exasperation wells in me until I'm overflowing. "Is this—" I jerk my chin, indicating the offensive finger, and speak against it, "—supposed to mean something?"

From beneath the hood, his aspect shimmers with a thousand painful threats. "It means answer me."

"Or?"

"Or be silent. Answer me or be silent. Comply or do not. Both options will suffice."

Because I don't know what to make of that, I furrow my brows. In response, satisfaction filters through his visage, as though he can see me. Not once have his lips twitched in anything remotely close to a grin. In fact, I have misgivings about whether he knows how to smile. All the same, his eyes betray him, revealing gratification. He likes that I'm baffled.

I recognize this trap. Regardless of whether I answer him, it won't serve me well. I'll be giving him an incentive to retaliate, which is what he's after.

Since when does this Fae need an inducement? He's my captor, a viper, and a ruler. Not to mention, I gave him a motive years ago to punish me, long before I'd trespassed into his world with my sisters. He doesn't need another reason.

His hand steals out, though not with the same rapid-fire speed as before. This time, his arms flow like he's swimming, or like he's stirring liquid, or like he's fluidly plucking the strings of an instrument. It's hypnotic and harmonious, the way his digits move. He captures a tendril of my hair and loops the teal lock around one digit, his sharp fingercaps winking as he thumbs the strands in contemplation. I suspect he's less interested in learning the texture of my hair and more preoccupied with how hard he'll need to pull it, to make me wince.

The Fae pauses with my hair shackled between his fingers. "I would not keep me waiting."

I can't take this. "Who are you?"

"You know that already."

"Yes, Ruler of the River and Lord of the Water Fae. But neither of those are your name, and they're not the entirety of you."

"Because you indeed know me."

So, there it is. He remembers me, just as I remember him.

Regardless… "No," I dispute. "I never knew you. Not truly."

"Yet I have not changed," he quotes, hurling my earlier judgment back at me. "Not. At. All."

The contradiction in his tone is unmistakable, the response teeming with malice because, yes, he has changed. Despite the little I know of him, this much is certain: The one secret time I'd encountered this monster, he hadn't been blind.

Moreover, unfounded accusation festers in his reply. That, I can't account for. In our past, I'd done something to this Fae that he likely hasn't forgotten, but it has nothing to do with his impairment. It's about something else entirely, so perhaps he's compiling his anger and looking for any human to resent.

Of all unforgivable reactions, pity leaks into my chest and deviates from everything else I presently feel. Although this monster doesn't deserve compassion, the impulse toward benevolence has been my salvation for such a long time. How ironic that I should experience it with the one being who's ever inspired the opposite in me, the one creature who taught me what it's like to feel absolute hatred.

I thrust up my quavering chin and channel my sisters' bravado. "It's partly true. You're still a monster."

"You are still a mortal," he counters.

Meaning, I'm still the weaker one, especially without my weapon. But what he doesn't know is I have more than one means to protect myself. And I may have been raised in a loving family, but that's not how I began. Before that, I'd survived on my own, with nothing more than ten fingers and a quick sleight of hand. "You may have taken my spear, but I'll get it back."

"Yes, you will try." His rippling accent deepens, submerging me within its confines. "I hope you will try."

What sort of mind game is this? Faeries are riddlers and tricksters, but I can't tell if he's being thus, or if he's in earnest.

We're speaking so closely, and we're pressed even closer together, with his dark form smoldering over my pale one, and his black robe grazing my white dress. The room blurs. His breath clashes with mine to the point where my head fogs, the way it would if I'd swallowed an intoxicant.

So much heat radiates from someone so cold. I wonder if all his body temperature resides in those golden oculi, so laden with color one could drown in them.

I will drown you.

The words from our turbulent past, from so many years ago, come surging to the forefront. Speaking of our mutual history, I muster what remains of my courage. "If you recall, I'm not as frail and defenseless as you think."

The Fae reacts just as he did in the shark pool, when I'd accused him of not changing. He releases my hair and burrows closer, so that it's a miracle I hold myself steady. Then he tips his nose down at me, and his words abrade my skin. "Let me remind you of one vital fact, mortal. In that pool, you were almost torn apart."

"I think not. The sharks became too alarmed by you to bother with me."

"I was not talking about the sharks."

That evokes the vision of his forked daggers. I suppose exercising my tongue during our battle had distracted him and spared me an untimely death at his hands. That is, after he'd realized the impotency of his greatest weapon. "Why did you try to blind me?"

"Why did you resist?" he demands.

At last, we've come full circle, though it's hardly a comfort. I shake my head, unsure of what this creature wants to hear. I'd already told him I don't know how or why I resisted. But if I ever discover the reason, I won't divulge that information. He must be aware of that.

The Fae's wayward gaze hops across my countenance, questing, probing.

My family says I have a gift for empathy. I've never confessed to them it's not a gift. To the contrary, it's my redemption. Yet even with an enemy, the sensitive side of me takes the bait. Maybe it's the way his eyes lurch from one side of me to the other, looking for a place to settle, a place to land.

Again, the raw and inexplicable urge to care worms into my gut. My fingers scale toward his face, about to trace a hazardous path along his eyelids. My voice thins to a whisper. "How did this happen?"

The Fae flinches, sensing my intentions. Surprise crinkles through his eyebrows—then his reptilian reflexes kick into motion. He snatches my wrist and extends my arm out to the side, all the while fixating on the general vicinity of my face.

I gasp as the peak of a fingercap nudges my skin, yet the ornament's tip twitches with sudden indecision. Suspended like this, I wonder how often he experiences such a lapse.

His palm warms the pulse thudding against my flesh, which accelerates the longer he holds me like this. Intimidation and hostility clash. They produce a heady sensation, a disturbing and shameful rush that tightens below my navel. How I wish this feeling would go away.

Notwithstanding, my hatred inspires a bizarre sort of thrill. I can't decide if I want to exercise my pity or unnerve him.

After a moment, his digits snap open to drop my arm. An invisible veil rolls down his face, further shrouded by his hood.

The Fae turns, his robe billowing and tossing shadows across the chamber. He seizes the door handle, his tendons bunching, and glances over his shoulder. His eyes swell with gold—the only bright thing about him. "I shall say this only once," he warns. "Stay in this fucking room."

Then he pounds from the chamber and shuts me inside.

"Fables," I exhale, my breaths ejecting in short bursts.

It doesn't matter if there's no lock on the door. I think about the stepping-stones rising and sinking for him, the guard stationed at the jetty's end, and a legion of Faeries beyond that. Yes, I could slink out and slip into the encircling lake, with the hopes of swimming out of here, provided the water isn't infested with carnivorous sea creatures. Yet if I manage to locate a nearby escape route, there's no guarantee I would survive this environment, its predators, or its residents. I could try finding an outlet despite the hazards, but only to the detriment of my sisters.

I'd been summoned here to play a game, in which not only my life hangs in the balance but theirs as well. Escaping this fate would hurt them.

All of us win—or none of us win.

There's nowhere to flee. I'm marooned on this isle.

My knees quake. I buckle in place and wrap my arms around my stomach.

Tell me how you did it.

His words represent a dreaded truth, one that had dawned while the water Faeries surrounded me, and I'd beheld their vindictive expressions. If I think I've evaded their leader's venom by resisting his magic, I'm wrong.

In fact, I've just made things worse for myself in this dark realm.

I'd rendered his power useless, and he's going to make me pay for that. If he can't penetrate me in one way, he will in others—harsher, more destructive ways that I haven't begun to imagine.

5

A puddle gathers at my feet. I shiver in place, rub my arms, and inspect the room anew. Before arriving here, I had imagined being dunked in a cesspool or shackled in a dank cell littered with fishbones and reeking of mortal corpses.

This setting is an utter departure from what I'd expected. From the window recesses, lanterns fling tints of orange across the surfaces. The water basin froths, tendrils of steam coiling from within like some type of bathing tub. Silken sheets cover the bed, the textiles dyed a variety of blues and whites, from navy to seashell. If I weren't a captive, I would call this space wondrous and tranquil, like something out of a mystical aquarium, where I'm a guest instead of a prisoner.

There may be a guard outside the chamber, but it could be worse. I could be rotting in an oubliette or at the bottom of the river. Why situate me in such a lovely room? Have the Faeries sequestered all their former captives this way? Are there any other humans in this world besides me? What befell the ones who trespassed before my sisters and I did, or the ones lured into this realm by glamour? Are they hurt? Do they need help?

The room swims, upending my balance. I stagger to the bed and sit, the mattress sinking under my backside. Fatigue, hunger, and thirst weigh me down, turning my limbs to putty. No matter the ambience, this room is little more than a luxurious cage. I refuse to trust it.

A picture flashes in my mind of a young male Fae with a pool of black hair floating around his face. I recall that creature flailing and slamming his fist into a plate of glass, trying to break through, to reach me, to catch me.

Until tonight, that had been the only memory we'd shared. It happened nearly a decade ago, during The Trapping. After centuries of torment and misery by the Folk, the people of my village—Reverie Hollow—had waged an attack on Faerie. Specifically, the humans had gone after the Fae fauna, who are the sacred life force of these Solitary lands.

Some of the Folk—including youths—had tried to rescue their animals but ended up slaughtered or captured. The latter had included my captor. At the time, my sisters and I were children, though I've never told them about the brief encounter I'd had with my nemesis.

In the end, the viper had escaped, along with two other captive Fae. Later, that infamous trio became leaders of the Solitary wild in Faerie.

Rulers of the sky, woodland, and river.

The residents of Reverie Hollow had only learned about the river ruler's power in the years following the historic massacre. In the aftermath, the Folk retaliated, glamouring and abusing us worse than before. On that score, people started whispering about the river ruler's ability to blind others.

Since I hadn't been inflicted back then, I had determined the iron weapons—which the mob had used to catch him in the first place—had weakened his abilities. That's why he hadn't been able to blind anyone. Quite simply, the viper hadn't had the strength to.

Yet why am I able to resist his magic now? Why, when no one else can?

And what of his own blindness? When had that happened? What had caused it?

A wardrobe stands across the room. I rise from the mattress to investigate, discovering an assortment of stunning textiles, from caftans to frocks, robes to nightgowns, all paper-thin or woven into diaphanous fabrics. Beaded trimmings. Tasseled closures. Ribbons threaded to form bodices. Flowing skirts that brush the floor and radiate with watery colors.

But Fables help me. The closet lacks undergarments and the clingy, swim-friendly styles I'd noticed several Faeries wearing. My modesty would be so lucky.

I peel off my wet dress and underthings, and shrug into the thickest caftan I can find, which isn't saying much. The short sleeves flutter like fins around my elbows, and the white textile is oversized but finely spun, pouring down my body in waves, as if sewn from the ripples of a spring. I've never worn anything tailored, rich in quality and stitching.

My index finger quivers across the chain resting along my throat. I twist the waterdrop pendant to the front and trace its tear shape. As I do, a sob lodges in my throat, then it catches as the door opens.

Earlier, I hadn't peered closely enough at the female guard. She's bronze-skinned and resembles a woman in her thirtieth year. Her fleshy curves draw warmth to my cheeks. Despite my limited experience, males and females alike have always had this effect on me.

A harpoon lance is affixed diagonally to her spine. Apart from that, she wears tapered, alabaster pants attached to a bodice, the ensemble loose and draping. Silvery blue locks encircle her head. Crystalline scales cap her shoulders, as though they've broken through her skin, and match the hue of her irises.

The guard's sandaled feet barely tap the floor as she sets a platter atop the bedside table, casts me an inquiring glance, and inclines her head before sauntering from the chamber. The stepping-stones leading to the jetty must work for her as well, though I don't have to be a seer to know they won't for me. That is, if I were planning to flee.

I scrutinize the provisions. Only one serpent could have requested sustenance be delivered to me, but I fail to believe it after the things he's done thus far.

Moreover, it's risky to accept food from Faeries. Poison comes to mind, as does a quick and painful death. However, I'm alone, without an audience, and it's too soon for my demise. Otherwise, the river ruler would have killed me several times by now.

Also, I can't starve. The platter is laden with succulent salmon, a pile of coiled shellfish I can't identify, and steamed grains swimming in butter. I pace myself, taking cautious bites before fully succumbing to hunger and wolfing down the fare. The accompanying contents of a goblet revive my blood, the sweetness of crushed white grapes leaking onto my tongue.

While chewing on a morsel of salmon, I comb through my hair, breaking through the knots and then twining the locks into a slouchy but intricate bun. Performing the menial task cinches my heart with wistfulness. Lark has always coveted my ability to plait tresses into elaborate styles without effort. I've tried to teach her, but she doesn't have the patience for it, since her cloud-white hair is even longer than mine and oftentimes unkempt. Juniper, on the other hand, has the patience but lacks the interest. She prefers her spruce green hair out of the way, fixed into tight and practical ponytails.

I falter, realizing my mouth has tilted into a sad smile. But instead of pushing away thoughts of my sisters, I let them in until I'm full to the brim with their laughter and voices. These pieces are all I have left to comfort me, and I won't forsake them.

A tiny splash rings through the chamber. I whirl, my eyes skating to the tub, where a glittering shape filters through the water. After the sharks, I should be wary, except animals have never frightened me as much as Faeries have. Besides, the silhouette jogs my memory, its slithering motions as familiar as the sights and sounds of home.

With a gasp, I hasten across the room and sink to my knees at the tub's rim. "No," I whisper.

Oh, yes. Two vertical irises surface, the yellow rings blasting the room with new color. The snake peeks at me from the deluge. From the eddies, the reptile's neck extends like a tube, the resplendent brown-marble scales gleaming.

Stress cracks through my voice. "Fables forgive me."

It's the male water snake from my family's sanctuary, a creature I'd rescued from trade poachers and became friends with. I'd built a pond at the back of our house for the reptile, but somehow, the animal had crept out of the pool and tracked me here. I have no idea how the wee one had managed this, what with all manner of mystical creatures prowling this land.

"What are you doing here?" My eyes jump from those yellow crescents to the tub. "How did you get here?"

But my companion's forked tongue just vibrates as it swims closer. Not that I had expected it to answer.

There must be a gap in the tub's foundation, some artery that leads to the river, which connects to the streams on the borders of Faerie. I can only guess the snake had trailed me to The Triad, accessed one of the springs, and...

"It was you," I realize. "In the forest, the noise I'd heard before entering the tunnel. Something had been following me. That was you."

The reptile just stares. I shake my head, tenderness and protectiveness welling in me. "Brave little soul."

My index finger strokes the reptile's head, then freezes as the door rattles again. I veer toward the partition, then back to the snake. "Stay here," I urge, then use my palm to shove the creature underwater.

I lurch to my feet and swivel. For the second time, the chamber door groans open. Though now, the curvy guard doesn't bother to step inside. Beneath the lintel, she stalls and announces, "Follow me, human. Your presence is requested."

6

As I rise, I resist the urge to glance at the tub. The female glimpses my bare feet and ticks her gaze toward the wardrobe. Taking the hint, I bustle over to the closet, where two pairs of sandals I hadn't noticed before perch on the bottom rack. The soles are sturdy, but the upper material is some manner of airy textile consisting of thin straps that crisscross and tie at the ankles. They're a far cry from the scuffed leather boots my family wears but more suited to this balmy atmosphere.

The guard clears her throat, pretension dripping off her like syrup. My bookish sister had said to be polite, which is an atrocious irony, but it's also common knowledge regarding the Fae. If I want to survive another hour, delaying is ill-advised.

I bind my feet into the sandals and trail the female out of the room, stiffening as she shuts the door behind us. It will be all right. The Folk have never harmed mortal animals. There are many rules in Faerie, but none against the fauna of my world entering this realm.

Regardless, I doubt these Faeries want their prisoner bringing a companion with her. The snake is safe, so long as no one enters and finds it there.

We cross the stones and jetty. I anticipate a return trip through the canal colony, but instead, my warden ushers me across a walkway and toward a set of descending stairs lined in seagrass.

The guard sidles down the steps, her movements sinuous. "Don't lag, human. You don't want to be left behind, do you? No, I don't think you do."

Her voice oozes like tar—glossy and easy to get stuck in. When she speaks, it's the culmination of a weary sigh and a nefarious taunt.

I cringe at the dark mouth below, then trickle after her. "What…that is to say, where…am I wanted?"

"The Grotto That Whispers."

"That what?"

"I do believe you heard me the first time."

I did, and forgive me, but the name isn't enough to go by. "Why does it whisper?"

"Because it's been destined to share the river's history for centuries. And if you did that for half as long—" she turns and lightly taps my chest, "—you would lose your voice, too." She twists ahead. "The grotto preserves itself, but don't assume you may ask questions. Apart from narrating The Deep's chronology, the grotto only tells you one other thing, and only what it decides, and only what you must know." The female shares this detail breezily, as though she's conveyed it countless times. "In The Deep, it's customary for every mortal sacrifice to have this orientation."

For your trespass, be our sacrifice—to surrender, to serve, and to satisfy.

I recall that part of the welcome note from when I'd stood at The Triad.

The pit sinks beneath the river. As we descend…and descend…and descend…billows echo around us, signaling the river rushing against the walls. Lanterns bloom along the floors, and the same teal orbs glow from the ceiling, just as they do everywhere else.

The serpentine passages glimmer with unknown locations and secrets, the likes of which mortal children would love to explore, whereas mortal adults would cringe. I find myself on the verge of both. This place is as muggy as it is mysterious, the stones more decrepit and ancient down here, tantamount to the ruins of an oceanic castle.

Our footfalls resound down the cavities. The farther we go, the more anxious I become, anticipation scattering from my stomach to my chest. Nonetheless, I lift my chin and marvel that the river ruler would summon me this quickly after ordering me to stay put.

That is, I marvel until the guard corrals me through a spore-riddled archway and into a hollow. At which point, the Fae departs. I wheel toward the exit and back, my throat bobbing. It's the most fathomless place I've ever encountered, sunken to the deepest level at which I've ever stood.

Murals of vegetation, similar to rosemary, cling to the foundations and low canopies, all surrounding a compact well in the ground. The watery depression shimmers like a melted star, filled to the rim with the blue of lapis lazuli, the royal color illuminated from below.

The Grotto That Whispers.

My fingers itch with curiosity. I shuffle closer, kneel, and reach toward the spectral pool. "Majestic."

In answer, words oscillate across the surface. Simultaneously, a faint intonation ripples into the air, as if reading aloud the liquid text. "Historic," the grotto amends.

I pull back as if I've been caught touching what isn't mine. Did the water just talk to me?

But isn't that what it should do, based on its name?

Awe and trepidation overtake me, so that my tongue flops about in my mouth. "I beg your pardon. It's just you're so vivid, though there's very little light down here, and I wasn't expecting nature to have a voice. Or rather, I was but not like this. That isn't to say I doubt what you are. No grottos in my world have your coloring, or if they do, they're located elsewhere in The Dark Fables. Matter of fact, I probably shouldn't have addressed you as *you* since you're not a physical being, and—"

"Come closer, into the light."

"Which light?"

"Whichever one you consider to be light."

All right, so we're doing this. I consider the ceiling orbs and wonder if my own irises have blended in with all this teal, and if I'll become part of the illumination. I settle myself within the spot where the watery sheen and vibrant beams converge.

The grotto appraises my presence. "Hmm," shivers across the water and floats audibly into the atmosphere.

Is that good or bad?

"Here you are," the words fluctuate over the grotto. "One-third of the sisters called upon to play with the Faeries."

Because the guard had said I can't ask questions, I reshape my inquiry into a statement. "I was told you've existed for centuries."

"I'm chronology itself. I'm The Deep's history."

"I was told that, too."

"Yet you haven't been made privy to the particulars. Likewise, you haven't been told one necessary thing, which I have decided upon, and which you must know."

The water falls silent, even while words scrawl across its surface. Sentences wobble and unspool, the lambent strands appearing and dissolving from one set to the next, like liquid calligraphy. Thus, the grotto informs me why I'm here.

It anthologizes The Trapping and how the attack had yielded too many lost animals, and how the creatures' extermination by mortals is leading to the wild's imminent demise, and how the existence of its fauna, flora, and Faeries are in danger of fading as a result, since they can't exist without one another.

Rapt and horrified, I lean nearer. My eyes cling to the water as it delivers my fate with vibrant, fluid strokes. To save the wild from extinction, human sacrifices must be made, not simply by spilling blood or flinging humans over a cliff. Rather, the sacrifices must be executed through games. For every mortal player that loses, one of the lost fauna will be revived in exchange, hence contributing to the land's restoration…its survival.

I feel my complexion turn ashen. Due to the notes my sisters and I had received, I'd known there would be a game for each of us, but now the brutal gist comes to fruition. My presence isn't merely intended for amusement or punishment for trespassing. It's meant for something more crucial.

The Faeries have until the thirteenth year to complete the sacrifices and bring life back to this world. Otherwise, the mountain, forest, and deep will perish. Since it's been nine years since The Trapping, the gradual decimation has already started, and while four more years may seem long, it's scarcely any time for immortals trying to save their world.

My stomach heaves, disgust clashing with a streak of sympathy. While I refuse to condemn my village for defending itself, nor do I spurn the Folk's desire to safeguard their existence. I can't muster a proper response other than, "I didn't know."

As additional words scroll across the grotto, its faint whisper resumes. "Were you supposed to?"

My lips twitch with something close to a lie. "I didn't engage in The Trapping."

"I never said you did. Granted, while I know The Deep's timeline as it happens, what occurs elsewhere is out of bounds for me. Though naturally, you're innocent. What child would take part in such a massacre?"

I swallow my guilt. "The Fables say nothing of the wild's fatal vulnerabilities, but I'm sure those narratives don't cover everything, which means my people have little to go by in the grand scheme of things, and I'm guessing that's how you want it. I mean, I *imagine* that's how you want it, which wouldn't be out of the ordinary, unless I'm mistaken."

The water goes smooth for a moment before fluttering, "You talk a great deal."

"Not on purpose. My family says I can be dramatic and antsy, so whenever that happens, my mouth gets cluttered."

"Quite," the grotto agrees. "Your tone has a soft transparency to it. As do the tempo of your pulse, the temperature in your cheeks, and the brightness of your eyes. Such a vivid teal, such a saturated blush, such an earnest heartbeat, and such a rambling mind could either work to your benefit or get you into trouble with the river ruler. It depends on whether you apply defiance or kindness to these facets. Both are your strengths, though one is greater than the other. It's up to you to fathom which. Let this be my first piece of advice."

"What will this advice cost?" I question, rather ungratefully. Not that I'll apologize. The Fables tell mortals to be wary of favors freely given here, since they're never truly free.

The grotto emanates a dignified sort of sheen. "Cost," it spells out. "Nonsense. I don't dabble in bargains. To that end, few water Faeries do. That is left to the lofty mountain residents and spritely woodland Folk, whereas river dwellers strike without ceremony. Consider this my second piece of advice. It's what I've decided you must know."

I frown. That's two bits of customized knowledge, not one. But maybe tidbits are counted differently in Faerie. Or maybe this is deception.

Although I have an aversion to confrontation, I must be hitting my threshold for civility. After a battle with sharks and being nearly strangled by an odious water lord, I find myself growing angrier and bolder by the second.

I cross my arms. "Forgive me if I don't trust the advice of a hole in the ground."

"So, you have a combative tongue, after all. That's new. I had expected to be dealing with another mortal guppy instead of a stingray."

"I'm neither. I'm a mortal woman, three months shy of my twentieth year and wise enough to dispute the words of an enemy. For one, I don't understand how the loss of fauna contributes to this realm fading. Animals die and get born all the time, in each of our worlds. It's a cycle, so how does losing any of them destroy your land?"

"It's the way they died—at the hands of outsiders, those who have no Fae blood. The fauna were taken from this land. They were stolen by humans rather than perishing naturally. That disrupts our life force."

I think about the animals and Fae who had suffered in The Trapping, as well as the humans who'd endured eons of wretched treatment by the Folk. Those villagers saw no other resort for protecting themselves.

Silence encourages others to keep talking. I bite my tongue and wait.

It doesn't take long. The grotto says, "As to what particular game you're to play, that's for Elixir to impart."

"Elixir," I repeat. "That's the river ruler's name?"

Of all the hypocritical monikers to choose. An elixir is a remedy, a means of healing, whereas everything that viper represents is corrosive and deadly. Truly, is he being sarcastic?

I taste the brine of his name, each syllable pinching my tongue. I make no effort to hide my repugnance. Whether the grotto notices, I have no clue.

"In the mountain, tradition decides the game's precedent and rules," the water continues. "In the forest, the woodland itself chooses. Here in the river, its leader bears that responsibility."

The muffled thrust of water resounds against the walls. A bead of condensation worms down my spine. "Your ruler confiscated my spear. I want it back."

"Then get it back," the grotto says without a shred of interest.

"I will, if you tell me where to find it."

"Mortal, when I said you have strength in defiance, I didn't mean you should apply it by driving a weapon through Elixir's heart. If that comes to pass, you will lose the game and endure the wrath of his subjects. Likewise, my own."

"He dumped me into a shark-infested pool."

"It's called The Shiver of Sharks. Many territories in the Solitary wild are named after the resident fauna or have sacred titles, such as The Twisted Canals, which is the hub of this realm, where the bridges and residences intersect. You saw it when the water lord hauled you through that area upon arrival, then led you to The Sunken Isle, where you're a guest."

"A prisoner," I correct.

"The isle's name comes from an event centuries ago, when the landmass sank beneath the ground. The surrounding lake has maintained that sinking effect ever since. Faeries have the vigor to swim through, but any mortal who tries will flounder just as the island once did. The water will pull them down."

I will drown you.

I shove away the memory. "We're digressing. When using me for shark feed didn't go to plan, your ruler tried to suffocate me."

"He's overly ambitious, a trait which your presence seems to have intensified."

"Then he tried to blind me."

"Yet he failed," the grotto dismisses. "Elixir is intentional. Nevertheless, that was a self-defensive reflex, a lifelong habit. Thankfully, the shock of his failure brought Elixir to his senses, enough for him to remember the impending game. He won't attempt to maim you again, so long as you play. Your point?"

"I can't play if I have no means to protect myself. Even if Elixir doesn't pose another physical threat, the water Fae do."

"They would never disobey his rule, however much they'd enjoy tearing you to ribbons for besting him today. They might engage in glamour and tricks that could result in a measly cut or two, or a depletion of your dignity, but that's hardly cause to wield a spear."

A measly cut or two. The depletion of my dignity.

Evidently, the grotto's being serious. "What about the fauna?"

I'm not as well-versed on the mystical animals of Faerie as Juniper, but if they're anything like mortal animals, some will be tame, and some won't. Beyond that, I'll have more than fangs and claws to contend with, if the Fables are correct. The predators of this realm have powers and strengths that I'll need to arm myself against.

"The spear is your concern," the grotto maintains. "I'm The Deep's history, not your mentor. This orientation is concluded. Now if I were you, I would make haste. As of three minutes ago, you were already late."

"Late? The ruler's expecting me?" I balk. "You mean to say, I've kept him waiting?"

I don't care a fig about Elixir's precious time or causing him offense. Nevertheless, it isn't in my favor to vex him further, however much I relish the thought.

"Waiting," the water echoes, the words lifting visibly to the surface and floating audibly through the air. "Elixir waits for no one. If you had kept him even close to waiting—"

"I would have come and snatched you," a masculine voice says.

I swerve from the ripples to the hooded figure looming in the doorway. Or rather, no. The lord of the water Fae isn't looming.

He's striding toward me.

7

I tense. The sandal straps constrict around my ankles, and my hand twitches toward my hip, searching inherently for a spear that isn't there.

The river ruler—Elixir—approaches without pause to consider where I'm standing. Even in the most cramped of environments, he somehow knows where to find me. A shaft of light from one of the ceiling globes splatters his chest with teal, marking a target straight to his evil heart. If I had my weapon, I might be tempted to run him through.

Like a reaper's garb, his robe slumps open, and his leggings cling to his thighs and calves. The mantle's wide hood flops around Elixir's face and conceals expression, so that only his irises are visible. They pierce through, incinerating everything in their path like a pair of suns.

He glances toward the rippling water, then swats his gaze my way. "Follow me."

He pivots and stalks from the grotto. I trail after the Fae who surges in and out of the shadows, his robe buffeting his limbs. Lanterns crackle and paint the ground in orange. Elixir navigates the network of tunnels while holding out his fingers, extending them to the side and letting them glide along the walls.

After a while, my eyes flicker to the adjacent passages. Shouldn't we have located the steps by now? It hadn't taken this long to worm through here with the beautiful guard.

I clear my throat. "Excuse me. Hello? Hey? Hey, ruler? I beg your pardon, but um, the stairs weren't this far from the grotto. I'm sure you know where you're going, but it's never a wise idea to travel while in a foul mood. It prevents one from concentrating rightly on their destination."

We've done this before, so it's no surprise when he doesn't answer. But at least my captor's not dragging me with him this time. I grasp my caftan and trot to catch up. And despite my long limbs, I now have a greater appreciation of what Juniper must go through with her petite height.

I watch as Elixir's digits continue to graze the walls. "What are you doing?" I ask. "Is that how you find your way around? I mean, is that how you navigate The Deep when you're out of the water and in humanlike form? Or not in *human*like form but, well, when you don't have a tail?"

Nervousness gets the worst of my tongue, in addition to annoyance. "I've heard of a visually impaired cobra that can find its way through rapids by using its tail," I ramble. "Though, I've never actually seen it. I suppose you haven't, either, since it's a mortal reptile. We have lots of those. In fact—"

Elixir swings around so fast that I stumble into him. My nose bumps his chin, my breasts knock into the plate of his chest, and my eyes stagger across his face. "Do you," he grates, "*ever* hold your fucking tongue?"

"Why?" Then a wonderful thought lurches into my mind. "Does it bother you?"

He tilts his head, not missing the enthusiasm in my tone. Our closeness brings his face into stark relief, with its scales and exquisitely harsh lines. He looms before me like a ship—a reinforced vessel with the ability to rip through monsoons.

His glare is quite reinvigorating, sparking the daring in me. I've beheld this phenomenon in other people, where they find themselves defying sense and reason, then doing things they never expected. I've been that person once before, with this very same creature.

"Does it bother me?" the Fae reflects. "Would you like to find out?"

I brace myself. "I do hold my tongue. Just not tonight."

And not for him.

He glowers, his reply coming out low and shuddering. "Provocation from a mortal."

"Has that never happened before?"

"I have never given them enough time, once they lost their games."

Horror seizes me by the throat. "Do you feel no remorse?" I spit.

"No shame?"

Elixir's eyes slit, the sight reminiscent of basilisks. "What use are those emotions?"

"They teach us humility and compassion. They redeem us, inspire us to be better and care for others."

"Mortal inclinations."

"But without them, we end up alone."

Some type of disturbance spasms across the ruler's face. "I'm not alone."

"I didn't say you were," I tell him, my breath mingling with his. "But if you have no regrets, change is impossible."

He whips off his hood, revealing the entirety of his glare. His black locks are cinched in a low ponytail, the mane pouring down his back. Those basilisk eyes kindle to their boiling point. "Do I look unchanged to you?"

Unlike him, I'm not in a rhetorical mood. I've always been attuned to someone's inner joy or turmoil. Usually, this helps me to see them more clearly, allowing me to offer a helping hand or a soothing cup of tea. I search his irises for any sign of repentance for all the things he's done to my people...for what he's done to *me*.

Does he look unchanged? We'd tackled this before, and I stand by what I've already told him.

"Yes," I whisper. "You've lost your vision, yet your soul remains the same as it's always been. It's still evil, and that's tragic, because whatever happened to you isn't the only thing that matters. What matters is also how you responded to it."

He blinks. Then he sets an index finger to his lips, the caps of his digits glinting. "Shh," he warns. "The more you speak, the more I hear."

And the more vulnerable things he knows about me.

For one who says so little, this monster manages to stuff enough meanings into a handful of words and still succeed in twisting my thoughts against me.

Not for the first time, we're standing improperly close, suspended beneath a constellation of teal specks. The lantern flames simmer, illuminating the outline of my body beneath the caftan. The vestment is graphically thin, the material grazing my breasts—a faint, teasing contact that causes my nipples to pucker in a most indecent display.

Although Elixir can't see this transformation, my cheeks sizzle with heat. And when they do, his head twitches in awareness, and his pupils shift, assessing something. "Your temperature has changed."

"No, it hasn't," I lie, flustered. "What a thing to say!"

"Your blood is restless."

"That's...private."

His baritone drops, the edges frayed. "Not from me."

Because I'm not an octopus, my hands can only accomplish so much at once. I fan my face, then fidget with my caftan, then cross my arms to hide the pits of my nipples. I've never been so mortified in my life, and that includes my first kiss with the cobbler's daughter, when the initial curl of her tongue had made me squeak, which caused the female to cough into my mouth.

A droplet drizzles down the side of my neck. The Deep is a humid place, but this is a new level of oppression.

Elixir's head ticks toward my throat. His pinky steals out to collect the drop.

My jaw unhinges as he pulls away, the globule quivering on the pad of his digit. He contemplates the droplet, then closes it in his fist and pockets the bead like a trinket. I open my mouth, but Elixir cuts me off by prowling away while ordering, "Do not talk."

His hood flops down his back, and the ponytail lashes about as he blends in with the murkiness. My legs carry me across the corridor. I remain close enough that he won't lose patience and haul me with him, but far enough that I won't slam into him if he turns abruptly.

Before coming to live with my family, I'd learned how to sneak around people, flitting in and out of crowds with targets none-the-wiser. That's how a little girl learns to take what she needs—through sudden twists, evasive maneuvers, timed tricks, and intricate sleights of hand. That's how a child trains herself to be a pickpocket.

I take note of Elixir's gait, angle myself with his shadow, and pretend I'm trying to see past his shoulder before presumably giving up. In the second between approaching and scuttling backward, my left hand dives into the pocket of his robe and fishes out the bead of sweat.

Instead of bursting or seeping into my flesh, the globule maintains its shape by some form of the ruler's magic. Smug satisfaction lightens my step as I cocoon the droplet in my hand. Gladly, my pickpocketing days were over the moment Papa Thorne got me off the streets. It's been years since my digits performed such an act, yet they haven't forgotten.

Elixir keeps going, and going, and going. Then without warning, he pauses. His body clicks in place. In a flash, he wheels toward me, upends my hand, and swipes the bead back.

While he resumes his path, I stall and feel my features clench in outrage. "How did you know?"

"You have impressive stealth," he answers without looking behind. "I would not have known, had I not heard the droplet rolling in your hand."

He pounds up a new flight of steps. At the landing, the atmosphere takes a much-needed breath, our path expanding and leading to a building etched into a cavern wall.

We pass through a doorway with interlocking serpents carved into the lintel, a replica of the design I'd seen upon first entering The Deep. The threshold is curtained in a sheet of falling water, and when Elixir stalks toward it, the liquid parts to allow us inside.

I stumble through, gawking as the water curtain closes behind us. Ahead, a flat stone walkway cleaves through a lush enclosure of plants that resembles a giant terrarium. Dozens of serpents curl and slither along the damp soil. Braided nests of scales, from waxy and radiant, fill the area with rings and ovals of blue, green, black, and gold. The reptiles range in size, from slim as strings to thick as tree trunks, from small as pins to large as anacondas.

Their tongues emit the loudest, most melodic hisses I've ever heard, the unearthly sounds vibrating like cymbals. Their eyes are so vivid, the colors rival priceless jewels.

From my experience, many humans would recoil and flee the scene, apart from reptile admirers, trade poachers, and my family. My breath hitches at the sight. Elixir is busy crossing the path, but I stay where I am, the better to admire these creatures.

I step into the vegetation and explore, filtering through the green stalks while feeling the water lord's attention slowly drawing my way. Footfalls double back and trail down my path. I glance over my shoulder and catch the Fae monitoring me, his glazed eyes downcast in awareness as he listens to my movements.

A serpent with opal eyes skates my way, the cord of its body unwinding. I hesitate, appraising the faint line down the center of its head. Although Fae animals are different, the Fables vow that many key facets are the same. This one looks harmless, its appearance reminding me of a boa constrictor. If so, it's nonvenomous.

Tentatively, I reach out and run my finger over the reptile's head. The creature sways from side to side, and I chuckle.

A masculine intake brings me up short. I glance at Elixir arrested several paces away. His head is slanted, the peak of one ear having caught the sound of my laughter, which causes his profile to crinkle in what must be repugnance.

I wince, offended and oddly bereft by the reaction.

Elixir's attention slides toward the animal that has come to greet me. The ruler's expression turns concentrated and inquisitive while focusing on the snake. If I didn't know any better, I would say he's sending a message to the creature.

I would also say the snake is responding, because Elixir frowns in displeasure, as if betrayed.

A moment later, the reptile slinks around my feet, then vanishes into the undergrowth.

I stand and regard Elixir's disgruntled expression. "What?"

But he just spins on his bare heel and strides to the walkway. I sigh and catch up to him. "You looked like you were asking that snake a question."

"I was," he says.

"You can understand them?"

"I can."

"Were you talking about me?"

"We were."

"And you're not getting to tell me what was said? Not even a hint?" When he makes no reply, I try a different approach. "Is the reptile your familiar?"

Elixir reaches the opposite end of the pathway. His reply drops like a stone—heavy and lifeless—in the space between us. "My brothers have animal companions. I do not."

Brothers? But the Fables say nothing about Elixir having siblings.

Where are they? Do they live here?

Those questions are worth dwelling upon, but other details take precedence. I pad into a dome-like room germinating with more abundant vegetation. Three crescent-shaped tables line the chamber, each surface weighed down by glass bottles and stoppered jars that glisten with fluids. Other containers hang from the ends of ropes affixed to the ceiling, the vessels suspended like mobiles. Milky liquids and sparkling mixtures swim inside the glass, dousing the room with light.

In the center, a vat of water burrows into the ground. The surface ripples, the noise trickling through the room.

Elixir approaches one of the tables. Dispassionately, he withdraws my sweat droplet from his pocket, tips the bead into a jar, and stamps a cap over the lid.

I step fully into the chamber. "Why would you take a bead of my sweat? What are you going to do with it?" No surprise, the Fae stays quiet. "How did you do that in the first place?" I persist. "You plucked that droplet like the bud of a flower and then solidified its shape. How?"

"I'm Lord of the Water Fae. Ruler of the River. One of The Three," he reminds me arrogantly and flatly, as if those titles explain everything.

"So far, that's more than you've told me about yourself in a single sentence," I reply while inching near the containers hanging like ornaments. I raise my fingers to a tall vessel filled with bubbles. "But like I said in the chamber, among all those titles, you left out—"

A hand snatches my digits before I make contact with the glass. My head swings toward Elixir, who hovers at my side although he was twenty feet away seconds ago. "You know my name," he says. "The grotto told you."

I jerk my fingers back. His moniker tastes brackish on my palate.

"Elixir," I say.

"Cove," he answers.

The names collide, quivering through the room. This confirms he'd heard my sisters calling for me outside the caravan the other night. One moment, Lark, Juniper, and I had been huddling together. The next, we'd vanished from one another's sight. In a panic, we searched and cried out for each other.

Unbeknownst to us, Elixir had been looming nearby. I'd discovered as much shortly afterward. That's how he must have learned my name, seeing as I'd never shared it with him.

Now I know what my name sounds like on a monster's lips. And I wish I hated it more. His raspy baritone makes an unsteady thing of those four letters. The intonation reaches bone-deep, the penetration disturbing and causing my cheeks to bake.

"When I got here, how did you recognize me in the first place?" I ask.

"Your voice," he answers.

"You remember how I sounded? But I said so little to you back then, and I was younger."

"I do not forget voices—or words."

Fables forgive me. He remembers the last thing I'd said to him.

That one abominable thing.

I wince, then remember he doesn't deserve an apology. "Earlier, I was going to say you left out how to address you formally."

Elixir grunts, "You may call me a fucking squid, for all I care."

I stiffen at the profanity. "Do all Faeries have a vocabulary like my feisty sister?"

He bends toward me. "Do not touch anything."

The urgency in his tone must be from possessiveness. Certainly, it's not out of concern for my wellbeing. "For a ruler, I had expected a subterranean stronghold. Is this where you live?"

"No."

"*Where* do you live, then?"

"Nowhere."

"You don't have a home?"

"The Deep is my home."

That's not helpful. "But where do you sleep?"

"Wherever I choose."

"But what about a refuge of your own?"

"I need no refuge."

"But everyone needs a refuge."

"But, but, but," he snaps. "Why do you care?"

Good question. As it stands, I would have more success pulling shark teeth.

I thread my fingers in front of me. "I would tell you it's a habit, caring to know about others rather than always focusing on myself, however I don't think you would understand. Maybe this instead: Why did you bring me here? What is this place?"

"The Pit of Vipers," he answers. "This is where I brew."

I take a second inspection of the concoctions. "Are these poisons?"

His mouth quirks, neither confirming nor denying it.

Bile washes up my throat as I reconsider the resident serpents. "Are you using them for venom? Are they trapped here?"

Elixir's face creases with anger. "You are trapped here," he grits out. "Not them."

Faeries don't abuse their fauna. Not like humans do.

That's what his glower says. That's what it assumes.

I sense this unspoken accusation, which strikes as quickly as a jab to the chest. He hates my kind for what happened during The Trapping. Moreover, he loathes me for my part in it. And beyond that lingers some other wound, one that's still fresh.

Elixir's voice cuts into my thoughts. "This is the vipers' territory," he tells me. "They may go and leave from here as they wish."

"Not all mortals harm animals," I say, thinking about my family's sanctuary and the water snake in my chamber. "The grotto told me why I'm really here and why this game is important. I'm sorry about what's happening, but—"

"You are sorry," Elixir repeats with a frown, as if apologies are foreign and, what's more, distasteful to him.

"It was horrific what my people did," I say. "Truly, I'm sorry. But as much as I wish it hadn't happened, and as much as your fauna deserve to be restored, I won't be a sacrifice. Neither me, nor my sisters."

As I'd dreaded, Elixir is unmoved by my speech, which is why I haven't explained about my family rescuing animals, a fact he wouldn't believe in the slightest. So instead, he draws out, "Then win."

"Against whom?"

"Against me."

My heart dives to my stomach. That's why he brought me to this den, to reveal my game: a one-on-one challenge against the lord of the water Fae.

I muster the courage to ask, "What's the game? When do we begin?"

His golden eyes blaze with ambition. "We already have."

8

His gaze reflects off the glass bottles, the likeness multiplying a hundred times over. I retreat a step, evicting myself from that glaring light. "What do you mean, we already have?"

Surrounded by countless poisons, Elixir absorbs the signs of my distress, his eyes slitting with concentration. "Based on what I'm sensing, you know what I mean."

"I can assure you, I don't," I argue.

"Your body knows. I see it."

Would it be terribly rude to remind him how that's impossible? Though, I hardly need to because he translates my silent gape. "I hear every swallow, scent every shift in your blood, and feel the tempo of your heartbeat. That is how I see."

Mortification pours into my face. In my world, and with someone different, I would have glanced away. Violated, I stomp back into the glints of light, my height nearly matching his, minus about five inches. "But who sees you? And how do you see yourself?"

Those golden orbs flap in consternation, then in aggravation. "I will ask the questions from now on."

"Can you handle stringing together that many words?"

In my defense, I don't know where this pluck is coming from. No matter how petrified I am, there's this persistent urge to spar with him, if only to pry his lips open.

Elixir bears down on me. After a moment's consideration, he reaches for one of the hanging bottles containing an orange fluid. The Fae strokes the glass, the point of his fingercap scraping lightly. "This one melts the scales from your body." He touches it with relish, then chooses an inky vessel. "Drink the essence of a midnight spring, mixed with the trapped vapors from smoked fish, and the victim shall experience perpetual hunger until they stuff themselves to death."

The monster continues by pointing out an opiate that will never wear off, thus perpetually distorting reality, and a drug that forces its drinker to feel the physical suffering of the next prey caught by a predator of The Deep.

He taps one more dangling vessel replete with rose gold swirls. "An infusion of siren's blood and the extract of berries from The Solitary Forest causes an addiction to pleasure, to the point where one shall not recognize pain from ecstasy," he says, twisting his nefarious gaze my way. "You shall moan with every lash of a whip, for instance. The rapture shall be your downfall."

Not just poisons.

Dark magic. Sinful magic.

I lick my lips, the movement consuming his attention, as if he'd heard the swipe of my tongue. "If you remembered me all this time, why didn't you ever force me into this world earlier and take your revenge? Why wait?"

To his credit, Elixir looks appalled. "You were a stripling. The Fae do not harm mortal children. By the time you were old enough, you trespassed into our wild on your own, all before I could act on my grudges. In that way, you made it easy for me."

"Please. If you won't spare me, then spare my sisters. I'll endure their punishment. I'll gladly pay their price. Only release them. For pity's sake, set them free."

His black eyebrows slam together. "You would play their games. In their stead."

"Yes," I implore. "A million times, yes."

He pauses for a beat, then swerves away. "No."

The reply catches me like a slap across the face. Not that I'm surprised, but for Lark and Juniper, it was worth a try.

From within the vegetation, serpents hiss, the noises short and shrill.

Anger simmers in my gut, where once there was fear. I bite out, "Then tell me this game we've apparently begun, and I'll win against you, as you kindly suggested."

Elixir stops mid-stride. He wheels, the hem of his robe a black disk swishing around his frame as he returns to me. "I'm more than your opponent. I'm your objective."

"Excuse me?"

"A curse. You must break a curse."

"On whom?"

"On me."

It takes a moment for the truth to sink in, along with a stunning bout of realization. "That's why you're blind."

No answer. No inclination of the head to confirm this.

His shadow dwarfs mine the way a rattlesnake's shadow would devour a dormouse. "Break my curse. If not, you lose. That is the game."

"This doesn't make sense. Breaking the curse would restore your vision. You would be invested in me winning."

"No."

"No?"

"Think. Harder."

I can't read him the way he reads me. It's easy to empathize with my people, but they're human. They're *humane*. I can't sense the inner workings of a viper.

But I do have a logical sister who's rubbed off on me over the years. Because this moment calls for rationale, there's only reason for Elixir to task me with breaking his curse—while also wanting me to fail. "It's a consolation prize."

Elixir inclines his head. "It is more. I have no grievance against my condition, for it is not a defect."

"I know it isn't. I'm not so narrow-minded as you think. What I meant was, gaining your sight back would become a weapon. You'd use it as a tool, an agenda."

"Yes," he confirms. "You do not have a prayer of winning, but should you prevail by luck, challenging you with this feat is the lesser of the two evils. Your victory might bring these lands closer to fading, yet I shall have my vision back long enough to see your face when I retaliate."

"Retaliate how? The rules say my sisters and I go free if we win. The rules say I live."

"You do." His irises spark. "The rules just do not say for how long."

Cold panic floods my chest. The Folk are masters of riddles and twisted truths, so my sisters and I should have anticipated something like this. The rules list nothing about what happens after we go free, how long we survive. The rules say nothing about us living in peace.

Elixir lets his silence and my imagination do the damage for him. He would rather win for the sake of restoring his world than lose for the sake of restoring his vision. But in the rare off-chance I succeed, and the curse is lifted, he'll exact revenge anyway.

All with his sight intact. All because of me.

It's clever. It's ruthless. It's very Fae.

If this is my game, what are the rulers of the mountain and forest putting my sisters through?

I'm not bookish like Juniper, but I won't get far without certain knowledge. "Who cursed you? How did it happen? How do I break the spell?"

"Figure it out," Elixir invites.

"How do I do that?"

"Figure that out, too."

"Do you know?"

He stares through me, deadpan. That means yes. This fiend knows, but I'm not going to get it out of him.

The empty threat pops from my mouth before I can stop it. "What if I refuse? If I don't play, the games are void. It's a draw across all regions. You can't touch my sisters, then."

Elixir rasps, "Are you naïve or merely a coward?"

"A coward?" I snarl. "You're calling me cowardly? Punishing people is the coward's way. Freeing them takes courage." I choke on the rest of my words as the Fae consumes the remaining distance between us, his approach forcing me to back away. We travel like this across the lush cavern, from one shrub to the next, while the orbs prick the ceiling with unearthly teal, and reptiles scroll through the underbrush.

"You caged our fauna and our children," Elixir seethes, his scales radiating like a thousand shards of glass. "Where was your courage, then?"

"Do you think sacrificing mortals in kind makes you any better?" I counter. "To say nothing of how you've jeopardized humans before that, what with your glamouring and harassing and pillaging, afflicting everyone with trauma and paranoia, all for your superior amusement. Not that you're the type of Fae who relishes diversion. No, you're the brutish type who prowls and then pounces, attacking mortals with those savage eyes. Well, it's no wonder you're cursed, and I don't feel the least bit sorry for you…you leviathan!"

A hedge with broad, tubular branches materializes in my periphery. I smack one of the boughs in his path, as though that will hinder his progress.

Elixir catches the branch and squeezes the stem, just like he once tried to squeeze my throat. "Fuck the game," he warns. "I could poison you. I could feed you to the sharks."

"Or you could blind me," I bait.

Elixir stops—and snaps the tube branch in half with a single clench of his fist. The sound cracks through the space. It takes a fretful amount of willpower not to jump. That bough had been three inches in diameter, but in his grip, it might as well have been a twig.

"I shall do worse." Without glancing away, Elixir drops the branch. "You know that now."

Yes. Being invested in winning means I'll still perish at his hands. Either way, win or lose, he'll inflict vengeance on me. In the end, I'll die.

"What game did the others play?" I demand.

"The same one," he answers.

The same one. Did any of them succeed? What happened to those humans when they lost?

Elixir anticipates this question. At his leisure, he gestures to the heinous collection of brews. "The ones who lost or forfeited outright had to drink from one of these."

Bile clots my tongue. "At least you gave them a choice between melted flesh and an addiction to fornication."

"I said they had a choice between mixtures. I never said that I'd specified in advance the vessels' effects."

Now I'll truly be sick. Those poor souls hadn't known their fates until after emptying the unknown contents down their stomachs.

"You merciless, unspeakable tyrant," I spew.

"I am," he acknowledges.

"That was someone's child, someone's parent, someone's sibling, someone's friend, someone's love."

"Do not worry. When you lose, you shall get your choice." He strides to one of the crescent tables, traces the stoppers, selects a pair of corked carafes, and returns to me. He holds up the blue vessel. "This one suffocates slowly." Then he exhibits the green container. "This one suffocates quickly."

I will drown you.

Somehow, he'd always known this would happen. Fables forgive me, but whatever my future holds, and until my dying breath, I shall never despise anyone as much as I do this Fae.

He's making me play a losing game. However, for my sisters, I'll do it. A thousand times, I'll do it.

Now it's me who draws closer, moving on quavering limbs until our chests bump. I feel anything but brave, yet I gather my wits and whisper, "If that's the way it must be, then tell me precisely when this game began."

Elixir wears a similar look of contempt and whispers back, "A very long time ago."

I falter. Half of me understands while the other half doesn't. He's been waiting to punish me for what happened between us nine years ago. The water lord has a vendetta against me, not exclusively the mortals who breached Faerie. This game isn't just about saving his world.

It's about us. It's personal.

But I was a child. Why hold our fleeting past against me for so long?

Elixir absorbs my distress, as one might a heady swig of wine—with indulgence and gratification. I search the inclines of his face for a shred of contrition, yet I find none. He's as solid as these cavern walls. Even Juniper isn't this impenetrable.

As for what dwells behind those imposing Fae eyes, I can't say. It's a shock to the system, encountering this much of a blockade. When have I ever had to work this hard to reach someone? Who has this amount of willpower to keep themselves shielded? To say so little yet wreak such havoc on others?

I inhale a quivering breath, then let it out. "You like having power over others, and you like unnerving them with few words, and you like striking them down when they least expect it, and you're good at it."

Elixir's eyelids hood to an unnerving degree. As my gaze travels across his countenance, so does his gaze seek out mine. And when my attention wanders to the rest of him, he does the same with me. I scan the toned bulk of his arm, and he locates the slender length of mine.

It's as if we're standing on opposite sides of a mirror. Wherever I look upon him, he looks upon me, from my bobbing throat to the ravine between my breasts, to the private recess between my hips, to the thighs flanking that intimate slot.

We move in sync, so that every place he traces scorches me. Morbid curiosity wells up. It's hypnotic and frightening, but not in a way that causes me to recoil. And I detest myself for that.

Our mutual inspection gives way to something new, something that leaks in and disrupts the pure, unfiltered hatred boiling in the cramped space we share. This new thing sparks a violent sort of friction, eliciting another treacherous invasion, a perverted and unforgivable sensation that tightens in a low, scandalous place. My core pulsates. I have no clue where this vile urge is coming from or why, but the hate seems to fuel it, the conflicted feelings surging together.

Our breathing escalates, equally scornful and roused. The impact causes my head to pound with confusion. I've felt scores of emotions in my life, but never this one, and I don't know what to do with it.

All that gold smolders in Elixir's orbs. When the flimsy bodice of my caftan brushes his robe, the tips of my breasts heave centimeters from his torso. The color of his eyes intensifies. It's not like the first encounter, when he'd sought to blind me. Instead of piercing like blades, this time the irises flow like lava.

"How brightly do they burn?" I wonder, then realize I've spoken aloud.

Elixir stiffens. I blink, astonished. And the trance breaks.

At some point, the surrounding environment had vanished. Now it returns, clearer and sharper than before, with hundreds of poisons dangling from nooses.

The Fae draws himself to his full height, his frame backdropped by writhing flames and resident serpents. He looms there, the ruler of all things cavernous and otherworldly. "Play and die later. Or condemn yourself now," he murmurs. "Make your choice."

Play and die later, but spare Lark and Juniper. Or condemn myself now, along with my sisters.

All of us win—or none of us win.

That's the rule. Yet I've been idling in this spot, lost in the hellish gaze of a villain. The shame of it!

He's playing mind games with me. That must be it. To that end, he'll continue to play them while I'm here, while I'm fighting for my life, while I'm seeking to break a curse he fully deserves to endure.

The last droplet of terror drains from me. "How long do I have?"

His face slants with gratified menace. "Until your first attempt."

In other words, I have until my *only* attempt. Rather than a shortened period with several chances at my disposal, he'll give me as long as I need, but I'll only get one shot to win. One move in which I'll have to be certain. That could take days or years, assuming my sisters have as long, a fact I can't rely upon.

Mind games, indeed. How sadistically clever.

I finger the chain around my neck. "I accept. See if I don't shatter you."

"My presence might do that," he promises.

"But what will my presence do to you?"

Disgust contorts his face. "Nothing. It will do nothing. For mortals are nothing to me. Understood?"

"Understood," I assure him.

"Good." He tilts his head. "Now leave."

Gladly. For once since he dragged me out of that shark pool, I've run out of things to say. I swing around and march from the den, bypassing the contaminated jars and bottles. He hasn't told me how to get back to my chamber, but I'm unconcerned about that. I need to get away from him as quickly as possible. I'd rather face the dark and unknown than spend one more second in the glare of those ruthless eyes.

Those eyes, which somehow follow me on my way out.

Those eyes, which have found a way to blindsight me, after all.

9

My limbs carry me at a swift pace down the terrarium walkway strewn with hedges. The reptiles drape themselves across the ground and dangle over branches like colorful cords. As I pass by, they hiss and rattle, but it doesn't faze me.

Only one type of viper has ever done that. Game or no game, I mean to stop him from succeeding ever again. Elixir has caused enough mayhem. He's taken plenty from me, and I won't let him take any more.

I retrace my steps from The Pit of Vipers and into the underground tunnel. The soles of my sandals thwack the ground. Occasionally, I glance over my shoulder, but he's not behind me, not following me, not coming after me.

The cavities are vast and numerous, some containing slender waterways. And where there is water, there are creatures. From an adjacent stream, I catch a glimpse of jeweled skin and spiked fins surfing through the water. In a storybook world, I would stop to marvel at these mystical dwellers.

But I'm not a player in some fairytale. I'm alone in a dark, dangerous world.

It was foolish to dash off without considering my direction. If I don't stop, I'll be lost.

Maybe this is why Elixir hadn't appointed my guard to fetch me, so that I might run rampant like prey, because no matter where I go, and no matter how far I travel from the chamber, I'll still be trapped. The Sunken Isle is merely a small cage tucked inside a much larger one.

I halt at an intersection and grip my stomach, fighting to control my exhalations. The ceiling orbs toss light onto the floor while a parallel brook emits its own blue-green radiance. I peek over the edge and study my reflection. My intricate bun is awry, the errant tendrils frizzy. My eyes are wide and as teal as my hair, just like the flecks overhead. I bear scratches from this journey, but I'm whole. That's more than I could have hoped for.

If I can find the outlet back to the grotto, I might be able to retrace my steps to The Sunken Isle. As a climber, Lark has taught our trio how to distinguish patterns in bluffs. As a huntress, Juniper has taught our trio how to chart paths through the wild. As a swimmer, I've taught them how to follow the water. As rescuers and survivors, we've learned how to move quietly and get home safely.

It helps, but this is Faerie. Nothing is ever as it seems.

I tread with caution while noting elevation dips, outcroppings, and springs cleaving through the tunnels. At last, I reach the passage connecting to the grotto and determine my way from there, ascending the original stairway and emerging to a familiar vista.

Nearby, The Twisted Canals glitter beneath stalactites, the buildings showered in turquoise cascades and foaming with multi-level ponds. The silhouette of a peapod-shaped boat glides beneath an arched bridge, and the waterways pour into the great river.

The memory of Elixir dragging me to The Sunken Isle is entombed in my memory. Therefore, the route from here is impossible to forget. Encouraged, I head in that direction.

Melodic laughter peals from the recesses, the noise stalling my feet. A figure spreads its arms, which are lined in broad fins, and dives into the current. The water Fae doesn't come back up for air.

Whispers and mutterings drift from the canals. Heads swerve in my direction, and several additional bodies hurtle into the river, their splashes growing nearer.

They've noticed me. And they swim fast.

Despite the game, what types of restrictions—or permissions—has Elixir given his kin about how to treat me?

I inch backward, then wheel around and sprint toward the stone jetty.

My chasers close the distance with lethal focus, their slick bodies shearing through the gulf.

Then they stop.

I glance over my shoulder. A tide cuts through the river and lashes toward the Faeries. They reel away, evading the onslaught thrusting across the expanse like a barrier. Sulky disappointment mars their features before they whirl toward the canals and slip into the abyss. Some force had thwarted them, though I'm not interested in dwelling on that. I just want to get away from here.

I spin again—and bump into the guard from my chamber. She catches my arm, steadying me from teetering off the walkway. Her crystalline scales radiate as she examines me, then slides her eyes to the current. The ripples shift beside us. She heeds something there, inclines her head, and ushers me to the chamber via the stepping-stones, which rise for her.

The female guides me to the door. "Rest, human. You've had quite the orientation," she intones.

"My name is Cove," I insist.

She considers me, then splays her fingers on her chest. "Coral."

"That's a lovely name."

"Of course, it is." She offers a devious smirk that isn't entirely friendly. "Lovely to behold. Sharp if you get too close." With that, she leaves, the harpoon saddled against her back.

I hasten inside and shut the door. My back slumps against the partition, and several weighty exhales siphon from my lips.

The central tub glitters, pouring a mellow blue light through the chamber. I hasten to the water and fall to my knees beside the rim, then peer beneath the surface. "Are you here? Please, be here."

The ripples twitch as a small head lurches from the depth. The snake's yellow eyes find mine. I gasp in relief, a lump hardening in my throat. My pinky runs along the reptile's skin, the waxen texture familiar and so very mortal. All this time, I had been worried about the creature, and I worry still for its safety here, but I'm also grateful to have one more reminder of home. After what just transpired, I don't know what I'd do without him or my necklace, the remaining relics of my life.

I feed my companion the leftover fish from my platter, and the snake lets me pet him until I grow sleepy. Recent horrific events catch up, engulfing me with the force of a typhoon. My companion dunks its head under the water, the slender rope of its body gliding through the tub.

Admittedly, the bed looks inviting with its silken coverlet, its texture reminding me of a woven lake. I could sink into it and fall into a deep slumber. I could flee to that bed and drown in its comfort.

But I know the value of comfort. This is one sort I won't trust, nor accept.

I cross my arms over the rim, forming a makeshift pillow. While resting my head there, I watch the reptile weave through the tub. I stare and stare and stare until the world blurs like the bottom of an ocean.

Or maybe that's just my tears.

Two days pass. The monster doesn't pay me a visit, nor summon me to his den. I pace the length of the chamber and ponder Elixir's curse. I consider our short history, as well as the history between my people and his kin. I go over as many Fables as I can recall, in case they contain hints about curse breaking. I remember every caution Papa Thorne has ever voiced, and I muse on every lesson my sisters and I have ever learned about Faeries.

I replay that last scene between Elixir and me. I envision every crease in his face and every flash of his pupils, every time he'd remained silent and every time his tongue slipped, provoked by my replies. I recall his proximity, the vastness of his body so near, the way my blood had responded, and the fact that he had known. I think of our mutual hatred and the inexplicable heat that had resulted.

My skin flushes a rosy hue, an invasive warmth gushing through me. I may be chaste and inexperienced, but I'm not ignorant. That would be impossible with a sister like Lark, who recounts every detail of her exploits, down to the size of her lover's phallus. Be that as it may, my sister has never mentioned how anger can spark the same kind of flame.

The anticipation of seeing Elixir again spurs me to restlessness. Every distant sweep of footfalls causes me to tense. Each time, it's only the voluptuous guard named Coral arriving with my meals. Whenever the door rattles open, I urge the snake underwater or beneath the nearest stick of furniture, as my little friend has taken a liking to exploring the room.

One evening, shyness overcomes me at the sight of Coral's plush figure trussed up in a netted dress. As tales have said, the characteristics of the Folk can be extreme—either devastatingly beautiful or fancifully eerie. I greet the guard with a timid smile, which earns me a quirked eyebrow before she deposits my platter on the table and leaves.

After the first meal, I had asked for a second helping of fish—raw this time—and received a queer look from Coral. Nonetheless, she had obliged, and I'd offered the raw portion to the snake, determined to prevent the animal from exiting the pool in search of nourishment. The amphibians and small mammals of Faerie are unlikely to be easily captured by a mortal water snake. They're faster and stronger, and if my friend sets his sights upon a frog, that creature could shift sizes and devour the snake.

But since my initial request, the platters have arrived with side portions of raw fare suitable for my friend, the repast provided without me having to ask again. Puzzled though Coral must be, I'm grateful for the offerings.

In these caverns, it might as well be perpetual eventide. Yet it becomes easy to distinguish night from day, based on the remote activity resounding from The Twisted Canals—fluid voices singing and bodies swimming in the river—as well as the orchestral chirp of crickets and the belching croaks of toads.

I maintain my normal, human sleep patterns. Unlike the Faeries, I keep daylight hours and dream at night.

Or rather, I don't dream, because none of this is a dream. It's a nightmare, and when I close my eyes, all I see are jars of poison and so much gold.

My muscles and joints ache from sleeping on the floor beside the tub. By the third day, my body hurts too much to deny myself. And although it's early evening, I need a quick rest. After bathing, I crawl into bed and drag the sheets over my body, cocooning myself in a waterfall of finely spun silk.

The respite is short-lived. I awaken and flop onto my back, concerns and confusions overriding weariness. Foliage quivers from the walls. Shadows swim across the floor. It feels as if my confines have begun to shrink. I need a walk. I need wide open spaces. None of the ideas I've conjured regarding Elixir's curse seem right or plausible.

Let's see. Curses are based on wrongdoings. They're the springboards for why curses happen in the first place. With Elixir, it must be something prominent.

An error in judgement? An act of stupidity? A passionate misdeed? Or a weakness? Yes!

In fact, stories would claim it's his greatest weakness. If I'm right, I need to know what that is. I need to unlock it.

Cloistering myself in this hovel won't yield the answer. Tarrying here will only compromise my ability to win this game. If hints and solutions exist outside this room, I need to learn the terrain, map out this place, and search for clues.

There's one problem: my weapon. I can't go anywhere unarmed.

I sit up, the sheets tumbling around my hips. The absence of noisy insects and amphibians means the Folk are still asleep, so I have a few hours left before they rise. If there's any better hour to do what I must, it's now.

I swing my legs over the side of the bed. The last time I saw my weapon, the river had taken it from me at Elixir's behest. Though I hadn't noticed the spear in The Pit of Vipers, I'd been distracted and frazzled, and only one knave could be holding it hostage. That domineering, control-obsessed heathen wouldn't entrust it to anyone else. And if a pickpocket knows anything, it's that people eventually let their guard down.

I rise to my feet and square my shoulders. It's time to get my spear back.

I close the door behind me. All is still and tranquil—precariously so.

The lake is a polished blue coin. The stepping-stones are nowhere in sight, nor do they rise for me as they have for Elixir and the guard. And according to The Grotto That Whispers, the water will suction mortals down.

I dip my foot under, and a current latches on, tugging me down past the ankle. Gasping, I yank my leg free and take a moment to regroup.

There's nothing for it. I'm a swimmer, and I can hold my breath longer than most.

Besides, if I can resist Elixir's blinding magic, what else am I capable of?

While knotting my caftan around my waist, I coax myself to disregard the lack of undergarments. This isn't a time to fret about exposing myself. After muttering a Fabled prayer and preserving my oxygen, I dive in.

The water catches me. Immediately, it clamps onto my limbs, urging me down.

A brief spell of panic churns in my stomach. I conjure every minute I've spent in the water and push, push, push against the pressure. My eyes whisk open and catch sight of the bank. I keep going, keep stroking, keep kicking.

Don't think, I urge myself. Just press forward, I tell myself.

My arms and legs move in sync. The water wrestles with me, but I maneuver in and out of its hold.

At last, the lake grows shallow. I totter upright and slog out of the water.

Beyond the fence of reeds, Coral stands sentinel by the jetty, the harpoon lance at her side. I hunker beneath the archway as she scans the perimeter. An intricate platinum clip shaped like a quarter moon sinks its teeth into her silver-blue hair, right behind her pointed ear. It's an object she might easily lose, a bauble that could fall without her noticing, especially while she's patrolling.

She paces every few minutes, enough for me to count her steps. When she moves to the right, I slip directly behind her, my nimble fingers plucking the comb from her tresses. The action requires no trick, just a seamless progression of movement, like a draft of air. I glide back to the archway and hurl the comb as far around the bend as possible.

At the clink of platinum, Coral's attention snaps toward the disturbance. She coasts in that direction, opening a path for me. The moment she vanishes, I dart up the incline.

From there, I traipse between the shadows, the hem of my caftan billowing around my legs. I had chosen a garment as dark as these cavern walls, the better to blend in, with a hood to conceal the brightness of my hair.

Little by little, I pass through lush recesses and rocky alcoves, some trickling with water. While the Faeries sleep, the mortal captive prowls their world in search of something that doesn't belong to them. I travel back to the grotto, through the passages, and up the stairs to The Pit of Vipers.

The spear must be in there. I must have missed it the last time.

I scan the atmosphere for signs of activity, but all is dormant. On the count of three, I hustle into the main entrance, through the water curtain that parts for me. I cross the terrarium lane, pass the glowing snakes that entwine the branches, approach the second threshold leading into the den, and—

I skid in place. I've made it inside the building undetected. By the grace of the Fables, I'm here.

But so is Elixir.

My pulse leaps. The Fae is wide awake and standing before the central vat, one bare foot propped on the rim. He's leaning forward, an arm draped across his bent thigh, his brooding features tipped as he contemplates the water. His onyx mane slides down his shoulders, a thick layer covering half his profile.

In his free hand, the ruler holds a chalice. He crushes the goblet between his fingers, the digits straining, as if thoughts plague him. Whatever the problem is, it's keeping him awake.

At length, the Fae straightens. He's wearing umber-dyed leggings this time, and the same open robe hangs off his frame; the material splits down the middle and sweeps the ground. A chiseled plate of olive skin gleams in the lantern flames, and his nipples are dusky, the disks tight.

My body tingles with irritation, plus another corrupt impulse.

Does this monster not sleep? Must he insist on getting in the way when I'm on a mission to ransack his den? And why does the sight of him cause the throbbing in my temples to travel down my body, to a forbidden and feminine place?

Elixir lifts the chalice to his mouth. My intakes grow shallow. As the goblet grazes his lower lip, I imagine a single drop of liquid teetering off the rim, ready to spill down his throat.

That's when he pauses. The chalice stills, arrested against his mouth. Slowly, his eyes slant downward in sudden awareness, knowing someone's there.

From my hiding spot, I hold my breath. But then I frown when Elixir's eyes slant sideways in annoyance, as if sensing a nuisance. "Go away," he snaps.

And a roguish voice responds, "My, my, my. Is that any way to greet a brother?"

Another male figure materializes from thin air. The Fae slouches against the opposite wall, his bulky arms crossed and a lazy smirk wreathing across his face. The pose is both swaggering and magnetic, his aura befitting the leather vest and knee breeches enhancing his broad frame.

Where limbs should be, furred calves and cloven hooves extend from the pants. My eyes lurch past his face and land on the sharp antlers sprouting from his very red hair.

This one's a forest Fae—a satyr.

Elixir growls, which doesn't faze his guest. If anything, it encourages the male. In the heat of the blazing lanterns, the satyr tips his head sideways and grins like the devil. "Miss me, luv?"

10

"Fuck off," Elixir spits, tossing the request over his shoulder.

The satyr tsks in mock offense. "That's not the merry greeting I was hoping for. Most Faeries sink to their knees when I enter a room."

"I'm not one of your lovers, you overstimulated prick."

"Bloody true. That would be incest. Still, you could be a little excited by my arrival. Currently, I'm in as shitty a mood as you are on a regular basis, which should please you."

Elixir slams his free fist into the nearest hanging bottle. Shards of glass fly, sterling flecks blowing into the air and evaporating. "I said: Fuck off, Puck."

"Such a temper and such a menacing octave," the satyr gloats. "I do love having that privileged effect on you. By the way, that was a waste of pixie dust."

His accent is as prominent as Elixir's, though more provocative around the edges. With that kind of intonation, one would think the first word the satyr ever learned as an infant was a vulgarity.

Elixir scoffs, returning his attention to the water. He tips back the chalice, its contents pumping down his throat.

I duck farther into the corner. From this vantage point, I study the woodland Fae. Whereas Elixir is fatally beautiful, this male specimen is fiendishly handsome. Despite his fair skin, there's an earthy roughness to the satyr called Puck, with his fitted leather garb and those stag antlers.

Another fact rises to the surface. Did this Fae refer to himself as Elixir's brother? I recall Elixir mentioning his siblings the last time I was here.

But these males look nothing alike. Nor do I recall any Fables suggesting that Faeries of the same bloodline can possess such different features. By the same token, how is it they hail from disparate regions of the Solitary wild?

Puck pushes himself off the wall and struts across the cavern. Based on his confident swagger, he enjoys being the center of attention, on filthy as well as formidable terms. Truly, his gait exudes both authority and lusty sensuality.

Humming to himself, Puck reaches one of the crescent tables and noses through them. Glass clinks as he rifles the contents, his attention halting on a vessel filled with a liquid as red as his shoulder-length waves. He plucks the container and examines it in the firelight. "It looks like you've stoppered an inferno in this one. What the hell is it for?"

"Pour it on your cock and find out," Elixir answers.

The reply dabs another smile into the crook of Puck's lips. "Now, now. My cock doesn't need any help."

The river ruler angles his head over his shoulder, that mane sloping across his cheekbone. He arches an eyebrow. "I never said it would help."

Puck swears under his breath and drops the vessel onto the table. The action causes a paradox. Upon hearing Puck's distress, Elixir's mouth tips in the faintest, rarest show of amusement.

"Motherfuck," Puck drawls. "You're one vicious bastard, brewing something like that." He stops and reconsiders something. "Then again, mind if I borrow that little concoction? Might come in handy if I need something for bargaining, or in case one of my woodland kin crosses a line with me." Sobriety creeps into his voice. "It's more likely these days."

"Paining your subjects?" Elixir contends, as if that isn't Puck's nature.

The satyr shrugs. "What can I say? I make trickery my bitch. Either that, or I want to grow up and be like you someday, silently striking by the balls—and not for kinks. Sure, that's what I have a longbow and a pair of knuckles for, but sometimes those weapons aren't enough to thwart our enemies."

"Since when are kin the enemy?"

Puck's brown eyes narrow. "Look at you, chattier than usual."

"That is not an answer."

"Do I sound like I give a fuck?"

In a flash, the river ruler turns. His orbs flame with gold, hurling the metallic color in Puck's direction. The satyr curses, his head twists, and he squints to shield his eyes. "You cunt," he gripes. "I hate it when you pull that shit."

The gilded light dulls from Elixir's irises. "You try my patience."

"Rubbish. You're about as patient as a faun in heat."

"What. Do. You. Want. Puck?"

The satyr wheels back to Elixir. "Hmm. A favor would be nice. I fancy favors."

"I'm out of aphrodisiacs."

"Let me know when you restock. Though, believe it or not, I have something else in mind." Puck resumes his inspection of the containers, his finger dancing from one stopper to the next, and selects a vial of white grains. "What about—"

"Not that one." Elixir stalks to Puck's side and seizes the vial, though how did Elixir know which one the satyr had chosen?

"I was jesting," Puck says, nonplussed. "You weren't engrossed in my request, so I needed to get your attention. I'm no expert, but in my humble woodland abode, I dabble in my share of cooking. I know salt when I see it."

With delicate precision, Elixir places the vial on the table, returning it to the same spot where it had been. "It is not salt."

"Care to enlighten me, then?" the satyr inquires, then sighs when Elixir doesn't reply. "Whatever. I need something potent."

"For?" Elixir prompts.

Finally, the satyr's glib facade evaporates. In its place is the same nefarious aspect as my captor, notwithstanding more artful. He rotates his wrist, and a weapon materializes in his hand. "For this?"

My heart stops at the sight of a crossbow and quiver trapped in Puck's grip. The bolts are tipped in iron. I know that archery.

"Juniper," I whisper, the name slipping from my lips.

Blessedly, the Faeries don't catch the sound, despite their impeccable senses. My head swerves from the crossbow to Puck's loathsome face. If they're so-called brothers, and if he has the crossbow, and if Elixir had been in earnest when referring to Puck's "subjects," that means...

That means he isn't a common satyr. Puck is one of The Three.

He's ruler of the woodland. And he has my sister.

My molars grind. Fables forgive me, I will slash that scoundrel to bits. What I wouldn't forsake to pierce him through the heart this instant.

So, the rulers of the Solitary wild are really brothers? Tales from The Trapping don't recount this.

I dig my nails into the stone wall. What in Fable's name is Puck doing to Juniper? What game is he making her play? If he has obtained her crossbow, does that mean she's hurt? How did he get it from her?

Elixir sets aside his chalice and gazes into space, concentrating as his fingers sketch the crossbow, the quiver, and the bolts. Puck tries to warn him, but the satyr doesn't need to. On a hiss, Elixir jerks his fingers back an inch before touching the tips. "Iron," he rasps, his gaze seeking Puck's face. "This is hers?"

Puck nods. "Smart girl."

I glare at him. It's precisely the sort of compliment my sister would love to hear from a person. She values intelligence above all traits.

Does Puck know this? But why would he? And why does he sound proud? Am I being as gullible as my family says I am, or is he being sarcastic?

Elixir must hear the same appraising tone. The water lord's features crease as he dissects those two words. In spite of Elixir's blindness, the satyr holds his brother's gaze. I grant, the woodland Fae is skilled at manipulating his features into nonchalance, yet there's no mistaking the underlining attachment Puck has to the weapon.

Nonetheless, the impetus for it escapes me.

Elixir's visage darkens in awareness and no shortage of repugnance. Like me, the ruler doesn't understand the meaning behind Puck's flattery.

The satyr rolls his shoulders. "What say you, Elixir? Can you remove the iron?"

"My mixtures serve only two purposes," Elixir says. "Either they poison or cure."

I give a start. He has remedies? Not all the bottles contain toxins and depraved brews?

"Soooo," Puck draws out, "cure the bolts. They're contaminated, aren't they?"

"You will use the archery against her, then."

"Meh. Something like that. Her game has begun, and I need leverage. Let's say it's complicated."

"I'm sure it is," Elixir is quick to respond.

A challenge contorts Puck's expression, and the moment stews between them. Eventually, the satyr smirks. "You have doubts about my evil nature? I'm wounded as fuck. Let no one call me disloyal to my kin."

The jaunty tone fails to sway Elixir, who grates out, "I said nothing of the kind."

Puck's gaze tapers, slashes of black and white lining his eyelids. "Whereas I say many things, and some of those things lead to other things, but all of those things always lead to the same end. I'm cunning for a reason, and I like to play with my food, and she's a tasty mortal. You fuck with your human in your way. Let me fuck with my human in mine. Or perhaps I'll just bend the huntress over and fuck her body, plain and simple."

Reprobate! Devil incarnate!

His crudeness provokes murderous thoughts to enter my soul. When this is over, I'll find and slay Puck, along with his brothers.

The river ruler's chest rises and falls in deliberation. He slants his head toward the weaponry and resumes mapping out the bolts, taking care not to get near the tips. "Leave them with me."

"I'll wait," Puck insists.

"No, you will not. It shall take a day."

The satyr hesitates before depositing the archery against the nearest wall. He maintains his hold on the crossbow for a moment, another strange expression cinching his profile.

What right does he have to gaze upon Juniper's weapon as though it's of immeasurable value? As though he cares a fig about its owner?

All the same, his index finger strokes the crossbow's handle once—a covert gesture Elixir can't see. But I can. It's the faintest of touches, hardly discernible even if an amphitheater of spectators was watching. Given my history, I know what it means to reach out when one thinks others aren't looking.

This is one incident in which Elixir is wholly blind. The water lord might sense every heinous emotion in existence, and he might be somewhat acquainted with the manifestations of respect, charity, or vulnerability. But can he discern amorous feelings? Likely not, unless he's ever felt those sentiments in his misbegotten life. For that, I should pity him.

If Puck believes his gesture undetected, does that make it genuine? The action tugs on a small, susceptible part of me that yearns to believe he's in earnest. The part of me that can't resist believing heroes can be found in the unlikeliest of souls.

Abruptly, I shake myself out of the fantasy. There's no fathomable way Puck cares about Juniper. Although promiscuous satyrs are the rare breed who design to indulge carnal acts with humans, bedding mortals and developing feelings for them are different scenarios. Besides, if my sister mattered to him, Puck wouldn't have the archery in his possession, nor would the rogue be here, talking about Juniper like she's a common trollop.

And beyond that, the feeling would never be mutual. Juniper is the most unflappable member of our family. It would take a century for her to stomach such a libertine, much less warm to him.

"Is there anything else?" Elixir inquires, his timbre snipping the quiet in half.

Puck's fingers snap open from around the crossbow. "Let's hope not," he mutters, then swings his full, cavalier attention to Elixir, the archery forgotten. "Well? Aren't you going to offer me a drink, luv? In my neck of the woods, we forest dwellers are generous hosts. You should follow our example."

"Call me 'luv' again, and I shall fill a jug with your blood and make you swallow it."

"Much as I fancy a fetish, blood is where I draw the line." Puck breaks from his stance and saunters to a dense bush. He sprawls on the ground, reclining against the foliage and crossing his cloven hooves, and flits his finger toward the tables. "You got anything with enough substance to get shit-faced?"

"Be very careful," another voice intones. "You're obnoxious enough as it is."

The lilting accent swoops through the room like a gust of wind. My eyes skid from Puck, to Elixir, to a third Fae whose blue wings inflate like sails on either side of his body. This new male presence sprawls on a bracket of rock jutting from one of the walls, one leg dangling, the other steepled on the ledge. With an elbow propped on another bracket, he balances his profile between a thumb and forefinger. Somehow, he manages to make this position look graceful and alluring.

If Elixir inspires a pounding heart, and if Puck inspires a wanton flush to the cheeks, this third being inspires a flutter in one's womb. Looking at the newcomer feels like being pushed off a cliff and then caught mid-air—breathtaking and surreal.

In addition to the wings, the Fae carries the midnight sky in his bearing, from the dark blue hair and lips, to the glittering irises of the same shade. Elixir is fit and athletic, and Puck is broad and sturdy, but this one is statuesque and toned. His cheekbones alone could whet a dagger. Airy linens billow from his body, an open coat and shirt expose his chest to the navel, and his posture exudes lofty elegance.

Lark would call him pretty. She would add sexy to that list.

Lark…

My attention rakes over the winged Fae. The ruler of the river and woodland are accounted for, so this must be—

"Cerulean," Elixir says, his gaze tipping in the male's direction.

"Well look at you, making a spicy entrance," Puck compliments. "Care to put those feathers away, luv? You're upstaging my antlers."

"Fables forbid," Cerulean teases as he vacates the ledge and strolls into the lantern light.

Cerulean. Ruler of the sky.

He's the final member of The Three, the one who reigns over the mountain and has Lark under his command. That is, if she's cooperating, which is anyone's guess.

Puck pouts. At which point, the wings retract into Cerulean's back, vanishing someplace beneath the long coat. Wicked amusement dashes across the mountain Fae's countenance. "Never fear. The wings are gone, and your antlers are free to reign supreme. I've learned my lesson there."

"Why does everyone take my quips so seriously?" Puck laments. "Your plumage can spread whenever they want. I'm not complaining. They're no match for my hard, high, erect crown anyway."

"Is that a fact?" Cerulean wonders. "Because I do recall how you reacted the last time my wings stole public attention from your attributes."

"Whatever you're about to say, I deny everything."

Elixir and Cerulean quirk their eyebrows. To which Puck flings his muscular arms in the air. "What? You may have the wings, but I'm a fucking angel."

"Correct me if I'm wrong, but you threw a tantrum."

Puck jabs a finger at him. "That never happened." A pair of dangly leaf earrings jingle from his ears as he swings his attention toward the silent member of this trio. "Jump in anytime."

"No," Elixir says flatly.

Cerulean's mouth twists with mirth. Puck balks, "No? I'm your guest."

"Cerulean is my guest. You are merely an impish whore—a pest hell-bent on scheming, if not on smut."

"Fables. If you're going to just stand there making sense, go fuck yourself."

The water lord banks his head toward the crossbow. "Do you still want my help?"

Puck scoffs at the warning, then chuckles. "Where's that drink, dammit?"

Satisfied, Elixir turns, his dark robe slicing around his limbs. At one of the tables, he skims his pinky over the stoppers and halts on a tall vessel filled with something that resembles melted honey. He collects two extra chalices, pours the liquid, and distributes it to the Faeries loitering in opposite corners.

Cerulean migrates back to the wall and props his shoulder against the foundation. Casually, he crosses one booted foot over the other and rotates his drink without taking a swig. A slender cord of hair extends longer than the rest of his unkempt layers; the cord dangles down the cliff of his chest, exposed beneath his open shirt and coat. The tail of hair ends in a single blue feather, which shifts as he regards the crossbow propped in the corner. "Care to explain that?"

Puck guzzles the chalice's contents, then licks his lips. "In the articulate words of Elixir, 'No.'"

"Oh?" Cerulean inquires. "And when did you become the taciturn one around here?"

"Ah, but you know how I like to dance around my words, especially when they're none of your business. Are you going to finish that beverage or just smolder at it? If the latter, give it to me. It's been a long day, and I'm thirsty."

"You'd be wise to answer the question, Puck."

"You'd be wiser to kiss my hot ass."

Instead of umbrage, Cerulean's eyes slit with intrigue. Puck's rich brown ones twinkle with mischief. Both wear identical trickster expressions, albeit one elegant, the other knavish.

They move in unison. Cerulean flicks his wrist, and Puck flicks his fingers. A torrent of wind blows through the chamber and charges toward the satyr. Simultaneously, a thick foliage root breaks from the ground like a rope, spewing clumps of soil as it emerges and slams into the current, blocking its impact.

The ground shudders. I jump in place as a tide of water rolls toward the other two elements and smashes into them like a wave. The collision splinters apart, causing the gust to vanish and thrusting roots back into the ground. As for the water, it retracts into the central vat.

Elixir has stationed himself by one of the tables, his hip leaning against the rim. He lowers the capped digits of his left hand, his face steely compared to the sportive mischief of his brothers. Although the space looks as though nothing just happened, he cautions, "Vandalize my territory again, and it will hurt. *Éck abürkist fick.*"

"Apologies and so forth." Cerulean inclines his head, then sips from the chalice with the mannerism of a disheveled prince.

"Sorry, luv," Puck adds to Elixir while setting down his empty vessel. "Being in proximity to the both of you brings out the brother in me."

After another pause, the sky and woodland rulers flash their vicious teeth—and Elixir follows suit, muttering something to himself and then surrendering to a subtle and reluctant grin.

"To answer the question, Elixir is helping me remove the iron from those bolts," Puck says. Except he notices something while indicating the archery. "My, my, my. It appears great minds think alike."

My eyes stray from the crossbow to another weapon ensconced just above, affixed within a recess embedded into the wall. My hunch had been right about my spear's whereabouts. Relief and indignation prickle my skin as I behold the weapon mounted there, not like a trophy but a condemned object or bad omen.

"I'm not extracting the spear's iron," Elixir says.

Cerulean and Puck glance at him, puzzled. I follow suit, taken aback.

"Relinquishing power doesn't become you. Are you in the mood to play with fire?" Cerulean wonders.

"Or do you have a thing for masochism?" Puck demands. "Planning to use it as some kind of elaborate sex toy?"

"Keep your perversions to your fucking self," Elixir advises.

"If you insist. Though in my defense, perversion is for amateurs, whereas sexual exploration is not." Puck tsks. "How many delicacies you miss. You would know this if you'd ever once been ridden."

Elixir's eyes gleam. "In hindsight, I forgot to blind the shit out of you."

"The iron will weaken your defenses."

"I'm aware of what the element does to us," the river Fae snaps, breaking from his position and striding toward the central vat.

"Then why in fuck's name won't you blunt the weapon before your human finds a way to steal it back and castrate you instead?"

"We agreed not to disclose our games."

"We're not talking about the games," Cerulean interjects, moving to the vat and stalling beside Elixir. "We're talking about the weapons these women outfitted themselves with."

"Bloody true, and we did agree when this entire shit show began to report on any problems, with any of our sacrifices." Puck rises, congregates with his brethren near the vat, and shrugs. "Soooo…?"

The pool's surface casts lambent strands across their expressions, which have grown collectively pensive. Elixir listens to a python in motion, angling a single tapered ear toward the snake that coils itself around a neighboring branch. "My intentions are my own. The human shall give me no problems."

I bristle. He sounds far too confident for my liking. I'll need to remind him that I refuse to be preyed upon by anyone or anything.

Cerulean shakes his head. "If my mutinous mortal had her weapon armed in such a way, I would have brought it to you without reservation. That is, if I could manage to pry it from the female—a debatable feat."

"Mutinous?" Elixir echoes.

"Debatable?" Puck quotes.

"She hasn't been very cooperative," Cerulean admits with dry irritation—and a modicum of fascinated admiration. "She's quite the mouthy, meddlesome mortal. You'd favor her, Puck."

"I've got my hands full," the satyr grunts. "My quarry is a scholarly huntress who's been violating me with her prudish scowls and sterile quotations. Is that why you're here, Cerulean? To hold court on someone else's turf and listen to our woes?"

"As you said, we agreed when the sacrifices began to relate any setbacks. I traveled to the forest to collect you for a conference, but you were gone, already here I'd presumed."

"And like I said, I had crossbow business to attend to. But as for problems, I've got no complaints." Puck slants his antlered head, a bonfire of red hair falling across his brow line. "The huntress is under control. You?"

"The woman has a feisty tongue," his brother grants, immoral blue lips slanting. "However, that vice can be tamed. Elixir?"

I brace myself. My captor's attention jolts from the resident serpent to the ground, the lantern flames sharpening his features. "The lady is no threat to me."

"Marvelous," Cerulean says.

"Excellent," Puck agrees.

Silence follows. It's the sort of unstable quiet that contradicts everything they've just declared. The Faeries tarry around the vat, each male figure growing distant, their expressions wrinkling with malcontent.

My abhorrence over the way they've been speaking about Lark and Juniper dissolves. Pride swells in the wake of those feelings.

The steep inclines of Cerulean's profile flex, his lips thinning in displeasure. Puck's square jaw hardens, determination eradicating his wily demeanor. Elixir's pupils fixate on a distant point.

There's a look people have when they're denying or hiding something.

At the moment, I'm privy to such a scene. Here I am, spying on The Three. Here I am, watching these imposing, magical beings brood over my sisters, burdened by things they refuse to name.

A victorious smile wreathes across my face.

My sisters are being difficult. My sisters are challenging them.

My sisters are winning their games.

Or if not yet, they're proving these bastards wrong, and the result is this: the most wonderful sight I've witnessed yet. Amidst the vegetation teeming with serpents, and ensconced in a mystical cavern, the rulers of this Solitary wild are having internal fits.

At least, two of them are. Elixir doesn't bother turning inward. He festers openly, his fingers curling, eager for something to grab and crush.

Puck circles his shoulders, visibly loosening a crick. His brawny muscles contort down his arms, and the numerous buckles and clasps of his leather vest strain across his chest. "There's one other thing," he broaches. "The soil's becoming less fertile in the woodland, particularly in The Gang of Elks."

Elixir's head snaps, jolting across the ground toward Puck's feet.

Cerulean's brows cinch tight. "Has it progressed to The Seeds That Give?"

"Not yet," Puck tells them. "Birth in the forest is still possible."

Cerulean's shoulders unwind, though I can't say the same for his countenance. "I've noticed increasing signs on the mountain range. Several cliffsides have grown unstable. I've ordered them barred from passage. It's a route some of the cougars take, which will force them to change their patterns and seek territory elsewhere, which could lead to carnage with the other fauna."

Puck spouts what I presume is an obscenity in Faeish. "Not happening. We have four more years to fix this. A pittance of time, but still."

"On this trajectory, it might not be enough. If our realm continues to wither at this fucking rate, the animals will eradicate themselves quicker, and we'll have less of our lands to thrive off. Our kin won't last." Cerulean's gaze jumps between his brothers. "We'll fade before then."

"Unless we change the plot." Puck swings his glower toward Elixir. "Anything ruthless to contribute, from the one who sees what others can't?"

The water lord's nostrils flare. "The river is draining."

After a moment of silence, the satyr mutters, "Shit."

"You're certain?" Cerulean asks.

"Yes," Elixir grates out, rage stalking across his visage.

If he means what I think, the water level in The Deep is sinking. At some point in the future, it might not supply its residents or provide sufficient depths for its aquatic creatures.

I recall the grotto's recitation about what will happen if the Faeries fail in these sacrificial games before the thirteenth year. I think about the animals and Fae children of this realm languishing, their population annihilated because mortals and Faeries have failed to come to a truce.

Sympathy worms into my gut. But I also need to survive, for my family and the animals back home who still have a chance of being saved, rescued from their own human threats. Fables forgive me, I can't allow myself to feel mercy for these villains. I can't allow it to cloud my judgement.

Elixir makes this task easier. When his head whips up, venom pours from his tongue. "Make the games hurt."

The words slice across the cavern. It's hardly a groundbreaking suggestion. Of course, these games are meant to hurt.

Yet Elixir's instruction penetrates to the core. I feel its malignancy in my ribcage.

He's not telling his brothers to proceed as usual. He's telling them to make it worse, to exceed anything that has come before. He's telling them to be crueler, more severe than ever, no matter what that entails. He's telling them to distort the rules, to skew them and make my sisters suffer.

Cerulean draws in a breath. "So be it."

Puck's chest rises and falls. "I'm in."

"Are you?" Elixir wonders, his tone deadly calm.

The satyr's jaw flexes. "Strip that sodding archery to the bone."

"Do the same to them."

Why does it look like Cerulean and Puck would rather smash that suggestion to a pulp? In their expressions, some private battle rages. I want to believe what I see, but how can I?

At last, Puck's face smooths out, and a grin surfaces. He winks, then vanishes without sparing the archery another glance.

Cerulean's wings break from his back with a harsh snap. The mantle of plumes spans a considerable portion of the den. Subtly, he leans into Elixir and whispers, *"Jún fúlkist mede ojjur."*

To which Elixir nods.

The ruler of the sky vaults into the air, evanescing before he hits the domed ceiling. A second later, Elixir swerves in my direction. When he does, his eyes pierce through the setting—and scour the room for me.

11

I jerk to the left, pressing into the slot behind the wall. Moving another inch is futile; he'll hear it. Instead, I hold fast, hold my breath, hold everything in. He might be able to detect my inhalations and exhalations, but that doesn't mean he can discern when I suppress air.

From around the corner, the vat makes lapping sounds, and lantern light bleeds onto the lane beside me, but the vipers are quiet. I force myself to be still and silent. I sense his ears listening, his eyes searching, both raking through the atmosphere for signs of an intruder or a mortal captive playing the spy.

This lasts a second before the rap of feet stalk in my direction. True to his nature, he doesn't waste time.

My eyes clench shut. The footsteps stall on the threshold between his den and the terrarium walkway. Under normal circumstances, the foliage and murky environment should be enough to conceal me. Of course, that's no barrier for this Fae; he doesn't need vision to see. Any minute, I expect his arm to lash sideways and snatch me from my hiding spot.

Elixir veers my way. I react on instinct and from memory. Channeling my past as a child slinking in and out of crowds, I duck and slip behind him. Synchronizing our movements, I become his shadow and swivel with the Fae as he inserts himself into the very spot I'd just vacated.

He stops, dumbstruck. His body tenses, aggravation and bafflement straining his profile. When he turns the other way, so do I. Elixir pivots here and there, circling with the stealth of an aquatic creature. Wraithlike, I mirror him, turning where he turns, shifting where he shifts, so that if he were to swerve and reach out, he would catch nothing but air.

A droplet falls from the ceiling, its descent as silent as an errant feather. Nonetheless, Elixir flits out his arm and catches the bead without looking. He rolls the drop in his palm like a marble, then tosses it over his shoulder. The globule splinters into thousands and forms a cascade, the curtain of water shielding the entrance to his den.

With that, Elixir strides away. As if nothing just happened, he heads down the lane and exits the building.

Oxygen washes into my lungs. On a gasp, I buckle in place.

The spear is inside his lair, as is the crossbow. The weapons are there, unmanned and exposed for the taking.

I spin toward the liquid curtain and crash through the deluge. The impact douses my caftan, plastering the fabric to me. I make haste to the spear but stop to glance over my shoulder, cautious that Elixir might double back. When he doesn't, I transfer my suspicions to the serpents reclining, coiling, and dangling amidst the foliage.

Are they his spies? No, according to the Book of Fables, these mystical animals don't serve the Fae. If anything, it's the reverse.

I pivot and swipe my weapon off the wall. With a click and thrust, the spear condenses.

Belatedly, I realize the archery is another matter. It's clunky and re-quires more arms than I possess to transport them, especially through water. Moreover, if a Fae happens upon me during the return trip, I'll need both sets of digits to fight.

An oath boils on my tongue. I'll have to plot another trip to reclaim the archery later, whether or not Elixir's in the room with me. That's as-suming I can achieve that feat within a day, prior to Elixir stripping the iron bolts and handing the weaponry over to Puck.

"I know you can't hear me," I whisper to the crossbow, stroking my palm over its spine. "But I love you, and I won't forsake you."

Summoning the will to abandon Juniper's archery, I rush to the wa-tery partition—and slam against a wall. I skitter backward, white spots cluttering my vision. I shake myself out of the haze, approach the thresh-old once more, flatten my free palm against the liquid curtain, and push.

Resistance greets me, the facade aqueous yet solid, refusing to let me pass. Again and again, I try to no avail. Placing my spear on the floor and using both hands doesn't work, either. I may as well be shoving against a stone door.

Although it had permitted me through, the opposite side of the cascade is a barrier. Elixir has enchanted it.

It's a trap.

"Fables curse you!" I trill, slapping the water.

Had he truly known I was here? Or had he been taking preventative measures?

I swing this way and that. My gaze stumbles upon the vat, a mixture of dread and relief seeping into my stomach. I haven't a clue if it'll dispatch me anywhere close to a passage leading to my chamber. And no, I don't know how long this voyage might take, or how much oxygen it will deplete from me.

But if I stay here, he'll find me, and there will be hell to pay. And if all else fails, hopefully I can vacate the water before suffocating.

I tear a wispy branch from the nearest bush and pad to the basin's rim. One last precaution. If Elixir uses this vat for mixing and testing ingredients, it could be perilous. I toss the branch into the water, and when it doesn't wither or singe, I figure that's the best I can count on.

After sucking in a deep breath and securing the spear in my grip, I slosh into the vat and plunge under. The well suctions me down, but because it's wide enough, I pump my free arm and limbs.

I open my eyes, grateful when nothing averse happens. Underwater caves open at the bottom of the pool. Leaves resembling seaweed sway from the bedrock and tickle my knees.

The cave's mouth opens wide, spilling into a vaster expanse. I paddle my feet and launch to the surface, careful to do so quietly. My lips part on an exhale. I kick in place and almost go back under.

Elixir is looming above me.

Like a specter, he stands on an arched bridge not three feet away, but—thank Fables—he doesn't spot me. Instead, he makes his way along the platform.

I get my bearings enough to recognize The Twisted Canals sprawled around me. I swim beneath the arc, wary of making noise, and watch

Elixir's silhouette progress. Maybe he intends to fetch an ingredient for removing the crossbow bolts' iron, or he's gone to meet someone new, or he's left for many other elusive reasons.

Make the games hurt.

I could go back to my chamber. Or I could follow him.

I could learn more about whom I'm dealing with. In doing so, I might uncover more about this Fae, his greatest weakness, and the curse. It's reckless, but no combatant wins a game without making a move.

I grip the spear and glide after him. It's arduous swimming one-handed, yet I make do. Half of my training had been in the creek outside my family's home. I'd practiced fighting my sisters in the water, acclimating myself to staying afloat with the weapon.

Except this place is home to predatory fauna that could materialize at any moment. What's more, the river isn't idle. The current is erratic here, and the river feels denser as my limbs siphon through the expanse.

Elixir's form isn't hard to make out, even in this subterranean pit. His robe is a black sail around his form as he prowls down lanes and bridges. He passes through a segment of the canals while keeping to nearby walls and ledges, his digits lightly scraping the edifices.

Those long, peapod boats sway against posts, and waterways supplant many of the streets, the river's surface licking the buildings. The base levels of numerous shops and homes are submerged, as if they'd sprouted from the sandy bottoms once upon a time.

Beyond the canal colony and river proper, my nemesis travels to the outskirts and marches down a walkway stretching into the void. Lanterns dapple the platform, which bears no rails or handles, the flat extension suspended on stilts over the water. Bulrushes line the rims, swaying from the water and creating a fringed border.

My joints sizzle from the effort of traveling one-armed. The platform offers a blessed respite, allowing me to grasp the ridge and coast alongside Elixir.

Halfway down, the Fae halts. I bob in place, nudge the bulrushes apart, and peek through the crevice. With his profile in my sights, Elixir tarries beneath the dome spanning hundreds of feet above. The hood of his robe hangs freely, allowing that mane to tumble down his spine.

He sinks into a crouch. I duck behind a thicket of stems and spy through the blades. Kneeling parallel to me, Elixir's hand thrusts past the sedges and settles flatly on the river's surface. Nothing else happens. His head slants toward the ripples, and he idles for longer than I'd have wagered him capable of.

What is he doing? Summoning a wave? Or an animal?

My eyes jump across the perimeter, unable to detect an approaching creature or vortex. Elixir's gaze fixates on something I can't see. It as if he's feeling for a heartbeat, a sign of life.

That's when I glimpse an outcropping jutting from the foliage. The craggy protrusion is laced with chartreuse lichen, which harkens to a Fable about The Deep. According to that tale, this type of lichen germinates only underwater, which might account for the sickly brown staining some of the filaments.

The lichen needs to be submerged. It once was, but it isn't anymore.

I recall what Elixir had said to Cerulean and Puck about the river drainage. It appears, the water level is lowering. It's depriving the plant life—and possibly the wildlife, along with the Fae—of sustenance.

Faeries can live forever without growing sick, but how long do they last without food or drink?

A strange clicking sound plies through the silence, coming from the opposite bank. I swing in that direction, glimpsing nothing out of the ordinary.

Then again, what is normal in this world?

A heavy splash resounds behind me. The commotion propels me back around, where I part the bulrushes and scan the walkway.

Elixir is gone.

All that's left are two articles of clothing—leggings and a robe. Moving at a snail's pace, I wheel toward the river. Despite its gemlike color, the hue is so saturated that it hampers my vision. I squint, floundering to see what lurks beneath the surface.

But I know. Fables help me, I know.

The placid river sprawls like liquid glass. In the near distance, The Twisted Canals glitter with a thousand pools scattered amidst numerous levels, some of the cascades tumbling off the chiseled rooftops. Except for the muffled echo of those falls, all is quiet in my immediate proximity.

My flesh pebbles. I'm well acquainted with the differences between real and fake tranquility. Such peace as this can't be trusted.

While peering at the river, I choke the spear. Slowly, I give the weapon a deft jerk, the ends lengthening. I close my eyes and feel the water, deciphering its current, which accelerates with the force of a wave. And my eyelids blast open.

I twirl and swing the spear downward. A single male hand punches through the surface, a forked dagger in his grip. The pronged blade impales the air and catches the spear, blocking the strike. Steel meets steel, the clang of weapons reverberating across the cavern.

A muscled forearm extends from the water. With my spear ensnared between the dagger's teeth, my opponent uses that leverage to drive me in a half circle across the river. The circuit spritzes water everywhere, then my attacker shoves me backward, the force so great that I shear across the expanse before losing momentum.

I screech, kicking in place. Without the ground to steady me, it's a cumbersome task to whirl the spear overhead. I manage to arch the weapon toward the figure's skull, the effort pulling a guttural noise from my throat. The figure ducks, my weapon whizzing over his head.

I windmill the spear and freeze. So does Elixir.

He angles his set of daggers—one high, the other low—while arrested in a fighting stance. Whereas I'm wobbly, scrambling to keep afloat and balance a weapon, he'd emerged from the torso up and gone still, impervious to the weightlessness.

Strands of dripping hair fall over half of Elixir's face. Rivulets race down his torso, the muscles packed and clenching, and his waist narrows into the gulf. Although visibility had been limited before, now I behold a tail swatting under the surface.

Golden eyes hook onto mine. We disarm in unison, jolting our weapons away. Our chests rise and fall in a hectic search for air, the panting sounds loud in this cavernous place. With all the water Faeries asleep in The Twisted Canals, we're alone. Every time when it has counted, I've been so very alone with him.

I shiver. "You knew I was following you."

His gaze tapers. "Is there a reason I should not have?"

"What gave me away? My temperature again? My blood?"

"The water," he corrects. "I heard how you moved in the water. It is unique from how a river Fae swims."

"How so?" I stammer. "What do you hear?"

Elixir's visage pulls taut, as though the answer disturbs him. "Your movements are calm," he says. "Humble and considerate. Faeries animate the water, but you..." The ruler marvels, and his baritone lowers with reluctant fascination. "You put the water at ease."

I blink. To be honest, I like the sound of that.

My chin juts toward his hands. "So that's how you navigate this realm? Your fingers graze the buildings and tunnel walls? I've seen you trace the air like a path, too. Is that another method?"

Futilely, I had asked about his sense of direction before. Either he's private about his blindness, doesn't trust my curiosity, or confides to no one. No matter the reason, Elixir's features scrunch together, shutting me out.

He flips the daggers and sets them atop of the water, where the blades float in place. He may as well have deposited them on a table. Come to think of it, he hadn't been carrying the weapons earlier, so he must have drawn them here, via the current.

His orbs tick toward the spear. "I should string you up like a flounder."

My fingers flex around the handle. "You took what was mine, you barbarian. I had a right to take it back. I didn't give it to you as payment for a favor, nor did I trade it with you in some frivolous bargain. Not that I would do either, and not that you're the favoring or bargaining type, even if you are one of the Folk. But if you want to reclaim what's mine, we could always take another battle lap around the river. Not that I'm anxious to do that. I'd rather keep my only means of protection. Unless of course—"

The current snatches the spear and pitches it into Elixir's waiting grasp.

My mouth falls open. "Conniving, thieving river!" I snap at the ripples.

The Fae's lips spasm with underlying mirth. "It is water. It cannot hear you." He runs his free palm across the surface. "But we are bonded. It will move if I beseech it. That is, when it allows me the power to do so."

His point is clear. If he wants my weapon, he can pluck it from me at any time. This ruler scarcely needs to lift a finger, much less combat a mortal over the spear. This isn't the first time I've seen him maneuver the water, and it explains the cascade wall he'd created in his den, and why the daggers don't drift away.

Withdrawing his hand from the river, Elixir runs his digits over my weapon, then tosses it to me. I catch the spear, nearly thrown off balance.

"I will not take it from you," he says with a grudge. "Faeries cannot take objects twice."

I puff out a humorous laugh while paddling to stay above water and simultaneously balance the spear. "And here, I'd anticipated you would actually say something honorable."

He closes the distance between us, runnels drizzling down the brick wall of his chest. "Is that what you desire in a person? Honor?"

"How does that concern you?"

"It does not," he acknowledges yet doesn't revoke the question.

If I answer, he'll dissect my response and manipulate it for all it's worth. "I would explain, but I'll spare you the embarrassment."

He frowns. "Embarrassment."

"Embarrassment because you wouldn't understand. Honor is a concept Faeries can't conceive of. Plus, you'd never be able to comprehend my desires, not even if I spelled them out to you."

Elixir's incisors flash. "Then what is the harm in trying?"

The air crackles. My eyes lurch from Elixir's face to his chiseled torso and back up, animosity converging with the stifling temperature. A discomforting warmth spools down my stomach. Suddenly, I want to drink something cool from a tall glass that sweats with condensation.

The Fae's nose twitches. He inhales, and his nostrils to flare as though he'd rather bite into something than sip from a vessel. For an instant, his face simmers, enthralled by whatever scent he's picked up.

Then he jerks back to attention and snaps, "How did you escape the cascade?"

That's an easier matter to deal with. "I dove into your brewing vat."

"Without knowing if it was poisoned." Those eyes glint with surprise, offense, and a third, farfetched emotion that visibly unsettles him.

Truly, there's no point in lying. Not only am I terrible at it, but I can't think of an alternative story. Although giving him cause to be more severe is unwise, I also don't want him underrating me.

"What choice did I have?" I tell him. "After that conversation with your so-called brothers about making the games hurt, I wasn't going to give you an excuse to up the ante. There was a chance you honestly didn't know I was there, a chance I could flee with you unaware. I had to take it. But you did know I was there."

Elixir nods. "We all did."

"Which means the three of you could have said whatever you wanted me to hear."

"What we wanted you to hear," he repeats while pushing toward me. "And what makes you think you're worth that effort?"

Meaning, I'm just that inconsequential, just that harmless a threat. I lift my chin. "Don't underestimate me or my sisters."

The Fae sneers. "Mortal confidence."

I would very much like to punch him now. Instead, my tongue gives this viper the lashing he deserves. "I'm worth the effort if you had to confiscate my weapon in the first place, if Puck has to deface my sister's archery as well, and if Cerulean's been contemplating the strengths of my other sister's whip. I'm worth the effort if you need to maroon me on an isle surrounded by a sinking lake. I'm worth the effort if I managed to get past that obstacle anyway, and I'm worth the effort if you conjured that watery wall in your den. Therefore, and in conclusion, and for all intents and purposes, I'm very much worth every bit of effort." I lick my lips. "The end."

Elixir's head jerks toward my mouth. And I think...I think he'd heard the wet drag of my tongue, because when he answers, his baritone is even deeper and darker. "Exercise that fucking tongue all you like, for it shall not be so powerful if it reveals a vulnerability."

I must have imagined the husk in his tone, which doesn't match the aggravated look on his face. I open my mouth to respond. The river jostles, the water swishing against us.

A fleet of creatures careens our way, their slick bodies leaping, arching, and diving like lances. As they sling toward us, their bottlelike snouts punch the water, and their mouths open wide to emit clicking sounds.

Awe steals my concentration. I've never beheld these fauna in my world, but my birth parents had described their mortal equivalents to me. All the same, the animals radiate with unearthly color, shifting from the copper of coins, to the bronze of statues, to the amber of gemstones. The tints fluctuate, shimmering from their snouts to their tail fins.

Before they reach us, the fleet splits and forks with giddy energy. Their sprightly behavior is infectious. A fin glides playfully across my elbow, the contact dabbing a smile into my face.

Reverence transforms Elixir's features. The heat and hostility from seconds ago disintegrate as he straightens formally. He bows, inclining his head to the fauna as they whisk past us, then scatter into various parts of the river, where they bound and caper like children.

I can't decide what to process first—our gang of visitors or the sight of a viper genuflecting to a party of river dolphins. Unlike with his kin and subjects, Elixir's willingness to relinquish authority is limited only to the fauna. That much is widely known, how the Folk worship their animals and consider them sacred above all else. However, knowing this and seeing it are two different phenomena.

My gaze transfers from the dolphins to the viper. "By any chance, is this—"

"The Pod of Dolphins?" Elixir supplies. "No, it is not. This is The Fauna Tides." He angles his head in inquiry. "Your orientation with The Grotto That Whispers was informative. I gather you were paying attention."

What a condescending brute. "May I presume you didn't inherit your social skills from these creatures?"

"They preside over this area." He glances in the mammals' direction, his voice thawing. "Yet they share it with all water fauna, enabling every dweller of the river to congregate here."

"That sounds like a watering hole."

"Something to that effect, yes. Though, despite it being neutral territory, it is a risk for prey and predators to share turf. That is why sharks rarely venture here, for instance. They fear mass dolphin pods."

A perturbed silence follows. Elixir's face clenches in belated realization of how much he'd said. He thins his lips, preventing him from confiding more.

I'm not about to discourage this Fae. Listening to Elixir express anything deferential is an experience I don't know what to do with. It's the same as an illusion—out of reach, unrealistic, and unlikely to last long.

"I think it's wonderful," I tell him.

"You would say that," he remarks.

"The dolphins are sages for sharing this territory. And yes, I would say that. Many people in my world base worth on one's possessions. I see a person's worth in what they contribute. That's what strengthens us."

The skin between his brows crinkles. I would have expected him to act noncommittal, yet this Fae gives the notion prolonged thought, to the point where he shifts in discomfort and then grunts in acknowledgment.

I gesture at the river dolphins. "What will happen to them if the water level keeps draining?" At his prudent expression, I confirm, "You already know I heard everything."

Elixir averts his troubled gaze. "The same that will happen to all of us. They will either dehydrate or suffocate, then fade."

From the way he drags the words out, the weight of them heavy and laborious, the empathetic part of me longs to say I'm sorry. As usual, this impulse is ridiculous where it concerns him, but I do understand the palpable dip in his tone. I've lived through it, as have my sisters. I can't spend years rescuing animals and running a sanctuary without knowing a bit about this feeling.

"How long can Faeries and fauna last without nourishment?" I broach.

It takes him another moment to reply. I suppose providing details would give me fodder to use against his kind, which is why he merely whispers, "Not long enough." After a brief pause, acrimony replaces his angst, and he glares my way. "You are not saying anything. Why are you not saying anything?"

"Am I supposed to say something?" I reply, softer than I'd care to admit.

"You always say something," he carps. "I would hear it rather than guess it."

"That would be a first."

"Yes, it would."

"It's just…the look on your face right now."

"What about it? How do I look? Choose your answer cautiously."

"I don't have to *choose* an answer. I'm a human, not a Fae who needs to dance around the truth."

"And what is this truth you behold on my face? Tell me."

"You must be the bossiest Fae on this continent. Tell you? Where are your manners? I thought the Folk valued politeness."

Another grunt. "I'm a ruler. My requests are law."

"We'll see about that. But if you must know, what I see is grave concern about the animals' welfare."

Mockery tightens his visage. "Yes, that would shock you. Unlike mortals, we revere the animals of our world."

"You ignorant bastard," I spurn. "Mortals revere the animals of our world, too. Not all of them, but most. I'm included among that lot."

"Are you?" Elixir grates, low and scornful.

"Yes. Anyway, I know it's a characteristic of your kind to hold the fauna dear. That isn't what strikes me. No, what brings me up short is that you're not hiding the emotion."

"There is nothing to hide. I'm not ashamed to grieve for these animals, to fear the loss of them. I do not care who sees it. If it is something I cherish, I will show the world what it means to me, consequences or judgements be damned." He frowns. "What now? Why are you so quiet?"

"Nothing, I…," my words trail off. "Wait. Can't you tell what I'm feeling? You've been able to read my temperature, my blood, and my voice, and you've been able to gauge my reactions, body posture, and how I sound while swimming. Why can't you read me now?"

He bites out, "That's assuming your inner reactions illuminate your thoughts. Sometimes, it is evident. Other times, it is not. What your body does and what comes out of your mouth can be distinct. That is why I'm asking you."

So that he might compare the two, I realize. "In that case, ask me anything you want. Sensory signals or not, it doesn't mean you'll have full access to me, providing I decide to answer at all. And I guess that'll depend on if I like your question, so no pressure. I'm not afraid of an inquisition."

I sense Elixir picking through my declaration like he would a pile of splinters, meticulously and tenaciously for about three seconds, right before his arm knocks the lot to the ground. "Are you certain? Or would you care to revise that very evident lie?"

Condemnation! "I'm sure I don't know what you mean."

"It means I have changed my mind." Inspiration tweaks his features. "I have a bargain to offer you."

12

A bargain from a Fae. If I could have imagined this scenario, it would have taken place in a prominent setting where incidents of ceremony occur, such as in a throne room surrounded by an oval of spectators. Or, in the case of this realm, I might have imagined this scene on a bridge in The Twisted Canals. I wouldn't have pictured myself waterlogged in the river.

"One question," Elixir proposes. "I shall ask you one pivotal question. Answer it genuinely, and I shall allow you to leave."

"Right now?" I squawk.

"Right now," he says.

That's the bargain. It sounds innocent enough, but nothing is ever innocent when it comes to making deals with Faeries.

A soggy blanket of humidity gusts through The Deep. Water rustles as I kick to stay above water. "I'm sure many rulers take inquisitive action while soaked to the bone, swimming with mammals, and in the company of an armed prisoner. If I try hard enough, I can see how this would make sense. Sarcasm aside, don't you have a dry room or dungeon where we might proceed? Not that I'm advocating for dungeons, or any enclosure having to do with imprisonment or torture. In fact, disregard that altogether.

"But I once read a Fable that stated magical beings have a penchant for symbolic locations and spaces designated for interrogations, persecutions, bargains, and even normal conversations. One pertinent detail was the participants could stand on solid ground, which made things easier. I think the Fable was about a kelpie and a tortoise who—"

Elixir threads his fingers through the sparkling water, which thickens and forms a fortification under my feet, thus alleviating me of the need to swim in place. It bolsters my weight as though I'm standing on a damp shore.

I gape at the aquamarine depth, then back at him. *Thank you* stumbles across my tongue, then skids to a halt. "Well, that's convenient."

Elixir's mouth twitches, but he smooths over the reaction with a glower. "One might also call it a favor."

Favor. The word flaps like a red flag in my head.

I leap off the invisible foundation. "Never mind. I can't afford to accept. You understand."

The Fae tilts his head. Once more, he fondles the water, and the same foundation solidifies beneath my toes. No matter where I relocate myself, I suspect this breed of magic will continue to happen. I slit my eyes toward Elixir, who maintains a straight face.

"I did not say it *was* a favor," he asserts. "I do not bestow favors. I leave that to the lofty mountain sprites and frivolous woodland nymphs. I merely implied that it *might* be called a favor."

Despite that impenetrable exterior, his irises gleam like the river. If I didn't know better, I'd say he was teasing me.

I'm surprised Elixir has allowed this much time to lapse. I'd love to take the credit for delaying him, but I'm sure he has other nefarious reasons. I can't imagine myself that much of an influence.

"Is this the penalty for sneaking out and taking what's mine?" I ask.

His mien falters in disappointment, then in fleeting embarrassment. It's as if I had been right about the teasing, and he'd expected me to thaw and play along.

He recovers with a scoff. "I do not need bargains to penalize you."

"So, is this an official deal or a casual one?"

"Why? Are you afraid of answering, human?"

"Certainly not, viper."

The moment I've taken the bait, Elixir strikes. "What do you desire?"

The question sears my cheeks. However, the answer comes quickly. It springs from my tongue, as if it had been waiting there. "Freedom."

He shakes his head. "What do you desire *above all else*?"

"That's more than one question."

"No, it is an extension of the question."

"I petition for a rule that you can't alter the question once it's been asked."

The inclines of his face shift into something resembling involuntary mirth. "I must have forgotten to tell you: There are many sides and layers to a question."

"You plan to peel back those layers like an onion, then," I conclude. "Are you going to keep extending the question, so you get a variety of answers, so you can wring a multitude of emotions from me until I'm worn out?"

The Fae crosses his arms over his naked chest, brackets of muscle flexing. "That depends on how you reply."

I believe him. And yes, I shouldn't be giving him ideas in the first place. But this is Elixir. He doesn't need suggestions on how to be manipulative.

He continues, "Lastly, in case I was not clear—"

"How would a Fae define 'clear'?" I ponder.

"—I shall decide when your answer is satisfactory."

"That's absurd," I protest. "You won't be objective."

"And I presume if you do not wish to go deep, you will lie."

"All this negotiation for an answer?"

"Which you have yet to provide."

"Because it won't be earned."

Elixir's eyes twitch. His next words come out unbalanced and unpracticed. "And...how is it earned otherwise?"

I stumble over that. Is he serious?

"Your Faeish nature is hardly trustworthy," I accuse. "Why else would you care to know me? I have no idea what you'll do with the truth."

"Let's find out," the Fae intones, turning this moment into something private. "Or perhaps you are more afraid of speaking the uncensored truth than sharing it? Perhaps what you desire above all else is too delectably controversial? Will you blush? If you do, I shall know."

His voice plummets so deeply it reaches the crux of my body, stroking that root until it begins to contract. How had Elixir managed to make a threat sound like a temptation?

It doesn't help that he draws closer. His formidable silhouette consumes my view, all that flesh and sinew within reach. The Fae's black hair hangs down his torso, the mane puddling around him and brushing the water.

Tendrils of my own hair tremble over my shoulders, my soaked garment clings indecently to my breasts, and the newly familiar aromas of bergamot and black pepper flood my senses.

I should move. Truly, I should move away.

Elixir's eyes fall half-mast as he listens to my reaction. That's when I stiffen. He may think he has the right to my fate, but he has no right to access the inner workings of my body.

What do you desire above all else?

I had been telling the truth when I'd said freedom is what I desire. But I'd been thinking about my sisters' survival, not my desire outside of that. Not the great desire of my whole life, of my very soul.

Maybe I'd already known this is what Elixir had meant, but I hadn't wanted to face it. Maybe he'd sensed it in me as well, or he heard it in my voice, or I had answered too quickly, too easily. Maybe the answer hadn't hurt me the way a different one—the right one—would.

Because what I want most of all, I'll never have.

What do you desire above all else?

I think of a night, nine years ago: eventide soaking my village in hues of emerald and indigo, the elderberry bushes hissing, and my body diving into a stream. The suction of water. The furious kick of my limbs. A dark figure trying to flee, and my fingers snatching the back of his neck.

My hatred. My yearning to make him drown.

I remember holding my breath for longer than I ever had—while watching him lose his. I remember that one night when I'd transformed from a sweet little girl into someone vicious.

I don't remember ever regretting what I'd done. But I do remember regretting that I'd enjoyed it. I remember regretting what he turned me into, even if just for one night.

What do you desire above all else?

"Forgiveness," I whisper.

The word ruptures through me, from my gut, to my throat, to my lips.

It falls out of my mouth like a stone, shattering the quiet. For some peculiar reason, I'm grateful that at least I've admitted it here, so far beneath the earth that no one—not my family, nor my people—hears my shame.

No one but a monster. Elixir's eyes stray to the water as he absorbs my answer, his body utterly still and his serpent's tail frozen beneath the river.

Forgiveness. That's what I long for.

This spawns another troubling question. I feel it surfacing at the same time Elixir gives it voice.

"Whose forgiveness?" he asks.

"I don't know," I grit out.

I'm lying. I'm doing it to him as much as to myself.

Elixir knows this. He doesn't need to say as much, in order to scramble my thoughts further. Denial is just that strong, just that potent, like an intoxicant or a poison.

I hate him for reminding me of this, just as I hate him for a thousand other reasons. My urge to remain quiet is only eclipsed by my urge to lance him through with my tongue, if not my spear.

"Have you been living in a fathomless void for so long, you have nothing more honorable or purposeful to do than play mind games with your prisoners?" I seethe. "Has languishing in the dark taught you this?"

Elixir's head snaps toward me. He'd been lost in thought, contemplating my reply, because it takes him a moment to respond. "The Deep is not a fathomless void. It has its purpose, which is greater than you imagine, from its dwellers to its waters."

An awful response shoots from my mouth. "I wasn't talking about The Deep."

The Fae's entire being pulls taut. His jaw hardens, and his eyes shout at me, the orbs blazing with hot gold.

It's a horrible thing to say to someone. If I had heard one of my neighbors insult a person that way, I would have rioted against their cruelty, insensitivity, and ignorance.

My tongue prickles from the words, the harshness and wrongness of them. Never have I spoken to someone with this much vitriol. Years ago, I'd rid myself of the capacity, purged myself of such an impulse.

Elixir isn't a human being, nor does he deserve my empathy or respect.

Yet my temper disintegrates. Just as he glowers to conceal any modicum of humor, so does this water lord glower to conceal any trace of hurt.

However, I see it plain as day. I witness it in the twitch of his eyelids and the stunned flap of his lashes. I behold it in the way he inches backward, as if struck, which causes the river to billow.

What's more, I feel it in the guilty twist of my ribcage. To say the least, I don't believe in the reprehensible words I'd spoken, much less endorse or tolerate them. My family would be as ashamed as I feel. They know my flaws as well as my strengths, but they've never seen this unforgivable side of me.

Only one other soul has.

Elixir recovers quickly, his tail swatting the water. "Lucky for you, your answer is the truth," he mutters. "As to why I inquired whose forgiveness you seek, I was merely being…thorough."

Do I believe that? Again, Elixir would never be interested in me otherwise.

Would he? For that to happen, this Fae would have to see me as an equal. He'd have to care about who I am. That's something he'll never do, nor do I want him to.

"One wonders why," I say, humoring him. "Why the need to be thorough?"

"Perhaps I would like to know who has that power over you," he husks. "Who can fulfill or deny you that desire?"

Promptly, I discard my guilt. As I sidle closer to him, the hard watery foundation he'd conjured balances me. "Or you hope that person is you. But I'll spare you the disappointment: it's not. No matter whose forgiveness I seek, it will never be yours. I don't pine for your forgiveness because I don't regret a single thing I did that night. I only regret I hadn't finished you off.

"Maybe I wish for fate itself to forgive me for that. Maybe that's my greatest desire. If you expect otherwise, you're sorely mistaken. One might even say you're in denial. One might call you stubborn."

The Fae dips his head and rasps through his teeth, "That makes two of us."

Yes, it does. If I keep lying to myself about whose forgiveness I seek, that makes me just as stubborn. If I rifle through the shards of broken glass inside me, I'll find the truth there, waiting to be acknowledged. And it will cut deeply.

Nevertheless, I want nothing from this ruler, least of all his pardon. The notion that I should is obscene, considering what he's doing to me, holding me hostage. I'm paying for the past enough as it is.

This Fae doesn't want to know me. He just wants to find my limits and expose them, to slip under my skin like venom until I can't recover, until I'm too emotionally weak to play the game, too lost to think about breaking his curse—or even wanting to.

I'll be so focused on my own demons, I won't have time to consider his. How deviant. How clever.

"You're right," I say. "I do know whose forgiveness I seek, but I won't tell you because I don't have to. Like I said, you haven't earned it. Do you want to know how things are earned? Through respect, friendship, and trust."

"Why would I aspire to that?" the Fae defends.

"Why?" I gall. "Have you never confessed anything to anyone?" But the irate Fae just stares at me. "Because that's how you form a bond. That's how you connect with others. Those feelings and thoughts are sacred, and if you can share that mutually, it becomes the most profound and meaningful attachment you'll have with someone. To be truly known by them, and for them to know you, is a gift. What's the meaning of living if you don't have someone to share secrets with, to share those raw experiences, to share everything?"

"Everything," he utters, floating nearer.

"Everything," I say, moving closer.

Our words flow like the river—seamless and clear, its bottom within reach if we plunge deeply enough.

"If you can bare yourself that way, that bond will be the most intimate, the strongest thing you've ever felt," I impart. "It becomes unbreakable."

"Unbreakable," Elixir intones.

The rasp of his voice, combined with our proximity, tells me I've gotten carried away. And so has he. All the same, I don't stop.

"What do you desire above all else?" I echo.

That I dare to mirror his question causes the water lord's pupils to simmer. But he doesn't hesitate to thrust his arm toward the mammals splashing nearby. "Their survival," he replies.

The answer wraps itself around my chest and squeezes. It's the sort of response I'd wish from any ruler of a wild realm, and it suits the nature of his kind. However, it's not what I had anticipated. And it's not the answer I'm searching for.

"What do you desire *for yourself*?" I clarify.

Elixir takes a long draught of air and turns away. "I want for nothing. I long for nothing."

I hear it in his voice, pulled taut like a rope about to shred. "Then either Faeries can lie to themselves, if not to others," I say, "or I'm sad for you."

He twists in my direction, his expression stumped. I understand this reaction, because it strikes me as well: That I would show this being the slightest compassion, even now.

Elixir glides closer still, and I don't discourage him. Our bodies brush, wet and tight.

"Sentimentalism and idealism," the Fae observes, his intonation rough and unsteady. "I should disdain your softheartedness."

"Do you?" I whisper. Again, he makes no reply. And so, I dare, "Or what do you feel instead?"

For the life of me, I can't say how I'd like for him to respond.

In unison, our gazes wander, mine toward his evil lips, his near my mouth. Like an animal, Elixir muffles a coarse sound from the back of his throat. Yet it penetrates me anyway, the noise throbbing within the slot between my thighs. Anger, stress, curiosity, remorse, yearning, confusion, and frustration surge together, pounding against that intimate place where my inner walls dampen.

Elixir's digits contract. They fluctuate between curling into fists or plunging under surface, where my dress floats and spreads open. I'd be mortified by my body's reaction, if I weren't determined to deny this Fae that power over me. He has too much of it already, and I have a mind to take that power back.

A hardy splash reminds us of the river dolphins. The noise coming from their side of the river breaks our trance and wrenches us apart.

Elixir shears his fingers through the water with more force than necessary, sending a small tide toward the creatures. Immediately, a lone dolphin breaks from the pod and propels in our direction. When its head pops above the surface between us, I marvel at the creature in a way I hadn't been able to before. Its majestic, charming clicks, whistles, and squeals travel beyond this space, unlike the call of any water animal in my world.

I hesitate, then set my hands on its cheeks and run my fingers over the creature's sleek skin. Laughter springs from my lips as the dolphin makes a noise of pleasure, then bumps its head against my shoulder.

Sudden movement grabs my attention. My eyes stray toward Elixir, who must sense my gaze because he averts his own head. A muscle ticks in his jaw.

I clear my throat. "You control the water."

"I told you before," he says. "The water and I share a bond. I entreat the river, and it replies of its own will."

"Does that mean the water is alive here?"

"Not like the trees in The Solitary Forest. The water of The Deep is a force, such as the wind in the mountain. Both can be prevailed upon, and they react to the request of a Fae. It is a union, of sorts."

"You speak to the fish and mammals, too," I summarize.

"I do," he says. "We communicate through the water. Or sometimes, through kinship."

"Like that snake in The Pit of Vipers. You two were talking about me the first time I was there, but you wouldn't tell me what you were saying."

"Ah, that. I asked it to pass judgement on your character. The snake approved of you," he begrudges.

"Truly?" I ask, flattered. "That explains the sour puss you wore. Do you always ask a snake to appraise each human captive?"

"No," he admits.

I give a start, unable to tell if being an exception is a good or bad omen.

The dolphin capers around us. When it completes a circuit, the animal bumps Elixir's hip, which causes his mouth to tilt—a little.

I smile in kind, then stop myself. To my dismay, I like what fondness does to Elixir's lips. Nonetheless, I don't like what it does to my pulse.

Thankfully, he doesn't detect this internal dilemma. He runs his palm over the creature's back. "This male shall take you to your chamber. Trust his direction. He will know where to go."

A thrill eddies through me when I realize the animal is waiting for me to climb onto its back. How quickly moments in this place fluctuate from one extreme to the other, from magical to gruesome, from terrifying to wondrous. Like water itself, sometimes the moments are still and peaceful, other times raging and unpredictable.

The creature snatches my weapon in its teeth and angles itself toward me. I waver, then gingerly loop one leg over the arc of its back, and we bob in place like a boat. Unsure of what to do with my hands, I set my palms on either side of its body.

Elixir lingers beside us, his voice firm. "Hold fast," he instructs. "Do not let go."

The animal springs forth. I have one second to glance over my shoulder, to where Elixir's towering form looms.

My guide launches across the river, abandons The Fauna Tides, and cuts through The Twisted Canals at lightning speed. After passing the colony, the dolphin veers into a tunnel where shadows consume us. My companion slips in and out of passages so fast it's difficult to orientate myself. I can't recall having traveled this far from my chamber, but the creature could be taking a longer route because of its size and to avoid areas too dangerous to enter.

We shave through the ducts, the animal submerged and shooting ahead like an arrow, and me exposed above the surface. Waves split around my hips and spray the crusted walls. Air whisks through my hair and lantern flames glimmer from crannies on either side.

The dolphin pokes from the water with a jubilant squeal. I chuckle and spread my arms, letting the gusts course around me. I'm lost in a dreamscape, a place out of a storybook where danger lurks on the fringes like in any wilderness, in any world.

Then I stop laughing. The dolphin wrenches to a halt, and my body flops sideways. I scramble to clasp its head at the last minute.

Arrested at a cave-like intersection of tunnel archways, the baffled dolphin paces this way and that in front of a particular threshold. I realize why. The conduit's water level is too low for us to pass through without the dolphin scraping itself on the foundations. My guide is confused, as if this hasn't happened before.

Trepidation crawls up my spine. The river must be draining here, too.

The dolphin lurches eastward, then stops. It leaps westward but stalls again, its flippers and flukes battering the water in agitation. Water levels in the other arteries seem fine, yet something about them discourages the creature from entering. The environments beyond remind me of swamps festering with some type of fermented algae, sickly green cesspools gurgling loudly.

After rejecting several passages as options, my companion emits a series of frantic whistles. My first thought is to return to where we'd started, head back to Elixir, who can provide insight and show us an alternate way. Unfortunately, the animal fails to draw that conclusion, and I'm unable to communicate the request.

The creature is in such a dreadful state that my second thought is to calm the male down. "It's okay," I coo, leaning over to pat him. "We'll be fine."

It's easy to see the bottom, despite the half-light. With my height, it's shallow enough to stand, but not so shallow that I can't swim through.

I swing my limbs off the animal's back, submerging only to my hips. My feet hit the sandy bottom. Although the water's clean throughout the intersection, sludge coats the depths beyond the archways. That is, all except the one we'd hoped to enter.

The mires' putrid odor singes my nostrils. My heart races as I consider the types of river predators that might exist in swamps.

"Shh," I whisper, running my fingers across the dolphin's back. I gentle my voice, the way I do when the animals of my family's sanctuary need taming. This one yearns for a soft voice and an even softer hand.

"I get lost all the time," I assure the creature. "You know what I do when that happens? I think of a story."

No, I don't. But the poor thing doesn't need to know that. Instead, I murmur a Fable about dolphins exploring the oceans and rivers of this world.

The animal slumps, its anxious whistles receding. When I finish the tale, the dolphin goes still and floats sedately beside me, though I barely have time to feel relief. The creature's whistles have quelled—and been replaced by another sound.

This new noise is bigger and bumpier. It's the sound of a creature with canine teeth.

Slowly, I turn and find a pair of reptilian eyes floating several feet from us. It's another dweller I've never beheld but seen in one of Juniper's books. Although only its orbs have surfaced, I imagine what the rest of it looks like, from its armored body, to the length of its snout, to the trap of its mouth hidden below the depth. The reptile's ethereal pupils blaze like malachite, and its scrolling grunt rises from under the pool, traveling as far as the dolphins' calls had.

Terror roots me to the ground. If Faeries name locations after their fauna, I make a horrible conclusion: This must be The Bask of Crocodiles.

The crocodile growls but doesn't move.

With painstaking slowness, I pry my spear from the dolphin's mouth and step in front of my companion, blocking it from our predator. Except a telltale lap of water alerts me to another presence behind us. Veering that way, I spot another set of malachite eyes slicing through the water. Another croc drifts our way from the opposite threshold, followed by another, and another.

They're fencing us in.

I raise the spear and broaden my stance. That's when I realize their growls aren't directed toward us but one another. Each creature is staking its claim, challenging one another over who gets the kill. I sense the makings of a fauna battle, with me and the dolphin caught in the middle.

The outcome depends on who gets to us first. That's how they'll decide.

The crocodiles let out a grating roar and launch at us.

13

With their mouths open, the beasts charge. A great roar of sound rents through the cave and unhinges the foundation.

I bolt, ready to dive in front of the dolphin. But the mammal is fast, springing out of harm's way, so I throw myself in the opposite direction.

We splinter apart. Hurtling from the snarl of reptilian bodies, I land on the fringes of the pool while the dolphin stashes itself safely on the other side. My frame hits a craggy facade, pain slicing through me.

The beasts collide. Their bodies slam together, the wet slap of limbs and crunch of bones earsplitting.

Curled against the wall, I grip my weapon and stare in abject horror. Water lashes the air, and muck splatters the walls as several fauna tangle together in a frenzy of tails and jaws and serrated growls. They snap, attempting to drown one another, to jolt each other into death rolls. One pair tumbles in place like logs, fighting for dominance, hurling wave after wave across the tunnels.

Another pair surges from an adjacent threshold and barrels into the skirmish. While rescuing animals with my family, I've never found myself at the crux of an assault between fauna, neither over territory nor prey.

I've been lucky. My family has been lucky.

I want the beasts to stop, but it's not in their nature to stop. I'm torn between worry for the dolphin and these otherworldly animals tearing themselves to shreds.

My eyes jump from one end of the pool to the other. I peer through the quagmire, trying to find a route to the dolphin, but I can't see an opening. Across the expanse, the dolphin scurries from left to right. I fail to interpret its cries because the cacophony is too overpowering, too deafening.

But I know it's frightened. And I know it's still trapped.

The only way out of here is to get past the crocodiles before one of them wins this combat. I can't do anything to prevent a slaughter. All I can do is spare myself and my companion, Fables willing.

One of the crocodiles swings its tail in an arc that slams into the side of another, sending the latter beast careening into a wall. The animal smashes against the barrier but recovers quickly and propels itself back into the fray.

Just then, the ring of crocs fragments apart, as if detonated by a submerged source. I freeze. A massive alpha crocodile breaks from under The Deep, the reptile's body having shifted to an unearthly size and inundating the cave.

The giant beast doesn't go after its rivals. It swerves toward the dolphin.

I catapult into motion, flinging myself into the river. The pool catches me, and the noise recedes. My eyelids pop open beneath the river, threads of teal hair floating around my head. Clasping the spear in one hand, I pump my free limbs, shooting across the divide while the crocs are dazed and disoriented from the volcanic arrival of their new opponent.

The force of the battle shoves me about. My lungs are charred, and my pulse rockets into my throat. Immersed with countless spurts of red staining the water, it's a nightmarish swim. I think of my family and the snake waiting for me in my chamber. Saving animals has always been a perilous risk, but I've never turned my back on a creature in need, and I never will.

I pump through the current, then loop upward and break the surface in front of my companion. I have no time to think as my body emerges. I suck in air and spin toward the colossal, incoming crocodile, then windmill my spear and thrust it against the reptile's splayed mouth. The weapon's angle catches the beast, the spear lodging between rows of teeth. My molars grind together, my joints spasm, and I cry out. The croc's weight is heavy enough to crack my spine.

I hold fast. The animal growls in furious surprise and pushes against me. From behind, the dolphin flops around while releasing a series of frightened noises. The beast and I throw our weight against each other, but this shouldn't be enough. I should have gone down in seconds.

By some miracle, I'm upright. Meanwhile, the bask of the crocodiles shred each other into green ribbons. The sound and stink of it are unreal. The reek of blood clogs my nostrils, guttural bellows grate through the atmosphere, and tidal waves smash into the walls.

My knees quaver with the effort to stay on my feet. This beast would be a force to reckon with at its normal size, but with its body swollen to behemoth proportions, this duel is an impossibility. It's only a matter of time—minutes, seconds.

The dolphin dunks itself and propels in a circle around my waist, creating a ring that broadens and travels through the tunnel. After that, the male hides once more behind my back.

My memory retreats to those training sessions with my sisters in the creek—the maneuvers I taught them and the ones they taught me. I have one option and zero time to doubt it. I release the spear, drop into the water, and roll. The sudden yield shocks the crocodile into plunging beside me. In the depth, I take advantage of the momentary lapse and ram the spear's tip into the cage of the assailant's mouth. With another cry, I tilt the weapon upward and impale the beast's upper mouth, striking deep enough to penetrate its skull.

The crocodile shudders and goes still. Right before it topples onto the river floor like a sunken ship, I pry the spear from its maw and veer out of the way, then resurface with a gasp.

This is far from over. Half of the crocodiles have either retreated or float in dead heaps. However, two of them are hale and barreling toward me.

I don't know how I'm still alive or where my fortitude came from. But then my eyes catch sight of the spear dripping with crimson.

The iron. The inlaid scrolls must have weakened that crocodile and enabled me to run it through.

The knowledge spikes me with adrenaline. With my chest heaving, I broaden my stance and spin the spear over my head. Hunching, I wait for the onslaught.

The crocodiles bolt forward—then backward as a new wave blows from the depth and plows into them. In the spot where they'd been, Elixir erupts from the water like a geyser, rivulets racing down his torso, and his scales flinging rays of light across the cave. With his forked daggers clamped in his fingers, his pupils two wells of black, and half of his viper tail visible, the water lord resembles an avenging merman.

Ripples flow from the spot where the dolphin and I hover. From that faint signal alone, Elixir's head snaps in our direction, and he determines our location. An emotion bordering on relief unlocks his jaw, which must be for the dolphin. He can't be worried about me, apart from my place in the game.

I remember the dolphin sending tiny waves across the river. The animal must have sent a distress call to the river's sovereign.

My gaze clings Elixir's face, then strays to a spot behind him, where two figures leap into view. My lips split to holler a warning, but Elixir's features warp from relief to fury. His countenance tightens, and his irises burn as he whips around to sling gilded beams from his eyes. The cast of light momentarily blinds the reptiles and launches them backward, but this only fuels their temper, and they charge again. Their hoarse bellows reverberate as they flank Elixir on either side.

I hesitate. This Fae can handle both foes; he doesn't need my help, and if these beasts rip him asunder, it's hardly my problem. Indeed, Elixir's demise would be a blessing. This game would be over, and I would be free.

Yet another memory flickers in my psyche. Me, nine years-old and engulfed in another body of water. Me, trying desperately to stop a villain from escaping. Me, clutching him for as long as I can while his face bloats with immortal anger and raw, youthful fear.

And me, failing to hold on.

Consciousness shoves me back to the present. I could root myself to this spot and do nothing. I could watch the crocodiles end my captor. I could watch them finish what I had started so long ago.

Elixir's head wrenches from left to right as he struggles to filter through the clash of overlapping sounds. The reptiles agitate the water. This produces enough turmoil to set the ruler's senses into disarray, which gives one of the animals the opening shot it needs.

The beast swings its armored tail and clubs Elixir's right arm, the tail's incrustations piercing his flesh. Blood spurts from the notches. The Fae groans but swipes his dagger and cleaves the reptile across the throat. Regardless, the plate of its skin is too thick to penetrate with only one lash.

They lunge into a fight. Elixir moves with the speed of a tidal wave, wielding his daggers with vigorous precision and momentum. Meanwhile, the second predator approaches from behind and opens its maw.

Terror be damned. I heft my spear and vault into the fight. Landing in front of the second croc, I spiral my weapon into a dizzying formation, then swing with all my might. The tip lances across the beast's chest, and the creature tumbles.

In that span of seconds, Elixir and I wrench around to face one another. We pause, our weapons arrested. A thunderstruck expression sweeps across his features, but there's no time to ponder it.

The reptiles unleash. We whirl, our spines slamming together.

It's a pandemonium of limbs, tails, blades, and teeth. The iron scrolls are my saving grace, enabling me to deflect and thrust. I react, blocking where I must, jabbing where I must.

Against my shoulder blades, Elixir's muscles contort and flex, and his bare body fits to my own. My calves align with his tail. The spear whirls in my grip, while his blade emits its own whizzing sound. We battle in sync, as if we've done this our whole existence. I would resent that, if it weren't keeping us alive.

The world reduces to growls and clangs, to punches and stabs. And then, with a sudden jolt, it's over. The lifeless crocodiles skim the water, their bodies pitted and oozing red.

I stumble in place, my thoughts hastening to catch up. Wheezes scrape from my mouth, whereas Elixir remains deadly silent. We pivot toward one another, our digits strapped around our weapons, which leak at the tips. Echoing drips of blood produce a wave of nausea in my gut.

I'd had no choice. The reptiles would have ended my life. Through me, Lark and Juniper would have lost their games. I'd been defending myself and my sisters.

The spear falls from my grasp and splashes into the water. Instantly, the surface catches the weapon and bolsters it, preventing the spear from plummeting.

Then I gasp as Elixir chucks his own weapons, snatches my wrists, and hauls me into him. His heart pounds madly against my breasts. My body goes rigid, and I open my mouth to say…I don't know what to say…but the inclination ceases as his palms roam my hips, arms, and shoulders. The movements are quick and frenzied, his digits vaulting to my neck and jaw, taking care not to scrape my flesh with his fingercaps. The sensation of his hands on me, coupled with the reality of what just occurred, renders me speechless.

As swiftly as he'd begun, Elixir releases me. "You are unharmed."

All the same, his eyes remain bright with alarm. I translate his actions for concern, then wisely remember the part I play in the survival of his kin. Elixir's ministrations had nothing inherently to do with my wellbeing. He needs me alive, nothing more.

That I have room left inside me for disappointment—inexplicable disappointment—at this moment, is a mystery.

My caftan has been slashed in several places, including one shoulder. The garment's fabric droops to my forearm, exposing the top swell of a single breast. My bones scream in pain, and lacerations enflame my right side, but yes, I'm in one piece.

My fingers jump to my necklace, the chain still mercifully draped around my throat, and the pendant tapping my back. "I-I'll live."

"You should have been safe," he rationalizes. "Outsiders can pass through crocodile territory without incident, so long as they do not stall or linger. The threshold to your chamber should have been passable."

"Why wasn't it?"

"You heard me speak with my brothers."

About the wild fading and the river draining. We'd previously acknowledged as much, but that's not an answer.

Because I'm too worn out to pursue the matter, I cast a dazed glance at the dolphin. From beside me, I sense Elixir doing the same. The male emerges from its hiding spot and dashes toward us, circling me first and then Elixir. The ruler sets his palm on the animal's back and murmurs in Faeish, the words raspy yet melodious. Usually, it's my task to do the soothing, but all I do is stare at the pair of them.

Eventually, the dolphin butts its head against my hip, jostling me out of my stupor. I place a tentative hand on its cheek and whisper, "It's all right. I was scared, too, but we're safe now."

As the creature nestles against me, I catch Elixir listening to us with an expression so transparent, it forces me to take a second look. His aspect slackens, the creases smoothing out, and the gold of his irises mellow.

Abruptly, he turns to inspect the drained tunnel where the dolphin had originally intended to pass. After running an investigative palm over the water, consternation warps his profile, though not for long.

It might be the current's direction, the texture of the water, or the harrowing sound of the crocodiles drifting nearby. Either way, the Fae takes heed of the casualties and cuts his digits through the pool. The water vibrates, then gently wraps itself around the reptiles and tugs their bodies beneath the surface, along with the remnants of blood.

"Where do they go?" I croak.

Elixir startles at my question, visibly stunned that I would bother to concern myself. I watch him grapple with that before he swivels away. "The water buries them," he answers in a gruff voice.

Mournfully, Elixir shuts his eyes. Then he opens them and runs his thumb through the pool, sending ripples toward the dolphin. The creature responds by gliding around us one final time, plunging into the river, and vanishing the way we'd originally come.

A sudden and overwhelming quiet fill the cave, except for a few droplets leaking from crannies in the ceiling. Though, the silence doesn't last long. Elixir makes a hissing sound as crimson leaks from the notches in his arm, the gashes made by the crocodile's tail. The clefts pour onto his scales and stain them.

I slosh over and grab his arm, which causes him to freeze like an animal caught in a snare. Then he jerks away, his confusion evident: *What are you doing?*

He looks confounded, as though he's never received such attention before, which I can't fathom seeing as the river Faeries worship him. Maybe for magical reasons, he's never needed tending, on account of being a Fae who rarely suffers from wounds.

"Just let me," I tell him.

Plucking the hem of my caftan, I use the fabric to dab the craters in his arm, pressing into them tenderly and patiently. I sense his attention riveted on me, so I duck my head to avoid his gaze. The flimsy textile shouldn't be enough to staunch the bleeding, but it is. It may have something to do with him being an immortal who heals rapidly. Whatever the reason, I refuse to consider the magnitude of my actions.

Elixir does it for me. Recovering from his paralysis, he jerks back with serpentine speed. "Why did you help me?" he demands.

He's not talking about his injuries. I retrieve my weapon with shaky fingers, retreat to an outcropping of rocks jutting from the walls, and crawl onto the mantle, my backside slumping. Cradling my upturned knees and resting my chin there, I stare at the place where the crocodiles sank.

A shadow moves closer, blending with mine over the depth. I drag my gaze to Elixir, who looms before me.

All I can manage is a shrug. "It was the right thing to do."

From the way that he tilts his head, I could be speaking in a language he doesn't know. "It's easy to be cruel to enemies," I explain. "It takes more strength to be compassionate."

Slowly, the numbness rinses away. I rub my arms, glimpse the place where the battle had ended, and let the remorse clot my gullet. "It takes more grit to heal something dangerous rather than hurt it," I say, my lips wobbling. "It takes more care to rescue something rather than turn your back on it."

The atmosphere blurs, quavering at the margins as saltwater builds in my eyes. I'm exhausted, relieved, remorseful, shocked, and I want to go home.

For the longest time, the ruler remains silent. I glance up to experience yet another stunning vision. His features have crumpled like a wad of parchment, and his eyebrows are fluted.

So, this is what sympathy looks like on him. Or rather, it's not sympathy but empathy. He's bewildered that I would care what happens to the predators who'd attacked me, that I would long to know what becomes of them after the water sweeps them away, that I would show consideration for the predatory fauna of this world.

Can he detect the trauma in my voice? The bereavement?

The pool laps at the walls as he glides nearer, liquid parting around his hips. I tense but don't move away, my limbs spreading of their own volition as he slides in between them. The sopping caftan bunches around my upper thighs, exposing too much of me. He's so close that I'm straddling him, his viper scales skating over my inner thighs and making me tremble. Wet heat emanates from his torso, and his breath coasts across my mouth. I find myself inching nearer to those inhalations, yearning to infuse myself with them.

Elixir's gaze strays. It follows the trajectory as his fingers steel out to brush the welts blooming over my hip. I can't move, won't move.

While glancing toward the lacerations, his accent turns ragged. "This was not your fault."

My lungs compress. Any second now, the floodgates will open, and I'll weep. But if I cry in front of him, I'm not sure what else I'll be capable of.

His pupils lift to search for mine. The angle draws our lips closer, our mouths consuming the same pithy slices of air.

Splashes invade the scene. Elixir reels away from me as Coral bursts from the depth. Her crystalline eyes shimmer as she gapes at the remaining evidence of anarchy—our wounds and the crumbling foundations. Considering the territory, it's easy to deduce what transpired.

My limbs clap shut, blocking out the nexus of my thighs, which had been so utterly accessible to Elixir. His inability to have seen a thing is immaterial; no matter what, I'd let it happen. I had parted my knees and allowed him to fill the space between my legs.

Nonetheless, my cheeks are too clammy to boil with humiliation. Far too much has occurred, and far too many other conflicting sensations take up residence in my being, for me to spare room for such a paltry feeling as mortification.

Either Elixir had summoned the guard, or the dolphin had acted as a messenger for him. Coral's presence snaps Elixir to attention. A myriad of emotions streaks across his visage, from irate that we've been interrupted to ashamed for feeling aggravation in the first place.

I relate to this, Fables forgive me. Regardless, I do my most to stifle that flawed impulse by lifting my chin.

Coral casts me a stupefied glance, debating my part in this chaos. However, because Elixir and I had been huddled together, with our weapons coated in red, I see this female draw the conclusion that her ruler and I had joined forces. She must also see the effect it's had on us, which causes a single, silver-blue eyebrow to arch.

Elixir glides farther away from me, his serrated baritone as sharp as steel. "Get her cleaned up," he orders the guard.

Without another searching glance my way, the ruler swipes his daggers from the water and dives headfirst into the void, his tail flicking behind him. The level is shallow, yet he vanishes as though the depth is bottomless.

The female attempts to guide me off the rocks. I insist I can swim, then descend into the pool and follow her out of The Bask of Crocodiles. As she leads me away, I recall how stumped Elixir had been when I tended to his wounds, how it had sidetracked him. I think of his reaction when I'd explained why I helped him. I reflect upon his haggard expression, the low murmur of his voice, the way he had touched the abrasions on my skin, and the words he'd spoken.

This was not your fault.

I fret over how it had made me feel, the solace it had offered. It couldn't have been an easy thing to say, not from a Fae to a human, not regarding the death of sacred fauna.

A crucial fact burns into my head: Elixir's capable of feeling something other than darkness. He can feel more than hate and cruelty. I had witnessed momentary empathy in him, pure and unconditional. If I can achieve that sort of reaction from him once, I can do it again. If that's possible, what other susceptible emotions lurk inside him?

If I find out...

If I tap into that...

If I can get close to him...

If I can win his friendship and penetrate the impenetrable parts of him, I might earn his trust, and he might slip. At my coaxing, he might accidentally expose his greatest weakness, or he might reveal how to break the curse.

If I do this right, I might win. And if I maneuver him into the right vulnerable position, Elixir might simply let me win. He might let me go and let it be.

The first step to any of these outcomes is endearing myself to the water lord. I need to find that crawlspace in his soul where I can burrow in and poison him with compassion. Because who knew kindness could become a weapon? Who better to wield it than me?

I struggle to tamp down the remorse. I've spent my life treating others with tenderness, not using their fragility against them. Yet this is different. If I want to outlast this world, kindness must become a tactic, an advantage over someone who's never experienced it.

Besides, nothing happened between us, and whatever transpired against that outcropping had been a mistake. It was a moment of lunacy. There may have been a flicker of mutual comfort, and we may have exchanged reassuring touches, and the result may have shimmied across my flesh. Nonetheless, the truce had been fleeting, an isolated episode wrought from the need to survive.

Coral swims several paces away, lost in her own assumptions and thoughts. I puff and pump beside her while the river's current ferries my spear, doubtless at Elixir's behest. Several times, the female casts the weapon a curious glance but makes no attempt to confiscate it. Since Elixir had issued an order to get me cleaned up, she must conclude the spear is forbidden booty.

With my energy renewed, my pace accelerates. As I swim, I think about Elixir's potential vulnerabilities and conjure a plan.

I'm not going to play his game. He's going to play mine.

14

Instead of returning to my chamber where there's a perfectly functional tub, Coral leads me to a place called The Mer Cascades. According to her, those waters contain special healing nutrients, their potency warding off aches instantaneously.

The enclave is a haven tucked amidst interconnected caves. In showering alcoves, condensation rains from the ceilings. Steaming whirlpools are chiseled into various levels, with water spilling from the rims. Torrents splash down brackets of rock into more tubs. Each area glistens a different hue of blue, green, or gold, the vibrant shades illuminating the darkness.

But that's not what causes me to halt at the threshold. It's the merfolk.

There are figures with ultramarine curls and tiny gemstones embedded into their temples, the skin of their waists merging with scales that narrow into fins or tips. Others have long limbs with webbed feet and hands, and their stringy hair hangs like seaweed, and they flash honed canines.

Mermaids, mermen, and sirens. The dwellers range from curvy and fleshy to lithe and toned, from beautifully intimidating to frightfully enchanting. Although they gather here, each of the Solitaries keeps their personal distance, enjoying their own pockets of space. They float in the pools or hum to themselves, their voices clear and fluid, producing melodies one could float upon.

Their scales glimmer like kaleidoscopes, changing color as the Solitaries move. Most of the females bare their breasts or wear bandeaus. The males don no such adornments, their flesh either splotchy or blazing with ink markings down their abdomens.

It must be nighttime by now, because they're all awake. I stand at the threshold, absorbing the scene until Coral nudges me forward. Despite my jellied muscles, my limbs carry me into the enclave.

The merfolk sweep their gazes my way. Their features pinch with hostility. The water sprites slink from the raining alcoves, shiver off droplets of water, and move sinuously toward me. The mermaids, mermen, and sirens swim nearer and grasp the pool ledges.

"What's this?" a mermaid inquires, bubbles spitting from the surface around her. "A treat from Elixir? Has she lost the game already?"

"I saw her first," a merman says.

"I really wouldn't try it, if I were you," Coral warns in a deep, sultry tone that sounds like a prediction.

"Then it's fortunate you're not me," the male dismisses.

I recognize this one. The swamp-colored hair and tar-black ink markings resurrect that incident in The Twisted Canals, when Elixir used a waterfall to lash this male to the ground.

So, he can shift from land to water like Elixir. That accounts for why he wasn't in mer form the first time I saw him.

Up close, I notice the smudges of black under his lower eyelids, as if the color is leaking from there. The Fae peers at me with spite, his visage implying that I'm to blame for what happened to him. He twirls his fingers in the pool and whisks up a length of water that shapes itself into a net. I feel the color leach from my face and imagine him snatching me in his liquid snare, then dragging me into the bath with him. He might ravish me, or shave the skin from my bones, or drown me as the crocodiles had failed to do.

But after what I've recently been through, I'm no longer in the mood to be afraid. My spear is up and braced before any of the Folk say another word.

The merman seethes in Faeish but stalls when he registers my weapon, its length inset with iron. Outrage purples his face. "He allows this mortal to bear such arms?"

With renewed contempt, the male lunges. An olive hand thrusts from out of nowhere and seizes him by the jugular. At which point, the water net dissolves into the bath with a splat.

Coral sighs, as if having expected this. The rest of us spin toward Elixir, who towers next to the basin. Out of the water, his limbs have materialized, and a filmy robe drizzles down his form, the tie loose around his waist and threatening to spill open. Beads of moisture cling to his collarbones and the tips of his hair.

His grip bears the full weight of the merman. "Do I allow her to bear such arms?" he repeats into the male's face. "Yes. I fucking do."

His knuckles delve, plugging the merman's gills. Those golden irises flare, threatening to blind my assailant, if not choke him.

Elixir murmurs, "Nod if you understand."

The gagging Fae hangs suspended, the object of public humiliation for a second time. Breaking from my paralysis, I'm about to demand Elixir show mercy and let him go, when the obedient male nods.

Elixir's fingers snap open. The Fae crashes into the water.

The merfolk bow in subservience, and the sprites drop to their knees. Their expressions are loaded with admiration rather than trepidation, as though applauding Elixir for this level of aggression.

The water lord slices his errant gaze across the caves. He speaks in rapid Faeish, rattling off what sounds like a sequence of events, then finishes with, *"Jún ferndadi mick."*

The incredulous Faeries glance at me anew. "Her?" a mermaid gurgles in disbelief.

Elixir inclines his head, then snaps, "Out."

My escort and the merfolk disband, the latter casting me affronted yet perplexed glares before plunging into the cascades. There must be an outlet from here. The depths reduce the river Fae to colorful blots before they disappear altogether.

I round on Elixir. "Why did you do that? This is their territory!"

"They will get it back."

"What I meant is, you didn't have to assault that merman! Fables forgive you, but you could have been lenient!"

He blinks, as if struck down. "That is not what they expect from me. I'm no lenient ruler."

"Ruler? This isn't being a ruler. It's called being a tyrant."

"No, it is called setting an example. Do your kings behave differently?"

"Fine, but I can defend myself against bullies," I assert.

"And by now, I am aware of that," he replies blandly, though with a tinge of uncensored admiration.

"What did you tell them?" I demand.

"That I had confiscated your spear, and you reclaimed it. That you came to my aid against The Bask of Crocodiles, and now I owe you a favor."

"They'll wonder how I fled The Sunken Isle in the first place."

"I told them you were with me."

Which is true, but... "Coral would have seen you fetch me."

"I told the merfolk you were *with me*," he restates. "I'm your captor and their sovereign. They will not ask further questions."

"Fine, but you came to my aid against the reptiles first."

"And then you repaid me in kind, so the favor has reverted to my side. I would rather choose my repayment before you seize the opportunity from my grasp."

Because he knows that if I did, I would likely request something more significant than a bath, even if it's a bath fit for a mermaid. "Faeries have a complicated way of saying thank you. You go to a lot of trouble avoiding two simple words. At this rate, we could be expressing our gratitude to another for eternity."

Elixir curls his nose in distaste. Prior to this, he'd said a Fae can only confiscate an object from someone one time; therefore, he can't take the spear from me again. Nevertheless, I clutch my weapon. That rule might apply to him, but the spear remains fair game to his subjects.

"They will not try," he says, evidently reading my mind. "To take what their ruler no longer can would undermine me."

"You could order them to do it."

"Issuing that command would still constitute me taking the weapon, for the very act of orchestrating it would be my doing," he grumbles. "I would not rejoice about this, if I were you."

I unpack his meaning. After eons of discord between our cultures, my actions on Elixir's behalf might be enough to stump the Folk, but not enough to sway them into benevolence. And while the spear may be set in iron, it doesn't guarantee full protection in The Deep. There are other ways these Faeries or the environment and its fauna can assault me, perils

I haven't yet begun to discover.

Another vital consequence surges the forefront. "Have I made things worse?"

Elixir should need more information, yet he doesn't. "The battle was a natural event in the reptiles' territory," he counters. "It was a scrimmage for food and part of the lifecycle between prey and predators. It was not the same premeditated slaughter as The Trapping. In that sense, you have not contributed to the land fading by defending yourself."

The Grotto That Whispers had indicated as much. Regardless, I'd needed the confirmation.

I marvel that Elixir had admitted to his peers how I'd bested one of their sacred predators to help their leader, after I'd retrieved my weapon right from under his nose. He'd confessed this without shame or umbrage. "You told them what I did, just like that?"

The Fae waves in dismissal. "I hide nothing from my kin—or from anyone."

"You'll forgive me if I don't believe that, coming from someone who's scarcely a conversationalist and unlikely to prattle about himself."

"Being quiet does not mean being secretive."

"Then tell me your most embarrassing moment," I quip.

He narrows his eyes, then relaxes them after realizing it was a jest. The quip had leapt off my tongue from nowhere. It had been a reflex, like many actions I've taken toward him.

The cascades plash and throw mist into the air. We pause, awkwardness settling in. I think if we hadn't recently combatted a battalion of reptiles, we might actually chuckle. Or at least, I would chuckle, and this taciturn Fae would scowl to conceal his amusement.

So, there. Elixir does have things to hide, namely any semblance of a grin or humor. And how I want desperately to laugh at something—at anything.

The welts on my body cause me to wince. "Are you here because you forgot to say goodbye?" I ask through the discomfort. "That was rather impolite of you earlier."

"I'm here for my own sake, not yours," he says, disgruntled.

If I grin, will he detect it? I stifle the impulse, just in case. "Yes, far be it from me to think you'd come here realizing the merfolk wouldn't take kindly to their latest mortal prisoner infringing on their turf, and you got worried they would eat me."

"They knew to expect you. I sent word in advance."

"Through the river?"

He clips his head in the affirmative. "They were not going to eat you. They only wanted to scare you. If they had intended to nibble on your toes, they would have done so before you drew breath."

Shivers rack my limbs. His eyes glitter, sensing what the comment does to me. Though, the glint in his irises makes me wonder if he's being serious or, in a macabre way, teasing me.

Even with the spear in hand, I cross my arms. "You're mean."

No, this doesn't warrant saying. And yes, he takes it as a compliment.

"I am," Elixir boasts. "And you're disheveled."

He gestures to the enclave blossoming with blue-green-gold tints. My cheeks detonate as colorful vapors from the waterfalls spritz my nape. Blind or not, does he mean to stay while I bathe?

Elixir turns—and whips off the robe with backward flaps of his arms.

No leggings. Nothing but the mantle.

My eyes goggle. I swerve away, shielding my eyes before the garment ripples to the ground. While my pulse drums in my wrist, I listen to the thunk of his retreating feet. Once he's put enough distance between us, my will takes on a life of its own and does something unforgivable. I tilt my head, split my fingers, and peek through the digits.

At first, I watch him trace the condensation. He follows the mist, using the fog like a path that guides him to a lower-level pool, where an emerald cascade topples down rocks and plunges into the water. As he approaches the ledge, my gaze trips over the plates of his shoulder blades, down the ladder of his spine, the muscles of his lower back, the taper of his waist, and...

And the swells of his backside. They're smooth and firm, the dimples flexing, the concave shadows shifting with Elixir's strides.

My flesh boils, my stomach flops, and the slit of my thighs aches. Worse, my attention fails to stray from his buttocks, from the way it contorts with his movements, which calls to mind how it might snap between a female's spread legs, his hips slinging in and out in a sinuous rhythm.

Elixir halts at the pool's edge. Slowly, his head lifts in my direction but doesn't fully turn my way. Still, it's enough to catch his profile—the keen awareness, which causes his irises to hurl gold at the water.

Instantly, his jaw locks. He knows what I'm looking at, and he knows how my body has reacted. The admiration of a human must repel him, as it does all Faeries apart from satyrs. My face scalds with humiliation and annoyance. I huff audibly and chastely to illustrate it has nothing to do with attraction and everything to do with discretion.

The moment I swivel from the view, I hear him exhale and slosh into the whirlpool. So, that's what he's doing in The Mer Cascades. Elixir intends to bathe as well.

Although the swim here had rinsed off most of the gunk, bits of dirt adhere to my scalp and encrust my fingernails. Plus, the memory alone of the swamps festering beyond the archways makes me feel soiled. I suppose if I'd inspected him more closely, and more platonically, I would have noticed Elixir's own ravaged state.

I consider my options. While the showering alcoves draw my interest—no such things exist where I'm from—I imagine Elixir listening to the downpour sluice over my skin, to the point where he'd make out the water's path around my curves, the deluge outlining my breasts and thighs. From that, he would know the shape of my body.

The prospect also causes a tendril of warmth to unfurl in my womb. I shake it off and pad around a corner. A set of steps etched into a wall spirals to an upper-level pool and a miniature waterfall of rich cobalt. Once there, I peek over the ridge, down to Elixir's bath.

The Fae reclines in the frothing basin with a groan. His glorious back faces me, and his biceps splay on either side of him, resting along the ledge. I discern the viper tail, which has replaced his limbs.

Confining myself to my own niche, I prop my weapon beside the stair landing, peel off the sodden caftan, and discard it to the floor. Several times, I instruct myself not to think about Elixir below. Even if this high edifice weren't separating us, and even if we weren't situated at different heights, it wouldn't matter.

He knows the emotions in my voice, in my breaths, in my blood, in my temperature, and in my movements. But he can't see my nudity. He can't see. He cannot.

I wade into the pool. The moment my soles plunge, the water churns and bubbles around me. I submerge myself and muffle a sigh while the temperature and pressure massage my joints. A crescent shaped bench lines the underwater perimeter, the seat carved from stone. I settle in, the hot bath dousing my shoulders and loosening the kinks. A crisp, aquatic scent I can't identify mingles with the essence of florals, the combination imbued into the mist, so that it reinvigorates my senses.

The foaming bath absorbs the grime from today's battle, the muck vanishing into nothing, as if I'd been unsoiled before entering. Amazed, I dunk my head under, then come up with cleansed hair. My intricate bun has long since unraveled. After combing my fingers through the teal strands, I melt into the pool. My body goes limp…until I hear him.

A masculine hum drones from below, deep and rustling. I've not heard this anomaly before, the sound of him satisfied. Nor have I ever been *in the nude* while keeping company with a male.

My limbs steeple. I strap my arms around them and curl myself in like a snail while listening to the echoes of the Fae beneath me. His faint movements disturb the water, the commotion louder than it should be amidst the cascades.

Against my will, I think of him scrubbing his flesh. I think of those fingers rubbing his skin, kneading it.

After a beat, I unfold myself and sneak to the ledge like a critter, my eyes popping over the side. The vision stalls my next exhalation.

He hasn't turned around, but he's leaning back far enough that he doesn't need to. His skull lolls against the foundation, and his tail extends. Elixir is so tall that while sitting on his own bench, the water only reaches his waist.

His eyelids are closed, his dark lashes fanning out. Sprawled like that, he resembles a sea king or a marine warrior luxuriating in a moment of pleasure, less than an hour after ripping the ocean in half.

One lazy palm drags over his abdomen. With each pass, my stomach flutters, feeling his touch there. When his free hand circles in the air, a slender cord of water plummets from an overhead crevice, and he rolls his head forward, so the surge beats against his nape. Then he flings his head back, the long layers whipping behind him, and he scrubs his digits through the roots.

Trapped by the sight, I watch what this does to his muscled arms and the grid of his torso. Then I watch the torrent reduce to a trickle before drying like an emptied pump.

And then I watch his eyes flap open in awareness.

I duck. Except I do so without finesse, my haste roiling the bath and chucking water over the side. The motions also aggravate my welts, so that I make another pained squeak, the racket giving me away more than anything. If I had stayed still, he might not have detected me being sneaky.

"I know what you were doing, mortal," Elixir calls out. "Why do you stare at me?"

Condemnation! With a groan, I curl my fingers atop the rim and poke my head over the side. He has withdrawn from the cascade, turned in my direction, and is presently cranking his head toward my voice.

"Was I staring?" I query.

"I heard the water molding itself around you, fluctuating with your motions."

Then it's fortunate I didn't opt for one of the showers, after all. "Well, I could have been gazing into space, but you got in the way," I protest. "Spacious enclave or not, you take up a lot of room in here. You're hard not to miss, like a shipwreck or a giant squid. I'm not speaking from experience with those things, but I'm sure I wouldn't miss the sight of either. Though, I once came across a beached rowboat in a lake on the outskirts of Reverie Hollow.

"Or rather, the boat wasn't stranded so much as detoured, but since it was moored on the banks and overrun by thieving beavers, I think it constitutes as the same thing. Any visual that a bystander isn't used to is difficult to overlook. Beavers pirating a skiff and tugging it away—while its passengers have temporarily gone ashore—will certainly get noticed." I pause and chew on my lower lip. "It's amazing how much more sense this comparison made in my head than it did aloud."

Elixir just gazes with a severe frown pinned to his countenance. Yet the skin around his mouth ticks, working hard to stay fixed in place.

I sigh. "I'm staring for the same reason you were listening to my movements: curiosity."

"I'm not curious," Elixirs scoffs. "I'm not a curious Fae."

"Says the villain who tried to bargain a personal question out of me."

"Curiosity was not the culprit," he replies, far too quickly for me to accept. "Like I said before, I was being thorough. I asked a penetrating question to discomfort you, purely because I felt like it."

I slit my eyes. "You're *really* mean."

This time, that pruned mouth loosens a fraction. "I *really* am."

"You need to stop doing that."

"Being mean?"

"Deciphering every move I make and every physical response I have."

"Trust me: It does not happen on purpose." Elixir twists and backpedals, his arms rowing through the water and carrying him to the opposite end. On that side, a larger cascade parts like a curtain and splits down the middle. He reclines on another underwater seat, spreading his arms across mantles of rock while the emerald water sparkles around him. "For instance, now you're holding still, waiting for me to elaborate."

He's right. I haven't moved.

And because the bath has put him in a rare, charitable mood, he muses, "The way you move in the river. It is not like other mortals I've dealt with, for I detect it more acutely. You swim like a fish, as if you were born in the water."

It hits me. Based on his inquiring tone, this is the perfect opportunity. If I want to unravel his inner workings and get close to him, it's my responsibility to make a willing move first. If I want to access his soul, I have to bare my own, piece by piece.

Time to make this Fae play my own game.

He'd said I swim as if I was born in water. At the notion, a smile tilts my lips. I inch from my hiding spot, fold my arms over the ledge, and rest my chin on my wrists. My limbs rise, extend behind me, and float on the bath's surface while I stare down at him. "That's because I was."

Reminiscing about my birth parents hurts too much, but I do recite the story of how my mother brought me into this world while squatting in a pond. Before that, I was also conceived in the same location. Not that I'm not about to share that information.

Upon hearing this tidbit, Elixir says, "And you fight as though you've trained in the water."

"That's because I've done that, too."

"Who taught you?"

"I did."

I'd taught myself how to wield the spear, Lark taught herself how to brandish a whip, and Juniper learned from trade poachers how to shoot a crossbow. While under Papa Thorne's roof, we'd honed our skills as best we could.

Elixir's tail sways. "You like the water."

"I love the water," I correct him. "Don't you?"

"Love," he mutters. "I respect the water and relish its majesty."

"All right, so you *like* the water. You do know how to *like* something, yes?"

"I am not an imbecilic dragon," he says, belligerent. "I know how to like something. Very well, I like the water. Satisfied?"

"Ecstatic." From behind, my feet kick like flippers. "My first memory is of the water. When I was four, I sat on the bank of a lake, rested my feet on the shoreline, and watched these teeny little fish gather around my toes. They poked and nibbled and tickled my skin, then scattered every time I twitched my legs. I laughed and waited for them to return, which they did relentlessly like one of those sandpipers who chase waves.

"I remember being so present in the moment, like the past and future didn't exist. That was the first time I believed I could become a creature of the water, if I wanted. Not that it was truly possible, but the belief itself was real."

I trail off, stunned that I'd gotten caught up in the tale. Elixir's head slants, his irises emblazoned with interest. His thumb had been idly tracing the water, but now it stalls in realization, his knuckles bending with tension. "You're grinning."

The Fae's gruff tone reaches from his end of the enclave to mine. His lethal timbre sinks below the whirlpool and licks the cleft of my thighs. I wiggle to rid myself of the forbidden sensation, then hiss when the motion aggravates the welts.

Notwithstanding, I strive for an animated mood. "What else can you tell? What am I doing now?" I straighten and bunch my features into a theatrical snarl. Elixir's mouth crooks, but I switch before he can answer. "What about now?" I part my lips in an oval and widen my eyes so that I look like a scandalized duchess. "Or now?" Then I compress my face into a miserly glower.

I see Elixir wrestling to preserve his frown, which emboldens me. "And now?" I cross my eyes and bloat my cheeks like a blowfish.

Then I finish by sticking my tongue out at Elixir. "How about that?"

"Cease, mortal," he concedes. "You have made your point."

Thank Fables. My blood, temperature, and breathing aren't the extent of me. There are some facets he can't detect. Not unless he traces my facial features.

And someday, I might pry a smile from him.

"Although," Elixir says, "I might guess one of those expressions had involved a tongue and a measure of defiance."

I glance heavenward and mock huff. "If I lie and say you're wrong, would you believe me?"

Then I swallow my gasp as his breath coasts up my ear. "Not a fucking chance."

My gaze falls to his bath, but it's empty. Heat radiates at my back, and a shadow flanks my body. I freeze. His arms fence me in, bars of solid muscle extending on either side of me, and his fingers seize the pool's rim.

My heart goes wild, pulse thumping in my chest. Sweat nestles in the dip between my breasts, the swells inflating and beginning to ache.

I'm naked. I'm naked and caged by an equally naked Fae monster.

My limbs and curves are indecent, exposed inches from the viper towering behind me. If I swerve to face him, my nipples will scrape his pectorals.

Elixir knows this. Yet instead of moving, he goes as still as I do. Though, when he balls his hands into fists and releases them, I see the tempo of his own pulse slamming against his wrists.

I think he'd meant to say more, but he doesn't. Oxygen siphons from his lungs and blends with my exhalations, both sounds amplifying despite the crashing waterfalls, churning pools, and hazy showers.

I could tell him to move, and he would.

I could plunge and swim around him, and he would welcome the retreat.

Yet neither of us seeks to alter the moment, to reposition ourselves, to veer away.

I stare at our combined hands, which grapple the ledge for dear life, for leverage, or for restraint. "What is this?" I whisper.

Elixir's head bows forward. "I do not know," he grits out.

The whirlpool emits steam like a cauldron. The eddies toss water at our hips, coaxing us nearer. I imagine him hauling me around and off the floor, my limbs splitting and clasping his waist.

A hoarse noise rumbles from his chest. "Do not do that."

"Do what?" I pant.

"Do not think what you're thinking. You will regret it."

"Will I?" I mumble, my skull reclining backward toward him. "Will you?"

Another masculine outtake, this one heavier. "Your blood. Your heat," he gusts. "They are too loud...so loud."

"I feel yours, too. In a different way."

His mouth charts a path toward my jaw and hovers millimeters from the place where it meets my earlobe. Tingles ricochet down my spine, his words blowing hot air into that sensitive place. He rasps thickly against my jaw, then switches to the other side, along my throat—and I let him. This precarious and pivotal moment distorts all rationale, my body becoming unrecognizable to itself.

I'm not the only one. Elixir trembles, his body a volcano—massive, explosive, and on the brink of something so apocalyptic, it will burn for an eternity afterward.

"Tell me," Elixir mutters, his tone feral, furious, and faint all at once. "I would see what you see."

A whimper curls from my lips, the sound fluttering into the space. "Your joints are quivering, and your tendons have risen, and your scales have tinted with threads of scarlet."

He utters through his teeth, "There would be more, if we allowed it."

"What more?" slips out before I can stop myself.

"I would sketch you from behind," Elixir swears. "I would trace your flesh, mark a path to your breasts, and thumb them until your nipples become ruched."

My hips squirm. They jut against the water pressure, greedy for friction, for relief. It's either that or buck my backside into his tail, into the spot where his pelvis should be.

"I would suckle your throat until you are wetter than this bath."

It's all I can do not to reach back, tangle my digits in his mane, and clasp his nape for balance.

"And then," he says. "I would take you like this, soaked and with your spine bowed. I'm of The Deep, and so I would fuck you that way. My cock would lunge into you until the pleasure hits your scalp. I would blind you with rapture, if not with magic. I would show you darkness. And you would take it so thoroughly, so genuinely—but not so purely."

"How do you know?" I keen.

"The way your mouth forms words. How your voice pours from your lips. The delicate slide of your lisp. They prove you have been tasted before."

Yes, by the cobbler's daughter. But what Elixir describes goes beyond a kiss and several attempts at fondling, which my sisters don't know about because I'd been too sheepish to tell them.

"What about you?" I murmur, recalling what Puck had said about Elixir never being ridden. "Have you been tasted? Have you been taken?"

"No," he hums without reserve. "I have not."

He's incapable of lying, yet this can't be the truth, no matter what that satyr had claimed. How can this specimen be a virgin? How can Elixir describe such fervid acts without having experienced them?

What's more, how could he have lived this long without satisfying his appetites? Who has that much willpower? And why is his confession all the more enticing?

Elixir seems to read my thoughts, because he intones, "Granted, I have a rather knowledgeable, and rather vocal, satyr brother. But Faeries are graced with certain sexual capabilities, such as sensory perception and stamina. If I were to fuck you, I would know what to do. And I would last as long as you wish."

Oh, Fables forgive us.

My back arches. I lean into him, the position shoving my breasts higher, the points of my nipples erect. We're relentless and mindless, yet not a single inch of him has made physical contact with me.

Mist laves our skin. The cascades simmer with cobalt and emerald. We quiver on a precipice, savage and turbulent.

My pendant taps his ribs. We go still. Then we shatter apart, breaking free from the spell. Sultry air rushes through and dampens my mottled cheeks.

What have I done to myself? What has become of me?

The pendant's weight lifts as Elixir plucks and raises it high. "What is this?"

I fortify myself, wheel toward him, and submerge my nipples under the whirlpool, preserving what's left of my modesty. I don't care that he can't physically see me. It hasn't stopped Elixir from doing so, in other palpable ways.

We've given ourselves enough space to maneuver, but only just. My back presses into the rocks, and with every inflation of his chest, we're still in danger of colliding.

Elixir winds my pendant to the front, rolls it between his fingers, and discerns its shape. I steal the bauble from his grasp and drape it down my spine, where it's secure. Instead of telling him the pendant is my heart, my refuge, and my love, I answer, "It's why we can't do this."

But the Fae detects what I leave out. He hears my impassioned, protective tone, and it stokes the gold in his irises, which jump all over my figure with no place to rest. Confusion stares back at me. This being grasps the emotions, but he can't identify with them.

As I gaze at him, the question emerges unbidden. "Why is your name Elixir?"

He startles, translating the implication: An elixir is a remedy, not a source of venom. That must have had some bearing on his choice.

It's not his true name, as Faeries keep their true names secret. But why did he select this particular moniker?

My palm itches to cup his jaw and discover what such a caring touch would do to him, whether it would cleave him in half or awaken something new. I think he senses this urge in me, because he backs away like a targeted animal.

His lips part as if to answer. For once, he doesn't act swiftly.

Afraid he will change his mind, I whisper, "What are you trying to heal?"

I'd meant to encourage him, but I'd forgotten he isn't like a mortal or anyone else I've ever met. So, it's the wrong thing to ask. Those pupils sharpen, as do his features.

Elixir snarls in Faeish. He whips around and thrashes out of the whirlpool, his tail hardening into limbs. I'm so stunned, I forget to conceal my view as the Fae storms naked down the stairwell, his backside and swimmer's form on explicit display.

Air dashes into my lungs. I wade to the rim and peer over the side, watching as Elixir charges across the lower level and shrugs on his robe. He pauses, thrusts a hand in his pocket, and flings an object into the emerald bath.

"Use this on the welts," he snaps. "I tire of hearing you make those wincing noises."

The Fae evanesces, disappearing like a vapor. A moment later, a glass vial pops to the surface of my bath—the item he'd thrown into his pool. The cascades must have carried it to me.

In a daze, I pluck the vessel from the water. A rosy, jellied substance fills the container.

My mixtures serve only two purposes. Either they poison or cure.

That's why he'd ordered Coral to bring me here, then joined me so soon after. He'd taken a detour to find me a restorative for my welts.

A translucent bead swims inside the mixture, reminding me of the drop of perspiration he'd extracted from me outside The Grotto That Whispers. He had pocketed the globule, transported it to his den, and dropped it into a bottle, then refused to tell me what he planned to do with the bead.

My head swings to where Elixir had vanished. When the reality of what nearly happened catches up, I plonk onto the seat. I'd been ready to set my own game in motion, yet I'd gotten lost along the way.

Lost in his scent, his voice, and his body.

I was so immersed in...in whatever we'd almost done...that my parting question hadn't been intentional.

At some point during the bath, I had stopped playing a game. At some point, I'd forgotten to even try.

15

Coral arrives to escort me to my chamber. I follow her into the tunnels and through The Twisted Canals, where the bridges sparkle, and boats shave through the alleys.

In my peripheral vision, a handful of Faeries watch me from their respective corners. Reclining in a cattail pond, there's a handsome merman with cyan hair. A Fae perches on a windowsill, fins sprouting from her arms. An undine lounges atop a boat, with splotches of blue coating the female's skin, as though someone had thrown buckets of paint at her.

Their expressions range from flummoxed, to skeptical, to amazed.

The guard's sultry voice curls toward me. "They heard what happened in The Bask of Crocodiles and wish to view the evidence for themselves."

That bit of news does little to pull me from the haze. I trail along, my head foggy, my skin roasting from Elixir's erotic speech.

I keep the vial tucked in my caftan pocket until ensconced at The Sunken Isle. Once inside my chamber, I reunite with the snake, who twines himself around my calf. His companionship brings with it the familiarity of home, the warm memories and reassuring sensations cradling me like a blanket. If this little creature hadn't followed me here, I don't know what I would do, how I would cope.

I don't relish leaving this room again, nor am I eager to be caged inside. I need to know Elixir's world, to learn more about who he is.

What I don't need to know, what I never again need to know, is the heat of his breath against the shell of my ear. What I should never know again is the weight of his mouth near my jaw and the bottomless depths his voice reaches when he's close to me. What I can never know again is the stifling expanse of his torso hovering inches from my back, the proximity of his hips, and the mutiny these details incited between my legs.

I don't need to know any of this, and I should never know any of this, and I can never know any of this, and I will never know any of this. Not again.

But I want to know. And while I should feel repulsed and repentant, I also feel deprived, from my lips to my breasts, from my fingertips to my knees, from my core to my toes. My body quavers with a yearning it has no right to, the upheaval gathering to a tempest. This, without Elixir having set one bronze-capped finger on my skin.

What can he do with those sharp caps? Would a light graze make me quiver?

Would I sigh, as I normally do when I cup myself? Would I whimper, as I usually do when I'm on the brink of climax? Or would I unleash a primal noise, as I've never done?

I'll never find out, and that's as much a comfort as it is a disturbance. I'll never again experience the sensations he'd wrung from me an hour ago, nor the ones beyond that…the corrupt possibilities that threaten to darken my slumber. I can't say what exhausts me more, the battle we fought together or that seductive episode in The Mer Cascades.

A platter of mackerel, potatoes slathered in cream, raw fish eggs—which I feed to the snake—and a goblet sits on the bedside table. After eating, I uncork the vial's contents. The gelatinous mixture smells of mint as I smear it on my welts, the ointment melting into the angry, red abrasions.

Finished, I land on the bed and tumble into a deep sleep. And sometime during the night, I awaken briefly to find my skin healed and flushing pink. The contusions have vanished, and my mind is clearer.

But I still feel his weight behind me.

꩜

The crickets and toads fall quiet, signaling the break of dawn. I take a risk, hold my breath, and wrestle against the suctioning water of The Sunken Isle. After that, I evade Coral as she patrols the reeds circling the perimeter. I skulk past her like the cutpurse I used to be, sprint up the jetty, and sneak into Elixir's lair once more, this time by swimming through the vat to rescue Juniper's crossbow. To my relief, the water lord isn't there, but neither is the weapon. Either my nemesis hid the archery after speculating I'd attempt a sibling-worthy heist—The Three had known I'd been spying on them, after all—or I've arrived too late.

Logic tells me it's the latter. Elixir had said he would require only a day to oblige the satyr, which means Puck of The Solitary Forest has already made a second visit to his brother and reclaimed the crossbow and bolts, now stripped of iron.

I return to my confines empty-handed and fretful about what this means for Juniper. That night, sleep evades me until my sanctuary friend slithers to my pillow and winds himself into a coil beside my head.

Time passes, with no visits or summons from Elixir. As ruler of this domain, he must be occupied. Besides, all he needs to do is sit back and wait for me to lose, to make a failed attempt at breaking the curse. To that end, there's no other reason for him to bother with his mortal captive.

Part of me wants to kick myself for confiding about my love of water, plus everything else I'd told him. Another part of me can't blame myself. The Fae could have been manipulating me into talking, a thought I nonetheless won't accept, however much it nicks my chest. His interest had rung so earnestly. Gullible though I might be, but I know the sound of sincerity, and I know the shape of it on a person's face. My heart tells me he wasn't being shrewd or deceptive, particularly not after we'd combatted a bask of sacred fauna, and not after I'd witnessed the bereft expression on his countenance, the empathy that had resulted when he registered my own sadness.

And yes, I don't want to believe otherwise because...it had been easy to talk to him in The Mer Cascades. Fables forgive me, I had enjoyed our conversation.

Elixir had stridden away, visibly unshaken by what transpired between us. But I had felt a difference, a shift in his exhalations and a change in his eye color, the gold burning hotter yet glossier. I had felt his uncharacteristic restraint. I had felt him yearning to breach the remaining distance and commit an offense he couldn't take back.

I know because I'd endured the same contemptible agony.

Did he think about it long after walking away? Is he still thinking about it?

This line of thought is ruinous and unsafe. I push it away and move on.

Each time this world falls into daytime slumber, I skulk from my chamber and explore, searching the environment for clues about Elixir. It's also wise to learn the extent of this wild, to know its weak spots and lethal corners, to understand its currents and animals, lest I'm forced to rely on this knowledge in an emergency.

At some point, if I manage to acclimate myself and figure out how to travel while the Faeries are awake, I'll be able to eavesdrop at night. But for now, I keep to my human routine.

Two obstacles need to be dealt with. Carrying a weapon slows me down, but condensing the spear while swimming is the best I can do.

The second burden regards my clothing. Because it's preposterous to slog around wet and barefooted for every outing, I stash a parcel of dry attire and the second pair of sandals from my closet in a crevice at the opposite end of The Sunken Isle. Once I've changed, I blend in with the shadows and slip around Coral.

I pass through conduits embossed in lantern light, obsidian caves garlanded in teal orbs, and murky tunnels bursting with florets of greenery. Dampness and scarves of mist saturate the air. Deft splashes and eerily aquatic croaks perk my ears. I tighten my grasp on the spear.

Once, I tread a stream populated by glowing eels that swish around my calves. Later, I swim amongst oversized tetras. I keep vigilant of dangerous freshwater fish or river mammals, but mostly I encounter toads that croak louder than horns and gilded lizards with tongues so long they shouldn't fit inside their mouths. I avoid the fauna with poisonous traits and lance the nontoxic quarry with my iron spear, moving quickly before the creatures have a chance to shift sizes, then parcel them back to the snake.

The expeditions demand a firm grasp of geography. To be sure, Juniper is better at this. She prides herself on being the wisest, most literate, most erudite, most encyclopedic, most scholarly, and most "everything" having to do with the Fae. And as a huntress, she excels at map reading.

Without her counsel, I do my utmost committing the river's terrain to memory, then use a rock to etch a map into the floor beneath my bed. As for hints about Elixir, I discover nothing beyond a greater sense of the cloistered life he's led, so far removed from the sun and sky, with no space for his emotions or thoughts to breathe. No room for him—or any of these river Fae—to think differently.

What must that be like?

Presently, I finish scraping a new portion of the map on the floor, then notice the crickets chirping outside. Has an hour swept by already?

I scramble from under the bed, my caftan wrinkled and scuffed. Whereas such clothing must be commonplace for Faeries, this precious garment is worthy of a queen's wardrobe in the human realm. The outfit could have been sewn from water blossoms. The sleeveless garment clasps at the shoulders, and the hem splits on either side of my calves, buffeting my limbs as I hasten about the room.

My friend had used my back as a nest while I'd been sketching, but now I pluck the snake off the floor and stash him in the closet, then perch on the mattress just as Coral enters. Without a word, she sets my platter on the table and saunters to the exit, then pauses.

The female ticks her silvery blue head sideways and addresses the floor. "You protected the river dolphin," she reflects, uncertainty in her otherwise hypnotic voice. "You helped save Elixir, although you could have let him be slain."

I waver, taken aback. Come to think of it, I wonder, "Would the reptiles have truly slain the ruler of the river?"

"But of course, human. They're the fauna. They're the wild and do as they wish."

Her tone implies she's expecting a duplicitous response to her initial question. I rise, putting us on equal footing. "I help people. I don't harm them."

"You and Elixir combatted The Bask of Crocodiles together, and then you mourned the predators' deaths. Is that right?"

"Some humans treat fauna poorly, but not all," I share. "Some of us have respect for them, and we understand it's in a predator's nature to attack, and not all of us condemn an animal for that." When she makes no reply,

I take a leap of faith and give voice to the gentle truth. "The Trapping…
it shouldn't have happened the way it did."

"You mean this, don't you?" she muses, intrigued. "You mean this, after what we've done to your people."

"We deserve our freedom and the right to defend ourselves, but we
could have found another way, and you never maimed our children or
animals."

She sidles around and drums her fingers on her jaw. "What a positively bizarre one you are. Quite extraordinary, indeed. But I ponder, what
precisely is the meaning of this?"

The mock-conspiratorial inflection flows like syrup. Nonetheless,
she's anticipating a farce or charade, so I mollify my words. "To be
compassionate."

"And why's that, human?"

"Because that's who I am."

That she doesn't leave the chamber bodes well. I step closer. "May I
ask, why do you follow him? He would just as soon cut you down, if you
cross him."

"Ah, that." She dismisses this fact. "Elixir became our savior in The
Trapping. He has earned our allegiance."

"What about the merman Elixir battered? The one he lashed while
dragging me through The Twisted Canals? The same male in The Mer
Cascades who—"

"Who was assigned to clear The Shiver of Sharks when you arrived,
which the oaf failed to do."

So, Elixir hadn't intended for the sharks to feast on me. I'm grateful
to learn this and realize I'd been hoping for a sound explanation. Now
that I've gotten it, I don't know whether to be alleviated or daunted that
I'd been wrong about his agenda there.

The guard sighs. "Scorpio is hotheaded. It has to do with the humidity,
you see. Unlike the rest of us, he's never quite grown used to this climate,
which makes him daft."

"Scorpio?" I ask.

"The merman," she clarifies. "Where you're concerned, he should have
known better. Now that Elixir's done with him, Scorpio would do well

to think twice about touching you. At least, if he prefers to keep certain appendages from being severed."

"What do you mean, done with him?"

"Why, Elixir poisoned the fool, of course."

My stomach drops. He what?

Coral's chuckle oozes through the room. "Oh, sensitive human. Did you really think Elixir would limit himself to a near-choking in The Mer Cascades? That would hardly make him a sound ruler. As it is, the message was clear from the beginning: You're *our* sacrifice, but you're *his* prisoner. And no one touches what's his. In any case, Scorpio will live despite his charred vocal cords."

My legs struggle to keep me upright. I should have remained sitting on the mattress.

"I wouldn't be quick to judge a ruler," Coral warns, her crystalline scales glittering. "His word is law, and Scorpio the Idiotic knew that. It was Elixir's right to set the example of punishment. He's volatile, yes. He's ruthless, indeed. I've seen him tear open the gills of a siren who bartered one of our youths to an unseelie visitor, spill poison on the tongues of human captives who praised The Trapping, and blind the rest who've threatened us. He's brutal and the most isolated of all Solitaries, but that's the epitome of a river Fae, you see. It's what we aspire to.

"To us loyal dwellers, he's just. If the water lord trusts you, he'll do so forever. He's vowed to save this land, to his dying breath. That gives us strength."

Her speech dilutes some of my ire. I think about Elixir, who acts more than he speaks. Elixir, who covets his authority and brandishes it with fists, daggers, poisons, and a surplus of scowls rather than words. I've ruminated about this before, but have I stopped to wonder why he covets power?

"Who gives Elixir strength?" I ponder.

"Himself," Coral replies. "The fauna."

"Comfort is strength, too. Who gives him that?"

Her demeanor changes, her eyebrows slanting into downward ramps. She turns while flicking an answer over her shoulder like an inconsequential pebble. "Idealistic human. Comfort will not bring back what he's lost."

Echoes from The Twisted Canals dwindle. Nightfall yawns into daybreak.

While the river Fae dream, I wind my hair atop my head, paddle from The Sunken Isle to my hidden cache of dry clothing, and change into a loose, sapphire dress. After donning my sandals, I wend my way through the lantern tunnels. As I sidle around the flaming vessels and several brooks, my mind wanders. I miss the sunrise dappling our village in shades of amber and rose. I miss the caravan where my sisters and I tell stories. I miss the morning calls flitting from our sanctuary, the sleepy groans of Lark and Juniper, and the stairs creaking under Papa Thorne's weight as he traipses to the attic to wake us up.

I miss them, and I miss home, but the farther I travel, the more my vision adjusts to the darkness. The more I long to discover what exists in these depths, from its fauna to its currents.

I want to know if it's possible to make a haven here, if the absence of light yields its own tranquility. Despite all I've witnessed, I want to believe solace can be found anywhere.

At length, I come to a dead end. Sighing, I pivot the way I came—but halt.

An overlapping melody rains into the passage, sprinkling the area in music. My pulse lunges into a sprint. Either these mystical fauna can sprout fingers and play instruments, or I have company.

The tune is metallic, tinkling across my skin. It's a hauntingly beautiful stream of sound that tugs on my limbs, urging me to follow it. All the same, I brace my spear.

The tunnel splits in two directions. Rather than retrace my path, I take the opposite route and migrate toward the music. I've never heard this type of instrument before, but it reminds me of how a river might sing if it could, or how a trickling waterfall might sound if it had vocal cords.

The channel's end leads to a small enclosure with ropes of foliage swaying from the rafters. A wide fountain resides in the center. There are no statues or cisterns, merely a ring of water hurling vertically into the air and splattering the ground. Yet the deluge is mellow, a quiet burst of liquid that illuminates the space.

What's loud is the Fae seated in the fountain's heart. What's loud is the instrument he strums.

I lower the spear, wonder loosening my grip. Settled upon a stool, Elixir straddles an upright, sinuous apparatus, the object as tall as him. Rows of vertical strings pull taut inside the slender frame, the strings vibrating under Elixir's ministrations. Although I've never seen one, I remember this tidbit from whispered tales of The Three: The ruler of the river plays a harp.

It's an object of enchantment, as curvaceous as a shell. His hands swim over the instrument. As his sharp fingertips pluck, melodic noise pours from the strings.

His open robe hangs off his shoulders. Leggings encase his limbs, and his legs flank the instrument. Black hair falls over his profile as he leans back with the harp balanced on his shoulder. His arms lash, and his fingers claw at the strings.

Soon after, he slows down and pinches the cords slowly. The music is conflicted, beautiful, and harrowing. The performance achieves too many things at once. It floods my stomach, eases my muscles, and chips at my chest.

My gaze swings from the instrument to Elixir's clenched eyelids. Pain flickers across his features, raw and tormented.

Comfort will not bring back what he's lost.

The harp cries out. It's the melody of grief, made manifest and resounding through this secluded room. It flows…and flows…and stops.

Elixir slumps, his digits curled over the strings, his eyes on ground. "Why are you here?"

Truly, I should have known. I pad inside the enclosure. "I was being defiant."

"I know." He drops his arms and flattens both palms on his splayed thighs. "You have done that often."

In other words, he's aware I've taken to scuttling about ever since the reptile battle. "The more I see of this world, the more I'll know about it. Why haven't you stopped me?"

"The more you act, the more I'll know about you," he echoes.

Meaning, the more he knows, the more he can distract me from winning?

Plausibly. Yet thinking about the mixture he gave me, I draw another conclusion. "That isn't the only reason."

His face shoots toward me, resentment drawing lines across his visage. That, and protectiveness. I wasn't supposed to witness this moment. And while he would have roared days ago, he merely glares while his eyes reflect something entirely different.

With a thudding heart, I test that. "Would you like me to go?"

A muscle hammers in his jaw, but he doesn't answer. That's enough to pull me deeper into the room. "Where are we?"

"The Fountain of Tears," he says. "It holds the tears of all who come here, so they may never forget what has ailed them."

I condense my spear, set it against a wall, and pause before the spurting ring of water. "Why do you think someone would want to remember that?"

Elixir detects where I'm standing, his eyes crawling across my form. "You know why."

Yes, I do. Pain eventually heals, and when it does, the scars teach us to value our happiness more. But that's my definition, not his.

I wait. In fact, I'll wait as long as it takes.

Though, just for good measure, I warn, "If you don't humor me eventually, I'll start talking, and I won't stop until I've covered every story ever penned, including my favorite romance of all time, about a gallant knight and his fair lady, with a detailed recounting of the sappy bits. There are lots of them. It's a three-hundred-page work. Oh, and did I mention it's told in verse?"

For a second, his mouth tilts. Then it flattens into a line. "You provoke me."

"That means we're even."

"Pain makes us stronger," he finally answers. "Come closer."

Half of me wants to, the other half stays still. "You play intensely. The music is so lovely, it becomes sad. It hurt to listen."

"That sounds like melodrama."

"You play angrily, too. And on such a delicate instrument, I worry you might break it."

"I prefer to break delicate things," he acknowledges. "I relish music, the way I relish water and brews. They are fluid and temperamental. Each can be pure or destructive, dangerous or…"

"A haven?" I volunteer.

He grunts in acknowledgment. "The harp is an instrument of the river. It is as graceful as water. But like any body of water, it can rage and drown its visitors. That is why I chose it."

"And is that why you play here? To remember your pain? To connect with it, so it keeps you strong? Against what, I wonder. Humans or yourself?"

"You tell me," Elixir bites out. "When you were listening, what did you hear?"

"I heard suffering and violence," I murmur. "I heard loss and sorrow. I heard darkness. I heard everything you don't hide and everything you don't realize you're hiding.

"I think you rely on power and magic. And that gnaws on you because you don't want to rely on them. You crave being a ruler, but you secretly wish you didn't. I think blinding others is a weapon, but it's also your downfall. I think you cling to these things to compensate for whatever you've lost. I think you know this."

An agonized flicker cuts through his facade before it tightens like a fist. Elixir releases the harp, the instrument thudding into an upright position. He stands and prowls toward me, stalling on the opposite side of the water ring. "I have changed my mind," he growls. "Go away."

So, I'm right. And I refuse to cower or obey. He doesn't want me to leave, or else he wouldn't have stood up.

My feet carry me through the water and into the fountain. "No," I whisper.

Tension emanates from his large body. Tension and heat and sadness and hate and fury and…need. So much need.

My fingers steal out to graze his jaw. "Whatever it is that hurt you, I'm so sorry."

Elixir shudders like a scaffolding about to collapse, fragments breaking and splintering apart. "Do not be," he rasps.

I hear the pleading, the resistance. If I pity him, it will be his mortification. If I care, it will be his undoing. If I feel anything for this monster, it might just shame him. Either way, it will lure him to me.

I would say he's playing my game, and I would be correct, if that mattered right now.

Does it? Or do I care beyond that?

He can't take my kindness. He doesn't know how. The water lord doesn't know how to withstand what I have to offer, because he's never encountered it before. Nor have I ever dreamed of offering this Fae such tenderness.

He was always my exception to compassion, but in this enclosure, that isn't so.

It's easy to hate villains. It's much harder to understand them. It's hardest of all to forgive them.

My digits trace from his jaw to the incline of his cheekbone. "What do you desire above all else?" I ask. "Why is your name Elixir? What are you trying to heal? What gives you comfort?"

Elixir shakes his head, his eyes bright and searching for mine. "You are too selfless. I do not understand it. I cannot...understand what it's doing to me." His hands leap to my face and seize my cheeks, his fingers digging into the loosely plaited bun. "Cove."

My heart stutters. He wants to let me in. He does.

The water erupts, wetting my hem and his leggings. I inch nearer, my palm encasing his profile. "Please, let me help you. Let me help you understand."

My thumb breaches his ear. The trance snaps. Elixir's eyes flare, gold spewing from the irises. I gasp and skitter backward, but the lights fail to blind.

The beams vanish. Stricken, Elixir registers what he'd just done—what he reflexively tried to do. Horror and self-loathing clash with outrage, yanking his expression in two directions.

"I need no one's help," he seethes.

The river ruler storms past me, abandoning the harp and quitting the chamber. I whip around and call out, "Elixir! Elixir, wait!" I snatch my weapon from the wall and chase after him.

He's fled one too many forsaken times. For once, I won't let him get away.

16

He moves quickly, prowling down a network of corridors. I dash several leagues behind him, reaching corners just as he charges out of sight and then reappears when I've rounded the bend. His robe flares out, the fabric lashing around his long limbs. Sizzling lanterns fling orange light at his silhouette and turn him into a specter, a darker creature than he already is.

The sight mirrors my first glimpse of him, when I'd peeked into a tunnel as his imposing form had stalked through. Except this isn't the same moment, and he's not the same monster, nor am I the same mortal. I refuse to be a captive, an expendable piece in this game to restore his world, and I certainly refuse to be left behind without having my say.

Elixir isn't fleeing because he doesn't value my word. He is fleeing because he's terrified of it, because it matters that much.

The evidence of this is clear from the speed of his retreat, his pace furious yet heedless. He storms into shawls of mist, the vapors puffing out of his way, though he could have simply vanished. His arms flex at his sides, whereas his fingers should be grazing the walls or tracing the air to discern his way.

He strikes forth erratically, his direction unclear. He pushes ahead, swaying one way, then the other.

"Elixir," I shout, the name ringing through the passage. "Elixir, stop!"

The viper tears around a corner and crashes through a fence of tall reeds. Blessedly, the thoroughfares of this place have dry floors rather than slippery ones. I plow after him. Releasing the skirt of my dress, I swing my free hand, smack the foliage apart, and enter a water garden tucked beneath a cave.

Elixir falters in place. His tapered ears click, perceiving sounds I can't detect, which identify his location. Evidently, this isn't where he'd wanted to go.

"Shit," he hisses and vaults around.

I'm right behind him, marching forward to block his path. Profanities teeter on the tip of my tongue, words I've never resorted to using. I'm so mad, so fitful, I'm quaking from head to toe. "Elixir, dammit," I gust. "You didn't answer me."

"Cursed woman!" Elixir seethes. He whips away in frustration, claws through his hair, and slams back around. "I do not have to obey you. I do not have to answer your fucking questions!"

I get in his face. "Only if you can't handle taking the brunt, just as much as you give it. You don't get to be the only one who chooses when things end and begin. You don't get to be the only one dictating what's said and not said. You don't get to be the only one who asks questions. Unless you're afraid."

His voice ruptures through the cave. "You are a human. Your questions do not scare me. *You* do not scare me!"

My voice ruptures back and hits the crusted ceiling. "Then answer this one: Why did you heal me?"

Elixir falls silent. Our shouts fracture apart, leaving silence in their wake. My hands ball at my sides, fingernails digging into my palms to prevent them from reaching out, from grabbing and shaking him.

The compact cave blossoms with life. Situated amidst lawns of grass, a pond—backed by a rocky edifice and overhang, both cushioned in moss—fills the space. The expanse is as still and polished as a coin, with pearlescent lilies floating like rafts upon the surface.

The water glistens with a blue sheen, and the pearly florals glow, their colors the only sources of light here. No teal orbs. No burning lanterns. The only source of gold is the one staring down at me.

Elixir's features warp, stringing so tightly they might snap.

A lump clogs my throat. I want this to end. I want to stop hating him. I want to stop sympathizing with him. Worse, I want to feel other things, if only he'd let me, if I only I'd let myself, if only it were that simple, if only it were that forgivable.

I chuck my weapon to a grassy mound, grasp the skirt of my dress with one hand, and raise the material. The balmy air caresses my skin. Before I have time to question the instinct, my other hand finds his.

Elixir flinches. His head ticks toward the spot where my fingers gather his. I place them on my bare hip and run them along the place where his mixture had erased the welts, the signs that we'd once worked together, protected each other.

I drag his palm over my flesh, the touch searing me with heat, from my outer thigh to the crescent of my hip. Elixir sucks in a ragged breath. He bows his head, his eyes drifting shut. "Cove..."

The shudder of my name on his lips is my undoing. "Elixir..."

"Get out of the fucking way," he demands, begs, pleads. "Let me pass."

I inch closer, trampling over his last effort. "You used that bead of sweat as an ingredient. You need a piece of someone to remedy them. Is that why you took the droplet, in the first place? Were you taking precautions for me?"

Still, he doesn't answer.

My breasts punt against his chest, our rampant hearts pounding into one another. "Tell me why," I coax. "With no one around, none but me to hear it. Tell me why you healed me."

Why did he create a salve for an injury that wasn't fatal, that only caused discomfort and temporary pain? Why did he bother to comfort me that way?

Elixir shakes his head, his gaze leveling with mine. Dipping so low that I almost miss it, he rasps, "I do not like the sound of you hurt."

This creature admits it as though such a desire is a mystery to him, such an impulse new and confusing. My pulse stutters. I don't know what's happening or why, but the hoarse reply surges through me—warm, swift, and unexpected. It's everything I needed to hear and everything I shouldn't hear.

But what's been spoken can't be taken back. Neither can this...

I lean on my toes, cradle his roughhewn face, and utter, "I can make other sounds for you."

The invitation pours from my mouth, heady and unrecognizable. I can make deeper, longer sounds for him. I can make them *with* him.

Elixir hisses, the hectic noise barely restrained. "What are you doing to me? Why do thoughts of you consume my every waking moment? From the moment you came here, why? You are playing with fire."

"You wanted it in The Mer Cascades. You were rather vocal about it."

"I was battle-wary in the Cascades. And damnation, you were naked."

"And a virgin like you. But how is that possible for a mighty water lord? So many Faeries must crave you badly. I feel for their anguish."

"Stop it."

"Make me."

His fingers dig into my hip, the caps poking lightly, and his free hand pursues the other side. Those brutish eyes hood, his gaze tracking the sound of my outtakes. He tilts his head, breaching the distance to mine, and I meet him halfway, angling my mouth.

We pant uneven breaths, our parted lips hovering inches from one another. But the Fae doesn't stop there. His muscled arms encircle me, his palms grinding over the curves and clasping the swells of my backside.

I gasp, the reflex tapping our mouths together. Elixir groans against my lips, the sound disjointed. His jaw locks, all hardness, because that's how he would kiss—hard, strong, and tireless. If I let him, he will strike quickly.

Our mouths slant and brush, hot and hectic and damp. It doesn't feel like a tease but a warning, a forbidden line about to be crossed. Any second, I'm going to cry out, or he's going to roar.

I don't need to ask. I see it for myself. I see *hard* in the gleam of his eyes. I see the *fast* in the quake of his body.

That's how he would take me. That's how he would…fuck me.

The word pours into my mind like a stimulant. Where once it held a coarse and vulgar texture, now it's as smooth and seductive as velvet.

The Fae's possessive grip on my buttocks incites a frenzy of sensation. The juncture of my limbs sparks to life. An ache throbs inside the cleft between my thighs.

My body's reaction sets my cheeks aflame. Elixir's nostrils flare, inhaling the private scent of desire. Quivers rack his frame, every joint on the verge of snapping.

I want that. I want this, and him, and us.

I'm prey trapping a predator. I'm a human ruining a Fae.

Out of nowhere, the notion reminds me of a Fable. It's one I haven't thought of in ages, about a snake and a viper.

Deep beneath the water, a Snake bewitched a Viper...

My fingers entwine across his nape, climb up his scalp, and dive into the thick fall of his hair. Elixir lets out a haggard noise. When I reach his ears, I stroke them with my thumbs, offering the sort of touch he's never known.

A tender touch that shreds him to bits.

Those pent-up irises blaze. He breaks down, the harsh edges cracking like a wave against the shore, every raging piece of him shattering.

I keen as Elixir whips me into his torso, our bodies colliding.

His mouth burns a trail across my lips. "Decide," he growls. "Make your choice."

Because he's already made his.

Do I want it gentle with a chivalrous man, a hero who would nobly peck my hand and nudge his hips into me, as if I'm made of porcelain?

Or do I want it rough, with a venomous monster? Do I want a villain who would kiss the living hell out of me, then strip me down, spread me wide, and thrust raw and deep, as if I'm made of something stronger? Something sturdier and more lasting? Something that won't break?

Do I want what I've imagined? Or do I want what's right here, right now?

Do I want to make love with a fairytale prince? Or do I want to fuck a vicious Fae?

Unleashing a primal noise, I grab the flaps of his robe—and tear it from his chest.

17

The material blows open, splitting to display an expanse of olive skin. A guttural noise claws from Elixir's throat, the sound cutting through the silence. He stands still, his chest pumping with rapid outtakes as I wrench the robe down his biceps and let it plummet to the ground.

The pond light etches his torso, highlighting the clench of his abdomen and the erect points of his nipples. His pulse rams into the crook of his throat. I feel that same delirious drumming inside me, the rhythmic thud slamming against my wrists and between my legs, where the intimate slot grows damper by the second.

Elixir's hectic gaze roves over me, a disorderly pursuit to seek me out. The black wells of his pupils bloat, and the gold reams of his irises incinerate every place they land. I yearn to melt with them, to swelter in their light.

My assault on his robe had forced us apart, but I consume the distance once more. Oxygen skitters from my lips as I press myself against him, and his hands return to my buttocks. The Fae palms my backside harder now, his knuckles curling, though not enough for his fingertips to pit my flesh.

There's no room left for words, no space to question what this is or how we arrived here, whether we stumbled or thrashed our way to this place, this moment. I don't care to reflect or agonize, to be modest or innocent. I have no urge to think virtuously, only feel passionately.

I'm unmoored, a vessel unbound and lurching into the raging sea. I'm pure instinct, my hands taking on a primitive life of their own. They race from the ridges of his shoulders to his pectorals, the muscles contorting under my touch.

Choppy exhalations rush from our mouths. He bows his head and follows my fingers as best he can. My forehead presses against his, and I watch my own hands moving, sliding down to his nipples and circling them.

We tremble, our mouths slackening as the peaks toughen. My mouth waters, longing to taste those hard disks of flesh. I thumb them, skating around the rim and brushing the tips, pride infusing my veins with every festering noise Elixir makes.

For the life of me, I can't remain still. My digits plunge to his ribcage, where I trace the lattice of bone, then the flexing grille of abs, his temperature increasing on contact. My ministrations descend to the valley of his hipbones, which slope into his leggings.

My mind fogs. The cave disintegrates around me, my focus narrowing to the texture of his body, the heat emanating from inches below my palm. The thought of what lingers farther down sends my mind into a tailspin.

It slickens the crease in my thighs. I scrape my fingers down the smooth flesh below his navel, sneak into his waistband, and quest to the bulging base of his—

A single, savage hiss pierces my ears. A set of fingers snatches my hand and uses the momentum to drive me against him, the impact rocking my head upward to meet a pair of viperous eyes. My breasts mash into Elixir's chest, our bodies going flush, and my gaze stumbles to his lips.

The water lord grips the back of my neck with his free hand, hauls my head forward, and sinks his mouth into mine.

It happens in one fell swoop. The Fae's lips crush against my own, seizing and prying them apart. He wastes no time, his tongue lashing between my lips and stroking me with deft flicks. A moan flutters up my throat, and a groan skewers from his. The sounds collide from where our mouths clasp, searing together in a soul-crushing kiss.

Fables forgive me, we're kissing.

My hands launch into his hair, getting lost in the layers, tangling in them. I taste fury, freshwater, and wine—satiny and intoxicating.

Elixir maintains a hold on my nape with one hand and drives his free digits into the side of my scalp. He holds me in place and fits himself to me, splitting my lips wider. The faint sting of his grip incites a brushfire along my spine. I curl into him, my mouth yielding under the strength of his jaw, the rhythmic swat of his tongue. Each lick of wet heat sends bolts of lightning streaking through me, so that I feel the punch of that tongue in my core.

Elixir hums, inhaling what his kiss does to my body. I should be embarrassed, but I feel none of those things. All I feel is dizzy for more. The lust refuses to abate, the craving only getting worse, more torturous. I'm so wound up, I pull on his roots, yanking them for leverage, to keep my balance lest I puddle to the ground.

Elixir likes it. A carnal growl rumbles from his chest. He lets go of my hair and clamps my rear once more, plastering me to him, nearly hoisting me off the floor.

We kiss madly, furiously, relentlessly. Elixir feasts on the scattered noises vibrating from my mouth, then seethes when my tongue winds around his. I lick my way into him, swabbing his heat, matching its pace.

Our feverish pleas knit and snarl into one. Our lips crash together, tugging, folding, opening, closing. Over…and over…and over.

Elixir wrenches back just enough for his teeth to come out. He nips my lower lip while his fingercaps graze my buttocks in a teasing threat, never actually puncturing me. I can't take this, yet I want to take all of this.

Pleasure gushes from my being, from my pores. I feel monstrous and chaotic, his scent invigorating me, his arms entrapping me.

Elixir bites lightly, then draws his tongue across my upper lip. Emboldened, I snag my teeth into the crook of his mouth, then swipe at it, laving the spot. Instantly, tremors wrack his frame. With another moan, he smothers my mouth with his, plying me with rough strokes.

My lungs empty. Our lips fuse and undulate, tongues thrusting and plaiting.

When my fingers scale his ears and fondle the peaks, the kiss roars to life. He heaves into my mouth, and I keen into his, and our lips grind together. I think my eyes swoop to the back of my skull. The strength of his mouth turns my knees to jelly.

Tingles fill my stomach, my womb, and my toes. We peel back, twist our heads, and slam into another kiss.

Vaguely, I recall learning that in addition to his virginity, Elixir has never kissed another living soul. If that's true, it must be in his lineage, this inherent ability to throttle my senses, to pulverize them to dust.

Then it hits me: I'm his first.

I'm the first to taste his tongue. I'm the first to mold my mouth with his. I'm the first to have this.

At the knowledge, a wet rush floods my center. I grip his tongue and suck, increasing the pressure based on the octave of his growls.

That's it. Give me that cursed mouth. Surrender it to me.

Elixir does, his jaw unhinging and his lips rolling with mine. For a little while, at least. He's not to be trifled with.

In a swift move, the Fae crushes me against him and seizes my lips once more. He traces the raw seam and thrusts inside, and I meet him with every slick pass. Our tongues work us both into a stupor, each of us seeking dominance.

He kisses like a villain—dark, lethal, and punishing.

A whine curls from me as Elixir veers back, prying his mouth from mine. My lips are as swollen as his own, yet not nearly satiated. But my protest ripples into a shocked moan when he dips his head and latches onto the flesh beneath my jaw. His open mouth drags down the column of my throat, at once suckling, then grazing his ivories along my collarbones.

I whimper and curl into him. His silken hair tickles my arms as he moves on reflex, impulsive and unpredictable. Sparks flare in the wake of his mouth.

Elixir reaches my earlobe and draws his mouth along the rim. Leaning in, he etches the same path with his tongue and ascends to the rounded top.

"Oh," I stutter.

"Fade jlvjode," Elixir grates out. *"Éck frái fade jlvjóde."*

Then he drives his tongue into my ear. My nails burrow into his shoulders, fastening him to me. I tilt my head and give him full access, keening aloud as he moves from one ear to the other.

Meanwhile, his fingers vault down my back to trace my shoulders, the rail of my spine, and the flare of my waist. He breaks away, wrests the clasped shoulders of my dress, and rips the garment in half. The urgent echo of sundered fabric tears through the cave. The frock shreds down the middle, from neckline to hem, and billows to the ground. Astonishment and excitement peal from my lips.

I stand naked before him, my body on display. Flushed breasts, my thighs quivering with need, and the patch of hair between my legs glistening. In his own unearthly way, I know he can picture this. A frightful, wanton thrill eddies through me at the raging look on his face.

The Fae slithers around me, stalking to align himself with my back. My heart is a battering ram, and my limbs wobble from the change in position. I gawk at our surroundings, having forgotten where we are. The lily pond bleeds light onto the grass and tints my sandaled feet.

That's all I have the patience to notice. Our movements haven't been leisurely thus far, but now they accelerate even more. From behind, Elixir grabs my hips, yanks me against him, and dives his palms down the front of my body. My arms shoot backward in invitation, and I hook onto his nape while he scrapes my collarbones. Small noises chip from my gullet. I arch, my breasts heavy, my nipples aching and pitting into the humid air.

We pant harder, faster. His hands skate along the sides of my breasts, then curve inward to cup the swells. He massages and fondles them. The sharp index fingers circle the nipples until they're as hard as shells, and I'm squirming and muttering something unintelligible.

At last, he swirls his thumbs over the crests. I choke on my breath. Elixir drops his head over my shoulder, his masculine husk beating against me. He traces and pinches, the sensations urging my thighs apart.

It's not enough. I want his mouth on my breasts, tugging on the studs until I'm writhing. But he continues to torment me, sketching the undersides of my breasts before resuming his assault on the buds.

"What color are they?" he demands.

"They're..." I lick my lips, my words faltering as he brushes them. "They're dark pink."

"And this?" he hastens. "Tell me about this."

His fingers surge down my stomach, past my navel, and reach the thatch of curls between my thighs. I give a stunned cry—and that's before he's done anything crucial. The heat of his palm cups me, his fingers scooping over my folds, where heat and wetness spill from my body.

Elixir twists his head into my neck, a muffled "Fuck" staggering from his mouth. He feels how drenched I am. The slot leaks onto his fingers, coating them in slickness.

"It's warm," I chant. "It's…it's throbbing…"

"And soaked," he mumbles against my hair. "And open."

I nod vehemently, about to describe more, but Elixir finds out for himself. His fingers draw through the curls and begin to trace the shape of my core, so that it forms in his mind. He skims the folds and etches the crease.

Whimpers squeeze out of me. He murmurs in approval, lightly skating over the groove, back and forth. I cling to his muscled form and fling my head back, labored breaths siphoning from my lungs, recitations shooting from my mouth.

He tilts his head as his fingers rustle, brushing my passage. They trace the oval hole—then two fingers dip inside. I gasp, realizing he must have knocked off the fingercaps, because all I feel are rounded appendages.

Yet nothing about this is soft. His fingers sink into the recess, my walls suctioning around him. My air supply drains. A silent moan gets stuck in my mouth, which falls open.

I've known rapture of the sweet kind, tentative and experimental. I've listened to many graphic stories of Lark's dalliances. But I never knew it could be like this, ecstatic and gut-wrenching, vigorous yet sensuous.

Elixir accomplishes several things at once. His mouth clasps the curve between my shoulder and neck, and he sucks my flesh into the cavern of his mouth, into the scorched wetness of it. He suckles there, feasting on me while one hand returns to my breast, scooping its weight. The other hand fills my entrance, his fingers stoking more fluid from my body.

It's all too much. He's everywhere, inside and outside, behind me and around me.

He pumps a steady tempo, his hard digits jutting into me. I melt around his fingers, coating them in liquid. Again and again, his hand enters and retreats, wetting me into shamelessness.

My hips gyrate of their own accord, seeking depth, cadence, and friction. Mindless, euphoric intonations fill the cave, one wispy and the other serrated, so that I can't tell where his voice ends and mine begins.

All the while, Elixir suckles my throat and palms my breast. My concentration scatters like debris, splintering into a tumult of sensation.

My backside rolls into his erection, rubbing against the stiffness. The long mast of his body thickens, rising high from his hips to plague me with curiosity, triumph, and a new type of yearning. That I've produced this reaction in such an impervious male—a Fae—intensifies the need.

I've always thought of this body part in demure terms: length, member, and phallus. To the contrary, wicked alternatives now swim through my head. One of them dangles on the tip of my tongue: His cock.

Elixir's cock is hard for me. I press into that ridge, savoring his stunted breath. In response, his lips and hands release me, and his fingers withdraw from inside me. I half-grumble, half-whine from the sudden retreat.

I blink, my mind still drowning in bliss. I twist partway, in time to see Elixir bring his glossy fingers to his mouth and suck them clean.

My face burns. Yet his eyes produce another reaction, one that eddies low in my stomach, as though someone has dipped a spoon into my veins and stirred them to life.

Elixir slithers to my front, completing a full circle. He hoists me against him, only to steal a quick and violent kiss—his lips snatching my own, his tongue flaying into me—before plunging toward the ground, his body dragging down mine. Along the way, the serpent's mouth wreaks havoc on the dip between my collarbones, the valley of my breasts, and the little burrow of my navel, his lips suctioning and blistering.

While kneeling on the grass, Elixir's mane falls over his shoulders, the mass of hair blocking out his expression. I gulp in anticipation. Wasting no time, he unstraps the sandals, tosses them aside, hitches my right leg over his shoulder, and returns his fingers to my passage. He swirls his hand to gather my dampness, then glides his digits along the split—up, up, up to the kernel of sensation that swells from the center. Oxygen vents from my lungs as he smears my dampness there, then a startled cry bursts from my mouth as his lips follow the same path.

I buckle and grip his roots, nearly toppling to the ground from the stream of pleasure. Elixir prevents me from losing balance by slinging one arm under my buttocks. With his head bent, he raises his free hand in the air and gives a flick of his wrist.

Trickles of water cascade from chinks in the ceiling, the downpour expanding into a wall of water. Elixir nudges me backward against the liquid partition, the water bracing me. I bow against it, still fisting his hair while his mouth tastes the delicate flesh between my legs.

If I thought I'd been making noise before, it's nothing compared to what happens next. Elixir laps at my folds, tracing me anew, only this time with his tongue. The tip curls along my opening and probes into me, re-establishing that excruciating rhythm. He mops up every drop that seeps from me, and as errant rivulets bead down my body from the waterwall, he swallows those, too.

My pulse pounds in that spot where the flat of his tongue flexes. He licks in and out of me, collects the moisture on his tongue, and slides the tip across the seam, to that pearl of nerves rising from the thatch of hair.

Nudging my left limb to the side with his shoulder, Elixir groans and brushes his tongue over that stub, swatting the peak with quick lashes that have me sputtering his name.

The sound only encourages him to destroy me further. The Fae fluctuates between etching the nub of my clit and thrusting back into my core. He follows the signals—my gestures and moans. I know because every place I yearn for him, he finds and tugs into his mouth until I'm a sobbing mess.

He straps his lips around the morsel of flesh and sucks on it, drawing, pulling. I might very well faint. My blood charges to that place, a crescendo building in that spot, the need winding tight.

Simultaneously, I writhe against the waterwall and grind myself onto his face, chasing something brazen and forever out of reach. Elixir palms my rear and shoves me closer to him, closer to his lips and tongue, which throttle me faster, harsher.

My head whisks backward under the flux. I tense…and spring apart… and give a wailing cry. The world blackens at the edges, then swarms my being in a profusion of warmth, a great rush flooding from the place where Elixir's tongue rides me. The climax rages. It spreads down my limbs and over my scalp. I weep with rapture, the sounds cluttered and shaky.

I'm barely coherent when Elixir unhitches my leg, reattaches the fin-gercaps he'd discarded, and rises. His body pitches off the ground, his body flush with mine, so that I feel his heart dashing inside his chest. He listens to my stuttered exhalations and the beat of my pulse, and I watch him relish the signs.

In response, his irises flare. The Fae lowers his head nearer to me, his expression sick with desire.

He's not done with me yet. Nor do I want him to be.

The waterwall rushes over us, then ebbs to a trickle, then dissipates.

He leans in. "Now I know," he rumbles against my mouth. "Now I see it. Your cunt is beautiful."

I keen against him, "If you take mine, I take yours." I drag my tongue across the slope of his jaw. "Show it to me—"

I've barely finished the sentence. Elixir swoops down and claims my mouth. Our lips spread and clutch, our tongues sweeping together. His hands and my hands have the same intention, both dropping to the waistband of his leggings.

I want this barrier off, gone, never to return. I grunt, trying to peel them down his hips, but Elixir helps by pricking the material with his caps and giving a quick yank. The leggings tear and slump low over his narrow hips, and he lets me take over, lets me wrench the pants from his limbs. The leggings shed to the ground and land beside what's left of my sapphire dress.

My eyes drop to the ramps of his hipbones and...

The vision depletes precious air from me. My lungs give out as I take in the size and shape of his mast rising high against his abdomen. It's long, straight, and stiff as a rod, the skin as burnished as the rest of him, the crown swollen and flushed.

His cock is divine.

I reach out, yearning to discover if it's as smooth as it looks. Elixir's arm strikes out and catches my wrist. Silently, he shakes his head, his eyes flashing.

"But why?" I ask.

"Because you will slay me," he implores.

I would smile at this admission, that he wouldn't be able to stand my touch, but I gasp instead when Elixir folds me against him and takes my mouth again. He kisses me into another stupor. I cling to his shoulders while he grabs me by the waist and backs me toward the water's edge.

His arms strap around me, and the world spins. Elixir twists me down, lowering me to the pond's rim, where the water mops at a small crescent of wet grass I hadn't noticed before.

My body puddles atop the bank. Elixir follows me down, every hot and heavy pound of muscle and bone hovering above me. His hair tumbles in a curtain around us, the strands pooling with my teal locks.

We move in unison, panting and restlessness and fed up with waiting, with everything that's happened, with everything that will happen later. I split my quivering thighs and coil my legs around his waist, and he sinks into the vent. Heat emanates from his cock, and wetness drenches my core, and it feels so terribly good.

My nipples jut into his torso. Sweat and mist glaze our skin, my fair complexion a stark contrast to his, the differences evidence despite the murk.

Elixir braces his palms on either side of my head. His upper body looms off the ground, while his lower half splays me wide, his limbs shorn like his upper half, as sleek as glass.

Like this, I get a peek at his backside...his firm ass, as my sister would call it...another sinful word I'm beginning to appreciate. That ass is toned, with dimples in the sides. My knees pitch higher, and my heels skid up his thighs, reaching the swells of his buttocks.

Elixir's irises cleave through the faint light and seek me out, always probing, always trying. Unbidden, the knowledge prompts me to cup his cheek. He twitches from the contact but allows me this moment of tenderness.

Like this, I remember several crucial details. I don't love him, and he doesn't love me. I'm a captive, and he's the captor. I'm a human, and he's a Fae. We're still enemies.

And I want him inside me anyway. I long for escape, release, and defiance. I yearn for the hard, heavy thrust of his weight pushing moans from me.

His cock wedges between us, the bulbous head nocked at my opening. Nervousness and desperation clash within me, because this is happening. It's happening with this Fae, the last creature on earth I should be giving this to, sharing this with. But it doesn't matter, none of it matters.

All I feel is want, want, want. All I can think is now, now, now.

Elixir nudges his prick against my folds and leans down to hiss against my lips, "How deeply do you want it?"

Because this doesn't mean anything, because it's not the romantic first-time fantasy I've nurtured all my life, I'm not going to be precious about it. This is something more, something potent, something imperfect. It's real.

I slide my palm along his jaw and whisper into his mouth, "Don't be gentle."

Rays of gold blaze from his eyes. My fingernails claw down his spine and dig into his rear. Elixir snaps, and I snap, and we lunge into one another.

With a forward pitch of his hips, his cock thrusts into me. I bow against him and cry out as his length fills me whole. My walls yield and grip him in a tight clutch, encasing him to the hilt.

"Ah," cracks from my lips. The pain sears through me in a span of seconds, the sheer size of him robbing me of breath. Just as swiftly as it comes, the pain changes, pricking into something sharply satisfying.

Elixir's eyes cinch shut, and he utters a hoarse noise. His muscles lock, and his body vibrates. I expect an instant pounding, but instead he doesn't move until my joints loosen around him. I sigh as the wet clench of my body sucks him in, my folds spreading to accommodate him.

He must feel that because his eyes rip open, and he slips out, and he whips his cock into me again.

And I like it.

"Yes," I plead. "Yes…there."

"So…deep," Elixir growls.

He withdraws and then slings his waist forward again, spreading me apart. The Fae's hips strike a serpentine tempo, lashing into me with deft stokes. Every beat of his hips causes moans to topple from my mouth. His rear juts back and forth, his hips swipe between my thighs, and his cock swats into the cleft.

Our groans collide, matching the pace of his length. My hips vault off the bank, meeting his thrusts, my body jerking across the ground. Water sloshes against us, licking our limbs. In several places, I catch sight of scales materializing along his calves but not developing fully into a tail.

Elixir's sinuous rhythm urges my head to fly backward. I whimper and sob, the pleasure-pain replaced by ecstasy. My nails puncture the divots in his ass, possibly drawing blood because he growls in appreciation and hooks my leg higher, bracing it between us and lunging his cock deeper, deeper, deeper. The angle of his prick and the position creates a depth I hadn't thought reachable, the result spine-tingling. I feel him so buried, so seated in my wet grip, that my cries solidify into shouts.

The pleasure goes on, and on, and on. Our bodies roll together, cries breaking from our mouths.

It's not enough. I want it quicker.

"More," I whimper. "Give me more."

Elixir nods. He lets out a jagged noise, hunches forward, and pistons into me at a maddening pace. He goes faster, harder, deeper. He makes love to me viciously, fucks me thoroughly, takes my virginity and hurls it like a boulder into the water.

Our hips slam against one another. His cock plies my walls, soaking me to the brim, the crown hitting a spot that sends us into chaos. We buck, frantic. That earlier crescendo builds again, a wave cresting, roaring.

Still, I can't reach it. Not yet.

I contract around Elixir, wrenching groans from his open mouth, my wetness dripping now. Muscles clench in his abdomen, contorting with each push of his waist. He bends, catches the shell of my nipple between his lips, and sucks while accelerating his hips, propelling into me over and over.

Elixir releases my nipple and switches to the other. I holler, rock my hips with his, and lodge him farther still. Fables above, he's opening me so wide, deepening me so much.

We drive against one another, pumping ourselves into it, the pond splashing around us. I'm drowning in my own arousal, in his weight, in his howls. A cord winds where Elixir plows into me, where I drench him from base to crown. It stretches us thin until we're manic.

Elixir lifts himself up, balls my hands into fists, and pins them above my head. With my wrists bound to the grass, he gazes down and charges. The Fae puts his entire body into it, his waist swinging with force and vaulting into my thighs, which fall apart beneath him.

We launch forth, our joints shaking. I weep from each pitch of his cock, the strokes long and far too deep to be real. Like he predicted in The Mer Cascades, I take it thoroughly but not purely. Fables forgive me, I take it again and again and again.

The cord snaps. The wave breaks and surges.

At the last second, my eyes latch onto Elixir's. And somehow, he finds me as well.

Our gazes cling as we ride each other into the ground. Our bodies give and release, spilling over in a wash of sensation.

"Yes," I shout. "Yes!"

"Come," he pleads. "Come with me!"

I heave into Elixir. My moan hardens into a deafening cry, the sound rushing out of me. Elixir stills and then roars. His body spasms, my walls constricting around him, and his liquid warmth spilling into me. We come at the same time, rocking our hips, exhausting the climax.

The cave vanishes. Darkness floods my head except for two rings of gold light.

We slump into the bank, into silence broken only by the pond's ripples and our combined, shattered breaths.

Elixir's mouth sags against mine. With my thighs spread around his hips, I sigh and sneak my fingers into his hair.

Don't be gentle.

For my sake, he hadn't been. But I can't tell if I'd asked for this because I want to remember the villain he is, to remind myself of that fact when thinking back on this, or because I don't want to discover he has a tender side.

Maybe it's all those reasons. Or maybe it's none of them.

Or maybe I'd wanted him just as he is.

Pleasure and turmoil clash. As I feel those emotions twisting my features, I'm grateful for one thing: Elixir might see what others can't, but at least he can't see this.

18

Images and colors drown me, the collage swirling too quickly to catch. At one point, the haze clears. A set of fingers traces my lips and brushes hair from my shoulders. A set of feet rubs against mine, warming them. I mumble something.

"Shh," a voice whispers, the tone quiet against my mouth.

Arms band around me, and I fold myself into them, all the while feeling someone's gaze fixed on my face, even as I fall back asleep.

Just as swiftly, I awaken to darkness and the sound of masculine outtakes, a steady stream of inhalations and exhalations as deep as a river. My head rests on the raft of someone's torso, which inflates and deflates under my cheek.

Am I with a lover? Since when have I ever had one? A male one, that is? Is this a dream?

His heart thuds into my ear, the beat slower than a human's but no less vital of an organ, nor less real. Yet it's a hard pulse, thwacking like a protective fist, a sound only I can hear. For some reason, it eases my soul, so that I snuggle into the body cradling me.

He's built like a ship, all muscle and firm lines. My head nests in the crook between his shoulder and chest. A cascade of hair falls over my arm, which is slung around his waist. We're braided together, limbs tangled.

Grass tickles my ankles, and damp soil squishes under my hip. The ripple of water sweeps through my awareness, a gentle lapping that sloshes over our toes. It's not a current so much as water stirred from my movements. The liquid slide alerts me to a foreign environment perfumed with blossoms and musk. The latter is a sensuous aroma, the scent of intimacy.

It smells of sex.

My eyes fly open. I jolt in realization, then wince at the soreness between my legs, accompanied by a stinging bite of pain. Memories come rushing back—lips clamping with mine, hips thrashing between my open thighs, and a tidal wave of pleasure culminating in flashes of gold.

So much gold.

Arms coil around my body—my *naked* body—in a serpentine embrace. I twist my gaze toward the sleeping face beneath me, the encrusted scales glittering from his temples to his cheekbones, the long eyelashes, and the swollen mouth. The lips I had kissed until we'd lost our minds. The body that had thrust into me.

Elixir.

I disentangle myself from his grasp, vault upright, and gawk. He's sprawled under me, his abs flexing and stacked like bricks, and the slope of his hips points to the masculine length draped between them. That mast had been erect for me, stiff and hot as it plied through my walls and pumped moans from my lips.

Despite having lost its rodlike shape, his cock is still glorious to behold.

Blue light from the lily pond bathes our entwined limbs. Green pads and blooming petals float atop the surface. That's where we are, entangled at the water's edge, where we had...

How deeply do you want it?

Don't be gentle.

Fables forgive me. Heat scorches my breasts and face. Shock follows, seizing me by the throat. I'd slept with him.

I had shared myself with a Fae, the ruler of the river, my enemy. A monster had taken my virginity, as I'd taken his. He made love to me roughly, fucked me fluidly, and I had enjoyed every moment of it. Like a raging wanton, I'd sobbed with bliss, crooned his name, and begged for more. With this viper, I'd gone mad with lust.

That's all it was. Primal, greedy lust. My treachery had nothing to do with the truths we'd shared in The Mer Cascades or The Fountain of Tears. Had it?

I can't tell what would be worse—to betray my people and my family for an empty tryst or to have an affair that actually means something.

The latter is moot, though. It hadn't meant a thing.

What have I done? What have I *done*?

The evidence comes into stark relief. His hair is strewn across his profile, while my own layers hang in disarray. Purple markings stain below my navel, over a single breast, and across one shoulder—the places where he'd sucked on my flesh.

We had fallen asleep afterward. We'd gone limp on the bank and knotted ourselves into a ball of limbs. Our feet and calves had extended into the water, where the pond had quivered. Faint patches of serpent skin—the fragments of a tail—radiant along Elixir's legs where the pond touches him. If he'd been submerged, he would have shifted fully.

As deeply as he'd been hammering inside me, Elixir sleeps just as deeply, not so much as a shift in breathing. With his head flopped sideways, the seam of his mouth relaxed, and his joints slumped, the water lord resembles a marooned sea creature, a beached Fae stripped of clothing.

Normally, his expressions are either harsh, as if in the throes of battle, or as inscrutable as a stone wall. Never has he looked so peaceful, so tender, so good. I tilt my head to stare at him, and my fingers reach out, intending to brush aside his onyx mane.

Before I make contact, my hand halts, and my knuckles curl. This is wrong. I'm ruined, disgraced, and a traitor. My heart clenches, which gives way to panic lancing through my stomach.

I can't do this. I have no right to do this.

I want to stay. I want to leave.

I want him to wake up with a sleepy, pouty face. I want him to fall into an eternal slumber, so he'll never harm another living mortal.

I want to talk with him. I want his silence.

I want him lunging inside me again. I want him as far from me as possible.

I hate him. I don't hate him.

I scramble to my feet, wrap myself in the torn panels of my dress, tether it closed with an errant reed, and dash from the pond. Three seconds later, I swivel back around, dart inside the cave, and pluck my spear off the ground. *Then* I flee.

It takes a while to gather my composure, to orientate my present location in relation to The Fountain of Tears, where I'd found Elixir strumming the harp, and retrace my steps back to The Sunken Isle. Anxiety prickles through me as I skulk through the tunnels and cross shallow brooks. While sneaking over bridges in The Twisted Canals, I grip my spear and cast furtive glances at every alley and shadow.

How much time has passed? The resident insects and amphibians haven't begun their eventide chorusing, so it can't be dusk yet.

At last, I stuff my sandals into their hiding spot and plunge into the lake. I swim mindlessly and forcefully, then plow from the surface, having scarcely felt the effort, much less the water pressure. Sloshing into the chamber, I find the snake curled on the floor beneath my bed.

I move in haste, afraid of stopping to think. I discard the frayed sapphire dress, dry myself with the towel hooked behind the wardrobe door, and throw on an ivory robe. Then I give into temptation. I seek out my reflection in the lantern-lit window and inspect my disheveled appearance, from my tousled hair to my bright eyes.

Do I look any different?

A breeze rustles the robe's sheer material and shivers the tub water. My eyes widen. I swerve toward the looming Fae several paces away, his eyes a mellow gold.

"Elixir—," I blurt out.

"Cove—," he rasps at the same time.

It happens again, both of us forging ahead.

"I was—"

"You were—"

We pause. The silence thickens, the air clogged with awkwardness, repentance, and dangerous longing. I feel it, sense it, lean into it.

Elixir claws through his hair. He looks utterly spent, his mane in shambles, and his leggings and robe rumpled. His expression is the tamest I've ever seen it, drained of creases and trenches. In fact, he looks washed ashore—befuddled and lost, unsure of how he got here.

The uncertainty gives way to distraction as he slants his gaze in the vicinity of my bare feet. "You should wear socks. Your feet were cold. I tried to..."

In the midst of sleep, I'd felt his toes rubbing warmth into mine. That had been real.

"I have poor circulation," I blurt out. "It runs in my family. That is, not my family by heart, but my family by blood. Meaning, the family I was born into, not the one that raised me. Winter or summer, tepid water or icy water, my mother had chilly feet and hands. It's one of the few things I recall, though I'm not sure why I'd remember that particular detail, but then, we're not in charge of what stays in our minds years later."

My chatter ebbs. That last part is far too accurate, far too glaring for this moment to handle.

Elixir clears his throat. "You did not wake me."

He waits as though I have all the answers, all the resolutions he lacks. I shake my head, hearing what he doesn't say—that I didn't stay with him, that I didn't say goodbye, that I denied us any closure. And that, although it shouldn't matter, it does.

"I couldn't," I tell him.

Because although what we've done can't be undone, and although it was the most painfully erotic thing I've ever experienced, and although he had been as crazed as I'd been, and although we slept so deeply and closely, and although we could have remained like that, and although he'd sounded concerned rather than inconvenienced about my cold toes, and although he's here, and I'm here, and my fingers itch to touch him, and I see his gilded eyes simmer: This was a mistake.

Elixir's eyebrows cinch. I don't have to announce my thoughts. My blood and pulse and breaths speak for themselves, and I know he's beginning to feel the same, the farther we drift from this spell. Maybe it wounds him, but more likely he's equally ashamed.

Remorse curdles in my gut. I had been lonely, overwhelmed, and recovering from several traumatic events. We'd been enchanted and temporarily ravenous. Had these feelings erupted out of hate-fueled attraction, or is this purely what happens when two beings live through an ordeal and save each other, uniting to survive a battle with predators?

Or is something more dangerous brimming?

Elixir straightens. His demeanor reassembles itself into the stoically brutal ruler he is. Then he gives a curt nod, and that's that.

Straightaway, a reptilian shape glides from under the mattress. I jerk toward the snake, but it's too late. The creature has made an audible appearance, his forked tongue vibrating.

When Elixir's ears click toward the sound, I hold up my hands. "I can explain."

Yet his features betray no astonishment. "No need," he assures me.

The snake is heading directly for Elixir. Stunned, I watch the Fae stride toward the animal, hunker to the floor, and offer his hand, attentive to the sensory signals. The reptile entwines itself around Elixir's forearm and rests its head there, its yellow eyes blinking at him.

Elixir lifts his bent arm, suspending the snake off the ground as if in greeting. For a moment, they regard one another, some form of communication passing between them. Mild amusement unfolds across the ruler's face. That, and awareness.

I think about the extra portions of raw fish that had been delivered when I'd requested it, and how I'd stopped having to ask. "You knew," I realize while kneeling beside them. "The whole time, you knew he was here."

"The first evening, I heard him enter the chamber tub before you discovered him. He was waiting for me to leave." Elixir's mouth slants wryly. "He is not my companion to reveal, but I give you my word: You needn't keep the reptile a secret. Mortal or not, he is a member of the fauna. My subjects would sooner disobey me and incur my wrath than harm an animal."

That's a relief and common knowledge amongst my people. Still, I hadn't dared take that gamble. The ruler had known a mortal creature had entered his realm, a companion for his captive, and he could have objected. He could have sent the snake away just to hurt me. But he hadn't.

Likewise, Elixir hadn't needed to send my friend nourishment. I wonder if he did so for my sake as well. I want to thank him either way, but knowing what Faeries think of gratitude, I restrain myself.

My companion stares at Elixir. After a moment's consideration, the Fae's eyes spark with newfound information. He sets down the snake, who winds away and flops into the bath.

Elixir and I linger. Our heads twist toward one another, our shoulders tap, and we exchange shallow breaths.

"I was young when I came into my rule over The Solitary Deep," he says. "Akin to a mortal of sixteen, despite my sixteen-hundred years."

"H-how many?" I balk, causing his eyes to shine with mirth, a reaction that dulls as just soon as it comes.

"After The Trapping, my brothers and I matured quickly. Over the next nine years, I aged like a human, rapidly and exceeding a Fae's physical capacity. Because of this shared fate, we became brothers-in-arms."

In thin slices, he tells me how The Three became full-grown Faeries—in mind, body, and soul—over less than a decade. That's why he resembles a male in his mid-twenties and a Fae in his prime.

Elixir makes it clear. "So, you see. I did not wait long."

I do see. For someone destined to live forever, he wasn't a virgin for very long, until last night. Regardless, I can only imagine how many of his kin have lusted after his dominance, power, and beauty. They must have tempted him, and for a male in my world, nine years is still a profound amount of time to abstain.

"But you still said no," I whisper. "You said no to conquests."

"I said no," he affirms, his murmur hot and gruff against mine.

"Why? What were you waiting for?"

"I wait for nothing and no one." His baritone lowers. "My thoughts were elsewhere these years past. I wanted to choke the enemy more than fuck a mate. Those urges did not wane or stray."

"What about now?"

It has to be different now. It needs to be.

I lean in, and so does he. Our mouths part, weighty and burning. Once again, we hover on that brink.

Then he emits a haggard noise and shoots to his feet. I lag behind, rising slowly. Elixir's dry, and I hadn't heard the door close, so he must have manifested from thin air instead of using the stepping-stones. But now he strides toward the chamber door rather than evanescing.

Before departing, Elixir glances over his shoulder and says, "His name is Lotus." Then he pushes through the door and closes it.

Lotus. The snake told Elixir its name.

I hear a faint splash, rush toward the door, and whip it open. Elixir is gone. The surrounding water quivers, rings spreading there. But why would Elixir dive into this lake? There's no way out of the cave except for the obvious.

Maybe he can evanesce from beneath the surface. That stands to reason.

I hasten to the rim, search the depth, and catch a blurry form with two arms and a tail vanishing. It resembles the same mottled, retreating figure I'd seen nine years ago, back when he'd tried to flee from me, back when he didn't see me coming.

Didn't see me coming…

See me coming…

That line is familiar. It's from that Fable I'd been thinking of earlier, shortly before seducing Elixir. It's called *When a Snake Bewitches a Viper*. While thinking of ways to break the curse, I hadn't gotten to that story yet, as there are so many tales in the Book of Fables. But suddenly, the pages come rushing back from the recesses of my mind.

Deep beneath the water, a Snake bewitched a Viper. For the Viper had thought itself so immune to folly, it underestimated the Snake's own power. Little did its enemy know, the Snake possessed the ability to see the Viper's true monstrous nature, to feel darkness in the Viper's presence, and to act fully on these truths. Thusly, these abilities became weapons.

The Viper did not see the Snake coming until it was too late. From three bewitching strikes, the Viper paid the price and endured an altered fate. Its perception dwindled and grew more repellent than before. In the end, the Viper became unrecognizable, even to itself.

Alas, such tides are not easily turned. Change comes only from the bewitcher, who must see, feel, and enact the opposite of old truths and past deeds.

While the Viper languished, the Snake's senses became sharper. With the passage of time, the creature beheld the dark Viper in a different light—and turned those tides at last.

Henceforth, no other magic drew them together, nor apart. For once magic has touched two beings, no other enchantments may prevail.

I stare at my reflection, my hair awry and my eyes a vivid, confused teal. Childhood memories and Fabled passages collide. The onslaught comes swiftly. I sink to my knees beside the bank and gape at my rippling likeness.

That's when the Fable's words become clear. To *endure an altered fate* is to be changed, possibly to be damned.

"Bewitched means to curse," I utter.

In such a tale, Elixir's the viper. But who's the snake?

I note the parallels to the Fable. Although they could apply to many experiences—and likely, that's the point—they connect seamlessly to our shared past.

I return to that era of The Trapping, both of us nine years younger, me struggling with Elixir underwater. I remember what I'd seen in him, how I'd felt, and what I'd done. Then I remember his sudden change, the way his eyes had shifted and become puzzled, distant, and lost.

Change comes only from the bewitcher...

But if only the bewitcher can break the curse, that means...

I clutch my stomach. In a ruthless twist of rules, Elixir had challenged many humans to accomplish this task, but they'd lost because they were facing an impossible game, because they hadn't possessed the power to undo the curse. The only person who can do that is the one who'd enacted it, in the first place.

All this time, I've been pondering what could be Elixir's greatest weakness, the impetus for the curse. Yet it was there, in front of me. So simply, it was right in front of me.

His greatest weakness isn't a random misdeed or error in judgement.

His greatest weakness is the person who cursed him.

"Me," I whisper to the water.

Fables forgive me. I'm the snake. I'm the bewitcher. I'm the water lord's greatest weakness because I'm the one who blinded him.

I'm the one who cursed Elixir.

19

And he knows. Elixir knows I'm the one who cursed him. In fact, he must have known from the beginning.

That explains his reaction during our first acidic conversation in this chamber. I had blustered, arguing he was the same vile Fae he'd been nine years ago, and he had gotten infuriated—and sarcastic.

Yet I have not changed.

Not. At. All.

Back then, I'd heard the serrated texture of Elixir's anger and the piercing sound of accusation. The latter, I hadn't comprehended. Yes, I'd wronged him before, though for an altogether different act. Why would he blame me for his blindness as well?

Now I know. I had affected Elixir in more ways than I'd thought.

Guilt and astonishment, shock and grief, tenderness and turmoil collide within me, along with a defiant passion I shouldn't feel, the same emotion that had swept me into his arms hours ago.

This is why I can resist his power. If I'm the one who created the curse, I'm immune to it.

During our first clash, Elixir had asked me how I fended off his magic, but he hadn't needed to. He's wise enough to have drawn the same conclusion. The only reason he'd asked was to confirm whether *I* knew about my role in his fate, whether I knew about my immunity to him. He'd been fishing, discerning the level of my ignorance.

He still thinks I don't know.

The Fables say knowledge against magical beings is power. That's why he didn't tell me, because it would have given me a potential advantage. Knowing who incited the curse would have been the first step to winning.

Fables forgive him. He made other mortals play the same game, aware they couldn't break it, that it was impossible for them.

Change comes only from the bewitcher, who must see, feel, and enact the opposite of old truths and past deeds.

Yet how did I bewitch—curse—him? To break this curse, what does it mean to see, feel, and enact the opposite? What old truths and past deeds is the Fable referring to?

Does Elixir know these answers?

What happened in the lily pond…that hadn't been a game. It hadn't been part of his agenda, nor mine. It had been genuine, hadn't it? Otherwise, we wouldn't have tried to resist.

We had truly desired each other.

But I still want to win this game. And he still wants to stop me.

My likeness wobbles in the depth, unsteady and on the verge of losing its shape. As harrowing as this knowledge is, I need to find out how this curse happened in the first place. I need to keep playing my own game, keep getting close to Elixir, keep chipping away at his heart.

I need to do one of the few things Faeries can't do. I need to lie.

20

I crawl into bed, hoping to recover some of the rest I'd lost while swept up in Elixir's embrace. In the lily pond, we couldn't have dozed for more than an hour. While Lotus curls against my feet, I fall into a deep, dark slumber.

The respite doesn't help. The moment I awaken, everything comes rushing back. I've cursed my enemy, yet he doesn't feel like my enemy anymore. I've betrayed my family, yet I can't seem to wish back what I've done.

I preoccupy myself with the map under my bed. In addition to sketching The Fountain of Tears and the lily pond, a new ambition inspires me. Using the drawing rock, I mark the places where the river levels have shifted. But without Lark and Juniper's help, I fail to decipher a pattern, any indication that the river's draining in a systematic manner. Maybe it's futile to hope this natural event can be prevented in some manual way, with the effort of physical work rather than magic and the extermination of my people. Regardless, if there's a remote chance to save the Solitary wild without sacrificing mortals, I won't stand by and wait for such a miracle to manifest.

If curses are possible, so are blessings.

Because we had agreed never to touch each other again, Elixir doesn't return. I imagine the water lord burying himself in pressing matters, including the river's demise. Yet I frequently catch myself glancing at the door, waiting, hoping.

But what do I expect? We had acknowledged our mistake, so I'd be a nitwit to assume things have changed. He has this world to preserve, the fauna and his kin to save. I have my own life and the survival of my sisters to think about.

As time passes, I keep my wits about me, keep the spear in grabbing distance, lest a certain resentful merman called Scorpio make an appearance in this chamber. Despite Coral's assurance that the merman won't disobey Elixir's command to stay away from me, Scorpio has already been punished three times because of me. Revenge is a powerful motive. Centuries of strife between humans and Faeries have proven that.

Finally, I'm ready to continue my exploration of The Deep. Yet when I tie the hem of my dress around my upper thighs, grip the spear, and prepare to dive into the water, bubbles well to the surface and spit out a boat. I stall at the ledge. Fluid rustles from where the slender vessel materializes. It's one of the boats I've seen at The Twisted Canals, though this one is less conspicuous. It has a prow but no lantern or rower.

The transport shaves through the water and halts at the bank.

The water and I share a bond. I entreat the river, and it replies of its own will.

I take a guess. Unlike the other bodies of water, this one has an embedded history. And because the lake will mimic its sinking descent forever, Elixir can't ask this water to cease its pull or keep me afloat. Nor can he command its stepping-stones to rise for a human.

But he can send a boat.

My heart winces. For a second, I consider refusing his offer. Lark and Juniper would, one out of defiance, the other out of pride. Now I love my sisters. I love them more than anything in this world, and I respect their choices. But for my part, there's a fine line between defiance, pride, and folly. I'm not so bullheaded as to refuse help.

I step into the boat, hunker into its peapod shape, and flatten myself along its base. Best to keep out of sight, secluded isle or not. Quietly, the boat ferries me across the lake, yet instead of mooring on the other side, it turns and keeps going.

I blink. "Wait. What—"

The transport drifts toward a gully camouflaged into the cave wall, which leads to a tunnel. All this time, this was here? Hidden in plain sight?

At the entrance, the current stills. My boat tarries beneath the rocky archway.

I hesitate. Presumably, this vessel's mission is to bring me somewhere. Or to someone.

The boat remains anchored, awaiting my decision. If I want to, I suspect the vessel will veer around and take me where I'd originally intended to go.

Make your choice.

How many times have I told myself I won't, can't, shouldn't? How many times have I listened?

If I turn back now, I'll be left wondering.

Ignoring the tiny thrill that eddies through me, I whisper, "Okay."

The boat jolts into motion and skates past the archway. Once tucked inside the passage with its teal-spangled ceiling, I sit upright and untether the skirt of my dress, the fabric dyed the color of a medallion and cinched with a plaited belt.

Balmy air brushes my shoulders, and mellow water licks the sides of the boat. My carrier glides down several forks encrusted in topaz foliage, then tumbles down a slide that sprays my face. I surge downward and land at the bottom while nervous chuckles lurch off my tongue.

"You enjoyed that," a voice says.

I swing toward that rasping baritone. While the boat slows to a halt beside a raised landing, a figure materializes from the shadows. First his riveted eyes, then his glistening scales, then the rest of him.

Leggings as black as nightfall mold to his limbs. Instead of his hooded robe, a paper-thin tunic billows across his chest, with the sleeves loosely rolled up his forearms and the crisp, white material stark against his olive skin.

I've been naked with this otherworldly specimen. I've tasted his tongue and felt the relentless pace of his hips. He's been inside me, thrusting so deep and dark.

To my dismay, those gilded eyes shimmer. My flesh detonates with heat. If my body doesn't shut up, it will continue hurling signals in his direction, and then I'll never have the upper hand, curse or no curse.

Elixir's right. I did enjoy the slide, but it takes a minute to remember how my laughter had rung loud and clear as a bell through this channel. My pleasure must have been lucid in his ears.

I swat errant strands of hair from my face. "It's hard not to enjoy a boat that rows itself, plus a waterslide in the dark. Things like that don't exist in my village, only in stories. But you already knew that, and…" I trail off. "It doesn't matter."

Fondness and intrigue simmer in Elixir's expression. "But it does. It matters to you."

"Why did you bring me here?" I accuse.

Is this a mirage, or does the water lord look insecure? Whatever he's about to propose, his tentative demeanor suggests he's expecting me to reject him.

Elixir clears his throat, concealing the noise with a baritone grunt. "I would…very much like…" he rubs the back of his neck, then squats at the landing's edge and extends his hand. "I would like to show you something."

I should recall accepting his offer. I should recall disembarking from the boat. I should recall standing before him.

But as he guides me down a series of lantern-lit corridors, all that lingers in my mind is my hand taking his, the warmth of his palm, and our fingers weaving together. The last time we held hands, Elixir had balled them over my head while thrusting feverishly inside me. This is different. It's consciously done and somehow riskier.

The Fae moves a step ahead of me, his free hand grazing the left wall and following its direction. His grip is neither firm nor loose, neither possessive nor indifferent. Until the lily pond, I hadn't thought him capable of maintaining such a hold on anyone.

Those honed fingercaps press to my knuckles without biting into my skin. I concentrate on the cadence of his pulse thudding against my own and growing more rapid the farther we get.

Actually, I think about one other thing: Elixir's face just after I'd emerged from the boat, when our hands made contact. The lines of his countenance had been soft for a span of only seconds. Then his brows had knitted, and he'd made a gruff noise while turning away.

As we wind through the passages, I get sneaky and lean sideways. A quick peek at his profile yields the same surly I-don't-care-how-good-your-damn-hand-feels glower.

I bite my lower lip to stifle a grin. It's rather cute to see him in the throes of denial.

At last, he ushers me from the corridors to a cave promontory overlooking a gulch twenty feet below us. The view is wondrous, with its glittering ceiling, sprays of jade foliage crowding every surface, and the aquamarine current gushing below. Grass carpets the overhang, the blades sinking under my feet.

Elixir kneels at the overhang's rim, his feet also bare. "We shall wait here."

"For what?" I hunker beside him, perch on the ledge, and let my calves swing over the side.

He shakes his head. "It must be seen, not told."

Anticipation creeps into his voice. Then I hear the rumble of a stampede.

The ground ruptures beneath us. The gulch roars to life, the current rolling into rapids that thrash over boulders and crash into the vegetation. As the raging tide grows, the waves solidify and take the shape of horses.

"Kelpies," I gasp.

The rapids manifest into a fleet of massive water horses galloping at breakneck speed, the equines' bodies translucent yet sparkling with color—from citrine, to pale green, to azure. Their manes fly like banners; their coats are gilled or covered in scales; long whiskers splay from several muzzles; and fins sprout from their withers and legs. The kelpies are made of liquid, yet the details froth into tangible shapes.

They're not illusions. They're alive!

A chorus of whinnies blast from their mouths, the otherworldly sound as cavernous and melodic as a siren's song. The enchanted spectacle robs me of breath. Dazed, I watch as they pass by us, spring into the air, and dive into the rapids with a tremendous splash that douses the gulch. At which point, they vanish into the water, becoming one with the breakers.

"It is called The Kelpie Rapids," Elixir says, breaking me from my trance.

I catch his face angled toward me, his Fae senses listening for my reaction.

The tides continue in the water horses' wake, rushing forth and soaking the environment. When the rapids show no sign of dwindling, I whisper, "I don't know what to say."

"Are you sure about that?" Elixir wonders.

With a startled laugh, I twist my body his way, only to be greeted with an equally remarkable sight. His head bows, and his lips slant, a close-mouthed huff of mirth escaping him. Is he teasing me?

Three seconds later, he sobers and regards the gulch with reverence. "Always, they run at this hour—the kelpies of old who created the tunnels and passages of The Deep. Millennia ago, they would race through this realm, forging rapids that dug craters into the walls. Now they content themselves to this place alone, to honor what they've contributed by sharing The Deep with other water fauna and Solitary Fae. They have given rather than taken."

He emphasizes that last tidbit, which makes me grin. He remembers what I'd said.

Many people in my world base worth on one's possessions. I see a person's worth in what they contribute.

My smile widens as Elixir grapples with his next question. "Does, er… does this view please you?"

Honestly? I want to kiss his cheek, but I'm not sure this Fae can handle that amount of sweetness. "Yes, it does," I reply. "Can't you tell?"

I'd been joking, but Elixir frowns in contemplation. "No," he realizes. "I…" After a moment's concentration, his frown deepens. "No, I cannot."

That's unexpected. But for some reason, I don't feel motivated to contemplate what that means. Later, I tell myself. Not now, when there's so much else to marvel at.

"They're stunning," I confess.

Rich gold floods his irises, and his voice grows animated. Elixir is still kneeling, but now he settles beside me. "Will you tell me what they looked like?"

Drawing in a breath, I describe the kelpies' vibrant colors and aquatic features, down to how fast they'd charged. I do my best to paint a vivid picture in his mind.

The river ruler gazes into the distance, as if imagining. When I finish, his accent dips low, the intonation melancholy yet alleviated. "They have not changed," he whispers.

I sketch his wistful profile. "When was the last time you were here?"

"As a child, I would watch them," he says, lost in a haze of memory. "My mothers would take me here."

"Your mothers?"

"Marine and Lorelei," he says. "They were mated mermaids. They loved watercolors, harp music, the smell of lemons, and the art of brewing mixtures. I adopted the practice in their names, as well as for myself."

In all sincerity, I hadn't thought of the river ruler as someone with parents. Back when I hated him, I had assumed he'd been spawned from the depths of this place or hatched in a den of anacondas. According to the Fables, it's rare for Faeries to sire children, but it does happen.

There's no mistaking the way his words shrink, reduced to threads of sound. I recognize the audible texture of bereavement firsthand. "Did they care for you?" When he nods, I coax, "What happened to them?"

Every muscle in his face tweaks, from haunted to livid. "They died."

My throat clogs. This violent, powerful being has made no home for himself. He has no family or animal familiar. He lost his mothers, and now he's losing his world.

He might have brothers through a shared experience, but that shared experience had involved a traumatic attack, in which the fauna and avenging Faeries of his land had been slaughtered. He might have rescued some of them, but he hadn't rescued all of them.

After what I've discovered, I shove my way past that brutish exterior. In this moment, I see what he can't. The picture is a devastating one—anger, beauty, and tragedy. What I see is a conflicted soul who would rather hate than hurt, who would rather punish the ones who've caused him grief than mourn what he's lost.

Did his mothers perish in The Trapping?

It's too soon to pry. I scoot closer until our shoulders press. "I'm sorry," I whisper. "I know how it feels to lose family."

I'm not only talking about my sisters or Papa Thorne. Regardless, the

Fae's expression twists, caught between penitence and vengeance. He knifes a hand through his hair. "You were not supposed to learn about The Sunken Isle's hidden outlet. Only my mothers and I have known. I do not know why I shared that secret with you. I do not know why the fuck I brought you here."

"You wanted me to see the kelpies."

"But I do not know why."

I have a theory, though it's too scary to acknowledge. It has everything to do with him admitting he hasn't been here since he was a child, back when his mothers were alive. It has to do with him sharing this isolated moment with me. It has to do with him asking if the kelpies had been a pleasing sight. Yet if I let myself think of him as a sensitive being, I'll never make it out of this place.

Instead, I confess, "My mother and father died, too."

Elixir's head jolts toward me. He had assumed I'd been talking only of losing Lark, Juniper, and Papa, but there's more to the confession.

The Fae doesn't ask, but he does swerve in my direction. If I speak, he'll listen.

In this dark abyss, I let the story unfold. My parents were sailors who loved the ocean. Although they hailed from Middle Country, they spent years exploring The Southern Seas. But for the first years of my life, they settled down in the land of their roots and showered me with love.

They told me stories about oceanic mammals and aquatic creatures—whales larger than pirate ships and fish with sword-shaped noses; cities of glowing coral; starfish and seahorses; and deep-sea fish that sizzled with light. Also, they told me about the southern dragons, not the ones that reign over the sky but those that dominate the sea like great leviathans, able to breathe fire beneath the depths.

Every day of my existence, my parents' hearts longed for the ocean. Unfortunately, seafaring was no life for a child, so although they vowed to wait until I was old enough to sail with them, they made a different choice when I turned nine. I promised I wouldn't be any trouble if they brought me along. When that didn't work, I cried my eyes raw and begged for them to stay. Instead, they left me with a kindly neighbor and swore to return.

I heard it in their voices, strained as taut as ropes. Rather than guilt, I heard passion. Or maybe it was obsession.

They adored me. But they adored the ocean more, as though salt flowed through their veins.

They weren't coming back.

Even if they'd wanted to, they wouldn't have had the chance. Their vessel got caught in a storm, never to be heard of again.

"Sometimes I wonder if my love for water is genuine," I confess, my throat clotting with unshed tears. "Or if I'm trying to connect with them, trying to prove what they didn't believe in the first place—that I could bond with the sea the way they did. Maybe I'm trying to prove myself worthy. Or maybe it's because the water's all I have left of them. Maybe it's because it's the last place they took a breath. Or maybe I'm trying to convince myself they're alive, that someday I'll be able to save them, wherever they are." I shake my head and tuck a lock of teal behind my ear. "Or maybe I love the water for myself."

Although Elixir is quiet, I feel him absorbing my words.

News of the ship's sinking had reached my ears in the worst way possible. Because my parents had owed payment on their vessel, the grizzly man who'd sold the ship to them arrived, intent on delivering the tidings and collecting compensation: me.

He had planned on selling me to a brothel in The Northern Frosts, but his carriage had barely gone a mile when I'd swiped a dagger from his belt and stabbed his palm, then threw myself out of the vehicle. My sleight of hand had been a moment of luck, but I'd wondered if I could teach myself to get better at it and, therefore, protect myself.

I developed that skill quickly, purely out of necessity. With nowhere to go, I became a pickpocket who wandered the countryside from village to village. The knack provided me with coin for food—until the day I wandered into Reverie Hollow and got caught. My hand had barely reached into a random pocket when a set of dark-skinned fingers snatched mine.

The man had a friendly face, a soothing voice, and he didn't drag me to a jailer. Instead, he became my father.

By then, Papa Thorne had already adopted two orphaned girls. One of them wanted to make me laugh by using naughty phrases, while the other had frowned at me, her expression and posture as rigid as a tree.

"They became my sisters," I say with a smile.

Elixir's expression had been murderous, his eyes fuming and his fists clenched, while hearing about the man who'd tried to sell me. However, while hearing the tale of my new family, the muscles in his face slacken. The Fae hesitates, his eyes tripping across the vista. During the tale, not once has he looked at me, yet I sense him wanting to.

I tell him about Lark and Juniper, about their quirks and personalities. I describe the jewelry we gave each other—Lark's thigh cuff, Juniper's leaf bracelet, and my waterdrop pendant, though Elixir already knows about my necklace.

Only when I talk about my family's animal refuge, The Fable Dusk Sanctuary, does the ruler's head whip toward mine again. "You rescue fauna."

I relish how his eyes flash with amazement. "Lotus was one of my rescues. Trade poachers were after him."

Recognizing the term, Elixir's face tightens with malice. I forge ahead, describing the sanctuary and gloating at his features, which range from awed to respectful.

Finally, the rapids stop, and the water calms.

"So, I lost my parents, and I found a new family." I glimpse his pensive countenance. "Then you happened." I watch the teal specks brush his profile in lightness and darkness. "Do you remember?"

"I do." Elixir swerves my way, his eyes sparking with all that gold. "I remember everything."

Yes. So do I…

21

Nine years ago

In the field at night, I wade through a brook that cuts into the underbrush. My bare feet splash through the water as I scurry across the plains. Alders and elderberry bushes shiver in the breeze and emit a soft, hushing noise. I tell myself it's okay, everything will be okay, not to worry, never fear.

But it's not okay. Nothing is okay. Worry crawls through my stomach, and I'm scared.

While grasping the muck-stained hem of my cloak and nightgown, I race through the icy water, which chills me to the ankles. Juniper had been right. We should have worn our boots. Whereas I had been right to whimper about us losing each other.

We're not allowed to be out this late. It was supposed to be a quick and safe game of hide-and-seek. That's all.

A serpent mask covers the upper half of my face, the visor falling lopsided as I dash over several rocks. Every few leagues, I stop and whisper-cry, "Lark? Juniper?"

There's no answer but for the quiver of stalks and the gurgle of water beneath my feet. My sisters could be anywhere. They could be lost, hurt, or kidnapped.

A sob bubbles from my lips. It's perilous to be out after dark, and the countryside is dreadfully silent. I had sniffled about this, but Lark had promised nothing would happen, had sworn it would be fun. I must remember what she and Juniper had also said, what the villagers always say: Faeries don't harm children.

Those magical beings might prey on the elders of our town, but my sisters and I are too young, only ten. The Folk have never stolen anyone our age.

Please, please, please let that be true. And what about other night walkers and prowlers? What about hags, bandits, pirates, or trade poachers? What about wolves? Are there wolves in Middle Country, or do they reside only in the north?

Fate may chastise us yet for being disobedient. In fairytales, children are often punished in some way, especially when they sneak out at night. If Papa Thorne finds out, he'll be so very angry, and we'll be in so much trouble.

The distant call of a nightingale's song flutters into my ears. That's Lark's favorite sound.

I bypass the entrance to the woods, where leafless branches crank and resemble stag antlers. That's Juniper's favorite animal.

Air rattles from my lungs. Fear propels me down the brook, the frigid temperature biting my heels and numbing my toes. Maybe Lark and Juniper are by the creek, expecting me to wander there. I pray to the almighty Fables I'm right, otherwise I'm destined for either the forest or nightingale territory. The latter is too close to the glassblower's forge, which is a creepy place with its rickety facade and the strange caws resounding from there.

I don't want to search those places first. The creek is safer.

High grasses fence in the babbling current, the surrounding foliage too condensed to scramble through. This brook is the only passable route. The icy current freezes me to the bone, and my teeth clatter like loose tiles. But the stalks towering on either side like sentinels protect my small body from the blue-black shadows of eventide.

At last, the brook winds down a little hill and spills into the creek. At this hour, the surface is as glassy as a mirror, reflecting a spray of constellations.

I halt at the bank, tears leaking down my face. "Lark?" I blubber. "Juniper?"

Branches crackle in the wind. A fish plops beneath the depth, its descent forming rings that multiply across the water's surface.

They're not here. They're *not here!*

I hiccup, shove the serpent mask to my forehead, and twist left and right. If I were to follow the creek, I'd soon find my way home. But I'm not going anywhere without my sisters, never without them.

If only I had brought my spear. Juniper had wisely thought to bring her archery tonight. Why can't I be as smart as her? Why can't I be as adventurous as Lark?

I would bet my favorite stuffed python that neither one of them is weeping. My hiccups stutter to a halt. I swipe a forearm across my wet lashes and suck up the last of my tears.

After tiptoeing closer to the bank, I squint through the darkness at the rings vibrating across the creek's surface. They're not branching out as they should be. No, they're traveling, as though someone's dragging the current.

A fleet of copper fish dart beneath the ripples, creating a miniature tide. Such freshwater fish are common here, yet there's something strange about the way they surf through the depth like moths drawn to a flame.

My unshod feet carry me down a lane parallel to the creek. I trail the school of fish, their journey ending half a mile down the path, where a flat expanse of grass stretches into the water like a short jetty. There, a decrepit stone rotunda rises from the ground.

Uh-oh. I stifle a petrified breath. This must be the ancient well that Papa had once talked about, the one long rumored to be cursed. The first residents of Reverie Hollow had built it centuries ago, but they stopped using it after the tales began to circulate. This harbinger has something to do with old dark magic, but I can't remember much else.

Chills race down my spine. I thrust the serpent mask over my face while scuttling backward. My gaze jumps across the landscape and returns to the well. Only the base remains, the blocks of stone weathered and barely holding together its cobbled shape. It looks like any old well, crumbling with age and disuse.

Except wait. Is that glass?

My flight stalls. Propped upright inside the well is a translucent chute, pipe-shaped and flooded with liquid. Murky water swirls inside the glass cylinder, bubbles frothing from within.

The creek fish gather beside the embankment, their animated fins and tails beating through the water in a frenzy. It's as though they're anxious to enter the well, to be invited into the confines, to join whatever's inside.

Whatever's inside …

Inside…

I don't know what comes over me, but I find myself floating toward the glass, toward my blurred reflection caught in the facade. Above and below, grids of iron are faintly visible, which means the glass must be hearty and thick to endure the weight. The grates seem to form doors, preventing entry and exit. The well drills into the grassy jetty, and the bottom closure cuts through the water leading into the creek.

The bubbles simmer and thrash about inside the cylinder. If I didn't know better, I'd guess the water has a temper, or something's trapped in there.

My fingers reach out. In my reflection, I see my wide, teal eyes peeking through the serpent visor.

Then I see gold.

Then I see a fist.

Olive-skinned knuckles punch through the murk and ram into the glass. With a shriek, I leap back. Rings of gilded light pierce from the container, followed by a pool of long, black hair.

A venomous face swims into view. Scales encrust the creature's flesh, from temples to cheekbones, the shingles glittering like plates of foil. Livid irises blaze through the compartment and find me.

It's a viper. No, it's a male.

A male Fae.

Pointed ears spear from the black mane swirling around his face. His chest tapers to a snake tail just as vivid as his scales.

Some type of water Fae? A merman?

He's bigger than me, halfway between a youth and a man. If I were to cross paths with him on the street, I'd say he's no more than sixteen.

My pulse catapults into my throat. I can't speak, can barely utter a noise.

The Fae peers at me, his gaze dragging down from my clothes to my bare toes, then back up again. Upon seeing my mask, his pupils flash with umbrage—right before he pounds his fist into the glass again, and again, and again.

I jump in place, a yelp popping from my lips. The panel ruptures so violently, I fear it will shatter. I'm staring into the vicious eyes of a Fae, a powerful one, a trapped one. A magical being who doesn't like what he sees.

I whip off the visor, which does nothing to pacify him. The viper pummels the glass like a baited bear. Does he think the mask is meant to taunt him?

"I-I'm sorry," I stammer, my lisp thick. "I'll put it down. Look, I'm putting it down." Slowly, I sink to the grass and place the mask there, then gain my feet. "See? I'm not mocking you. I mean no harm."

The Fae stops battering the tube, yet he glares with those knuckles still curled. Can he hear what I say? If not, he certainly sees what I've done.

How did he get stuck inside this cylinder? Is he hurt?

I take a second look at the chute's upper and lower iron grilles.

I gasp, "The Trapping."

This Fae was caught in The Trapping, the revolt my neighbors had staged only days ago, when they stormed into Faerie while armed with iron weapons and cages. Sick of the Folk tormenting them, the people of Reverie Hollow had blindsided the Fae by attacking their sacred fauna, knowing the mystical animals give Faeries their life force. Without nature and its animals, the Solitary wild would fade. And with it, every magical being who dwells there.

Papa had protested the attack, to no avail. My sisters and I have been suffering from nightmares about this. We'd hated what our people were doing but were unable to stop the massacre. Did they have to hurt the animals who'd done nothing to us?

And the villagers took Fae children, too? No, there must be a mistake. Or there must be a reason this male was caught.

Papa says when animals are trapped, that's when they're most dangerous. I shuffle closer to the glass, moving at a snail's pace. The viper festers at me, his eyes liquid gold. Yet he floats in place and doesn't move, which emboldens me to get closer, closer, closer until my nose hovers an inch from the container. At the same time, in the same direction, we tilt our heads and stare at each other.

I raise my palm, and so does he. When I flatten my hand against the glass, he moves to do the same thing. Then he strikes.

His palm hammers into the facade with a single thrust. Again, I lunge back.

Satisfaction gleams in those orbs. He breathes heavily against the glass to create an oval of fog, on which he scrawls a message.

I will drown you.

It's not a warning. It's a promise.

Heat drains from my cheeks. He can't hurt me. He's trapped, and the chute is sealed with iron bars. It's okay, everything will be okay, not to worry, never fear.

But the viper glowers at me, watches me, sees me.

I spin and run.

My blind sprint takes me home, where my sisters and I collide on the porch. We throw ourselves into a hug and blabber over each other. What happened? Where had we gone? At that last question, we clam up, duck our heads, and shuffle our feet.

"Nowhere," Lark and Juniper say.

I nip my lower lip. "Me, too."

We'd just stumbled around, searching for one another. That's our unanimous answer, though I'm the only one who's lying.

The fib tastes like rotten cabbage in my mouth—disgusting, unhealthy, and hard to digest. I don't like it. Fate will punish me for this someday, I'm sure of that.

Although I've never kept anything from my sisters or Papa before, I can't bring myself to utter the truth. What if it's dangerous for them to know about the viper? What if Lark sneaks out, intending to see him for herself, and gets hurt? Or what if Juniper does the same for research purposes? What if he threatens them?

Once I start talking, I won't be able to stop myself, and they'll know he's there because of The Trapping. What if that alone traumatizes them?

More than not wanting to lie, I don't want to scare my sisters. Loyally, I bite my tongue and live with the knowledge alone.

We're a dazed trio, though Lark has a fascinated gleam in her gray eyes, as if she's been on an escapade. Between the three of us, she's the type who would see getting lost as a thrill. That explains the sparkle in her irises.

As for Juniper, her cheeks are uncharacteristically flushed, either from exertion or embarrassment that she hadn't been able to track us down, her being the huntress of our family. Juniper loathes incompetence, so that accounts for the rosy puddle in her cheeks. Otherwise, she never blushes.

I don't need a mirror to determine how I look. All the color has leached from my face, and no amount of cooing from my sisters alleviates it.

I stay close to home every morning and night, barely venturing out except to minister to our sanctuary animals. Every evening, I slumber deeply, engulfed in visions of golden eyes probing me through a plate of glass.

I will drown you.

A few times, I stir at the sound of Lark or Juniper's feet padding to and from our room, probably to relieve themselves. Other than that, the nightmares consume me, pulling me under the surface.

A week later over breakfast, I wonder about the viper. No doubt, the translucent cage fitted inside the well is the collaborative handiwork of Reverie Hollow's glassblower and glazier. As for the iron grilles, the villagers have the blacksmith to thank for that. But is this how all the cages look? Or is it just for the water fauna?

"Cove." Papa Thorne's gentle voice breaks my spell. "You're not eating."

I blink at the apple pie and eggs set before me, then meet my father's kind eyes. The truth sits heavy on my tongue, but so does another question. Cottagers have been whispering how some of the Folk had attempted to rescue their animals but met a gruesome end against the rebels' iron weapons. And so, I wonder, "Did any Faeries get caged during The Trapping?"

From their chairs, Lark and Juniper's heads snap up, their eyes flaring wide with alarm. Lark's cutlery clatters onto her plate. Juniper chokes the stem of her fork. One would think I had asked a naughty question, but since when does Lark care about discretion? And since when does Juniper fear asking questions?

All the same, guilt pinches my ribs. I hadn't meant to upset my sisters.

I must look equally dismayed because Papa's brows furrow with concern. He reclines in his chair and ponders for a moment. I know that conflicted look, when he doesn't want to tell us something, but he also won't lie.

"I won't pretend you haven't experienced darkness in your short lives, and I can't shelter you three forever," he sighs. "Many of the avenging Faeries were slaughtered, but others were indeed caught along with the fauna. They're being kept in different places, spread throughout the village and on the outskirts. They didn't have room for all the cages in one enclosed place, nor did the townsfolk think it wise to store all of them near one another." He pats my hand, a forced smile cutting through his face. "Don't worry. There are no cages near our home."

Lark and Juniper collapse in their seats, air spilling from their chests. I'm not so relieved. Did that male Fae try to save the animals of his world, and that's why he'd gotten caught?

Unable to evict the question from my mind that night, I wrap myself in a frock, cloak, and boots, and grab my spear. At the last minute, I snatch one of Juniper's pencils—I make sure not to take her favorite—and several leaflets of parchment, stuffing them in my pocket.

From their beds, Lark and Juniper rest peacefully. Under their blankets, bundles outline their forms. Odd that Lark isn't snoring or tossing and turning, nor is Juniper mumbling in her sleep. I mull over that for a moment, then take care to shut the door quietly behind me.

It's long past midnight, far later than I've ever been out on my own, including the last time I stood beside the creek. I walk quickly, glancing over my shoulder every so often, lest a mythical beast is following me.

The journey to the ancient well passes quicker than expected. Before I know it, I'm dashing behind a crochet of bushes and squatting to the ground. To my left, dozens of rings ripple across the creek and head toward the embankment where his cage stands.

The world smells of damp foliage and distant elderberries. I part the shrubbery like a curtain, my breath catching at the scene playing out before me. The Fae floats in his watery cage, that black pool of hair spilling around him. His head is cocked, and his lips are slanted. An intrigued expression—a friendly expression—lights his face.

He's still trapped, but he's no longer alone. The fish that had been lured to the well seven nights ago now swarm the glass tube. They spiral around him like leaves caught in a whirlwind. Joining them are other breeds, including eels and snakes that must have ventured from the outer sea. I recognize many of the species, whereas he seems fascinated by the fish, so they can't be Fae, right? Otherwise, they would be caged like him, and he wouldn't be so fascinated by their presence.

He must have welcomed them inside. At which point, they must have wedged themselves through the bottom grilles. The fish corkscrew around his tail, the eels ricochet through his hair, and the snakes coil around his arms.

The Fae's mouth compresses, holding back a grin. A sad one but a grin, nonetheless.

The sight pricks my chest. I lean into the bush, the better to observe.

His tapered ears pick up the sound, and those eyes skewer in my direction. The gilded light hits me square in the face. I release the shrubbery, the bush's panels thwacking closed.

My pulse rattles. It's no use. He already saw me.

Cautiously, I rise from my hiding spot and meet his blustering gaze. That almost-grin has vanished like mist, replaced by the meanest glower I've ever beheld. With a gulp, I pick my way toward him.

The fish keep swimming around his form. In the eventide shadows, I pause before the glass and brave his glare. His eyes trace me, slithering over my dress and the spear clutched in my fingers, then strike back to my face. At least I didn't wear the serpent mask this time.

Tentatively, I withdraw the pencil and leaflet, balance the sheet on my palm, and write. I know he understands the mortal tongue, if he was able to threaten me the other night.

I flatten the paper against the glass: *Are you hurt?*

He scans the question. Those orbs blaze with contempt because, of course, he's hurt. Not only do iron rungs prevent him from escaping, but upon further inspection, crisscross welts mar his neck and tail, the pattern recognizable. One of the villagers in the market had mentioned iron netting would be used for trapping any water dwellers of Faerie.

I try again: *Who did this to you?*

Which of my neighbors? Someone I know?

This earns me nothing but a scornful look. I keep scribbling on new leaflets.

What's your name?

This time, the Fae shakes his head slowly, protectiveness burgeoning in his pupils. Oh right, Faeries safeguard their true names.

Did they come to take care of you?

I jab my finger, pointing at the snakes, eels, and fish. The Fae's black brows slam together in puzzlement. Yes, I'm asking if these mortal fish were worried about him and came to offer companionship and comfort. I suppose it's a silly question, but I need to know.

Suspiciously, the young viper nods. Encouragement blossoms in my stomach. My breathing evens out, though my fingers quiver as I pen another question, because he couldn't have meant what he'd said that first night, could he?

Why do you want to drown me?

Hateful trenches dig into the Fae's countenance, his eyes flaying me with more wretched gold. His breath fogs the glass, and he writes back, his reply cutting through the vapors.

You hurt them.

The leaflet and pencil slip from my fingers and hit the grass. I see it on his face—grief and fury and vengeance. I can defend myself, tell him I'm only a girl, that I'm not the one who laid siege to the fauna, but it won't make a difference. Regardless of whether he believes me, I'm a human. From now on, that's all I need to be for him to hate me. In this Fae's mind, all mortals of this village are to blame for The Trapping.

It's true, I haven't tried to help those animals, much less aided this creature or brought him food. He must be starving. I've stayed away, leaving this Fae harnessed and hungry like a monster, because maybe that's what he is, after that deadly threat he'd tossed at me. If I'd had an ounce of doubt after that, I would have at least considered freeing him.

But I've done nothing wrong, nothing wrong, nothing wrong. I wouldn't hurt a single living being. I'd never do such a thing!

The Fae's vehement stare lances through me. I swipe the leaflet and pen from the grass and march from the creek, my pace quick but not hasty. The last thing I want is for him to see me run like the last time, just like prey.

Though Faeries don't harm mortal children, I realize one detail stands apart from that rule: The tales are referring to adult Faeries. Elder Faeries might not attack human children—but young Faeries might.

I resign not to pay a third visit to that sinister place, a pledge I keep as time passes. On the thirteenth day, it's my turn to do the laundry. I'm behind on this chore, and it's almost dusk, so I'll have to be quick. While kneeling beside the creek and scrubbing stains from a towel, I notice the fish coasting by, their bodies glistening in a vivid tide of scales and fins.

They're swarming in one direction.

One very unfortunate and doomed direction.

The towel falls from my hands. A haunting premonition pebbles my skin. Maybe the creatures are simply fond of him. He's a water Fae, after all.

Or maybe it's something else.

Intuition is both a wondrous ally and a strenuous foe. I awaken at midnight and think what if, what if, what if. A thousand plots, cautionary Fables, and moral lessons plague my mind until they pry me from bed.

Again, Lark and Juniper's forms are bundled under their blankets. They dream as silently as mice, which neither of them typically does, but I don't have time to puzzle over that. Within ten minutes, I'm dressed and slinking out of my family's house.

Ripples multiply across the creek's surface, a fleet of rings vibrating toward the well. I cast the water furtive glances while tracking beside it. All manner of aquatic dwellers swish through the depth, with more and more joining them.

I marvel that none of the villagers have noticed this phenomenon. Either the townsfolk aren't paying attention, or these dwellers only congregate at night.

A terrible screech pierces the night, the upheaval sharp and high. It sounds as though hinges have broken, the sort of hubbub one might hear in a dungeon when things go wrong. Seconds later, the creek sloshes about, and the fish scatter.

I jog toward the commotion while gripping the spear. It's heavy, more so than usual, but Papa says I grow taller every day, so the weapon isn't as unwieldy as it used to be. I'm not planning to use the spear, but I feel safer having it with me, especially while remembering the Fae's fists ramming into the glass.

Yet it isn't the glass I need to fret about. When I scurry behind an ash tree and peek around the column toward the grassy jetty, I realize this at once.

I realize this because the well's glass tube is empty.

Terror clamps around my throat. I dash toward the chute and peer inside, which is still packed with freshwater but no fish. And no Fae captive.

The viper is gone.

The bottom lattice hangs ajar, swinging just under the creek's surface. The rungs are caved outward, as though someone had pulled them from the outside, or as if someone had punched from the inside. It's hard to tell which.

Although the court of fish has vanished, a host of eels and snakes remain. I squint into the water cage and spot their lithe forms coiled around the lower lattice.

Did they force open the bottom door?

Fables. They did!

They weren't gathering to keep him company, at least not tonight. They had gathered to help him.

A small group of dwellers couldn't have achieved this. But legions of them might have.

The creatures must have exerted pressure, and the Fae must have done the rest by giving the iron a solid punch, just like he did against the glass. Thirteen days of pent-up rage and captivity could have accomplished that, regardless of what the iron had surely done to his hand.

Splashes resound from the creek, forming a wave that scrolls across the surface. I race in that direction and halt beside a tuft of reeds. At the opposite embankment, the water churns and swats the surrounding foliage. Based on the ripples, something much larger than a goldfish just harpooned through here.

I should run. I should run home and hide before he catches me and makes good on his promise.

No, I can't. That may lead the fiend to my house, to my family. He wouldn't harm the sanctuary animals, but my father and sisters are fair game.

What about the other families of Reverie Hollow? How might he retaliate against the ones who had entrapped him?

I spring along the creek, but I can't see him, can't find him. As eventide deepens, I plow through bracken and vegetation, finally reaching the fields. Oxygen dashes through my lungs until they burn.

Stars cut into the night. Clouds slice through the constellations.

At length, distant shouts lurch into the sky. The overlapping hollers and bellows aren't otherworldly; I've heard those voices before. I know them from townhall meetings, market festivals, and jubilees. They're made of sweat, laughter, and tears.

They're my neighbors—shocked, disoriented, outraged, and scared. It's a rampage of sound hailing from the cottages and farmsteads.

Additional commotion resounds from near the glassblower's forge. And the same type of ruckus echoes from the woods.

All this, just for one young Fae?

I hasten back to a new part of the creek, located nearly a mile from the well, and stumble in place. Cages and tube-like containers lay overturned or shattered across the bank. My eyes widen at the ethereal mutiny of a dozen water creatures plunging into the depth. Blue vipers, copper reptiles, and green crustaceans charge across the creek and shoot toward the channel, where the water broadens and splits into streams…one of which leads to the valley…where a mountain range, woodland, and a network of waterways converge…where The Faerie Triad stands sentinel…where the Folk live.

More shouts erupt from nearby. "Get him! Kill the fucker!"

Him. The Fae.

But how can he travel on land? And is he tracking my scent home?

"No!" I scream and fly toward the chaos.

Yes, he freed the animals of his world. Yes, it's the one thing I understand. Yes, I'm glad he liberated the fauna.

But no, I don't trust that Fae.

My feet barrel across the Hollow, past creepers, alders, elderberry bushes, and nightingale song. Human voices scramble, making it hard to distinguish their origins now.

I stop.

And I see him.

Beneath the chalky moon, a silhouette pounds toward one of the streams. I would swear it's not him, because this Fae has two solid legs, a flash of moonlit skin telling me he's naked. However, the onyx mane and that furious aura are unmistakable.

Magic must enable him to travel on dry land, so that he runs like he'll tear the world to shreds. The faces of my family blast through my head. He could harm them tonight, or someday in the future. Or he could harm another villager, someone innocent.

I run as fast as my legs can carry me. I can't let him get away. I won't.

I will drown you.

"Not if I drown you first!" I scream.

And I don't know if it's possible, since he can breathe underwater. But with all my might, I'm going to try.

Although I've been training with the spear, I haven't progressed to fighting in the water. But one thing I know is how to hold my breath for a long time. At the last moment, I chuck the weapon aside, because I'll need both hands to take him down.

The Fae's hair thrashes around him like a sail caught in a storm. Scales glint from his joints. With a battle cry, I focus on nothing but those details and run, run, run.

I tackle him from behind. The impact shoves air from my chest.

The Fae growls. I make a garbled noise.

Together, we crash to the grass, roll across the landscape, and plunge into the stream. The icy water takes a million bites from my skin, liquid floods my throat, and we tumble through the void.

A briny flavor pours into my mouth, potent enough to make me gag. My eyes pop open, then sting shut. Saltwater.

I'd forgotten. In Reverie Hollow, this is the only watercourse that leads into the outer regions of Middle Country, which runs into the sea, which leads faraway to the southern ocean. The Fae and I have managed to plummet into the only saltwater source in my village.

We wrestle. My nails scratch and claw at his arms as I try to shove him down, down, down, so far down he can't hurt anyone. His fingers grapple for my elbows, and my eyes finally twist open. It's so hard to see, but I manage to glimpse his face shadowed in darkness, his predatory eyes blazing with rancor and something new, something that stunts his movements and causes him to slip several times.

He flounders, those orbs swelling and his body spasming. That vicious glare tightens, and with renewed determination, he fights back. He will drag me to the bottom, and he won't regret it, because I see nothing but vengeance staring back. Nothing but wrath.

Monster.

You're nothing but a venomous monster. You're blinded by hate.

A moment later, his grip on me loosens, and his irises swirl with an unearthly light. The gold spins into whirlpools. When they stop, shock and confusion overwhelm his face.

Those eyes dart about in a wild search for...what?

He's paralyzed and sinking. I don't need to push him down anymore. I watch his head lash from side to side, his eyes frantic and lurching about. I don't know what just happened, but hope and triumph and guilt snarl together. I could take pity and help this creature, but I won't.

Right then, a figure swoops overhead, its outline reflected across the water. I pump my arms to the surface and crash through, just as a broad set of wings veers from the stars, then catapults toward the stream. It's too big to be a falcon, too small to be a vulture, and too blue to be mortal.

A Fae of the sky.

I spot a fringe of blue feathers attached to a male body, and a face partially covered in an owl mask, before the figure dives into the stream.

On a shriek, I careen back and hit the embankment. Water spews everywhere, followed by a series of liquid crashes. By the time I cling to the edge and open my eyes, the winged Fae is soaring, his plumes flapping madly and sprinkling water. A flock of other avians flank the silhouette, banding around him like a shield. Slumped in the Fae's arms is the viper I'd just attempted to drown.

"No," I whisper, my chest heaving. "No."

No, indeed. Helpless, I watch them fly into the clouds and disappear.

After retrieving the spear, I manage to slog home without my family discovering I'd been out. My sisters lay bundled in the same position, and Papa is a deep sleeper despite the uproar coming from town. Our house is located far enough away to blot out the shouts.

I'm not sure what else is happening out there, be it in the creek, in the woods, or where the nightingale sings by the glassblower's forge. I don't care to know. All I want is my bed, so when I arrive home, I change into my nightgown and crawl under the blankets. But it's a long time before I can breathe again.

The next day, news of the escape reaches my family. Three young Faeries had broken free from their bonds and released the surviving caged fauna. I had witnessed two of them, the viper and that winged figure. As for the third, I don't know. But when that infamous rebel is whispered about later in the market square, Juniper's face turns pasty.

Apparently, a fourth captive had tried to get away—another Fae with wings. Though, that one had died in the attempt, a fate that makes Lark's eyes glisten. My sister isn't one for sentimentality, but she has a soft spot for any creature that can fly.

That evening, I simmer hot chocolate for the three of us and read from the Book of Fables, using a soothing voice while Lark rests her head on my lap, and Juniper balances her cheek on my shoulder.

The villagers mention blue hair, stag antlers, and golden eyes, but they never say just how young The Three are, and as with any tidings that pass from mouth to mouth, the details vary. Some accounts place them younger than us, while some say they're older. The villagers who originally trapped the Faeries, and the ones who'd chased after the captives, also disagree on the ages.

Even the glassblower, who had confined one of the Faeries in his forge, can't get his story straight. I have a feeling he doesn't want to admit the

Fae's age and appear incompetent or weak. In any case, the tidbits range from vague to elaborate.

I never confess. Instead, I keep what I've witnessed to myself. I volunteer no information or corrections, not even to my family.

Months pass, but the viper doesn't return for me. Eventually, remorse squats in my gut—the shock of what I had attempted to do, without truly knowing who he was.

The feeling never goes away. I rescue animals with my sisters, give counsel to my neighbors, and donate my free hours to worthy causes and charities. I spend my time comforting others, offering tender words and a willing ear, drawing blankets over shoulders, and chatting woes away.

I know how to distract and console, so long as I'm tending to someone other than myself, because I don't deserve to nurse my own wounds. Kindness and generosity become my safe havens, my chance to atone for what I can't undo, for the one moment in which I was anything but good.

New details manifest about The Three. They arrive through messages and warnings from the Fae, delivered to Reverie Hollow in the form of glamoured humans or threats penned in the water, carved into the trees, or whispered in the air. That's how we learn about the weapons they brandish and the instruments they play to enchant mortals.

The viper's ability to blind others is a parcel of knowledge that comes later. A peasant who'd been bathing in the creek stumbles into the square, his vision blurred before disappearing altogether. "It was him," the man croaks, his words tripping over themselves. "One of The Three, the one w-with the g-golden eyes. He d-did this, I s-saw those eyes right before it h-happened."

But why hadn't the Fae blinded me back then? At any time, he could have robbed me of vision.

Maybe the iron had weakened him too much, along with being in captivity for thirteen days without nourishment, then trying to outrun his captors. It would explain why I'd almost succeeded in drowning a water Fae. He'd been struggling against me, after all. And he began to sink before that winged savior came to his rescue. Yes, that must be it.

Years pass. I'm still alive, but I've never recovered.

Three months shy of my twentieth birthday, my sisters and I trespass into Faerie.

That same night, my sisters vanish while we're huddled together in our wagon hideaway, where we'd been recapping the incident. A moment later, I hear splashes outside the vehicle, and I race outside to follow the sound. The noise is impossibly loud, stretching a distance it shouldn't be able to. It guides me to one of the streams—the saltwater one I haven't dared to revisit since that night.

There, a black silhouette ripples from under the surface. I blink at it for several awful seconds before the figment disappears, a message vibrating in its wake.

I have not forgotten.

A petrified scream lodges in my throat. Had he taken my sisters hostage? Is this delayed retribution? Is this about The Trapping or the trespass? Is this punishment for *then* or *now*?

The next thing I know, my sister's voices carry on the wind, a blessed sound that shouldn't reach me from the wagon but does. I rush back to join them, only to learn they're just as confused about my whereabouts as I am of theirs. If this world were exclusive to mortals, our disappearing acts wouldn't make sense.

Yet more than humans thrive in The Dark Fables, so this trick makes absolute, vicious sense.

The following night, the envelope arrives. The missive surfaces in the pond where my rescue snake lives, while I'm taking solace in the reptile's company. The woven paper floats to me, a puddle of blue wax sealing the closure and embedded with two interlocking sea serpent tails.

The instant I fish the message from the water, the paper dries. My fingers shake so wretchedly, it's a chore to break the seal, the cracking sound puncturing my ears. I read the message and heed the call.

An hour later, I stand at The Triad with my sisters and cry while they embrace me. "We did nothing wrong!" I insist.

But I'm lying. Years ago, I did something very wrong. No, I haven't forgotten, and neither has the viper.

He's expecting me. Tonight, I'm being fed to a monster.

22

Sitting together on the ridge overlooking The Kelpie Rapids, we regard one another, my vision clear, his hooded. Unspoken memories flash through our minds, the silence more prolonged than it's ever been between us.

How do his recollections compare with mine? I want to ask, but I'm afraid to, and I see the same misgivings in his own eyes.

Countless emotions surge through me. Just as many radiate from him.

Aside from our mingling breaths, it's quiet. The rapids have calmed, the water placid now.

I swallow. "The creek dwellers helped you escape, didn't they?"

Elixir's fathomless eyes probe the half-light and stray across the ground. "The iron was too strong for me otherwise," he reflects. "They loosened it. After that, I was able to punch through."

"And Cerulean is the one who saved you from the stream," I assume.

Elixir nods, then grunts, "The bastard can see from the greatest of distances, particularly while airborne. He was freeing the mountain fauna when he caught sight of me in the water." Despite Elixir's gruff tone, gratitude and fondness slip through the cracks in his voice. "Though, I have never told him how I escaped or about you. My brothers and I do not speak of our experiences in the village, what the humans did to us."

I cross my legs under the medallion-colored dress, take his hand, and cradle it. Our fingers bunch together in my lap. Elixir's breath hitches, and he goes still while I examine his knuckles. Aided or not, he must have struck the iron hard to blast the cage door open.

"No scars," I marvel.

"I removed them," is all he says.

Oh. I think of the mixtures in his den and wonder which one of them he'd used to erase the wounds. However, those injuries evoke other grievances, as well as my own spin on this game, the need to get close to him.

I release his hand. "Why do you hate us? You don't even know us."

"I know what you did," he snaps, but with less venom than usual.

His accusation applies to more than one offense, and not only to me. All the same, I reside at the nexus of his anger, because I'm the one who attempted to thwart his escape.

Somehow, I had cursed him that fateful night. During our brawl, my actions had changed his fate. That's why he'd acted so strangely, flailing in confusion and shock. In that moment, I had changed him. He'd been so frazzled by the transformation, he hadn't had the capacity to retaliate.

That's why he hadn't blinded me in the stream. It had nothing to do with the iron cage weakening him. Likewise, Elixir's counter-ability must have developed because of the spell, but he hadn't known about that right then, much less how to wield such magic.

To this day, he knows it was me. He knows I cursed him, but even now, Elixir doesn't confide it.

The confession sneaks up my throat but gets stuck on the edges of my lips. That's where it stays.

Besides, something else lurks behind his words, his raspy intonation frayed. I've heard many renditions of this tone coming from my neighbors, particularly after burials. It's the sound of bereavement. It goes beyond the fallen Solitaries and fauna, beyond the fate of his subjects.

Elixir's loss is intimate, as deep as the sea. It's the loss of family, a feeling I understand well. I think of his mothers—Marine and Lorelei—and remember what Coral had told me.

Comfort will not bring back what he's lost.

"Every time I thought of humans, all I thought of were the Faeries and fauna they butchered," he growls.

"Elixir, please," I say. "Think past your anger. Not all of us took part in The Trapping. Some were too young. Did you ask any of your former sacrifices how old they were when that night happened? Have you asked those captives if they even lived in town that year, or if they had moved there afterward? You would have gotten those answers if you'd bothered to ask, to understand who they were. You've been punishing people without knowing who they are."

Elixir frowns. "You were young. That did not stop you."

No, it didn't. I could claim I was just like any innocent child who grew up being persecuted by the Folk unfairly. But while that rule applies to my neighbors and my sisters, it doesn't apply to me. I was ten when it happened, but I knew what I was doing that night.

I made a choice to attack him. I made a choice to act.

I twist toward the vista, wishing the kelpies would come back, wishing this Fae and I could return to a happier moment, a mesmerizing one. "How can you despise someone you don't know?" I utter. "Someone you've never met? How do people do that?"

How did I do that? How did we both do that?

In my periphery, Elixir's gaze trails my lips before whipping toward the view. "When you say these things, I cannot respond. I do not…remember how the fuck to answer."

Good. I speak to the panorama. "Then do you still want to drown me?"

"I never wanted that," he whispers.

I shake my head because this wasn't how it was supposed to be. I was supposed to cross paths with a dashing prince or a beautiful maiden. We were supposed to court each other, gift each other flowers, and murmur endearments into one another's ears. My fantasy suitor and I were supposed to fall in pure, tender, uncomplicated love. We were supposed to get married and live happily ever after.

Once upon a time, I was destined to choose the hero or heroine. I wasn't supposed to desire the villain.

"What are we?" My voice breaks. "Are we hateful enemies who've become reluctant enemies? Are we enemies who crave each other and became lovers for one moment in time? Because I know this can't be about more. I know this for thousands of reasons. We can't be anything but adversaries, much less friends, or even friendly, for that matter. And don't get me started on becoming allies, because in what universe would that ever happen? So, what are we doing?" I implore. "What *are* we?"

The questions simmer between us, impossible to grasp. I can't muster a response.

However, Elixir can. I glimpse his face dipping to where our hands thread. Then his eyes lift and search for mine, and he inclines his head in a truce. "We are a human and a Fae, taking the time to know each other."

And just like that, a grin tilts my lips upward.

23

On route to the boat from The Kelpie Rapids, I halt in the corridor and grab Elixir's elbow. "What if there's another way?"

He frowns. "Another way to what?"

I tell him about my goal, that I'm searching for a pattern in the river levels or clues to stop this world from deteriorating, to find some way that doesn't involve games. Because he's Elixir, he hasn't admitted it, but his actions prove he wants me to be safe. He protected me in The Bask of Crocodiles. He choked Scorpio, then poisoned the merman for trying to harm me. Elixir may have used the public excuse that I'm the river's newest sacrifice. Therefore, it's necessary for me to live, to play the game.

Still, that's not the only reason he defended me.

Upon hearing of my ambitions, Elixir's features slacken with stupefaction, deference, and something close to humility. He shakes his head in amazement, then drizzles his knuckles down the side of my face. "You have been trying to help us?"

"All of us," I declare, itching to cover his hand with mine.

Elixir continues to gaze at me, then he sighs. "There is no other way, Cove."

"When was the last time you Faeries checked? You see things others can't. You see inside me, for instance."

"I did, for a time."

"What does that mean?"

"It means I cannot read you the same way any longer. The heat of your desire is still there, but not..." His scales radiate with color, the effect

215

reminiscent of a blush. "I knew how to follow the sounds of your hate and lust, but I do not…" When he grunts, I hear the belligerent vulnerability. "I do not know how to follow the sound of your affection. I do not know what it sounds like."

My heart twists. It seems the tides have reversed. Knowing what I do, I'm able to read him better, whereas he doesn't understand the sound of emotions like fondness or love.

I cup that harsh jaw, which softens under my touch. "I like you."

"I like you, too." He leans into my hand, his eyes drifting shut. "That is why we cannot fucking do this."

"No, we can't. But we already have."

His eyes flap open. "And if I do not send you off in that boat at once, I shall take you in it."

Heat rises from my toes to my lips. The craving simmers from me to him, our breaths growing shallow and hectic.

At the distant call of a water mammal, we vault from the trance and spring backward. Elixir scrubs his face, mutters something in frustrated Faeish, snatches my hand, and charges down the tunnel while scraping the nearest wall with his free digits. We walk quickly, quivering and in a sudden hurry.

Swiftly, he deposits me into the boat. "Go," he snaps.

"Now," I beseech the water, as if it will listen to me.

Elixir swats his hand through the air. The current latches onto the vessel and surges off, heading to my chamber, to my bed, and to my dreams, which have become infinitely more shameful. I sag in the transport, my lungs heaving and my head slumping forward.

Because it had taken a trip down that steep waterslide to get here, the boat cruises in the slope's direction. The flux pulls me toward the incline, the transport bound to shear through the gush.

On the brink of ascending, I grip the rims on either side. Elixir's right about this anarchy between us, because a truce is one thing; but what could have happened seconds ago is another offense entirely. We can form a treaty, continue to bond, but we can't stray like we did in the lily pond. Never again can we get swept away like that. We'd be committing the worst of sins. It's corrupt, forbidden, reprehensible, disgraceful, and selfish.

Except for one problem: I want to do it again.

Except for another problem: I change my mind, tear off my sandals, grab my spear, hasten to the boat's prowl, and dive.

Right before the boat coasts up the slide, my body hits the tepid gulf. The current stalls. The vessel bobs in place like a cork, the eddies foaming around it. Thankfully, it doesn't seem to be going anywhere with the shoes or without me.

The boat can wait. I can't.

I breaststroke through the depth, then lose patience and kick in short bursts of adrenaline. Despite the dress and spear hindering progress, the distance isn't vast. The landing comes into view, but Elixir's not there.

It couldn't have been more a few minutes since I left this spot. I grasp the ledge and slog out of the water. Drenched and plastered in a film of fabric, I hustle along the passage while glancing in all directions, noting several arteries he could have taken, if he hasn't evanesced altogether.

No, he hasn't. I squint at the traces of water trickling down one of the thoroughfares where lanterns burn from recesses. My feet slap the floor as I cross through the conduit.

Around a bend, the area becomes achingly familiar. It turns out, this network connects to the special places I've already been, only from a different end of The Deep. I pad down the channel, following the drips of water and knowing where to turn, knowing where he's taken refuge.

I push through the reeds and step into the lily pond. The pool glistens with its blue sheen, and the lilies blaze white, their vibrancy lighting the cave. On the opposite end of the pond, the waterfall sprouts from the overhang and creates a partition, separating me from the naked figure shielded behind it. Although the downpour isolates Elixir, it doesn't blot out the sight of what he's doing to himself.

With his back facing me, the Fae stands before the mossy facade, his shoulder blades drawn in tightly and the muscles of his backside flexing...pumping. He arches, his head flinging backward while additional threads of water leak from crevices and splatter down his arms. Like this, he braces a flat hand on the wall while the other hand is concealed, tucked in front of his pelvis. With strong, rhythmic motions, his right arm siphons up and down.

If the vision hadn't made the location of Elixir's hand clear, his groans do. The waterfall does its best to shroud the frenzied noises, but I hear them. They rent the air, the texture hoarse and tattered. He moans bitterly, wildly, desperately, each sound in tempo to the jutting motions of his arm.

My lungs constrict. I shouldn't be watching this. I'm about to swerve and leave, but then I hear the most damning noise of all.

"Cove," he grunts.

The word reaches my ears, harsh and quivering. I stall, frozen. My pulse smashes against my breasts, flames singe me beneath the sodden dress, and the lustful sound of my name on his lips probes the cleft between my legs.

He's thinking about me. The lord of the water Fae is pleasuring himself to visions of me.

Is he remembering the last time we were here? How it had felt, how deeply he'd lunged into me, how wide my thighs had parted around his snapping waist? How soaked I was? How hard he'd been?

He wants that again, as much as I do. Isn't that why I came here?

His clothes have been discarded at the water's edge. Though drapes of water and mist plummet around him, he's not fully doused, and he's no more than ankle-deep in the spring, so his limbs haven't shifted. Moisture coats Elixir's smooth back. That long hair sweeps his hips, and his rear—that firm, wet ass—undulates toward his hand.

It's a miracle I haven't dropped the spear. I set my weapon on the grass and move forward, drawn to the scene, to the cadence of his body.

I halt beside the pond and stare openly. The sight of him is erotic, sensual, and savage.

However, it's not enough. I don't want to be limited to fantasy, reduced to fleeting images. I want his hand to be my hand. My flesh chafes so terribly, I long to peel this frock from my body and step into the torrent with him.

A whimper curls in my throat. And Elixir stops.

His body goes rigid, cutting short his moans. The sight of him caught and suddenly aware only increases my need. Yes, he had admitted he can't detect my softer emotions, but he can still sense my desire.

I wait for him to face me, but he remains anchored, riveted to the spot. I'm near enough to glimpse the flush of his scales. I've seen this ruddy tinge before, when he was on top of me.

It's not shyness. Rather, it's from satisfaction unfulfilled.

The strong hand that had been strapped around his cock falls to the side. The other hand burrows into the foundation, about to break chunks of mossy stone.

He pants, his baritone heavy, winded, and plaintive. "Leave."

I grip the sides of my dress, strip it over my head, and drop it to the lawn. "No."

The Fae grits out, "You take many dangerous liberties with that word."

My feet dip into the water and pick their way toward him until I'm hovering at his back. I set my palm on his lower spine, relishing his oath as I brush my free hand along the ovals of his ass, then slide my fingers around his waist to trace the incline of a hipbone. My hand skims down the steep V to the firm length, to that place where heat emanates.

I pause at the base of his cock, on the brink of strapping my fingers around that high, thick erection. "Then offer me something I'll say yes to."

Elixir shakes, his arms tensing like they might snap. His fingercaps dig into the edifice, and his second hand joins the first, bracing him there.

How did he manage to fondle himself with those sharp ornaments? Is his flesh that tough? Or was he being careful?

I could demand he turn and face me, but I like how his spine feels against my cheek, how his shoulder blades quake under my breath. I like trapping him this way, and I like feeling him this way, and I need more of it. So, when he swears and juts his hips toward my palm, giving me leave to dominate his body, I seize the offer. My greedy fingers brush the stem of his prick, tracing the ridges and width with gentle ministrations.

So very tender. So very unlike the life he's led.

The instant I touch him, he belongs to me. This Fae is mine.

Elixir shudders, a garbled noise spilling from his lungs. I etch his mast, skimming around the shaft, grazing its height, and feathering over the crown. He's long and firm, the head of his cock swelling under the pads of my fingers.

He mutters in Faeish, the intonation severe and transfixed. It sounds as though he's never been handled intimately before. In The Mer Cascades, he'd confessed to having limited experience, and since we were both virgins that first time, this might be true.

I might be his first in every way.

I close my eyes, picture his length flushing darker, stiffening further. I imagine it the way he had imagined me. Possessiveness, sensuality, and power guide my hand as I find the head's slit and flick my thumb across it.

Elixir groans, helpless.

"That's what I long to hear," I whisper into his ear. "I want to be so delicate, I'll ruin you for eternity. I want you so pliant, you forget what violence feels like. Will you let me? Can you do that for me?"

That rasp hardens into a growl, and his hips lurch into my palm. I take that as a *yes, do it, please.*

My fingers sink to the base and wrap around him. I gasp at the size, at the hot weight balanced in my hand, my fingers unable to encompass his width.

I lick my lips. I've never done this, but a certain promiscuous sister of mine has been expressive about the experience. Back then, I had tried to plug my ears—a regretful action—but I'd heard enough to guide me now.

With my fingers gripping Elixir, I draw my hand up and down, up and down, up and down, while recalling the tempo he'd used on himself. As I do, his body trembles. Groans pump out of him, in cadence with my hand as it siphons from the seat to the head of his cock. I stroke the length, captivated by all that solid yet malleable flesh. Every carnal sight, sound, and touch wets me between the legs.

"Harder," Elixir mutters. "Take it harder."

I do, gripping him, pulsing him. I fist his shaft, tugging on it, drawing out his moans, yanking them from his throat.

He seizes the wall. Unable to keep still, his hips snap into motion. They jab upward, slinging in and out of my palm. His cock twitches, slickens from the mist, and broadens more.

Elixir hisses, agonized, overwhelmed. "Faster."

I give it to him, over and over. His backside clenches beautifully while his cock rides my hand. The Fae's pleas roughen, beginning to splinter.

My forehead drops between his shoulder blades. I sigh into his skin, press my lips there, and coax, "That's it. Just like that."

The cascades drown out his pleasure, so that only I can hear it. A thin stream of water splashes onto us, not enough to soak our bodies, but enough to dampen us. I pump him to the brink, until we're chanting into the lily pond.

He's smooth and solid and scorching. I clamp around him, claiming him with gentle firmness. And when I thumb the slot of his crown, swiping it once, twice, three times, Elixir spasms. He hunches forward, a final growl suspending itself...pausing...building...and erupting.

He shatters apart, his body convulsing. A gritty howl rages from his mouth as he comes into my hand. His cock bucks, warmth seeping from the crown and spurting down my knuckles.

Oxygen blasts from my mouth. The noises we make tangle together, keen and fearless. I roll my hand over his solid length, the motions slowing, growing languid.

"Say it," I order. "Let me hear it."

"Cove," he heaves. "Cove."

That's the sound. I nod, my heart swimming.

Aftershocks jolt through Elixir's frame. He slumps and folds his hand over me. We stay like that, gulping and panting, while I run my thumb over his spent cock.

Although I'd very much like to keep touching him, Elixir reluctantly maneuvers out of my grasp and whirls to face me. He stares down, captivated. A mesmerized light smolders in his eyes as he strays over my features. It's a private look, new for him and meant only for me.

I glance at the fingercaps, then sketch their points. "May I?"

Elixir nods. I pop the caps from his digits and toss them to the bank. Shedding the accessories reveals the olive skin and groomed nails underneath. His fingers are lovely, strong like the rest of him, yet defined.

And scarred.

The Fae tenses, but his joints unwind as I twist his hand to examine the burn marks rising from the pads of his fingers. I gulp, sensing what these are from. "You said you erased the wounds."

He shakes his head. "Not these."

The iron door of his cage. He'd used a mixture to cure the wounds on his knuckles, but he kept these ones.

"Before the fish helped you," I say. "Did you try pulling open the door yourself?"

"Yes," Elixir says, his words devoid of self-pity. "After they sealed me inside. The mob had several river fauna with them, and I watched the humans take the animals away. I tried…" He clenches his eyes shut. "I tried."

"Elixir." I press kisses to each scar, because it wasn't his fault, and I want him to feel something other than pain.

His head ducks, watching me soothe him.

When I look up, our fingers knit, and our foreheads rest together.

"Um…" Bashfulness heats my face. "Did you feel good?"

"Good is not the word," he husks. "I felt as I never have. I felt euphoric."

With my free hand, I map out his eyelashes. I think about how I'd touched Elixir without looking at him, and I imagine what that everlasting darkness must be like.

Balancing on my tiptoes, I speak against his mouth, "Show me what you feel. Show me the darkness."

Elixir pulls back, arousal swirling in his orbs. His fingers steal out to sweep a tendril of teal from my shoulder, then he brushes his hand through the nearest cascade, and all the lights in the pond snuff out. Blackness eclipses the water's blue sheen and the pearl radiance of the lilies.

Elixir runs his lips across my profile until he locates my ear. His deep, silken voice rumbles, "Close them."

My stomach flips with anticipation. I obey, letting my eyelids flutter shut.

The universe reduces to pure sensation. Taste, touch, smell, and sound.

The whiff of bergamot and black pepper. The sweet tang of humidity, an unexpected flavor carried in the air. His firm grip on my hips and the tingle of his skin pressed to mine. Fluid smacking the banks, the clapping sound of waterfalls as they hit the pond, and the jangle of lily petals—noises I hadn't registered before.

How he sees this world is beautiful.

I feel lost yet hyperaware of Elixir's movements. He spins me away from him and traces my curves, from my hips to the ruched tips of my breasts, showing me what it's like to feel without sight. It's an ambush of sensations. Knuckles skate over my ribs, gooseflesh pops across my flesh, and masculine outtakes puff along my neck.

My backside grazes his cock, the length still erect against my spine. I gasp and rub myself into him.

He grunts, "That is fucking evil." Then he jerks me into him, my shoulders mashing with the plate of his torso. "As am I."

To demonstrate, Elixir ushers me forward. The ground slants downward into the pond, and the water rustles around us as we descend and begin to glide. Swathed in blackness, I float with him, our bodies weightless.

Fully submerged, his limbs disappear beneath us and shiver into a tail. I feel it swaying, driving us toward another part of the pond, where a thin stream leaks from someplace overhead. When it grows louder, the droplets plopping into the water, we idle in place.

A squeak pipes from my lips when Elixir cups my buttocks and hoists me to the surface. Humid air caresses my skin. He palms my thighs and spreads them, his hands bracing me wide, so that my core floats exposed.

His teeth graze my earlobe. "Savor how the air touches you. Inhale the pond's scent. Listen to the water's direction and the cave echoing. Feel yourself amidst this land. Feel yourself naked and filling this space. Do you feel it?"

My sigh is tremulous. "I do."

Like this, the atmosphere combs through the patch of hair between my legs. My clit throbs from the shift in temperature and the way my folds splay open, bare and swollen.

Elixir's timbre floods my ear. "Will you trust the darkness?"

My hands reach backward to clamp his nape. "I will."

His answering hum skates across my jaw. With that, he swims me to the slender cascade and hovers me beneath it. Or rather, he settles my core beneath the stream.

At the first drop of water on my folds, I arch in surprise. A pleasured gasp lurches off my tongue. "Oh, my Fables."

"Feel it," he urges, his tongue swabbing the flesh of my neck. "Open your pretty cunt for it. Let the darkness taste you."

Whimpers dash from my throat. The narrow trickle of water pours onto me, beating gently on my cleft and leaking down. The contact produces a liquid friction that has me aching, because this feels too wonderful.

My thighs tremble and split wider. I dig my fingernails into Elixir's skin for leverage, his hair tickling my knuckles. My backside grinds and lifts, wanting more.

The water soaks my walls, dripping down the slot. I gyrate beneath the onslaught and follow the sensations blindly. The nub protruding from the center of my body swells, needing to make contact. I angle my hips, elevating the kernel of nerves beneath the cascade, and cry out.

The stream taps gently at that spot, relentlessly hitting every spark. My blood crackles to life, my cries hardening and growing in volume. In the background, I hear Elixir groaning, feel his palms spanning my rear, feel him bobbing me up and down, creating more friction, more rhythm.

Endlessly, the water abrades that crest of sensation, drenching it, patting it. I cling to Elixir. Together, we drive my body into the water, my legs sprawling, my clit pounding.

Elixir curses and plants my feet flush against a wall I hadn't known stood before us. The foundation braces my movements, allowing me to intensify the motions and go wild. I lash upward, and the stream lashes downward, the pressure building.

Then it happens. The wave crests and crashes, rapture bursting at the seams and coursing through my veins. I flake apart, shattering into particles. My inner walls pulsate, the climax wrenching an endless moan from my mouth. I shout, pleasure infusing every fiber of my being.

Then I collapse, sinking into Elixir's embrace. I whine, depleted as he wheels me around and scoops me into his arms. My legs hook around his waist, and his viper tail swishes, keeping us aloft.

My head sags on his shoulder, and I taste freshwater and wine on his skin. We pant, our chests brushing. Elixir drags his fingernails down my spine, making me shiver.

I let my eyelids fan open and tow my head upright to meet his gaze, except it's too dark, liquid black surrounding us. All I see are rings of gold. We map each other out, our fingers scaling into one another's hair. Our foreheads crumple together, and our mouths slant, exchanging pants—which surges into a kiss.

With haggard breaths, our mouths launch into it. His tongue plies the seam of my lips and flexes into me, his mouth crushing mine. I keen and vault against him, my breasts mashing into his torso.

Our lips fuse and fold. My tongue whips into his, lapping up the taste of him, the heat of him.

I nip his bottom lip, making Elixir quake and heft me closer. He anchors my body higher, so that I straddle him and bear down on the kiss while our hands destroy one another's hair, knifing through the roots and tugging. Elixir braces the back of my skull, his lips driving against mine. I consume every rasp and muffled curse.

My legs tighten around his waist, my heels hooking above the smooth viper scales. A bulge swells where his pelvis should be, and I realize his mast is rising from the tail, able to separate from it. He's been erect the whole time.

It should be over, but it's not. He's still hard, and I'm still wet.

We wrench our lips apart and move simultaneously. Elixir clutches my buttocks and pivots his waist deeper between my legs while I spread my thighs astride him, our outtakes erratic and impatient. I cradle him in the split of my thighs, heat brimming where his crown nocks against my entrance.

I whimper at the tease of contact, his tip grazing the slot. Elixir hums, kicks his hips, and skims the head over the tiny root of my core. Ecstasy and frustration clash, prompting me to grind myself into his lap.

We move wordlessly, helplessly, desperately. In unison, we fasten ourselves around each other—and he pitches into me.

Elixir's cock lunges through my folds and sinks inside, my walls sucking him deeply. My cry collides with his moan. I can't see it, but I feel our mouths falling open and hovering an inch from another.

The wet clamp of my body seals around his length. And just like that, we're bucking. I bound atop the Fae, his thickness plying through me, his cock striking high and withdrawing completely before sliding back in. My moans echo the harsh beat of his hips, the snapping tempo of his abdomen as he works himself into me, fucks so deftly into me.

The tempo's brisk and fluid. Water buffets our movements, sloshing into us.

My shaky hands remain buried in his mane. Elixir gropes my back-side with one palm and braces the other around my nape, the better to maneuver me up and down on his prick, his thrusts tireless.

I arch backward into the cave, into the air while clinging to his neck. My body juts from the thump of his waist, my thighs flaring wide.

"Ah," I sob. "Elixir."

"Again," he growls. "Close them again."

He must have guessed. Despite the glossy blackness, I cinch my eyes shut and submerge into a void, a place where nothing exists but this—his wet body, steam coating the air, and my lungs emptying. This stifling wilderness of cascades, blossoms, and pleasure.

At my rapturous moans, his thrusts accelerate.

At my stuttering pleas, his cock strikes quick and shallow, repeatedly hitting a spot that destroys our vocal cords. And…it's…so…good. I'm clamoring, and he's shouting, and the waterfalls catch the sounds.

My walls yield around Elixir, the inner muscles constricting around his length. Blood whittles to the place where we're joined, our waists slamming together now, charging toward the precipice. I can't think, can't speak. I'm a wild creature, nothing but raw sensation and dire need.

Fables forgive us. We grind, and grind, and grind.

Elixir clasps me harder, bows me farther. The angle of our coupling shifts, his cock reaching a new angle and striking there, over and over. The pressure mounts, the decadent strain of it coiling in my bones.

I become inconsolable, and he becomes irredeemable, the pound of his body devastating. I squeeze Elixir inside me, my folds tensing around his cock. He moves with abandon, his hips driving into me, spurring us toward the edge.

"Take it in," he entreats. "Take me in."

"Oh, Fables," I shout. "Yes."

And the wave crashes. My walls contort, his cock shudders, and we climax in a tumult of noise. I cry to the ceiling. Elixir hollers into the depth. We expel ourselves, my wetness seeping onto his hardness.

For the second time, we dissolve into the pond. I tumble into his arms, and Elixir anchors me to him, his own muscles slackening.

Like one of the lily pads, we float aimlessly. Elixir reaches past me and swats his arm. At once, the cascades drain, the deluge ceasing. The pond goes silent.

We heave, sucking in air. Overwhelmed, I twist my cheek into his shoulder and nestle my lips into the crook of his throat, which flexes as he swallows. We linger, hidden in the darkness, the world obscure yet somehow clearer and more vivid than I'd known it could be.

My eyes sting, but I mustn't let the tears fall. I must *not*.

Elixir goes still. "Are you...crying?"

"No," I sniffle.

He reels back, agonized. "Did I hurt you?"

Days ago, he would have smelled the saltwater and heard the tears leaking, even before I made a noise. Now he can't read me. But of course, fibbing isn't my best skill, which is why he licks that single traitorous drop from under my eyelashes.

"You are a poor liar," he murmurs. "And you are not ashamed of tears."

He says this without the cynicism, distaste, or rancor I'd expect of his kind. Instead, he speaks with admiration, because he knows me.

He's right. I have no qualms about crying. But I don't want to leave here, and I don't want to return to the world outside this pond, and I don't want to regret this.

"It's just," I blubber. "It's just I never knew."

Elixir shakes his head. "Neither did I."

That fucking could be so exquisite, nor lovemaking so primal. That they could be one and the same. That such a vicious touch could be so sweet.

I never knew it could be like this.

The Fae's voice is brittle, like shredded paper. "You will be my undoing."

I never knew an enemy could become a friend—or a lover.

"You are like this water, illuminating this world."

I never knew a monster could find my heart—or that I'd let him.

"Fú ert livjoside," the Fae whispers against my temple. "You are the light."

24

We drift from one minute to the next, the lily pads rustling around us as he encircles my midriff and coasts me through the water. Elixir has an unbreakable grip, his arms like reefs of muscle.

This Fae kisses with stamina, his tongue teasing me until my head dissolves and my body melts. Our lips layer and fold, our tongues seeking to dominate, to delay the inevitable. The moment when this will end.

I run my palm over the back of his tail, tracing the faint swells of what should be his buttocks. "If your mothers were mermaids, then you're a merman?"

"Yes," he says while nibbling on my throat. "There are different kinds. Some can shift between land and water, others cannot. I'm of the former."

His ravenous mouth snatches the pulse point of my neck. "Every piece of you has its own taste. I could sample your body until you come. I could drug you with pleasure. I could fuck you into delirium, my cock spreading the hot clamp of your walls to the hilt. Would you like that? Tell me."

My head lolls to give him access. "You're a viper."

But I say it affectionately, until I can't say anything at all because I'm too busy whimpering when his lips fasten onto my nipple, and my head flings back.

I return the sensual favor, bracing my mouth over his clavicle, tonguing the disks of his own nipples, and caressing the grid of his abdomen. I lick his throat, suckle under his jaw, and nip the honed tip of his ear.

We do lingering damage above the surface, branding one another, savoring every shudder and groan. I want his cock again, and he wants my clit again, but the Folk will awaken soon.

Elixir's lusty frustration could hammer through a cliff. The distant echo of crickets peals into the cave from the tunnel, signaling dusk. With his face burrowed in my hair, he thwacks the pond and snarls, "Quiet!"

The wave launches into the reedy threshold and slaps the walls. It doesn't silence the dawning insects, but it does make me laugh. The chortles pop out of me, multiplying tenfold when his head lifts, his expression one of disgruntled amusement.

"You find my agony humorous, do you?" He tugs me into him. "Wait, my light. You shall know agony."

My laughter catches as he seizes my mouth, his tongue pulling moans from my lungs. We're ravenous but out of time. I pry my lips away and trace his lower lip, yearning for one final growl. He lets it out, then husks out a baritone chuckle. It lasts half a second. I commit the rare sound to memory, tucking it inside a forbidden place in my chest, along with Elixir's grief over the mothers he lost; his fondness for water creatures; the furious poignancy of his harp music; the mixtures he brews to cure; the food he'd ordered for Lotus; our time in The Kelpie Rapids; and every heated touch I've known from him.

His light. This dominant, powerful, impenetrable Fae had called me his light.

With a groan, Elixir releases me and sweeps his fingers through the pond. The cave ignites once more, the lily petals blazing white, and the blue sheen spilling across the depth like a watercolor across parchment.

We swim out of the pond. Even then, we linger to dress one another. He drapes the dress over my head, feeling his way through the motions. Truly, it's the slowest I've ever seen him move.

I pull the shirt down his torso, comb out his mane, and set the caps on his scarred fingertips. He rubs a strand of my teal hair between his fingers.

When there's nothing left to do, and no other touches we can use as an excuse, I collect my spear and take his hand. He guides me to the landing, an uncommon chill sneaking through the passage. Droplets leak from the ceiling when they hadn't before, which is odd.

Elixir extends his free palm to catch one of the beads. He rolls it in the basin of his hand and frowns. "The fuck?"

"It was dry when we came through here earlier," I agree.

He nods and makes a fist, encasing the droplet. The farther we go, the tighter our fingers lock. When we reach the landing, Elixir tosses the globule into the depth, where it dissolves into ripples, which drag the boat into view. My sandals are still resting inside.

Although I'm only returning to my chamber, it feels like a certain type of goodbye, and I hate that. I step forward, then gasp as his hands find my waist, and he hauls me against him.

This is how he moves—sudden and strong. His forehead lands against mine, his hair a black curtain around us. "I do not want to let you go."

The confession sinks into that hidden place where I store the rest of him. I balance my weapon while hooking my free fingers around his nape. "What happens now? Where do we go from here?"

He takes a mindful breath. "Middle Moon is tomorrow."

Middle Moon? I've never heard of such a thing in the Book of Fables, and if Juniper hasn't schooled me or Lark on this enigma, then it mustn't exist in the pages.

Elixir explains it's a tradition in The Solitary wild, a night when the Folk celebrate the origins of the Fauna, the ancient date of their birth, when they first came into being in Faerie.

In the mountain, Faeries of the sky host a masquerade. The festivities forbid human captives to attend, not that such a rule would discourage Lark.

In the forest, home to the rowdiest bunch of Solitaries, revelers enjoy a feast. There, the current human is expected to join for reasons Elixir can't impart. He doesn't know the particulars, since it has to do with the woodland's game, which is kept secret until it's over.

"The Deep hosts a sail," Elixir tells me. "Every vessel of the river voyages down serpentine canals and isolated passages—the darkest, deepest, remotest corners known thus far. In one of those recesses, the sail ends with a race."

"What kind of race?"

His eyes glint. "A dangerous one."

When I shiver against him, his palm roams over my pebbled flesh, the motion soothing. "In general, the race is not for the faint of heart, nor for one lacking endurance. Though, that hardly applies to you." He clears his throat. "Might you consider…will you…"

I smile, enjoying his brutish awkwardness. "Will I…?"

"I would like to show you how we honor our fauna."

Genuine hope flickers in his gaze. That, and the knowledge I might refuse him.

He could order me to go. His kin would expect no less.

"You said it was dangerous," I remind him.

"The race is not for mortals. You will not be harmed," he swears, and the lethal tone sounds like a command to everyone who exists beyond our little bubble, every river Fae who would like to claw me into filets.

Elixir's whipcord arms fasten around me. The look on his face could slice through iron. "No one shall touch you."

"Will Scorpio be there?"

"I will kill him if he comes near you again. It will happen before he can blink. The merman knows this, and I have loyal eyes watching him as well. As for the rest, my subjects revere me, honor my law, and want to restore their fauna more than anything. They would not dare."

"Did your kin harm the mortals who've attended before?"

Elixir's mouth compresses. "None have survived that long."

The chill from before rushes between us. None of the humans had paced themselves before trying to break a curse they had no power to break. When they lost, Elixir likely hadn't given them much time to choose their losing brew.

This is the Fae I've shared myself with.

Anguish strains his features. "Cove, I…I do not know how to…make amends for that."

"You can start by finding a way," I insist. "There must be some way around the sacrifices."

"I told you. There is no way."

I lurch from his embrace and shove him, for all the good it does since he doesn't budge. "Are you saying that because you've tried? Or are you enjoying your power too much?"

His jaw clenches. He follows the sounds of water, and his finger stabs toward the exit, where his kin reside beyond. "My power keeps them hopeful. My power keeps them alive. My power has cured allies and poisoned enemies. My power has made the games unbeatable. My power has restored many of the fauna we lost to your people. My power keeps this river from crumbling sooner rather than later. My fucking power is mine."

"It also compensates for what you've lost. How convenient."

Those eyes flash with pain, then spark with fury. "Do not speak about my mothers. You did not know them."

"You don't know my sisters!"

Anyway, I'm not talking about his family. I'm talking about the thing I took from him, the thing I cursed him with. I hate that I did it, even though it had been out of my control, and I hate even more what his blindness has turned him into. If I'd shown Elixir kindness nine years ago, maybe I would have thought of him differently, and this wouldn't have happened to him.

Still, no one forced Elixir to be evil. No one forced him to use his anger as a weapon, nor to supplement his losses with violence, dark magic, and rigged games.

He twists away. I shuffle back and cross my arms. What I'd said hurt him, and I don't like hurting him, because I know what it's like to lose my parents. I hear the adoration in his voice when he talks about them.

I don't want these hours to end like this. I don't want to bring this quarrel into my dreams tonight. I want what we had in the pond. I want that to last.

Elixir's chest heaves. "The Middle Moon Sail begins at midnight. If you want to, the boat shall be waiting."

"Why do you want me there? To show off your captive?"

"No." His voice dips low. "I want you there because you will enjoy it."

Tears spring to my eyes, but I suck them up like Juniper would. I don't answer before stepping into the boat, and I don't look back as I leave him behind.

In my chamber, I dream of a thousand drowning faces. I dream of hate and love, of viciousness and kindness. I dream of mortal worlds and immortal lands. I dream of a cursed wishing well and a lily pond.

I dream of crickets and toads, then flip my eyes open. The eventide chorus of insects and amphibians resounds outside the door. The window lanterns bloom with orange light, and the central bath gurgles, wisps of steam curling from within.

Lotus is snoozing beside me, rolled into a spool of reptilian skin. His tongue flutters from his mouth as he rests, his body satiated from the feed I'd brought him after leaving Elixir.

Nevertheless, a covered platter and tankard wait on the table. I stare at the offering, knowing the trencher will contain nourishment for us both.

If you want to, the boat shall be waiting.

What time is it?

I rustle out of bed, scurry through the chamber door, and pad outside. Sure enough, the vessel is there. Anchored against the bank, the transport sways over the water, a lantern brimming from its prow this time.

A netted bag sits in the boat. Pulling on the rope closure, I find one of those strappy, clingy suits the other Faeries have worn. This one is backless and extends only to the buttocks and hips. It's cut from the softest material, reminiscent of brilliant, white petals.

It's also tiny. The garment reminds me of the lacy underthings Lark favors, though in one piece rather than two.

But there's also a skirt. I tug it from the bag and gasp. It's like nothing I've ever seen. Layers of scales cascade like a waterfall, the white shingles etched in tints of silver. The colors throw prisms into the air, every plate shimmering like liquid and light strewn together.

"Mermaid scales," I whisper.

It's exquisite. And it's daring. The skirt is some type of wrap style, allowing the front panels to split around my limbs. Lark would approve, but never mind what Juniper would say. She hates skimpy clothing as much as she disapproves of wearing the color red.

But my sisters belong to the sky and roots, whereas I belong to the tide.

The ensemble is immodest but stunning, the fabric as supple as water. I've found nothing of the sort in the chamber's wardrobe, and I realize why. The style and unearthly textiles are tailored for swimming, a pastime Elixir hadn't wanted to encourage in the beginning.

But now…

Make your choice.

I shouldn't be near him any more than I need to be. My heart can't risk it. He won't let anybody harm me, yet he has the power to hurt me the most. He won't help me find a way to abolish this game, to stop the wild from fading without sacrificing humans. He won't relinquish that power. He thinks it's all he has left.

I won't change that. I can't change him.

That's not my quest. No, my quest is to find a solution myself, to map out this realm, to explore this domain, and seek out another way. If I don't, my quest is still to win this game. Either way, I won't surrender.

It's time to show these Faeries that mortals are stronger than they've been given credit for, to show them a human can survive the harshest of elements. Even gentle mortals can be fierce. Even mortals are paragons of nature. If someone never proves the Folk wrong about this, nothing will change.

Sorrow, anger, and tenderness work in tandem. Standing beside the water, I peel the nightgown from my body, then step into the filmy garment, which clings to my form like a second skin. I swirl the skirt around my hips and jerk on the tie, strapping it in place. I shimmer with every move, flinging brightness into this sunken cavern.

You are the light.

Yes, I am. The clothes fit perfectly, an outfit made for the depths, made to find its way through dark and dangerous places.

An hour later, I'm standing on the boat with the spear in my grip. The waterdrop pendant hangs down my back, and Lotus has strapped himself around my bicep. Elixir had vowed his kin won't injure my friend, and I believe him. I trust this much about the history between mortals and Faeries.

I would impale any Fae that came near Lotus, but that won't come to pass. Here, he is cherished. The snake ventured into The Deep to be with me. We have a bond, and the Folk need to see that.

Balmy air caresses the bun I've plaited against my scalp. The boat cruises through the secret tunnel, but before it reaches the waterslide, my transport rounds a sharp bend, heads in an unfamiliar direction, and enters another passage. I commit to memory as much of the route as possible. Beyond the exit, a vast dome of teal constellations spans a cavern.

My mouth falls open. I lunge sideways and grip the archway, halting the boat before it can fully materialize into the scene.

I've gone through a shortcut, a shielded route from my chamber to The Twisted Canals. Ahead, the river proper bears the weight of countless vessels. River dolphins lurch through the aquamarine depth, zipping around spiked and fanged fish, including several sharks who glide in and out of sight.

The ships aren't large enough to cross oceans, but they consume my vision like great whales from the storybooks. Their broad hulls curve into otherworldly shapes chiseled from obsidian mineral rocks. Lanterns burn from the masts. The sails are diaphanous, yet there are few examples of rigging.

It's a painting come to life, a fleet of mystical ships at eventide, a midnight parade of fire and water glowing in the darkness.

The Middle Moon Sail.

Peapod-shaped vessels slide between the larger transports, carrying Fae children who snack on roasted crustaceans and pet the sharks.

Faeries clutter the boats. They perch on the ledges or sing from within the decks, their voices braiding together and vibrating across the dome.

Any jubilee or festival in Reverie Hollow involves barrels of ale and dances where stomping feet shake the ground. Here, the music drifts rather than pounds through the atmosphere, and the Folk either toast to the splashing fauna, swim with them, or duel in mock battles across the decks, their weapons clanging while spectators watch.

Beneath the skirt, my knees quiver. They haven't spotted me yet.

But I see him.

His arrival causes a tidal wave of reaction, every member of the Folk sinking to their knees and bowing their heads. The water lord stalks from one of the passages leading into the canal colony. Followed by an entourage that includes Coral and half a dozen other figures, Elixir draws this legion of Faeries to him without uttering a single word. His long limbs carry him across a planked crossway, his strides imposing, his profile hewn from stone.

A long robe splits open and flares around him like a black sail. A loose shirt slumps down his chest, his pectorals rippling into view, and ebony leggings clutch those athletic limbs.

Onyx hair tumbles from a low ponytail gathered messily at his nape. If he were human and unshaven, he would be a pirate.

Elixir's gait is swift and domineering, as though he'll trample anything that gets in his way. He storms past his kin, his fingercaps scraping the air, which guides him to the largest vessel in this port.

Right before he turns to board the ship, an undine child points his webbed finger. "It's her!"

His melodic accent carries through the silence and reaches Elixir's tapered ears. He pauses midstride, his hand gripping the ramp railing. He stares ahead for a moment, then whips toward the boy's voice. His Fae senses strain, reaching out for the slightest hint, but it's no use.

I do not know how to follow the sound of your affection.

Because he can't hear my rapid exhalations the way he used to, nor my blood racing, nor my body heating, Elixir follows the sound of the river, the sound of my boat. Those eyes were dull a moment ago, but now they gleam with hope.

At that look, the wind drains from my lungs. He didn't think I would come.

Every head slashes in my direction. Murmurs dice through The Twisted Canals.

My heart rate quickens, more from the expression on Elixir's face than the onslaught of glares I receive. Lotus nestles himself around me, the slits of his eyes scanning the environment for signs of hostility. I run my finger over his head to ease his vigilance.

That's when then my enemies notice the snake around my arm, and the murmurs reach a fever pitch of awe and confusion.

"A mortal snake?"

"She has a familiar?"

"What's the meaning of this?"

The whispers reach Elixir, whose expression doesn't alter. Yet prideful gold simmers in his irises, the metallic shine clear from my vantage point.

Without breaking his gaze from my direction, the river ruler lifts his arm. The voices from every vessel fall silent. Then he extends his hand, palm up, in invitation.

I release the tunnel wall. My boat drifts, the current guiding it to the pier, where the craft bumps against the planks. Swallowing, I take his fingers and step onto the crossway, his warmth burrowing into my fingers.

Covertly, his pupils stray over me. I wish he could see my face, but more than that, I wish he could see himself, could see what's hidden there.

Elixir releases my hand. As he does, his knuckles graze the scales of my skirt, and his chest rumbles.

"You're wearing the light," he murmurs under his breath.

My pulse leaps. "Yes. And I've got company."

We pause for a beat, then he glances toward the snake in acknowledgement and steps back. "The mortal and her companion shall attend," he announces with a subtle growl. "That is my word. Let her see how we honor the fauna, and let her know that bond reigns eternal. Let it be so."

I know this is a performance. I know he has to say this, has to exercise his authority, and has to make sure they don't sense more between us. I know it must appear as if he's forced me to be here. I know it needs to appear as though he's amused, rather than proud, that I've brought Lotus. I know it needs to look as if my demonstration makes no difference, because humans will never be stronger, because we're the lesser beings, because we're of a lesser nature.

And I know I've had enough. I fist my spear and lift my chin. "Actually," I amplify my voice. "I'm here to race."

25

It takes Elixir a moment to process what I've said. His eyes widen, sharp and piercing.

Mutterings filter through the scene. Elixir's nostrils flare. Without breaking his attention from me, he swats his fingers in silent command, as though smacking a monsoon back to the place it came from. The commotion dies instantly.

He stands there, in all his Fae glory, and ticks his head to the side, waiting for me to continue.

"I'm not here to watch," I say. "I'm here to race against one of you."

Astonishment slices through the crowd. From aboard every ship and boat, stunned gazes level on me as my words hang in the air, overflowing in this expansive hub.

Then laughter breaks out. The incredulous Faeries erupt in a stream of cackles and titters and guffaws, the noise resounding from the vessels and echoing across the river. Despite this rare fit of hysterics, the merfolk, undines, and water sprites sound like liquid music, their voices reverberating like cymbals and chimes.

My cheeks roast, but I trace my necklace for support and keep my chin raised. Lotus strains toward the sound and hisses, which snags their attention.

But it's the rasping baritone of their leader that makes a greater difference. "Silence!" he booms.

Again, the congregation goes still. They swallow their mirth and watch with rapt intrigue, some of them coiling around the sails or leaning at steep angles from the serpent figureheads.

Tension radiates from Elixir in waves—a geyser about to burst. He's caught between me and them, between his influence and my wellbeing. He's searching for a way out of this, but this ruler is too visceral to handle tact.

From the one of the ships, Scorpio and his swamp-colored hair materialize in my periphery, ink markings clawing across his torso. He leans over the craft's rail and crosses his forearms, his black-smudged eyes waspish as they target me. "That's no race. It's an insult."

"No, it's an execution," an undine trills, correcting him.

"What Fae would lower themselves to race you?" a sprite warbles.

I open my mouth.

"I will race her," a syrupy voice says.

From behind Elixir, Coral steps forth, her gaze arched with neither scrutiny nor superiority. Sheer pants balloon around her limbs like smoke and cinch at the ankles, and her dark thighs and calves are visible beneath the textile. One of those clingy bodices adheres to her bust and stretches to cover her backside and pelvis; the swimming suit is also visible under her transparent pants.

My stomach flips with nervousness. Although she looks only a few years older than Elixir, the slight difference is considerable for immortals. And Faeries grow stronger with age. The Fables say as much.

Someone nearer to my equivalent would be easier. But they might also play dirtier.

This female has no interest in that. Matter of fact, I see a measure of intrigue staring back at me. She would be a good option if she weren't several times more robust than a younger Fae.

Have I thought this through clearly? Because right now, neither option seems promising, not if I want to win.

"I will race her," the guard announces louder.

Elixir shakes his head. "No. I shall."

His voice grates, the texture sounding aggressive to the spectators. To me, it sounds protective.

A thrill washes through the cavern as the Faeries murmur. Coral had been a mighty choice for an opponent, but a lukewarm form of entertainment. This twist is more enticing.

Condemnation! I should have known Elixir would volunteer. It's all I can do to stop a protest from lurching off my tongue.

I can't race him. He's not the same venomous ruler he was when I'd arrived in The Deep. I need this victory against another Fae, not him. I need to win against one of them, against one of his subjects. I need this race to be genuine. If not, they might see right through us.

Versus Elixir, the race will be compromised. Winning reinforces his authority. But the problem is, he doesn't want me injured, and he'll shield me through the whole thing, shredding any danger that gets near.

When Elixir makes a choice, he makes a choice. His word is final, and no one contests it.

The crowd stirs with excitement. They bow in ready acknowledgment, sinking fluidly to their knees. These subterranean beings know it's a predictable race with uneven odds and an impossible outcome. They must also know Elixir won't let his sacrifice perish. Nonetheless, they expect the challenge will be painful for a measly human, and they'll relish the exhibition.

Elixir inclines his head toward me, his jaw ticking. For one so uncivil, he's good at striking cleanly.

Yet I know better. He's holding back. He's mad.

He's very mad that I've put myself in this position.

At the same time, his throat contorts because he's also scared. So am I.

Make your choice.

Surrounded by the masses, I sidle up to the water lord and offer the bait. "Don't hold back."

In the light of hundreds of lanterns, Elixir looms over me, fury and pride tweaking his features. That's when I know: He understands what I'm doing and why.

His temple throbs, but his eyes tell a different story, burnishing with admiration. "Challenge accepted."

That gets another rise out of the Faeries. They sing their approval, their melodic voices dancing across the muggy air. However impressed, they must think me foolish. Let them for now.

The water lord whirls and strides away, his robe thwacking behind him.

A sea of Faeries parts as he ascends the ramp and steps onto the deck.

"Can you swim, human?" Coral asks, her silver-blue tresses sleek around her dark face.

Unlike beloved Juniper, I refrain from bragging. The last thing I need anyone to know is just how well I can answer this question. "I keep my head above water."

Her mouth twitches in amusement. "Hmm. I must say, you're either clever or positively stupid. I can't wait to find out which." She sweeps aside and extends her arm toward the plank leading to the ship, with its interlocking serpent figureheads. "And it won't be about keeping your head above water. Not when you reach The Fever of Stingrays."

"The what?" I squeak.

But when I show no sign of moving, she shrugs and struts off without me. I follow, ascending the plank with a thousand eyes cast my way, including the spiteful orbs of the merman stationed in another craft.

However, Scorpio's glower drops the moment Elixir's head snaps in the merman's direction. From across ships, the river ruler bares his teeth until Scorpio retreats several paces. After that, it takes a moment for Elixir to pry his attention from the merman and offer me what the spectators assume is a mocking hand.

Hidden in plain sight, it's him and me. It's us.

My fingers drape atop his, heat rushing from his digits to mine. Stepping onto the deck, I let go first and shuffle past him, the mermaid skirt brushing his robe, the contact sending a bolt of longing straight through me.

Elixir shows no sign of it, but I glimpse him making a fist at his side. I wonder if he's debating whether to shake me or drag me into a dark corner and ruin the skirt. Without a backward glance, he turns and marches to the quarterdeck, his serpentine movements claiming the space around him.

I see the way heads turn as he passes. I see the way males and females color in his presence, their eyes lustful and lingering.

Embers of jealousy skid across my knuckles. I'm not supposed to matter, not while crowded in a snake pit. Though his dismissal is for my protection, it stings nonetheless.

Is this all we'll ever be? A scandalous secret? A forbidden complication?

Pain clogs my throat. I swerve away, relieved by the distraction as a flurry of activity resumes, Faeries casting glances my way but keeping their distance. Though unlike with me, they regard Lotus with esteem.

Somewhere, a horn blows. And we're off.

The vessels set sail. Faeries chant, their song filtering through the environment. We leave the river proper behind and shave through the water, coasting into the widest tunnel.

And into the outer reaches of The Deep.

I install myself in a corner and brace my forearms on the ship's rim, the wind combing through the intricate bun. I peek over the edge where merfolk spear through the depth alongside sharks and dolphins.

"What do you think, Lotus?" I whisper to the snake. "Terrifying or enchanting?"

Lotus curls into my bicep, his head bumping my shoulder. I chuckle, fear and anticipation clashing. I'm on a Fae ship, sailing through an underground world.

We cruise through passages, canals, and plummet down slopes.

I marvel at the scene. The lanterns burn. The teal orbs glisten. The aquamarine surface tosses strands of light across the craggy ceilings. The fauna leap beside the hulls.

The smell of wine—crushed white grapes, plums, and citrus. The sensation of humidity soaking through my bodice.

The hot weight of his attention from across the ship. In my periphery, I sense him inhaling my scent and listening to the rustle of my skirt. The other signals he used to read might be out of reach now, but others aren't.

It's no different from being watched. In fact, it's more intense. It forces him to penetrate deeper, to slither beneath my clothes and skin, in order to see me.

We pass waterfalls and rapids and secluded grottos. The fragrance of damp foliage and water florals permeate the balmy eventide air.

I shiver in awareness, a bead of condensation drizzling down my spine.

"Look up," a deep voice says from inches behind me.

On the surface of the river, the water lord's shadow bleeds with mine. His breath stalks between my shoulder blades, and my nipples toughen from that Fae accent.

Beside me, Elixir leans casually against the ship while I look up, gazing high, high, high into a crater. Beyond, a ring of white blazes in a fathomless sky littered with teal, gold, and white stars. The vision resembles the base of a circlet or crown, a globe missing its center, or an iris surrounding a pupil.

"The Middle Moon," Elixir intones. "The one night when the moon's center goes dark, as it did millennia ago when the fauna first appeared in this wild."

"It's surreal," I say. "Beautiful."

"Yes."

That voice is directed toward me, furious and ravenous. I can't say anything. The Faeries make enough noise for us, cheering at the sight as we drift past the open firmament.

"You are wearing the clothes I sent you?" he rasps, referring to the fleeting caress of my skirt earlier.

"I'm wearing them," I confirm. "The outfit is lovely. It fits as if it were made for me."

"It was. In The Solitary Mountain, my brother Cerulean is well acquainted with an expert tailor. The Fae wove ripples from the lily pond for the suit, along with mer scales for the skirt. I did not foresee this race, but a garment from the pond shall enable you to bond with any body of water and pass through it like a fish."

"It was made from the lily pond?"

He lowers his voice. "I wanted you to feel that place. I wanted you to feel it holding you."

His accent is equal parts desire and uncertainty, as if unsure whether he's explaining himself correctly. But I understand. He's explaining himself so well, I feel his response swirling around my knees. I'm wearing the lily pond, where are we gave ourselves to each other.

We wheel to face one another, my breathing shallow, and his deep. The proximity stunts my intakes and his outtakes.

Elixir's black eyebrows crinkle, plagued by a sudden thought. "I wish I could see you in this outfit. I should like to trace it, peel it from your body, and bare your exquisite tits while you moan. If we were alone, I would take you against the prow of this ship, while the water rages beneath."

"They can see us," I say once sanity returns.

"They will think I am tormenting you," he dismisses.

"You are. I'm sufficiently tormented."

His lips skate across the sensitive crook behind my ear. "As am I."

I want to swallow those words. I want them on my tongue.

Even so, "What did you expect?"

Elixir turns, grips the rim until his knuckles strain, and speaks to the waves thrashing below. "Not. This," he bites out.

Conflicted emotions tangle between us, cinching tightly to the point of suffocation.

What will it be? Desire or anger? Collaborators or competitors?

Lovers or enemies? Friends or foes?

Sink or swim? Win or lose?

That horn blares from one of the ships, and the crafts anchor, bobbing in place beneath the Middle Moon.

Elixir straightens, his teeth clenching. "Hand Lotus to me."

I spin toward him. "What?"

"It is time. He cannot race with you, but he will be safe here. Hand him to me."

My heart hammers. I pet my companion's head and whisper, "I'll see you soon. Promise."

I lift my bicep, and Lotus listens to whatever Elixir communicates, then my friend uncoils and winds his brown-marbled body around Elixir's forearm. The ruler settles Lotus on a cushioned bench, where Coral stands post and regards us with a shrewd twinkle in her eyes.

Elixir strides ahead, saying as he passes me, "Relinquish what you consider useless."

The spear warrants debate, but I can't race one-handed, and Elixir isn't armed with forked daggers, either. I remove my sandals and blush while untying the skirt, only the clingy suit remaining. I offer the items and my weapon to Coral, ignore the weight of Scorpio's snide glare from the neighboring ship, and catch up to Elixir, falling into step with him.

On the way, Elixir strips off his robe and lets it puddle to the floor. We mount two ramps with springboards extending over the river. In a terrible dose of reality, mist sprays my face from below.

Logic wrestles to catch up. "I don't know where to go."

"Straight," Elixir says under his breath. "Always straight until you reach The Creep of Tortoises. It is an impasse. You will recognize it."

Poised on the ship's planks, we hover side by side above the mouth of a wild current swirling below, the depth about to consume us. Silhouettes of finned creatures slice through the depth, and the sharp cave walls arch overhead, stalactites piercing from the dome like tusks.

Elixir snatches my hand and squeezes it. "You have infuriated the fuck out of me tonight."

"I know," I say.

"And you shall pay for this."

"I know that."

"Cove, I…"

Because we don't have a choice anymore, and because I don't know what awaits us at the bottom of the abyss, I squeeze his fingers back and speak gently. "I know *that*, too."

His shaky thumb brushes my wrist. It takes Elixir a moment to recover. "Do not tarry. Keep to the west side," he rushes out, nipping his chin in that direction. "The current is lighter. At the waterfalls, pass through the central cascade, and hold your breath for as long as you can. Do not touch the stingrays. If you founder, reach for me. I shall be close." The water lord hunches into a diving position. "For as long as you can. Whatever you do. Heed this warning."

I nod while bending into the same posture and gazing down. "Will the boats follow?"

"No, they must wait here. My subjects take signals from the water and fauna. That is how they will know our trajectory. Faeries who try to follow disrupt the race and incur public wrath, along with retribution from me. They will not pursue us, but they will know what is happening."

My lips tremble. What was I thinking? This is madness. I haven't trained for an otherworldly race through canals in the dark, with predators lurking in the recesses, nor without knowing what else lies ahead. I'm in no shape against a Fae.

My panic must be audible because Elixir says, "Cove, listen to me. I'm here. I'm here, and you can do this. I will not let anything happen to you."

I nod vehemently while gawking at the churning abyss. "Fables have mercy."

"Trust the water," he coaches. "Remember how I showed you darkness. Remember how you mastered The Sunken Isle's lake. Remember that, and trust yourself. Remember that, and trust me."

I do as he bids and remember, remember, remember. As that happens, my blood slows, the flux calming.

I can do this. I need to do this.

In the hot glare of the ship lanterns, Elixir's profile wrestles with itself, struggling to tamp down his own emotions. He's distraught because I'm important to him. No matter what, I've made that mark. I know because I feel the same way about this Fae, because he's become my weakness, too.

But weaknesses can turn into power, can become forces to reckon with. The promise of that works its magic. Despite the Faeries chanting from the ships and boats around us, faith loosens my muscles, and determination fuels my blood. We can race, and we can play this dangerous game, but we'll find a way to do it with each other, not against.

"Fall with me," I say into the void. "Go deep with me."

Elixir is quiet for a moment. "It is too late. I did that long ago."

Together, we jump.

26

My body springs off the plank, my arms extending toward the water. I turn myself into a spear, conjuring the times when I've dived off tree limbs into the deepest parts of the creek.

The plunge is swift yet endless, time advancing and slowing. Air pressure rushes through my limbs, the velocity turning my hair into a kite. Wearing nothing but this elastic suit, I feel the descent in a way I never have, my body cutting through the atmosphere.

My stomach lurches, freedom and terror converging. Maybe this is why Lark loves this feeling—the rush of flight, the surrender, the leap of faith, and the power that comes with it.

Mist launches from nowhere, spraying my flesh. A second later, I break through, lancing into the gulf. Water surges around my limbs, suctioning me down. The world grows silent, gravity disappearing. I hear bubbles bloating around me and muffled waves rolling from above.

It's a clean landing, my body knifing into the depth. Leveling forward, I vault ahead and then loop upward, following the current, following the noises. The surface spews into fragments as I emerge, oxygen flooding my lungs. For an unfortunate moment, I'd forgotten how much thicker the water is in this realm, how sometimes it moves differently. That's going to make it hard to pace myself, to preserve my breath.

Against the ruler of this land, I shouldn't stand a chance. Yet there's one advantage to remember, one vital straw to grasp at: Immortals of the river don't know how to swim for survival, because they don't need to.

Mortals like me do.

My eyes blast open, scanning the perimeter. Ships and boats tower above like ancient monuments, their hulls croaking, the tunnels magnifying the noise. Thankfully, the eddying river washes out the hollers and songs of the onlookers.

Droplets plunk from my eyelashes. The setting wavers, turning my vantage gritty and uneven as I bob. Glimpses of writhing flames, craggy foundations, and boulders covered in filigrees of lichen fluctuate in my vision.

A shark fin cuts into view, then vanishes in a slap of water. Fear knots into a fist and punches me in the ribs.

Where is he?

Do not tarry. Keep to the west side.

The shark will identify me as prey if I linger, but like the first time I had this problem, speeding away will also seal my fate. I barrel toward where the fin had plummeted. The flux sloshes around me with every kick and beat of my limbs, hopefully sending a message to the dweller that I'm not its target, nor am I in the mood to be eaten.

I recall the direction Elixir had indicated—I need to remember this mental compass for the map etched into my chamber floor—and veer west, careening forward, bounding in and out of the water. Several slick bodies race across my calves, and I don't know if the aquatic creatures are about to shift sizes, but I keep going, keep plowing straight.

The river flows against me, burdening the momentum and scorching my muscles. This is Elixir's idea of a lighter current versus the east? No surprise, considering the Folk's stamina. For me, it's the lesser of the two evils.

The tunnel narrows to a sliver and begins an unearthly zigzag. At last, the current shifts and flows with me, but it also accelerates, driving me into the winding flux and threatening to fling me into the serrated walls. I harpoon left and right, left and right, left and right. Any second, the sharp turns could either capsize or hurl me against the foundations, where I'll splatter to a pulp.

I deflect and push, deflect and push. Inhale, exhale. Inhale, exhale.

River water sluices down my throat. My joints scream from exertion.

A force catapults from somewhere below and cleaves past me. On the way, a set of fingers brushes my knee, and a tail grazes my ankle. A quick glance into The Deep reveals a dark outline coasting beneath and then shearing ahead.

Searching for me must have slowed him down. If I want to win authentically, having the ruler looking out for my benefit isn't going to help. Then again, that's his choice, not mine.

Energy renewed, I speed forth, putting every ounce of strength and faith and love into it. I conjure the faces of my family, the voices of my sisters, and the scents of the sanctuary. I remember my birth parents, lost to a raging ocean. I recall a young, forbidden enemy caged in a liquid tube and pledging to drown me.

He could do that now, but he won't. He's not that Fae anymore.

Even if he were, I would never let him. I won't drown for these Faeries, and I won't sink like my parents, and I'll never fear swimming.

The curves straighten, dashing into a new artery where three cords of fluid pour from craters in the canopy. The lantern flames have long since vanished, and the aquamarine water has darkened, leaving only the teal orbs to illuminate the passage. A fluid screech peals through my ears, the fathomless call belonging to an unknown sea creature.

Don't stop, I will myself. He told me not to stop.

The trio of slender cascades shower down as I approach.

At the waterfalls, pass through the central cascade—

I shove through the middle deluge.

—and hold your breath for as long as you can.

Suddenly, the ceiling grows shallow, declining into a blockade. I suck in a deep gust, packing my lungs to capacity, and plunge under the hard foundation. Again, the world goes silent. My eyes pop open, but it's dark. So very dark.

My digits grapple overhead, and a jagged facade bites into my skin. It's like I'm beneath solid earth, with no way to hammer through, no way to go except forward. I pump my arms and legs, fling myself into it, and count. Two minutes pass, then another fifteen seconds, and another, and another, and another. I've practiced this many times before, but it's too much, just too much.

I'm not a water Fae. I'm not Elixir, who can breathe down here.

Panic skewers my womb. I keep checking the edifice, but there's no sign of an opening or groove. My head fogs, dizziness tugging on me.

I think of an infant being born in the water. I think of a child sitting on a bank, chortling as a gaggle of tiny fish peck at her toes. I think of a young girl learning to wield a spear in the creek. I think of a woman bathing in that same creek, loving the depth and flow—my anchor and my haven. I channel that watery love and battle my way through.

Visibility returns. Blue-green gradients flow around me like melted jewels, the colors glazing the underwater architecture of sculpted rocks and coontails that latch around my calves, so numerous they could form a net and trap me.

I kick the plants away and propel myself, then reflexively lurch backward at the sight ahead. A legion of wide, thin figures surf toward me like spotted cloaks, the long strings of their tails whipping behind them.

Do not touch the stingrays.

The Fever of Stingrays.

Elixir had cautioned me. And before that, Coral had mentioned this area.

The squadron accelerates, swinging from side to side, a few spooling like rolled bolts of cloth that cannon my way.

If you founder, reach for me. I shall be close.

But I won't do that. I won't because maybe part of me is as stubborn as my family. I need to do this.

The creatures move like water itself, their stingers whipping behind them. They flit by like a stampede, but the crush is so dense, it blocks out portions of the abyss. I'm not small enough to pass through while avoiding those tails.

Some shrink and skate just below my thighs, others bloat to the size of canopies or tents. I twist and duck, dive and rise. A cry of pain pops from my lips, more bubbles foaming as one of the tails whacks my shin.

Nausea roils in my gut. It's not a puncture wound, but stingrays carry venom. If any of them thrust their tails into my upper body, I'll be in trouble.

Is this how I'm going to die? By doing what I had sworn not to do? By drowning or from suffering a thousand stings?

Will my bones become part of this earth? Will the only proof I've been here be my pendant necklace?

The necklace! Fables forgive me, I forgot to remove it before the race!

My desperate fingers cling to my throat, but when the digits skate across my clavicles, all I feel is skin and bone. It was there. I know the necklace was there because I never unclasped and handed it to Coral for safekeeping. Somewhere between the ships and the stingrays, the necklace had snapped from my throat.

Grief stunts my pace. Yet loss tightens into determination because my sisters are alive, and they know I can weather this.

So does the water lord. The memory of Elixir's baritone sweeps through, low and private and mine.

For as long as you can. Whatever you do. Heed this warning.

I soldier forth, pumping, kicking. The stingrays disband, splitting and forming a trench that I slip through. They fork around me, then dissipate.

At the same time, a familiar serpentine outline materializes and slithers past my vision. A reptilian mer tail flexes in and out of my periphery. His fingers race across my limbs, my shoulders, and my cheeks.

Then I swerve, and he's there. Elixir snatches my face, his worried eyes punching through the vibrant depth. His tail strokes the place where the stingray got me, telling me it's okay, I'll be all right.

And the way he's grabbing me, the way he's searching for an impossible glimpse of my face, the way his eyes scour for something, anything to hold on to, and the way he falters when he can't find it, when he can't see me...

That same look, and that same hold, and that same falter blitzes through me from nine years ago. It's familiar but different. The way he's swimming off kilter reminds me of how he'd swam that night in the stream, when I tried to catch him.

There's something about this visual I hadn't recognized back then. I don't know what it is.

A sturgeon sails past us, dissolving the moment. My lack of oxygen catches up with me. Elixir must sense that, because he presses his forehead to mine and nods in encouragement.

Just a little more. Almost there.

We twist and zoom forth. The fortification overhead vanishes, giving way to a rippling surface. I lunge upward and crash through, a great wheeze escaping my parted mouth, blessed air siphoning down my throat.

Elixir catapults from the surface, registers I'm all right, and gives me an ardent look that communicates everything I need to know. I return the look, and we vault beside one another.

He swims like he's mated with the water, seamlessly and beautifully and violently. His body dives in and soars out of the gulf, again, and again, and again. I put my heart into it, pour my soul into it.

All the while, I pay closer attention to how he swims, his sculpted muscles rotating, his speed and agility rivaling any sea serpent in this world. I memorize his pace and rhythm. I surge his way while learning every contraction, sequence, and stroke of his body.

Yet I can't erase that one submerged instant when he'd wavered and tried to catch sight of me, as if he could.

Leagues ahead, a rocky impasse marks The Creep of Tortoises. Rocks form different levels and outcroppings, where babbling streams tumble down the brackets. Emerald tortoises hold court atop the foundations, one of them as large as a dolphin, with reeds germinating like a garden from atop the amphibian's shell. Although they're land creatures, the dwellers seem to make their home in this place. They clutter the niches and crevices, and paddle through basins.

I do a mad sprint, reaching Elixir and aligning myself with him. I don't know if that moment between us has depleted the Fae, or if it has spurred me into action. Either way, we're neck and neck.

The water level rises, shallow enough for us to run. Elixir's tail shudders into limbs. Our heads whip in the other's direction because when all is said and done, we want to prevail without the other losing, and at some point since I arrived in this realm, we've become one force.

Also, who's to know? His kin can follow the signals of our limbs in the water, but can they sense what our upper halves are doing when not submerged?

Our hands shoot out and clasp together, and we charge toward the first slippery outcropping. Then our free fingers land on the same boulder, at the same time.

Gasping, we peer at each other. Elixir's chest pounds, corded muscles bunching down his wet arms. His eyes flare with wonder and wrath, those pupils straining for my countenance. I can't tell if he wants to shake me for endangering myself or strip the white garment from my body.

"We win," I choke out. "It's over."

My hunch about what the Faeries can and can't follow must be accurate, because Elixir whisks his arm around my waist and hoists me against him, our drenched and exhausted bodies colliding.

"No," he growls hotly against my mouth. "It has only begun."

His mouth crashes onto mine, and my arms fling around his neck, but instead of robbing us of oxygen once more, this kiss does the opposite. Finally, we can breathe again.

27

Time blurs. Sometimes the days float by like gentle streams, whereas other times they rage by in waves. It's painful when we're together because there are so many places to touch, so many places that make him groan and me cry out, so many body parts to taste and fit together, yet there are never enough hours. We savor them in slices, in fragments of dawn and dusk, in my chamber or his den, in light watery gulfs or dark corners of The Deep.

In shallow pools, we practice crossing weapons, which usually ends in a toe-curling kiss.

In shadowed recesses, we drown ourselves in one another, whispering and confessing and moaning.

When we're apart, it's no less excruciating. I feel the separation like a wound. I feel the loss of him in every place his mouth has been.

I know he feels it, too, because the instant we reunite, the air crackles, and the humidity thickens. His eyes smolder. In seconds, Elixir is on me, and my clothes are reduced to ribbons, and his cock is lunging inside me before the garments have fluttered to the ground. I cry out to the rhythm of his thrusts, my body aching everywhere, feverish and intoxicated and insatiable, as if I've consumed one of his sinful brews.

I take Elixir while overlooking The Kelpie Rapids, straddling him on the vista point and riding his cock. My fingers skewer into his mane, and my other digits splay over his taut cheek, holding his face to mine. Our pants beat together. Elixir clings to my hips like he wants to either yank on me harder or surrender himself completely to me. Spurred on, I batter my waist on to his lap until he loses his voice.

Another time, he fucks me naked against the wall in a pitch-black tunnel, where vertical sheets of water cascade down the foundation. As the deluge slides over us, he hitches my right leg over his waist, grips the facade overhead for leverage, and pounds his hips hard and fast, his wet buttocks slapping, his prick rushing into me. Like that…and that…and, Fables forbid, like *that*.

He covers my mouth with his. This way, he devours my hollers of pleasure, keeping them from trembling down the passages and fracturing into pieces, keeping my orgasm between us, keeping it secret and safe and—

"Mine," he growls.

"Yours," I keen against him.

And another time, we take each other in the lily pond, where I bend over a bank and press my upper half flush against the grass. Under the water, my backside snaps into Elixir's stiff length, and he rolls his hips, thrusting from behind. The sensuous and repetitive lurch of his cock jostles me upward. I reach back, clutching his nape while he cups my breasts and thumbs the nipples into tight buds, and we pant into blue-white cave, and there's nothing else but this, and this, and more of this.

Always, it's long, fierce, and desperate. Always, it isn't enough.

In between these interludes, we become a single force. We band together, striving to find another way to save this wild. Elixir wants me to preserve my sleep, so I maintain my human routine, slumbering at night and sneaking out when the crickets stop chirping.

Elixir sends the same boat to The Sunken Isle, so I don't have to struggle against the water's pull. Through the secret tunnel, down the waterslide, and at the landing of an uncharted channel, that's where we meet. While the river Faeries dream or bed their mates and lovers, Elixir and I journey into the remotest confines, the arteries connecting populated caves with areas less traveled.

We note shifting water levels, leakages that give Elixir pause, and the sounds of nearby currents he doesn't recognize from previous trips. In certain terrains, the foundations are crumbling, liquid spritzing through the nodules. The water bodies appear to be thinning in places and rising in others.

"The river is not merely draining," Elixir realizes. "It goes beyond that."

I watch a brook fork around us. "The waters are changing course."

It's affecting the faunas' habitats, disturbing the environment's natural order and, thus, forcing the animals to migrate. We discern this while roaming amidst the dwellers. We swim amongst sharks, sturgeons, stingrays that double in size, and reptiles that bring miniature dragons or leviathans to mind. We breaststroke through lime-colored reefs and groups of whiskered fish. Half of me is petrified, the other half is mesmerized.

Sometimes Elixir's able to communicate silently with the creatures. Other times, not. It depends on the animal. Even so, a crocodile leaves us alone, content to float in its corner, so long as we don't get too close.

Occasionally, we sit near the animals and observe them. Elixir gives me ample time to watch this world live and flourish where it still can. I laugh, and he smirks as a raft of buoyant otters slides in single formation down a liquid ramp. They waddle back to the starting point and plunge again, and again, and again.

Whenever we say farewell, Elixir kisses me until my mouth is so swollen and my hair so mussed, I feel his mark until the next day.

I've sought high and low for my necklace. Elixir has searched on his own, swimming to depths that he says I won't manage without holding my breath for hours.

It's no use. The necklace is gone.

While perched next to him, with our legs in the water, I give up. Resigning myself, I hunch forward and weep.

For a moment, Elixir doesn't move. Then he clears his throat. "May I…can I…hold you?"

I bob my head. "Yes, please."

Most of my life, I've been the one holding the people I love, bracing them from collapsing. Seldom have I reached out for the same relief, apart from when I last saw my sisters. Even then, our little huddle had been for mutual comfort.

But now, Elixir slides his arms around me and tucks my head into his chest. And he doesn't let go until I'm ready for it, which isn't for a very long time.

⟋⟍

I listen to him play the harp in The Fountain of Tears, and I think of our families, and how none of this is fair, and how both sides are good and bad.

⟋⟍

He brings me a stack of parchment and a quill, so I don't have to scratch the map on the ground beneath my bed. Along with those, he offers a copy of the Book of Fables to assist with our crusade. He also presents me with another beautiful swimming suit made of interwoven water petals and additional salve for the stingray wound, although he'd already taken care of the injury immediately after the race. Lastly, Elixir presents me with a sachet.

With an awkward thrust of his arms, the water lord extends the bulk of items and clears his throat. "I, er, thought you would like these."

Inside the sachet are round confections shimmering like limestones. "These are for me?"

Elixir grunts, about to take them back. "Fuck. Never mind. I wanted to give you...something. It was a foolish idea."

I pull back, cradling the parcel. "Wait. Aren't you going to let me try one first?"

He stalls and waits, scratching the back of his neck and looking agonized. My teeth flash at his discomfort, my smile wider than a clam's. The confections melt on my tongue, leaving a cool, refreshing residue behind that oozes to my toes. "They're delicious."

Elixir lifts his head in my direction, his shoulders rising with confidence. The reaction hits a tender spot in my chest. He doesn't know how

257

to provide things without a bargain or favor involved. Living down here all his life, I wonder if this Fae knows the difference between a present and a deal, or what constitutes as a gift.

I lean in and peck his cheek. "I love them."

His pupils flare, and he inclines his head. Then he grabs me and licks the flavor from my mouth while I chuckle.

After that, Elixir brings me wedges of something pink, green, and seeded called a melon, preserved from The Southern Seas. After that, a soothing concoction of crushed ice, sweetened with a citrus flavor. Each treat is a balm to the humidity, replacing it with a chilled sensation that makes me sigh in comfort.

Elixir stays awake when I'm dreaming, going about his hours like the rest of his kin. He tells me about it when we're together, about conserving the environment, checking on and tending to the fauna in each territory, and holding court atop a bridge in The Twisted Canals.

Ah. So that's where he reigns supreme.

Elixir talks about leading his subjects, setting an example of power and resilience to assure them they'll survive the thirteenth year. There had been the stalemate between Elixir and me during the Middle Moon Sail, in which the congregation glowered my way when their ruler and I faced them afterward. Compiled with me reclaiming my spear and then felling the crocodiles with Elixir, I'd already been pushing my luck. As a result, the Fae are hissing more and more about the need for sacrifice, how humans don't deserve to live amongst nature, how the people of Reverie Hollow are fated to pay for what they did to the Folk, and that I won't last, no matter how fortunate I've been.

To that end, they look to their ruler, expecting him to stoke that flame as he always has.

"I want to drown them when they speak of you this way," Elixir confides to me through bared teeth. "I want to peel the scales from their flesh. I want to poison them."

"But that's not all," I murmur as we lie tangled and naked together.

"You can be better than that."

Wrath isn't all he feels. I see the remorse for his treachery taking its toll, the conflicted expressions across his countenance. What he truly wants, and what we need, is an antidote to the Folk's way of thinking.

Elixir no longer snarls in agreement to his kin, nor stokes their ire with handfuls of potent, tyrannical words. He senses they're trying to convince themselves, trying to reassure themselves after the crocodile battle and my triumph at the Middle Moon Sail.

I agree, counseling him that withholding is more powerful than striking, because it plants doubt in their minds. Elixir is good at that. When this Fae isn't growling, he's attacking with deadly silence.

It's difficult not to lash out, but I advise him to go slowly. During those canal gatherings, he towers from the bridge, clenches his fists, and redirects the Faes' attention to saving the land. He raises questions about history, the river's geography, and the water levels. He nudges his audience with the possibility of an alternate means to survival—merely as a precaution. It's prudent to have a safety net, isn't it?

Coming from him, the suggestion is unexpected. Yet the Faeries don't question the need for a preventative measure because it makes sense. Anything to preserve The Solitary wild, even if it doesn't involve mortal sacrifice.

At my insistence, he cites me as another reason for this effort. No human has ever paced themselves this long to break the curse. No mortal has ever felled a predator of this land. No mortal has ever sailed at Middle Moon, nor raced, nor tied with their opponent.

After holding court with the Solitaries, Elixir retires to his den where he shatters every empty bottle and unused jar he can find. I see the evidence of his self-destruction bleeding across his knuckles, which he doesn't bother to heal. No, I do the honors by dabbing cloth on his injuries while his eyes close in pain, though not by the glass cuts.

When I first found him playing the harp, and I'd asked why he didn't stop me from exploring, Elixir had said the more I act, the more he knows about me. Back then, it was a tactic. Now it's much more than strategy.

My family says I'm unapologetically, radically, defiantly hopeful. With affection, they tease me for being determined to see the best in people.

While that hasn't always been true with Elixir, maybe it can be now, if we keep letting each other in.

I refuse to believe that people can't change, including enemies and villains. If I prescribe to that grim notion, what promise is there for a better world?

"Tidings have come from the mountain," Elixir tells me the moment he enters my chamber. "Your sister has won."

My heart bursts, and my hand shoots to my mouth. Lark is alive. She survived and won.

Elixir is sober, yet his eyes kindle at the choked sound of my joy. This is tragic news for his kin, and he doesn't know Lark, but he knows and cares about me. He nods, and I do the same, because we each need a moment alone.

When he's gone, I buckle and sob with relief.

Days ripple into weeks.

Elixir hands me a pair of his leggings for momentary safekeeping, then tells me to mount his back and strap my arms around him. "Hold your breath," he instructs, aware of how long I can manage this.

I do as he bids, and he plows underwater, surging through the billows at an unearthly speed. His muscles revolve, and his tail strokes beneath me. We plow through the secret tunnel, along the route that had led me to The Twisted Canals for Middle Moon, across the river proper, and into another passage where the shore merges with dry ground.

From there, Elixir changes into the leggings and guides me to The Drift of Swans, where graceful birds glide in a vast hall encapsulating a lake. The swans rustle their plumage, each feather capped in metallic jade.

One of them shifts, growing as big as a skiff. Elixir runs his fingers down the creature's neck and introduces it as the first river animal that was restored in place of a human sacrifice. He says this without victory or resentment, only as a fact and part of history.

The swan is captivating and regal. I wince, remorseful that a human had to perish for this creature, though the rescuer in me won't spurn the animal's existence. I need to look upon this reality, need to face it, to see both sides.

Afterward, we sit facing the lake, and I describe the things my sisters and I have done for animals, plus the things mortals have done to honor them. I list the ways in which my neighbors have contributed to the land, fitting so much life into so few years, and describe how we leave our mark in every stream nurtured and every seed planted. That's magic, too.

Elixir listens, absorbing my words. He doesn't speak, but I don't need him to say anything.

I know he hears me. I know he sees what others in his world can't see.

In The Pit of Vipers, Elixir shows me his refuge in a way he hasn't before, giving me a tour of the bottles and jars. A tea to distort one's vision, so that while bedding a lover, the drinker will envision whatever face they fantasize about, lest they don't care for their partner. An infusion that will supply one's teeth with venom, enough to last one bite against an enemy.

Elixir is mindful not to hand these mixtures over to just anyone. Ruler or not, outside of remedies, his price for dark magic or wanton pastimes is steep. Ingredients that are perilous to find. Favors that last a hundred years. His blends don't come cheaply.

I recognize the vial of white grains Puck had selected while I'd spied on The Three. Plucking the container from the table, I quip, "And salt for garnish?"

But I remember Elixir saying it's not salt. And Elixir doesn't compress his lips as he usually does to hide a grin. Instead, he grimaces and takes the vial from my hand, balancing it precariously between his fingercaps. "It is the hydrated essence of sea air—a dragon of The Southern Seas owed me a favor. Pour this into any pool, however vast, and it shall salt the water. It is highly effective and helpful if an ocean dweller needs it."

His expression doesn't look like he finds the ingredient helpful. He regards it like melted iron, capable of blistering him to the bone. Carefully, Elixir sets the vial on the shelf, far away from the others.

The next time I'm there, I visit with the snakes and then find Elixir hunched beside his brewing vat. From the depression rises a tangy scent. "What is that?"

He doesn't look up but swishes a capped finger through the milky fluid. "I thought it would regulate the currents and cure them from withering, but…" He hisses and slaps the water. "It is not fucking working!"

Up until an hour ago, while I'd kept the vipers company, Elixir had seemed eager. I think he'd had this mixture planned, hoping it would work, so he could present it to me.

I swallow and comb through his scalp. "Elixir? Are you sleeping as much as I am?"

"I do not need sleep."

"But it's nice." When a mirthful scoff escapes my dark Fae, I hunker behind him, hug his waist, and set my cheek on his spine. "Sleep in my chamber with me."

28

Although we've kept our bond a secret, thanks to The Sunken Isle's tunnel—which I've learned connects to every other territory in The Deep—it's best for us to arrive separately. I take the boat, and when I reach the bank, Elixir manifests there, his hand already extended.

I smile. For someone so menacing, he can be the most attentive villain.

Disembarking, I barely have time to draw breath. Elixir grabs me, and we stumble across the isle, our heads pressed so tightly together, it's going to leave an imprint. Without turning away from me, Elixir lashes out and blows the door open.

By the time we make it into my chamber, our mouths are locked. Elixir kicks the door shut behind us, never breaking the kiss.

But I do. Prying my lips from his, I pant, "Lotus."

Elixir groans. With a laugh, I wiggle out of his embrace and find my companion gliding across the floor. Before I have a chance to cradle him off the ground, Elixir gets there first. He hunches and communicates something to the snake, and Lotus slides onto his crooked arm, after which Elixir brings him outside, where my friend will be free to roam among the damp grass and slink into the water if he likes.

I'd started allowing this once Elixir had assured me the water won't pull Lotus down. Mortal or not, Lotus is a fauna of the river. Therefore, he's immune to the lake's pressure. Apparently, that's how he'd managed to reach me here in the first place.

Elixir seizes my hips and claims my mouth. He walks me backward to the bed, and I drag him as well, both of us working in tandem. Our mouths unseal, open lips grazing, hot and hectic puffs blasting between us. I tug on the waistband of his pants, a loose material versus the customary leggings.

Our fingers drift absently, then intentionally. Fingers dive into hair and pull, eliciting pleasure and pain. His robe hits the ground, then my dress when he yanks it over my head.

The backs of my knees bump into the mattress, where we halt in the lantern light. The central tub bubbles with heat. Black, blue, and green shadows splay across the room, shafts of lightness and darkness running across the contours of our bodies. I'm naked, and the pants slump low over Elixir's olive skin.

His eyes grow hooded. "I'm going to fuck you so deeply in this bed."

My core throbs, but I shake my head while clinging to his shoulders. "No," I whisper. "You're going to make love to me."

Elixir jolts in my arms, a confused expression slackening his features. "Is that your wish?" When I nod, he looks spooked, out of his element. "I do not...I do not know how."

My palms glide to his cheeks. I'm careful to pace myself, the tender contact causing him to flinch. He can't trust it, doesn't understand it. With aching slowness, I frame his harsh face and wait for him to relax. "Neither do I. We'll show each other. All right?"

At my touch, he wavers. His eyes clench shut. "I might fail you."

My heart cracks into pieces. "You won't."

Nervous excitement eclipses lust. We've never done this—made love without a modicum of tension or frenzy. I want this to be different, as quiet as his nature, as gentle as mine. I want us deep and languid and patient.

Finally, Elixir twists his head to kiss my fingers. "Yes."

Yes. That's my harsh, complex, secretive, beautiful, vulnerable villain.

And then we're sinking onto the bed, our hands wandering, sketching each other. He bites my nipple gently. I lick the peak of his ear. His tongue runs across the inside of my thigh. My teeth skate over his abdomen.

My heels push down his pants, and his waist nestles between my spread thighs, the width and weight of him a harbor, a safe place.

Words pour from us. Here and here and here. Like this. Yes. That. Does this please you? Does it feel good? Slower. Yes, slower. Much slower.

As his cock nocks against my entrance, I brush the hair from his face. The gesture nudges a soft growl of surrender from him. My body kindles, flames licking my skin. "Do this with me," I coax, whispering the invitation against his mouth. "Make us come until we fall asleep."

The plea wracks Elixir's frame. "That, I shall."

I grasp his waist, directing the tempo as his hips swing forward, the swollen head of his cock plying into me. Slow, then slower. Deep, then deeper. We drag it out until he seats himself fully, his firm length slipping inside.

And then we're moving. His palms flank my cheeks as he rolls his hips, the pace leisurely and excruciatingly new. I grip his buttocks and rotate my waist, my core meeting his cock in long strokes that make me dizzy with want.

I whimper, he groans, and we gyrate in sync. Soon, we're panting in astonishment and releasing heavy drafts of air. My ankles link across his ass. Elixir sprawls me beneath him, his waist undulating between my hitched thighs. He hisses in my ear and nips at the delicate flesh. I shiver and take the brunt of his cock, taking it dark and deep.

His eyes seek me out, yearning for a place to land. That's when I see more than lust or desire, more than friendship and fondness. I see trust mingling with passion. I see affection, protectiveness, and a seed of something more, something scary and forbidden and defiant. What I see is unconditional, and I feed it back to him, using my moans and movements and lips to convey the emotion.

I show him what he can't see.

A strangled sound wrestles from Elixir's throat, encouraging him to burrow his body farther, the fluid slide of his cock stealing my breath. "I would keep us here," he husks, then kisses me. "Always like this."

"Elixir," I plead, rocking with him.

"Cove," he utters against my mouth. "I don't want it to end."

That's it. That's why he hasn't asked about me breaking the curse. That's why he hasn't broached the subject.

Maybe that's why I haven't plotted more ways to unravel him, because I'm no longer sure I want to, because I scarcely need to, because it's happening on its own, without duplicity. And because the more we're together, the less I know where our games end and the truth begins.

All I know is right here, right now, in this bed, away from everyone. Our reality is the place where we're joined, where we pulse together like a heartbeat.

This is what it's like to fuck sweetly. This is lovemaking. This is real.

We beat our hips languidly, yet it remains as intense as the other times with him. Everything has changed. It's nothing like I once imagined, fantasized, or dreamed of. But it's everything I want because I'm his light, and he's my darkness, and I want us crying out in unison, and I want us to confide everything, and I want us to fall asleep here, and wake up here, and fight as allies once we leave here.

Perspiration beads across our flesh, and our bodies quaver. My spine curls, my breasts lurch into his chest, and my limbs hook onto Elixir. He grinds his waist, his cock striking me to the wet core until we're a passionate mess, until my eyes lock with his.

The climax fractures through us. A convulsion spreads from the spot where we're linked, and shouts fall from our mouths, the noises filling the chamber.

Elixir roars but keeps thrusting, riding out the orgasm. He heaves over me, sucking on my lips and muttering, "I'm sorry. Forgive me. Please. Please, forgive me."

My throat swells. I've wanted him to say this, and I deserve it, and I want to purge myself in kind. I want to tell him I know about the curse, that I know what I did, though I hadn't been aware at the time, and I didn't mean it.

I don't want it to end
Make your choice.
I will drown you.

But Elixir didn't drown me that night. He never even tried.

I did.

"I'm sorry, too," I choke out while my hips undulate with his. "I'm so sorry."

Just like that, Elixir's tempo ebbs, slows, and ceases. As his hair falls in a curtain around us, alertness brightens those irises. His ears slant, detecting something in my voice. It's not affection, therefore it's not inaccessible to him.

No, Elixir hears what I hear: guilt.

That, and hurt. That, and a tinge of anger.

The emotions collide in me—guilt over a curse, along with pain and anger that he hadn't told me about it himself. After what we've been through together, he still never told me. I'd had to find out on my own.

We were supposed to make love and then dream. That's all. We were supposed to fall asleep like lovers do.

Instead, awareness unspools across Elixir's features. "How long have you known?"

29

The question suspends between us like a held breath. Shadows and flames glaze our naked bodies in washes of spectral blue and chimeric green, illuminating the beads of sweat covering us. We lie tangled together. My legs are snatched around his waist, and his cock is still lodged inside me, his hardness coated in my wetness. I want us to stay this way—joined, united, one—but I have a terrible premonition.

How long have I known? Far too long.

"Since our first time," I confess. "At the lily pond. That is, I realized it later, after I left you sleeping there. What we did…it jogged my memory of a Fable."

His eyebrows slam together. *"When a Snake Bewitches a Viper."*

I nod. "That one."

Abruptly, Elixir's cock slips from my body, and he lurches upright on the bed. He twists away and then whirls back. "Why did you not tell me?"

I vault to a sitting position beside him. "Why didn't you tell *me*?"

"And give you that power from the onset. Give you that advantage in the beginning." Elixir listens as I shift the blanket and use a corner to shield my breasts. His jaw clenches. "Why are you covering yourself? I have already touched and tasted them."

He's not being crude, only honest. And befuddled and irate.

And something else. Something frail.

Truly, I don't know why I've covered myself. It was instinctual. Suddenly, it's clear that's what upsets him.

"How long have *you* known it was me?" I ask.

His expression cinches as he glances toward my hands. "To answer that, I must tell you the history first."

So, he does. It's a history that isn't found in the Book of Fables.

I scoot closer as Elixir brushes his fingers against mine. "Long ago, there lived two ancient Solitaries—a female of the seelie court, another of the unseelie court," he narrates. "Both were the last of their kind, Fae witches who deserted their homes in favor of the Solitary wild, where they could practice their magic freely without the intervention or manipulation of political intrigue. They were the first of their kind to inhabit the landscape amongst the fauna. After that, more Faeries came to the mountain, forest, and river, and then more were born here…"

By the time three mortal scribes began traveling the environment and collecting research for the Book of Fables, the Solitary wild was thriving and populated. The two original pioneers of this world maintained differing opinions about this: The seelie witch supported the scribes' endeavor, but the unseelie one didn't. The latter feared it would inevitably condemn Faeries if humans were to learn about their culture. She sensed this wasn't just about educating humans but empowering them, protecting them.

However, the rest of her kin either hadn't taken the book seriously or translated it as a tool to appear even more frightening to mortals. Regardless of the guidelines and morals for survival, Faeries have always been too self-assured in their power and imperviousness. They take this privilege for granted, scarcely believing mortals wise enough to outwit or outlast the Folk.

Besides, there was only so much they'd permit the scribes to learn. Because of that and several convenient bargains, the scribes had been tolerated by the Solitaries and received a guarantee of protection from the seelie witch.

"Enraged by this, the unseelie female had lashed out in the only way she knew how: vengeance," Elixir continues, the word trapped between his teeth, as if he understands its flavor.

The unseelie witch had placed a curse on Reverie Hollow, a newly established village outside The Faerie Triad. She performed a spell on the town's first and only water source—the ancient water well, where I first laid eyes on Elixir.

In storybooks, wells grant wishes. But this one forged curses.

Should any humans make contact with this well, they would have the power to curse the next individual with whom they interacted. That's how it had linked me and Elixir. I'd pressed my hand to the glass that night, and then he'd responded by ramming his fist into the partition.

Such vile enchantment. This unseelie spell not only deterred mortals from using the necessary well, but it was also a means to incite disorder and sabotage progress, a weapon to disarm humanity despite the Fables. This, because the superior Fae witch foresaw destruction within the scribes' book.

Elixir expels a coarse breath. "You see, the unseelie witch was my ancestor."

At first, I assume he's speaking figuratively, the same way he calls Cerulean and Puck his brothers. But no, Elixir's being literal.

"I'm an offshoot of a line on my mother Lorelei's side," he sneers. "Ironic and a gross oversight, how my ancestor had not foreseen a human cursing another Fae, much less one of her descendants. To combat this, her seelie opponent had placed a counter spell on the well: To break a curse, the bewitcher must see, feel, and enact the opposite of old truths and past deeds. Naturally, the seelie witch did not tell her nemesis about this. Instead, she had the scribes tuck the breadcrumbs into a Fable entitled *When a Snake Bewitches a Viper*. That is where it has been cemented ever since."

It takes a while for his attention to stray from our hands to the vicinity of my face. "I knew you were my downfall from the beginning. It happened that night, in the stream with you. One moment, we were combatting underwater. The next, I could not see your face. When I returned home, I knew the well had given you the magic to curse me.

"To that end, I did not tell you what the curse-breaking entailed for the same reason I did not tell you *who* cursed me. For this game, that would have given you leverage, a greater chance of winning. As for the Fable, I trusted you would not know or remember the tale, among the hundreds that exist."

Considering the water well's age, few of my neighbors recall the particulars of its curse. Over generations, it's been reduced to variations and hybrids. The villagers of Reverie Hollow have always said the well was damned, but none could say exactly how.

Presumably, the former players of Elixir's game hadn't made the connection, either. Otherwise, those mortal sacrifices would have questioned when they'd had the chance to curse him, since only the bewitcher can break the spell.

I can't decide what staggers me more. The ancient tale, the length of Elixir's monologue, or the details of his confession. "Do your kin know?"

"All the Solitaries are aware I was cursed," Elixir says. "But none know it was you."

I can fathom why he'd withheld this in the beginning. A while back, I had theorized as much. Learning what I'd done could have been a vital clue to breaking the curse, a situation he wouldn't have wanted.

"I understand why you clammed up at first. But that was then," I say, my heart stuck in my mouth. "What about now?"

Elixir opens his mouth, then shoots off the bed and turns.

I rise to stand behind him, refusing to be denied. "You bastard." Rancor sizzles across my tongue. "It's been nearly a month since the Middle Moon Sail, and after all this time, after all that's happened between us, you still never said a word. Whether or not the information would help me, there was always the possibility of an advantage. You willingly denied me that!"

His shoulders pinch, as if the words have stabbed him. Here we are, unclothed, stripped bare, and separated by inches while the bath hurls steam into the air. We could have slept, like a normal couple. We could have woken and made love again, like a normal couple. We could have eaten together and bathed, like a normal couple.

But we'll never be that.

A human and a Fae are never normal, much less possible. Long ago, we'd crossed those enemy lines. It's too late to undo everything, and if I had that chance...I wouldn't want to.

I wouldn't undo this, even while a single question terrifies me, even while I don't believe he'd ever give the wrong answer. Despite that, I have to ask, to purge the question from me before it expands like a blister.

My voice fractures. "Do you want me to die?"

Elixir vaults around and clasps my face. "Never!" he swears. "For you, I would sunder The Deep. I may not have told you what I knew, but I never wanted to lose you. I have sought to protect you, to keep you safe while ruminating on how to fix the game, how to free you." He flinches with uncertainty. "And you? Do you want my kin to die?"

"Never," I croak, framing his cheeks. "I've never wished for anyone to die."

Again, he winces, because we both know that's untrue. As a child, I had wanted him to die, and I'd tried making it happen.

"We're at an impasse," he reminds me. "That is why we're seeking a way out of this. Has our mission changed?"

It hasn't. I haven't given up, and his tone avows that neither will he. Elixir will stay by my side, band with me.

All the same, my mouth feels heavy, weighed down by stones. "Did you know what seeing, feeling, and enacting the opposite meant? Did you know that, too?"

"I did not." His voice turns acidic. "Yet I have ideas about the first two now. From the sound of you, they're feats impossible to achieve."

"What does that mean?" When Elixir doesn't reply, I push him away. "If you care for me, you could have told me of your own volition."

"You found out for yourself."

"Yes, I did! But I wanted you to tell me, too. We have enough between us as it is. I wanted us to be open and honest with each other." This is moot, yet I can't stop myself. "Would you have gone on keeping this to yourself?"

His silence reveals plenty, cutting to the quick.

My stomach hitches. "Why?"

His eyes close, then whip open, emitting a flood of gold. "You tried to kill me."

I step back, the truth burrowing deeply, opening me like a gash. His irises swirl with residual fury, hurt, and…fear. The feelings igniting between us are so out of his realm, so foreign that he doesn't trust them.

He doesn't trust me. Because nine years ago, I attempted to drown him. Nine years, which is no time for an immortal Fae, to say nothing of the scant time we've spent together in The Deep. This isn't even considering what's happened to my beloved sisters, that he conspired with his brothers to imprison them.

That's it. By force of will, he was guarding himself, lest I endeavored to defeat him despite what we've shared, despite our crusade to find a way around the game. Elixir did this because he can't bring himself to completely believe in my change of heart.

Why would he trust my affections when he's never experienced them with another? When they're so new and fragile?

"What did you see in that stream?" Elixir mumbles. "When you looked at me, what did you see? Do not think. Say it."

"Evil," I admit, and it falls from my lips effortlessly.

"What did you feel?"

"Hatred."

Elixir's chest caves, as though I've flung the answers at him. He waits for me to make the necessary connections. The bewitcher must see, feel, and enact the opposite of old truths and past deeds.

That night, I had seen evil and felt hatred.

To see the opposite is to see goodness.

To feel the opposite is to feel love.

Yet I have ideas about the first two now. From the sound of you, they're feats impossible to achieve.

My chin wobbles. "Elixir."

"Tell me, Cove," he mumbles. "Am I a monster?"

I open my mouth, but nothing comes out. He's done vile things to my people, and if we don't find another way, he'll continue to do them after my game. I'm his exception, but that doesn't make it right.

By no means is this an epiphany for me. Nevertheless, it's there.

This Fae ruler doesn't care if the world deems him a monster. But he does care how I see him.

He would tear my world apart for his kin. But he would make sure I'm the only mortal left standing.

He won't protect my world. But he will protect me.

Is that enough? Does this absolve him?

I've taken too long to respond, too long to decide, to make my choice. His outline stretches across the ground, the shadow catching my attention like a net since it's easier than looking at him. It's easier to watch that silhouette reinforce itself, steel itself. It's easier to watch that figure storm away. It's easier to hear him wrench on the doorknob, throw open the door, and slam it shut. It's easier to hear the water splash as he dives in. It's easier to hear him rage than to see him in pain.

It's easier to let him walk away.

Several seconds pass before I muster the will to glance at his discarded clothes. Only now do I recall his initial response. He'd wondered the same thing: If I'd known, why hadn't *I* said something?

Because I had hoped he would speak up first, hoped I wouldn't have to announce it myself. I'd wanted him to trust me that much.

I scoop the pants and robe off the ground, and press the garments to my nose, inhaling the scent of bergamot and black pepper. My face burns, and my heart burns, and everything burns. I never knew it could be this beautiful, nor this imperfect. It's how I feel for Papa, Lark, and Juniper— for our home, our sanctuary, and our animals.

Only it's different, the emotion. It's his mouth on mine, his body inside mine, his shouts to my whispers, his rage to my calm.

He sees what others can't, but no one sees him. No one but me.

He's a monster, but that's not all. He's evil, but that's not all.

I felt hatred once, but not anymore. Now I feel…

The clothes fall from my hands. "Elixir," I say, then sprint out the door, because it's only been seconds, and maybe I can catch him before he reaches the hidden tunnel. I spill into the isle grounds and dash across the grass. "Elixir!" I call into the void.

But he's gone.

I stall in place, then buckle onto the ground and dump my face in my hands. My bones shake, but my eyes remain blessedly dry.

A slender cord glides over my foot. I blink at Lotus, who nestles against my calf and lets me stroke his head.

We stay there for what must be hours. Me, still naked and keeping company with a viper of my world. Never have I looked more like I belong in this realm, though I never will, and I never should. Eventually the crickets chirp, toads belch with unsavory noise, and somewhere beyond, the Fae awaken.

I offer my arm for Lotus to coil around. As I move to stand, a flash of white ripples across the lake. A closer look brings the object into stark relief—a paper boat sails across the surface toward me, the tiny makeshift vessel perfectly folded and perfectly dry.

That's impossible. Though, didn't Juniper once drill into me and Lark a Fable about the Solitary waters? How they always convey messages in whichever way they're sent?

The boat cruises in my direction. Sometimes, my sisters and I would enjoy paper boat races in the creek. The loser had to buy the other two trinkets from the star peddler's coach.

I tilt my head. The boat's shape, and the way it's assembled into neat corners, reminds me of only one person.

My pulse beats a wild tempo. On a gasp, I reach out and snatch the boat from the current, my hands trembling as I unfold the paper to reveal the tidy handwriting, achingly familiar to me.

"Juniper," I whisper. "Lotus, it's from Juniper."

And from Lark. Beneath the missive, their combined signatures loop across the vellum. My palm shoots to my mouth, tears pricking behind my eyelids. This must mean Juniper won her game, too. They're alive, they're together, and they've sent me a message.

My free hand settles on my chest. I'm shaking so terribly, it's hard to read the note at first.

Two victorious, one left to triumph. The wind is a force, the tree rises high, and the water runs forever—just like us.

We're closer than you know. We have faith in you. We love you.

The letter ends with the mantra we'd spoken on our last night in the caravan.

Whatever happens to one of us, happens to each of us.

Together. All or nothing.

"All or nothing," I repeat, the paper crumbling in my grip. I rock forward and backward, in gratitude and grief, while Lotus keeps me anchored. I want my sisters back, and I want Elixir back, but I can't have them both. No matter what, I'll never be able to have them both.

Make your choice.

I take those choices to bed, unable to weather them for a moment longer. At some point, I awaken to darkness etched in lantern lights and a tall form in the doorway. I lunge from the mattress while swaddling myself in the blanket, not because I don't want Elixir to see me naked, but because I need something else to hold, otherwise I'll grab him.

He lingers on the threshold and grips the frame, his expression wrung out like a towel. "I should have let you sleep."

"No," I blurt out. "Please, don't go."

Don't go. I can't let you walk away because I need, and I want, and I'll miss, and I can't, but I must, and I hate, yet I care, and I see, and I feel, and I feel, and I feel.

He stalks forward, stopping within arm's reach. His loose shirt and leggings are dry, which means he manifested here, but an unlikely fragrance wafts off him. It's the aroma of pine and bark, mixed with the river, though no trees grow down here.

He clears his throat and levels his gaze off to the side. "You have missed this," he murmurs, then extends his upturned palm.

Sitting in his hand is a necklace, its pendant glistening like a tear. "How did you..." I accept the dainty chain and drape it over my head, letting it fall down my back. "Where..."

"In The Solitary Forest," Elixir confides. "I met your sister."

"Juniper?" I move forward, but he jolts backward. "I don't understand."

Brevity is Elixir's first language. In short bursts, he confesses that he'd meant to swim in isolation after our quarrel. His journey took him to the woodland streams, where he sensed the presence of a human. Still festering from the words we'd spoken, he didn't rationalize it could be one of my sisters.

"I attacked her," Elixir says.

"You what?!" I shout, ready to bury my fist in his face.

"She is unharmed. I'm sorry, I did not know it was her. I heard your necklace resting in the grass beside a creek—it must have washed up there, but a small portion of the chain was still touching the water. I detected someone nearby, just as they grabbed the necklace. I was livid and could not...I'm sorry." He expels a guilty breath. "I dragged the figure under with me. But then I felt a leaf bracelet strung around her arm, as you described it once, and realized it was your sister."

I gather the blanket tighter around me as he explains the rest, that he released her just as Puck arrived and threatened him, that Juniper and Puck are lovers, that Juniper won her game, and now she's reunited with Lark, who's mated to Cerulean.

Lark and Cerulean are mates. Juniper and Puck have bonded with each other.

My sisters and their enemies have fallen in love.

While I struggle to wrap my mind around the shock of this, Elixir collects the clothing he'd left behind earlier. Then he makes for the door. With his hands clenching the knob, Elixir's head slants, and his profile speaks to the ground. "Sleep well, Cove."

"Good night, Elixir," I whisper.

And then he's gone once more. And I'm still here.

I could have asked him to stay, and he would have. I could have told him to fall asleep with me as we'd planned before, and he would have. Yet there's a difference between what my sisters have and what I have.

By whatever twist of fate, Lark and Cerulean are magically united and able to share an extended life together.

In a miraculous change of heart, Juniper and Puck have pledged themselves to one another, a union made possible because she took half of his immortality. Because the satyr had willingly confided his true name to Juniper, she was granted this power, according to Elixir.

Both pairs will endure. Elixir and I won't.

We have a dark history, and Elixir doesn't believe my affection overrides how I ultimately see him, and we have a curse wedged between us.

Also, there's this: *Henceforth, no other magic drew them together, nor apart. For once magic has touched two beings, no other enchantments may prevail.*

That means once a curse links two souls, that's the only magical bond they'll ever share. We won't have the chance to become mates through a mystical force, nor to share his immortality. It will never last between us, which means we have two options: delay the hurt until later or end it now.

I'd wanted to tell Elixir about the paper boat, but it's between my sisters and me. Based on the timing of things, Lark and Juniper must have sent it sometime before Elixir had encountered Juniper. Other than that, one thing is certain: Both couples want me to survive, and if they can help, they will. My sisters would accept nothing less.

I sniffle, then collect the paper boat from under my pillow, along with the quill Elixir had given me to draw the map. Quickly, I scribble on the boat's reverse side, fold it into a less refined version of Juniper's vessel, and pad outside. Kneeling, I set the boat free and watch it embark toward the hidden tunnel, back the way it must have come.

Somehow, the river had delivered my sisters' tidings. Somehow, it will convey my reply, my hopes, my secrets, and my heart. Somehow, it will keep those treasures safe before I lose them all.

A week passes in which Elixir and I continue our sojourns into the caves. We rarely speak except to swap observations about the terrain, potential clues to this world's survival, and places where the river levels are either draining or rising. When I catch him tilting his gaze my way, he evades my eyes. When he catches me doing the same, I duck my head.

My fingers itch to touch him. And I notice every time his knuckles curl inches from my body.

On the seventh night, I lay sleepless in bed with my flesh aching and the space beside me empty. That's when the door rattles. Clad in my nightgown, I leap upright and tuck layers of loose teal hair behind my ears while my pulse does a mad sprint.

Then I think twice. It can't be him. It can't be Elixir coming to see me, unable to resist, wanting me, needing me.

It can't be him because he knows the door isn't locked. Whoever is on the other side hasn't tested the knob yet; the rattle isn't from trying to open the door. To the contrary, it's from someone placing an ear against the partition.

There's a second thump, followed by a muffled curse, then a muffled lecture. Feminine voices. One is vexed, the other brusque.

I'm fluent in those voices arguing over each other, one snapping, "My damn way" and the other clipping, "The correct way." I know that reckless rattle and practical thump against the entrance. I recognize the overlapping count of "One…two…"

I'm vaulting out of the bed, snatching the knob, and whipping open the door as they reach "Three!" As the partition swings into the room, two females tumble like burlap sacks onto the floor, the busty one landing beneath the petite one, glossy layers of white hair tangling with spruce green.

I chirp, scuttling backward to make room as my sisters land in a heap at my bare toes.

30

They puddle on the floor like a pair of starfish, their legs sprawled akimbo as they grunt and smack each other across the shoulders.

One sister snaps under her breath, "I told you, on *three*."

The other scoffs, "I heard you, dammit. It wasn't me who—"

"Lark?" I whisper. "Juniper?"

The names drift from my lips, a rippling tendril of sound. Their bickering ceases, as though clipped by shears. My sisters go still, then their heads whip upward, and the beloved sight threatens to buckle my knees. Our breaths fill the room, louder than the bubbling tub or the subtle licks of water resonating from outside.

I must be dreaming. This is a chimerical vision, a figment of my imaginings. If I touch them, they'll disappear in puffs of smoke, or I'll fail to reach them no matter how close I get, as if they're a mirage or a glamoured mind trick.

They can't be real, yet they are. They can't be here, yet they are.

The proof of it wafts off their clothes—the fragrances of rainfall and chopped wood. The trueness of it swirls in their wide eyes, the irises I know so well—the gray of a morning tempest and the green of a resilient tree. The realness of it resounds in this space, in Lark's feisty tone and Juniper's smoky voice as they gasp, "Cove."

Lark. Juniper. Cove.

That's us. That's our family.

My heart bursts. We gawk, suspended and shocked. And then I'm flinging myself to the ground just as they're scrambling to their feet. We collide in a fit of limbs, tumbling back to the floor. The exclamations surge and flow together, our tremulous voices inundating the room with "You're here" and "You're alive" and "You're safe" and "Lemme look at you" and "We came for you" and "I've missed you so much!"

Lark whips her arms around both of us, crushing us to her while she plants kisses all over my face. I cradle Juniper's jaw as she checks me for injuries and bruises, her fingers hunting for signs of the enemy. Our movements shift from one reflex to the next. We're hugging, then pulling back to gaze, then clasping hands to make sure none of us will disappear, then hugging again.

Saltwater leaks down our cheeks, our forms shake with elation and astonishment, and we start laughing. Cries of worry and relief segue into teary mirth. In the lantern light, we nestle close to form a knot like we used to in our caravan, our sacred place where stories had been safe, and nothing could break us apart.

When the tremors subside, we wipe the tears from one another's faces, content to just look at one another. Until this moment, none of us had known if we ever would again.

"Lark. Juniper," I choke out, weaving my sisters' fingers together. "You won."

"We did," Juniper says, her voice cracking.

"She's being modest as hell," Lark adds, sliding a lock of teal behind my ear. "We kicked Faerie's ass."

We chortle through our sniffling. As we do, I notice the weapons they'd been carrying. Lark's whip and Juniper's archery, sans the iron tips of her crossbow bolts, lay scattered like detritus across the room. They must have clattered to the ground during the fall.

"Make no mistake, you'll win too," Lark professes. "We're here for you. Let any Fae try to get rid of us, and they'll see what's what."

"We can't help you win," Juniper amends. "But we're not leaving without you."

My spirits lift. "Then you've already given me everything I need."

Juniper is the first to rise and help us to our feet. To my surprise, they're wearing the appropriate garb, down to the sandals. The latter is a far cry from our matching scuffed leather boots.

Lark dons a strappy yet loose frock that trails to her upper thighs, the gauzy material suitable for the humidity. Juniper wears an airy, oversized tunic that ends several inches above her ankles, which she's tied with a matching fabric belt. Someone must have advised them on how to dress for The Deep's climate.

We collect the weapons and set them in a corner. I lead them to the bed, where we huddle atop the mattress. My sisters fight over who gets to speak first. According to their overlapping words, they had assumed stealing into my chamber would be the first task, that maybe the dwelling was bigger than it had looked from the outside, and they'd need to hunt for me, or that I'd be sleeping as deeply as I usually do. Either way, they hadn't anticipated encountering me so quickly.

In the midst of that explanation, my sisters falter in surprise as a brown-marbled reptile with familiar yellow irises weaves from under a pillow and twines himself on my lap.

"What the hell?" Lark exclaims with a grin. "Is that runt who I think it is?"

"From the sanctuary," Juniper marvels. "The pond snake."

"He followed me here." I beam, petting him. "His name is Lotus."

They coo over my companion, taking pleasure in a reunion with one of our sanctuary rescues while I recount the details of discovering him in my room shortly after I'd arrived.

Juniper appraises the chamber, doubtlessly searching for reference points or extra clues about my wellbeing. She frowns at the bath, the wardrobe, the nightgown I'm wearing, the water pitcher and drinking glass, the parchment and quill, the satchel filled with morsels Elixir had gifted me, and the comfortable bedding. Her studious eyebrows crinkle, then she slaps her palms on her thighs and temporarily dismisses whatever hypothesis she's drawn.

"First order of business," she begins. "Are you all right?"

"I'm well," I assure them. "I'm unharmed."

"Mentally? Physically?"

"Both."

"I have a whip that's ready to do damage on a certain viperous ruler, so you'd better not be saying that just to alleviate us, hon," Lark demands.

Juniper gives me a stern look. "The Great Camping Incident of the year 15—"

I cross my arms. "I can't believe you're bringing that up."

With her memory jogged, Lark snaps her fingers. "Shit, that's right. I'd forgotten."

Unfortunately, Juniper hadn't. Her lips purse into a dried fig of disapproval. "We're hiking for half a day, having a pleasant time, and through the whole thing Cove fails to tell us that she's been bitten by an insect the size of a walnut and that her leg is covered in red welts from the venom."

"You were both having such fun. I didn't want to worry you and ruin the trip," I defend.

"Exactly! Cove—"

"I promise, I'm fine."

After a wary moment, Lark and Juniper slump, and Juniper gives a quick nod. "Good. Second: We…" She swaps delicate glances with Lark, then clears her throat and admits, "We have something to tell you."

Her practical demeanor doesn't fool me. At their guilty expressions, I pat their hands to console them. "Tidings reached me from the mountain and forest. I know what you'll say."

Now it's their turn to flush, rueful and afraid I'll despise them for bonding with our enemies. What they don't know is that I'm no less susceptible. To that end, I wiggle nearer and gentle my voice. "Peace, my family. I could never hate either of you. Now tell me about them."

Solace washes away the dregs of their remorse, and their smiles illuminate the chamber. Suddenly, we return to that caravan, where our innermost secrets and uncensored dreams had been protected. While Lotus makes himself at home in the center of our huddle, my sisters launch into their tales and share what happened to them in the mountain and forest—their games, their histories with the rulers of the sky and woodland, and their bonds with Cerulean and Puck.

What they feel for these males is genuine, and those emotions are reciprocated because my sisters wouldn't have it any other way, because they know what they're worth. I hear it in the soft but sturdy textures of their voices, tender as a breeze yet lasting as an oak tree. I see it in the unconditional blazes of their eyes and the lifts of their shoulders.

Despite Lark's saucy descriptions of her mate Cerulean, her words are airborne as if she's free falling yet certain someone will be there to catch her.

Despite Juniper's ramrod posture and levelheaded narration about Puck and his roguish ways, a grin cuts through her perpetual frown.

They love their males, and they're loved in return.

That's all I've ever wanted for them. Far be it from me to question their judgment, nor to mistrust it. I never have before, and I never will. That isn't to say I won't protect them.

My chest twists. Not only do I envy their good fortune, the luxury of being with the partners they adore, but I'm gladdened for them. It's strange to feel sorrow and joy at the same time.

My sisters appear the same yet different, each wearing a few scars courtesy of Faerie, scars visible above and below the surface. But their eyes are brighter, happier than I could have imagined, and topped to the brim with new memories.

Juniper, especially. There's an effervescence in her pupils that I've never beheld, and her pert features are more relaxed, her skin peachier than usual. She's always had an earthy appearance to her, an organic beauty despite people calling her plain and prickly, but now...

"You're glowing," I muse to her.

I can't tell what it's from, but it feels unique to Juniper, elemental as though she's become connected to the earth and its soil and all that grows there. Or as if she's carrying the life force of a woodland from within. She would accuse me of being silly and poetic, but this newfound radiance suits her.

It must stem from her lover's touch. Nevertheless, she blinks, clearly having no inkling of the source and unaccustomed to being the recipient of such an observation. "Well." She analyzes the compliment like it's the moral to a Fable. "Well, that would make sense."

It would, after falling in love and losing one's maidenhead to a satyr. However, it's less about her complexion suffusing with crimson and more about the vividness of her irises. Were they always this verdant green?

Now that I mention it, Lark takes a second look as well, her eyebrows vaulting skyward in contemplation. "Cove's right. Told you, didn't I?

You've been Pucked," she singsongs.

Juniper has never liked being the center of attention, so she insists we move on to industrious matters, and I smile wider. How I've missed them.

She and Lark had planned to see Papa Thorne, if only briefly, while I continued my game. Instead, their paper boat had returned to them, the vessel including my response to their own message, plus a copy of the map I'd drawn of The Deep.

"We belatedly recovered the boat," Lark says, elbowing Juniper in the ribs. "Miss know-it-all found it nearly a week after it had washed ashore in The Gang of Elks."

"The what?" I ask.

Juniper turns up her righteous chin as she cuffs Lark's shoulder. "I was indisposed."

"She was—" Lark cups her mouth and leans in, "—fucking."

"Well." Juniper scowls, then smooths out her tunic. "Fine. If you must know, Puck and I spent a handful of days in solitude cohabiting and solidifying our relationship. And yes, that included sex. Puck's a satyr and very...knowledgeable, skilled, and um, inventive. He has an exuberant degree of stamina."

"Reckon that's one way of putting it," Lark teases. "Our Faeries have energy in spades."

Although I can attest to that as well, I maintain discretion and try not to turn beet red.

Juniper continues, "So I was a bit tardy in realizing that if you responded, the boat would end up where it originally was sent from. Furthermore, I resent being singled out when you're one to talk," she accuses Lark. "You once said Cerulean's private about consummation, yet the second he gave you permission to get chatty, you hit the ground running. Since then, how many times have you subjected me to a dissertation about his prowess in bed?"

Lark's sigh is almost a moan. "He does this thing with his hip, and it makes the angle of his cock—"

I set my palms over the sides of Lotus's head, as if he has external ears. "In this, you haven't changed."

My sister flips a pile of long, white hair over her shoulder and winks.

"Why, thank you."

"To the matter at hand." Juniper gestures around the chamber. "So, this is where he's been keeping you."

"Not what we expected from a serpentine prick," Lark concedes, jutting her chin to the bath. "It's still a cage, though I had visions of dungeons, shackles, fishbones, and piss puddles."

"Many things regarding Elixir aren't what you'd expect," I murmur.

Hearing the slant in my tone, they swing their heads toward me.

"Elixir, eh?" Lark inquires. "First-name terms with the asshole?"

I twiddle my thumbs. "First-name terms are inconsequential in Faerie, as you're well aware. It's their real names that are sacred, and anyway, I have to call my captor something. He goes by Lord of the Water Fae and River Ruler, too, but that's hardly practical. It's a mouthful, really. The point is, it's just a title. I can't simply call him, 'Hey, you.' That would be impolite, not to mention tedious."

My sisters stare at me. Indeed, my cheeks are roasting, my lisp had thickened, and I'm babbling. Three, two, one—

"Uh-ohhh," Lark chirps.

"What does *uh-ohhh*, mean?" Juniper interrogates, her words sharp enough to hack through a redwood.

When I delay answering, my astute sister scans the chamber with renewed vigor, her eyes skidding from the furnishings, to the snake coiled between us, to the parchment and quill on the side table. Juniper draws out her words the way she does when quizzing our family on anything bookish. "How do you know the snake's name is Lotus? And how do you know so much about The Deep's geography? When did you have time to anthologize it?"

Snakes don't talk to humans, but they do communicate with Faeries. And educated in the Fables or not, mortals don't traverse this landscape as if it's their home while also assembling enough details for a map. That's what she means.

"I...that is to say..." My sisters watch as I stammer and wiggle in place. "Lotus revealed his name to Elixir. And the river ruler gave me the materials to draw the map, once he provided me an outlet to explore."

Which aren't the actions of an enemy or captor. To say nothing of the heat detonating across my face.

Silence. Steam rises from the bath. The lanterns sketch the room in amber.

"Why would he do any of that?" Juniper grills.

"Son of a bitch," Lark breathes, her features slackening. "For fuck's sake, Juniper. Do you really need to catch up? Look at her."

Juniper glares in bafflement, loathing to be the last one to draw a conclusion.

Amazement kindles Lark's gaze. "You're smitten, hon."

"She's *what*?" If Juniper were wearing her reading spectacles, they would have fallen lopsided from how violently her head whips toward me. "No."

"Hell yes," Lark insists. "Seems our sister did what none of us thought possible. She brought the irredeemable to his knees." Just like that, without an explanation, my sister links her arm through mine and gives me an encouraging shake. "What's he like? Leave nothing out, including the spicy stuff for grown-ups."

Juniper's mouth opens and closes like a blowfish as she observes my expression anew. "You and him?"

I take a deep, deep, deep breath. "You're not the only one who has a confession to make."

The floodgates open, and the story cascades out of me, and I let it flow like water. Every hateful and beautiful word, every harsh and passionate look, every vicious and penetrating touch. I start with the night I met Elixir and continue to the present, including each gruesome and painful and forbidden thing that has happened since I arrived here.

I tell them about Elixir—his darkness and ruthlessness, along with the facets no others see, the quiet crevices where empathy, bereavement, and dedication hide within him.

With his curse being common knowledge—apart from the bewitcher's identity—there's no reason to omit it. I admit my role in the spell, lament what I did to Elixir, and admit how I've never been able to forgive myself for trying to drown him. It doesn't matter that he'd been able to breathe underwater, that I hadn't known whether suffocating him was even possible. Intentionally, I had tried to harm another living being, someone young like me.

My sisters hold me while I push the words out, and they whisper it's all right, it wasn't my fault. I was defending my people, and I was a child.

I beg Juniper's pardon for wanting the very Fae who had attacked her, and she hushes me with a pragmatic sense of diplomacy. She harbors no fondness for the ruler, but she reasons that he didn't know who she was.

I tell them how the mutual hatred between me and Elixir had thawed into friendship, then ignited into something more in the lily pond, and how we've begged one another's forgiveness, and how we found a miraculous type of serendipity in one another's arms.

I allude to the caresses, kisses, and sensualities. Yet I leave out the finer specifics, such as the heat of his tongue sliding between my lips and the hard sensation of his length filling me to the brim. I share only enough for them to empathize, because it's personal, and it's special, and it's mine. They would understand that, too.

I cite the curse—how it's the only magical bond we'll ever share—and our extreme differences in lifespan as reasons it will never work between Elixir and me. I explain that it's over, that the experience was worth it while it lasted.

Besides the particulars of my intimacy with Elixir, I withhold the object of my game, that breaking the curse is my actual quest. I hadn't revealed it in my note to them, nor am I allowed to do so now. From the beginning, the rule had stated in our welcome letters that we can't impart our games to each other. Not until they're complete.

We fall quiet, stunned by the similarities and differences of our stories. That we snuck out at night as children to meet forbidden Faeries.

I thread our digits. "Whatever happens to one of us, happens to each of us."

"Together," Juniper recites.

"All or nothing," Lark finishes.

Our heads land together. Echoes of the crickets and toads have long since faded, signaling the break of dawn.

Something else occurs to me as I pull back to glance between them. They could have been sighted during their journey to my chamber. "Wait. How did you get here? The map, yes. But how did you get *here*?"

Lark shrugs. "We had escorts."

"Bloody true," a rugged timbre announces. "Aren't you going to introduce us?"

"A name for a name," a more refined voice adds.

Lounging in the doorway are two figures I've seen before. Except the first time, I had been spying on them.

Now the rulers of the sky and woodland are standing much closer—and staring right at me.

31

Ten surreal minutes later, the five of us have packed ourselves into the boat that's been arriving every morning for me. The vessel bobs, anchored in the hidden tunnel leading from The Sunken Isle. Orbs glisten overhead and fleck the walls in teal.

The transport is large enough to accommodate a dozen riders without feeling cramped. It enables the winged Fae to stretch his plumes and the satyr to extend his limbs, right down to the cloven hoofs.

With his blue-black hair and wings, Cerulean blends into the shadows. Puck, on the other hand, burns right through the murk with his wavy red hair and honed stag antlers.

Neither couple can interfere with my game, but my missive had given them sufficient details to conclude that a reunion wouldn't break a rule or skew my chances of winning. Though from what they've told me, their journey to The Deep had been a cautious one. Armed with a javelin and longbow, and using my map as a guide, Cerulean and Puck had manifested to scout the vicinity first. Then, one by one, Cerulean had fastened Lark and Juniper to his body and flown them to the isle via the hidden tunnel.

While my sisters and I had been reuniting, the males had patrolled the area until they'd grown concerned and came to check on their partners. After a series of introductions, my sisters had ordered the males out of my chamber so I could change into a caftan. Our small party had agreed the isle wasn't the ideal place for a conference. We'd needed a location shielded from any stragglers who hadn't yet retired.

Presently, Cerulean is settled between Lark's thighs, his head resting on her chest and one of his arms looped through her steepled limb. His thumb strokes the scars on her kneecap, the pulped wounds harkening to Lark's childhood as a chimney sweep. In turn, Lark sketches the shelves of Cerulean's collarbones, the area exposed beneath the navel-deep V of his shirt.

Juniper perches against Puck, who reclines into a lazy position, frames her hips with his splayed limbs, and twirls a lock of my sister's hair around his finger. Although she folds her hands primly in her lap, Juniper inches closer to give her lover better access to the green locks.

Their weapons rest on one side of the boat. By contrast, I maintain a grip on my spear and contend myself to the opposite bench, the better to judge the Faeries. While I've pledged to give these males the benefit of the doubt for my sisters' sake, I cast them periodic looks of scrutiny. I've never been one to intimidate, but my time in The Deep has been long and arduous, and I've had enough practice dealing with a certain water lord to muster my own version of a silent warning. Conjuring my best frown, I lob the expression in Cerulean and Puck's directions.

If you break their hearts, I will run you through.

They see the look. Cerulean inclines his head in acknowledgment. I inwardly approve of the way he's thumbing Lark's scars, as if offering her infinite comfort and support, the very balm Lark has never received from the men she's bedded in the past.

Puck nods to me as well, yet he punctuates the motion with a conspiratorial wink that nudges a reluctant chuckle from me. He's a charmer, although that alone would never win over someone like Juniper. If she can love him the way she does, my sister must have seen beyond his coltish veneer and unraveled someone with depth and intelligence. Someone who's her intellectual equal and worthy of her respect.

Besides, if I can fall for a monster, can see beyond the viper and find Elixir's beating heart, who knows what Lark and Juniper discovered in these two.

Apart from that, worry churns in my gut. The only thing keeping Juniper from making any logical connection between the curse and my game is that she doesn't know Elixir like I know him.

But his brothers do. Even if craftiness weren't in a Fae's nature, these males don't strike me as the oblivious types.

The satyr wrinkles his nose at the environment. "It's humid as fuck."

"You've been here before," Cerulean remarks. "Did you expect the temperature to change out of fondness for you?"

"I told him not to wear leather," Juniper says while patting Puck's thigh.

"Smart girl," the satyr flirts while unclasping one of the upper buckles cinching his vest. "Maybe I wanted a merry excuse for you to be right. I like when you're right, and I like what it does to your mood. Look any more correct, and I might have to take you home for a quickie."

"Flatterer," she quips.

"You two want your own boat?" Lark jokes while flapping her digit toward one of the shadows. "Maybe stationed over there?"

"Why choose when there are so many darkened corners to enjoy, and life is long?" Puck replies. "Always have something to say, do you?"

"You might not know, but there's a Fable that warns against judging people for the same things they could easily say about you."

"*The Dragon Rivals,*" Juniper says in admiration. "It's one of the most influential tales."

Puck slings his arm around Juniper's midriff while replying to Lark. "Guess it does go both ways, doesn't it? My woman says I like to hear myself talk, and your level of snark is so abundantly capacious that soon you'll need your own territory in The Solitary Mountain."

"Be very careful, Puck," Cerulean remarks, his blue eyes glowing in the dark.

The satyr perks up at the notion of a threat. "Or you'll what?"

"Not me." Wryly, Cerulean knocks his head toward Lark. "Her."

At which point, Lark directs a challenging mien toward Puck, silently telling him to do his verbal best.

"Oh, I should hope so," the forest Fae gloats with the sort of unadulterated and gleeful antagonism reserved for kindred, if not siblings. "Did you know a group of larks is called a Chattering of Larks?"

"Did you know a group of satyrs is called an Asshole of Pucks?" she volleys.

I've never heard someone snort eloquently before, but Cerulean manages it while Puck clutches his chest in mock offense. "Egad, did no one tell you? It's actually called an Orgy of Pucks. Either get your facts straight or consult my woman. She knows everything."

Lark playfully sticks out her tongue at Puck, Juniper shakes her head in amusement, and I grin at the scene. It's clear the time this unlikely group has spent together prior to their arrival has inspired a camaraderie.

Puck's mouth quirks, then he casts another glance at our surroundings. "Never mind. The banter was going so well, yet I'm back to feeling sulky. This place is as bright as Elixir's disposition."

I'm fully aware he's speaking out of anger at what his brother did to Juniper by mistakenly trying to drown her. For my part, I still want to strangle Elixir for that. Nonetheless, the mirth evaporates as I fist the material of my caftan. "When you've lived in darkness for most of your existence, that's what you become. This is how he grew up. It's what he's used to, and it's all he knows."

Four pairs of eyes study me across the divide. Two of them are overcast, subdued by their affinity for me, whereas the other two spark with intuition. My feelings for Elixir aren't my sisters' story to tell, so they've imparted nothing to their lovers. Yet against the power of a Fae's perception, I might as well have worn my heart on my sleeve.

I shift, causing the boat to rock and slosh water against the jagged walls. "True, this environment isn't customized to Elixir. The darkness is a natural facet of The Deep, and the water lord isn't the only Solitary who resides here. He's brooding and violent, but where we live is part of who we are, so it stands to reason a dark setting would yield a dark soul. Yet where there's depth, there's *depth*—much more lurking below the surface. I would say the darkness doesn't get enough credit for that.

"There's also the matter of his blindness, which is another form of darkness entirely, though Elixir is hardly feeble because of it. In fact, I've never once seen him wallowing in self-pity, so I suppose this point is moot. As for the rest, I think we should all take a moment to appreciate how strong light has to be, to flourish in the dark."

My words echo through the cavernous tunnel and taper into the void. Lark and Juniper watch me with concern. We're attuned to the sounds one another makes, so during my rant they'd heard my voice splinter several times. I'd heard it, too.

The Faeries gaze at me, speechless. Cerulean leans back, his hair slumping across his face and a finger draped over his mouth while he ponders my words. Puck sobers and quirks an eyebrow. Neither of them regards me with the distaste or condescension mortals expect from their kind. Instead, they consider my speech with objectivity.

"My, my, my," Puck says, his tone mellowed. "Like sister, like sister, like sister."

Cerulean leans forward. "May we assume you've spent significant time with our brother?"

I meet his keen eyes. "You may."

"Fables and fuck," Puck reels. "It's not just venom. Elixir actually has warm blood pumping through his veins. Who knew it was possible?"

"It was with us," Juniper asserts.

"And us," Lark says, poking Cerulean's chest.

"Well, we do like our humans mutinous," her mate replies with a smirk.

"Baby, you didn't know mutiny by half until I showed up," she purrs, tapping the wing ornaments capping his ears.

I narrow my eyes at the males. "You speak of Elixir as though he's the only Fae in this wild without a beating heart. What made you two any better before my sisters came along?"

Both males accept the hands of their women, who gaze at me with love but hold their partners with just as much devotion.

"Fair enough," Cerulean concedes. "Except we never said Elixir was missing a heart."

"It's that we thought he'd lost it," Puck explains.

My grasp on the spear loosens. "Lost it," I repeat in confusion.

"Meaning?" Juniper prompts.

"Meaning," Puck obliges, "I assume if you and Elixir have gotten cozy, you've been here long enough to know he's cursed."

My sisters and I exchange glances. Again, they clam up on my behalf, since it's my business to confirm what I know and don't know about the river ruler. Though, they do frown in puzzlement when I hesitate.

"Yes, I know about that," I say. "It happened the night of The Trapping."

Cerulean's expression strays into the tunnel's black pupil. "That's not all."

"You gonna keep us in suspense?" Lark persists, at which point Cerulean breaks from the trance and strokes her knee.

He and Puck trade grave looks, then the satyr murmurs, "It's no secret."

Cerulean nods. "As fledglings, I was raised by animals, and Puck was born from a woodland seed, but Elixir had Fae mothers who were alive that night."

Anticipation drums in my temple as I scoot nearer. The Faeries and my sisters do the same, closing the distance while the boat sways.

"After my future mate freed me that night—" Cerulean gives Lark a look of candid admiration, "—I saw the carnage of my kin, the fauna, and the animals who raised me. I managed to save the owl who became my father, along with several avians caged nearby, but there were more scattered across the landscape. I knew this, so I circled the village from above, and that's when I caught sight of Elixir in a stream. I have no idea how he freed himself, but he was struggling to stay afloat, and there was something else in the water with him, but I couldn't make out the silhouette, and he's never told me what happened.

"I plucked him from the water and flew him to The Deep's entrance. I didn't have time to resuscitate Elixir or take him underground, not when other animals of the mountain needed my help. I left him there, intending to return later.

"At some point right before then, he was cursed, but he didn't know it yet. Because of that and his age, he couldn't control the power yet. The only thing that spared me from going blind was his unconsciousness, and I was already gone by the time he woke up."

Cerulean's eyes flash like a storm. "But his mothers were there." His throat contorts. "Like him, they had the ability to shift between land and water. Shortly after I'd disappeared, Marine and Lorelei arrived to find their son just as awareness overtook him. He was disoriented when he opened his eyes, and he panicked, and…" Cerulean shakes his head. "And that infernal curse. He was too young and didn't know what he was doing. He couldn't fucking stop himself."

Lark swears in horror, Juniper gasps, and I go utterly still. Dread crawls up my throat because I hear the devastation in Cerulean's speech.

"Some of the villagers attempted to hunt us down." Cerulean clicks his head toward Puck, who locks his jaw. "The humans were so desperate to catch us, they stormed the Solitary wild for a second time—scarcely a handful of them armed with iron weapons, but it was enough."

Because Cerulean can't continue, Puck speaks through his teeth. "While Elixir was waking up, his thoughts too scrambled to fathom why the fuck his mothers were shrieking and why he couldn't see them, only hear them stumbling about. That's when their attackers took aim. The mermaids were blind and didn't see the iron blades coming. But Elixir heard the onslaught. He fucking listened to his mothers die, right in front of him."

My hand vaults to my mouth while Puck grates, "I got there just as the mermaids fell, still clutching their eyes. I'd escaped and was mounted on my companion, Sylvan. We'd just made it past The Triad when I heard the shitstorm and galloped in that direction. The humans barely had time to target me or Elixir before I planted a shower of arrows in those fuckers."

The tale rattles in a deep, dark place within me, the same impulse that once wanted to destroy Elixir. History shakes from its confines, breaks from its hinges, and collapses into a heap.

Comfort will not bring back what he's lost.

That's what Coral had meant. I know Elixir doesn't mourn the loss of his vision, because it's not a deficiency, so that's not what ails him. Rather, he mourns what his condition did to those he held most dearly.

That's what I've heard in his silence, and in his malice, and in his harp music.

I had cursed Elixir, and that curse had blinded his mothers, and the villagers had killed the mermaids. That's the source of his pain. That's the true curse. He couldn't save them, couldn't heal them. In addition to The Trapping, that's why Elixir had vowed to take revenge on the mortals of Reverie Hollow—and on me.

Someday in the future, a child from my village and one from Faerie might feel the same way about each other. They'll rue the other's existence, and the cycle will never end.

It will reign like the sun and moon. It will endure like the wind, earth, and water. It will burn like fire.

And for what? More of the same?

For ages, the Faeries assaulted and abused my people. Eventually, we repaid them in kind, and they spurned us as a result, damned us to punishment. And soon enough, humans will rise again. There's only so long we'll remain fearful and docile before my world is driven to act once more, until the lines between right and wrong, innocent and monstrous, malevolent and compassionate are blurred.

I sling my arms around my stomach, lest I keel over and retch into the water. "Fables forgive us all," I whisper, and everyone understands.

Water rustles around the boat as silence engulfs our small band. We bow our heads, remembering, harkening to those nights years ago, seeing it from endless vantage points, both human and otherworldly. I sense each of us retreating into our own memories, picking through the shards and deliberating whether the fragments can ever be reassembled.

I see the same rawness in each of us. The goodness and badness. The merciful and unforgiving. The lightness and darkness.

Like creatures of nature. Like nature itself.

What is so different about us, then?

A dry sob tumbles from my lips. Lark can shield her pain with snarky comments, Juniper with willful determination. I do neither. I need my hurt, because if I didn't have it, nothing I feel for Elixir would be real.

His past doesn't absolve him, nor does my past render me innocent. Yet he'd wanted me, and I'd wanted him. I still do. And isn't that better than hating one another?

"You've shared this in confidence," I say to Cerulean and Puck. "Thank you."

Cerulean studies me, his words a breeze that reaches out tentatively. "You feel that much for him."

"He feels that much for me, too."

"Dare we ask, how this phenomenon happened?" Puck asks.

I hedge. As Faeries, the two brothers must know the old tale of the water well and the Fae witch's spell. They also know Elixir enough to figure out the game if I speak too freely. Moreover, I'm a terrible liar, especially in the presence of my sisters. Potential fibs sit on my tongue like feathers or leaves, about to flit away at the slightest gust of wind.

A baritone voice cuts off my attempt. "Well met."

My heart stops. We swerve toward the Fae looming in the water, his silhouette a monolith of black and his golden eyes spearing through the murk. Shadows lace his face and highlight the fingercaps, which bunch into fists.

His head clicks toward me, the pupils wavering. He heard us. Elixir might not have entered during the story of his mothers, but he'd heard the last of our huddle, the part where I'd admitted our bond.

Puck's timbre cuts through the space, the texture of his voice suddenly hardening into something one would need an axe to chop through. "Caught us talking about you behind your back, did you?"

Only then does Elixir drag his eyes from my direction and slant toward the satyr. "Nice of you to return, Puck," he replies without an ounce of sincerity.

"Oh yes, I feel so welcome. By the way, do mermaids find that deadpan expression titillating? Go on. Teach me something I don't already know."

"I'm going to say this only once—"

"That's predictable. To think someday you might repeat something twice."

"Puck," Cerulean warns. *"Fardun farleka."*

Whatever the winged Fae cautions, his brother ignores it with a bulky shrug and continues to address Elixir. "Sorry, luv. Here I was, too busy fuming over your tormented soul that I forgot to be pissed at you for recent events. Not to worry, though. My anger's back with aplomb."

Tension thickens in the tunnel as Puck reflects on Juniper's near-drowning.

Elixir's fists unlock. "Anger," he repeats.

"What can I tell you?" Puck remarks, a lethal threat brimming under that smarmy veneer. "I've had that emotion set aside for a rainy day, which ended up being yesterday, so I'm overdue. Or do you need another colorful fucking word? Because my woman comes fully stocked, and trust me, you've inspired her."

"If you are here to take revenge—"

"Who me? I'm but a spectator," the satyr hisses. "Juniper's the one who'll verbally wipe the floor with your ass. Unless she goes for the crossbow, in which case, you'll need a head start to dodge her aim."

"Enough," Juniper barks.

"Both of you," I add, because for Fable's sake.

The males yield, but only just. Lark mutters in Cerulean's ear, and he nods while scrubbing his face. "In the interest of communal self-preservation, I suggest we relocate to drier turf before the whole Deep overhears us." He swings an arm toward the river ruler. "Elixir, if you will."

*

We gather in a circle on the grassy promontory of The Kelpie Rapids. After my sisters and I discard our shoes, Juniper glances about with wide eyes, her green gaze bright with the excitement of a scholar. Puck, who can't seem to cease touching her, tucks my sister into him and watches her enthusiasm with unbridled warmth.

Lark and I swap knowing grins. Our bookish sibling is bursting at the seams, a hundred questions battling for dominance on her tongue. To begin with, she'll want to know the origins of this place. Generally, she prefers to research in chronological order.

She takes in every scrap of detail about the vista while Puck whispers in her ear, making her playfully elbow him in the ribs. That is, until Elixir's shadow casts over my petite sister. He takes his place in the circle, armed with his forked daggers and his limbs now clad in leggings, both of which he'd stored at the waterway's landing.

His movements draw all of us. After a quick glance toward the place where I perch across from him, he clears his throat. First to Puck: "When I mentioned whether you had come to take revenge, I was not talking to you." Then to Juniper. "I am sorry."

My sister, being the practical sort—who values assertiveness over waxing poetic—appreciates his inclined head. Even more, the simplicity of his apology wrings approval from her eyes.

She nods back, then remembers he can't see the gesture. "I accept."

"Then state your retribution," Elixir prompts.

Heads veer between them. My sister blinks, not having expected this offering. It's neither a bargain nor a trick.

After a moment, fortitude rinses away the haze of indecision, and my sister's face narrows in thought. That she silently consults Puck is a pleasure to witness, the final confirmation that she's found an equal partner.

"Here we go," Lark predicts, and I agree.

"They say you see what others can't," Juniper begins.

"They say many things," Elixir answers.

"Spoken like a quintessential Fae."

"Ah, but humbleness doesn't become him," Cerulean tells my sister. "Lack of vision has attuned Elixir to sense acutely what's occurring inside us, from our blood to our heart rates." Those midnight eyes dash toward his brother, and Cerulean quirks a single brow. "Isn't that a fact?"

Elixir's pupils click in my direction, and my blood spikes. "Sometimes," he and I mutter in unison, because while it's true, I'm no longer susceptible to his sensory power.

"My point is this," Juniper persists. "As the ruler of this land, and as one who sees beneath the surface, my price for forgiveness is simple: Join with us."

"Join with you," Elixir inquires, his brows snapping together. "In what capacity?"

"Reformation," Cerulean supplies. "A mutiny of sorts."

"Another word for it is anarchy," Puck inserts.

Hope lifts my shoulders. "To what end?"

"Possibly death," Puck remarks. "Starting with disorder, leading to upheaval, and resulting in potential war between mortals and Faeries. That is, if opposing sides can't come to an agreement, or if we fail to unravel a Fabled mystery. We're not sure yet. Though, our band did predict having a much shittier time convincing you."

Juniper sets her hand on the satyr's tanned arm. "History says the way to restore the fauna and save your world is by human sacrifice." She draws herself up, ambition cementing in her voice. "But there's a second way."

Elixir's head snaps toward me. At the same instant, mine swings his way.

My sisters and their loves have discovered an alternative. There's indeed another way to salvage the lost fauna and preserve the Solitary wild, after all. This is what Elixir and I had been scavenging The Deep for.

I'd told my sisters about this crusade in the chamber, yet they hadn't said anything, maybe because they'd been pacing themselves.

Elixir's eyes blaze with uncertainty. "A second way."

"Truly?" I ask Juniper. "How?"

"I found it myself," she declares with a rise of her pert chin.

"Show-off," Lark and Puck say affectionately.

At which point, a stream of information pours from Juniper's mouth about the original Book of Fables and how she'd come into its possession, which has to do with a male centaur named Cypress, a friend of hers and Puck's.

Juniper narrates her discovery of a Fable that includes a hidden message, the secret missive crafted by one of the ancient scribes who'd penned the book. Then Juniper recites the message from memory.

"*Immortal wild. Immortal land. Dwellers of the mountain, forest, and river. You are born of eternal nature—of the wind, earth, and water. Yet that which is everlasting is not unbreakable. And should you wither by the hands of others, look not merely to sacrifice, for another path to restoration lies in wait. Therefore, follow your Fables, heed your neighbors, and look closer.*"

From there, she summarizes the rest. That their group hopes to translate the passage's meaning and yield a solution to the Solitaries' plight. That the solution could be a spark, the beginning of peace between mortals and humans.

Because of circumstances having to do with Lark winning her game, Cerulean has transferred his rule to the mountain fauna, who are just as equipped for the role. Cerulean's no longer in charge there, but he's maintained his influence with the animals and a handful of former subjects who haven't snubbed him.

As for Puck, he still rules the woodland. As such, the satyr, Juniper, Lark, and Cerulean have been taking precautions, recruiting alliances and support from the Solitaries who have adopted the cause.

Because Elixir reigns over the river, the group had intended to approach him about this endeavor. They'd been meeting to discuss when and how, considering it's no secret Elixir relies on his power and authority. As the only member of The Three who'd yet to experience a change of heart, and as the least likely Fae to relinquish his thirst for vengeance, the group had anticipated a dangerous response from him. And amid my game, they couldn't move recklessly.

"Until you replied to our message, we weren't sure what we'd be dealing with," Juniper explains.

At this, Elixir breaks from his stupor. His attention strays toward where I sit with my arms strapped around my upturned limbs. Awareness and hurt converge across his countenance, pulling his features taut. I'd made a choice and acted despite our attachment, and I hadn't shared this with him.

I hadn't known where we stood, not with everything that divides us. I couldn't place full stock that our bond would endure despite whatever came to pass.

Besides, if my sisters call out to me, I'm going to answer no matter what.

This, Elixir comprehends. Understanding infuses his irises, and those orbs anchor upon the ground, at the grassy center of our band. A muscle ticks in his jaw, though not for long.

I know what the rigidness of his profile means. My sister is asking him to betray his subjects by aligning himself with mortals, as well as the two leaders who've already been shunned by their own lots. Elixir would be turning his back on the river Fae who idolize his silent strength, aspire to his fluid brutality, and follow his example.

Thus, Elixir's not hesitating to join so much as contemplating how his kin will react—and how fatal the result will be for us. His subjects will feel disillusioned at best, lethal at worst.

"I shall join you," he says, much to the others' shock.

Juniper balks, "You accept?"

"I do. Though, I offer fealty of my own volition, not as compensation for misdeeds."

"Well. Agreed, then. As for additional retribution, your apology is enough, so long as my sister vouches for you."

While glancing at Elixir, I say, "You have my word." Then I reach out and clasp hers and Lark's hands. "And my loyalty. Always."

When we sit back, Juniper extends her hand toward Elixir. "Allies."

Elixir must detect her movements and the nearness of her voice, because he reaches out to locate her fingers. They shake. Faeries rarely use this custom to seal bargains, so he's awkward about it, his brows crinkling.

However, the awkwardness gives way to a deeper frown. While touching my sister, Elixir senses something and freezes mid-handshake. His startled eyes leap about in concentration, his head tilts in consternation, and his ears perk…listening. It happens too fast to react, like a knife slipping off a counter. Those gilded irises flash, and Puck and Cerulean jolt forward at lightning speed, each of them about to knock Elixir from Juniper before she ends up blind.

Lark and I shift, ready to fling ourselves in front of our sister. Yet Elixir remembers himself swiftly, the vibrancy dulling from his gaze enough that Juniper merely winces. It had been a reflex. His brothers pause, though only marginally, whereas Elixir drops Juniper's fingers as though he's been scalded with an iron poker.

"Elixir, what the everlasting fuck?" Puck snarls while harnessing Juniper to his side.

"It's all right," she assures him. "I'm fine."

Lark dumps herself back onto the ground. "Then what the hell was that?"

Cerulean is quiet, monitoring his brother alongside me. Elixir looks visibly shaken, as if stumbling through foreign terrain, as though beholding something in his mind.

But he shakes himself. "Nothing," he stammers. "It was nothing."

It wasn't nothing. But if anyone knows Elixir, they know not to waste their breath prying. He won't answer until he's ready to.

"It happens to me often," I say, to placate everyone. "I go into a trance, and sometimes it's hard to pull away. Or a sudden thought comes to me, and I react absently."

It's hardly convincing, and although Puck still looks as if he'd like to decapitate Elixir, my words do soothe everyone's nerves. Whatever just occurred, it's over for now.

The promontory glitters with a tapestry of teal specks, and the rapids below hasten, the current accelerating. An indistinct floral fragrance mingles with the muggy heat. The foundation trembles, the barest rustle of movement, like a shifting blanket.

Juniper folds her hands in her lap. "Perhaps you might use that power to a beneficial end."

Clarity returns to Elixir's gaze. "You have a tactic in mind, then."

"Like I said, we're lacking valuable information about this Fable. Perhaps you might enlighten us."

I translate her meaning. "Are you suggesting that he…?"

Elixir peers, incredulous. "You believe I know the second way."

"We believe you have *greater access* to the second way," Puck amends. "Your senses go deeper than ours."

His brother scoffs. "Not with this. You are mistaken."

"I don't think so. You've got the capability."

That rumble from a second ago magnifies, yet it doesn't feel like the kelpies are approaching. It's too soon for that spectacle. While the group debates, I rise and shuffle to the nearest wall tufted in foliage, then flatten my palm on the facade, which also begins to tremor.

"You're even more attuned to the land than we are," Cerulean insists. "Your senses exceed that of any Solitary. If you were to try—"

"The Horizon That Never Lies told you—not me or Puck—about the first way," Elixir lashes out. "What makes you think I'm privy to the second?"

Puck grunts in frustration, "What makes you think you aren't? And what the fuck is that fucking noise? The kelpies?"

I shake my head while Juniper answers, "That's not the sound of a stampede." She pauses, then suggests, "A wandering stream?"

"Another mountain peak rising from the earth?" I hear Lark guess with forced humor.

The earth shivers, then jostles. I yank my palm from the wall and swerve toward the group, who all rise to their feet. Elixir's eyes lurch along the ground, feeling and listening, then soaring toward me, aware of what I suspect and agreeing with it.

He knows the sound of water, and he knows the difference between a rapid and something harsher, and I've learned those differences as well, because we've been roaming these tunnels for weeks, examining the shift in water levels, the drainage, and the overflows.

"It's not wind or the earth," Elixir says to me.

I whisper, "No. It's not."

"Cove." His voice blurs, calmness layering over deadly urgency. "Get away from the wall. Now."

That's when I detect what he must hear—the river building, rolling, and rushing toward a barrier. That's when the wall cracks open. And that's when a tidal wave swallows me whole.

32

Once, long ago, I dove into a stream and tried to drown a young merman—a Fae with a viper's tail. I remember the fall, the splash, and the quiet. And finally, I remember the swirl of liquid drawing me in, tugging on me as I tumbled through the depth. I remember the paradox of weightlessness versus suction.

Since then, I've experienced this onslaught numerous times while in Faerie. I'm no longer a stranger to violent fluxes. Except each time in memory, dating back to that first chaotic dive nine years ago, I had been prepared. I'd had time to fill myself with air, to store my breath.

This time, I have no warning.

It's as if a giant pump has burst. Chunks of rock catapult from the wall and split into a gash, through which a great tsunami of water spews. The wave shoots forward like a predator, spreading and striking quickly. Stones crunch, and boulders roar, and the surge opens its mouth, then closes around me.

The impact flings me backward, hurling me into the void. Everything is slickness and silence and speed. It seals out the muffled bellows. Darkness envelops me as liquid drenches my lungs until I'm heaving.

I flail my limbs, wrestling against the liquid pressure. But it's too strong, too violent, thrusting me across leagues.

For an instant, time suspends. In the span of seconds, I think how many times nature has been my ally and savior. Other times, it's been my enemy. And yet other times, it's been neither. It's been a victim freeing itself from its cage, although it's already been hurt, the damage already done. Here, now, someplace inside me says it's the latter.

Hints flicker through my frazzled mind. The places where the river has drained, the areas where it has overflowed, and the territories where it has altered course. This isn't random or the kelpies' doing. With all those changes in levels and currents, and with its foundation weakening, eventually the water would end up someplace that couldn't hold it, somewhere that would eventually break.

This is what happens when the Solitary wild gets closer to fading.

Elixir was right. This isn't the wind or the earth.

It's a flood.

The river buries me alive. It sinks me into an abyss while a vignette of images splinter through my head. Lark, Juniper, Papa Thorne, and Lotus. My birth parents, who became part of a raging sea. Cerulean and Puck, who might have become my friends.

And a viper who's become more than that.

No! Please, no!

Where is everyone? What's happened to them?

Panic grips me by the jugular. My eyes fly open to an underwater world, the promontory and gulch submerged. Clouds of dirt and sand and foliage spiral, blotting out the aquamarine expanse, so that I only see a few feet in front of me.

Whiskered fish dice across my vision. They must have been tossed here from another part of The Deep.

How far has this flood reached? How much of this realm has it consumed?

Fear cracks through my ribs. My fingers dash outward, but they slip through the nothingness, the intangible force reminding me it's impossible to hold water. I grapple for another set of fingers, my digits slicing but failing to latch onto anyone. I fight against the river's pull and search for an anchor—a jutting bracket or a boulder, but there's only the current, and the vortex, and the tide.

A blast knocks me sideways, the honed teeth of a wall chomping into my thigh. Crimson tendrils swim before my gaze. The river clogs my scream, and the crash rattles my bones, and dizziness swarms my consciousness.

It's so quiet and warm. Yet my lungs burn, and my flesh stings from where the wall took a bite out of me.

Like threads of seaweed, my arms tangle as they strain to carry me upward. But the river's too heavy and swift. Wave after wave pushes me one way, then yanks me in the opposite direction.

The promontory looms above now, which means I've tumbled off the edge, which means I'm floating somewhere over the gulch. Suddenly, the fall becomes deceptively tranquil, a gentle whip of motion coupled with deadly, blurry quiet.

Instead of rejecting it, I let it in, let the darkness in, let it enfold my body. I allow the slow drag of water to calm me, to soothe me until I'm a part of it.

In the throes of violence, I've learned how peace can become a weapon, something to wield, a means of survival. I know how to embrace this darkness now.

Peace washes away the terror, eases the lack of air, and settles my mind. For good measure, my fingers land on the necklace around my throat, the dainty talisman still there, still holding on, holding on, holding on, holding on.

Elixir. Lark. Juniper.

Adrenaline surges through my veins. I preserve what oxygen remains inside me and thrust my limbs, kicking with all my strength. My teeth gnash with the effort, clamping until my jaw aches.

As always, the current is different in Faerie. It's denser in places, swifter in others. While I've had practice with this, my sisters haven't. And while Cerulean and Puck might get to my sisters in time, I can't take that chance.

I siphon through, climbing upward, more and more and more. I pray there's a surface and the river hasn't filled this area to the domed ceiling.

The flood intensifies once more, whisking about like a raging squall. It pounds the walls, ramming its liquid fists into the crevices.

A glittering tail flaps in my periphery. I swerve just as a female whisks past me. Her arms are little more than strings of yarn as she battles with the profusion. Then I see another form careen past, this one marked by gills and translucent fins.

Merfolk. Several figures combat the flood, their jeweled eyes glistening with fright. This is more than they can withstand, which means it could be more than Elixir can withstand.

Terror magnifies tenfold. The promontory's lip juts out within arm's reach. A siren darts by, her body shoved by the onslaught. In a rush of energy, my arm snaps out, and my fingers snatch her wrist.

The Fae's pupils dilate with shock, yet she straps her digits around me. Together, we haul ourselves over the precipice and break through the surface. My lips part, wheezing a mouthful of air. The flood races over the edges, turning the gulch into a wild sea.

The promontory is a wasteland of crumbled rock, torn vegetation, and cavities pitting the ground. Our weapons are gone, washed away by the deluge. There's no sign of my sisters, Elixir, or his brothers.

The waterlogged siren slumps onto the grass and glances at me, then nods in gratitude. I nod back. Then I fill myself with air, flip sideways, and dive back in.

If they're not above the flood, they're submerged. It's fortunate my sisters and I had removed our shoes when we'd gotten here. I cannon downward as fast as I can, my cheeks bloating and bubbles churning from my nose.

Midnight blue plumage swoops across my vantage point, the shingles of a wing vanishing before I can flag Cerulean. Moments later, fiery red hair blazes in the distance, then disappears too quickly for me to locate Puck.

I race after them, stroking at a breakneck pace, crashing through wave after wave. Beyond a patch of ripples, four silhouettes huddle atop a mantle of flat rock protruding from a wall. I crash through and brace myself before smashing into the edifice.

"Cove!" Lark yells.

My sisters scramble toward me on all fours, with Cerulean and Puck bringing up the rear. They're alive. They're soaked, clothes and hair plastered to their faces, and a series of bloody lacerations pouring from foreheads and shoulders. But they're alive!

A wave slams into me.

Cerulean's wings retract and merge into his back as he extends his hand for me. I ignore it. "Where's Elixir?"

"Searching for you," Puck shouts over the quagmire while bracing Juniper. "He'll come back! Now get the fuck out of the water!"

That's what a rational person would do. The river is Elixir's domain, and he can breathe in the depths, and his viper tail will do the rest. That's what I should believe, should trust.

Any swimmer understands logic and basic survival instincts. Never willingly dive into a rapid, or a tidal wave, or a flood.

I rip off the necklace and slap it into Cerulean's waiting palm. Then I glance at my sisters, who see the look on my face.

Juniper barks, "Cove, no!"

Lark squawks, "Cove, don't you fucking dare—"

"I love you!" I shout to them. "Count to three hundred."

I drop below the surface, the descent blocking out their cries. He's down here, and he moves fast, so he should have covered every inch of ground by now.

Something's delaying him. Something's wrong.

I make for the kelpie tunnel—then reel back, my scalp shrieking with pain. A set of fingers hooks onto the roots and yanks me around. I fight to keep my mouth closed, to keep from chugging gallons of water, to keep my oxygen preserved.

A pair of spiteful eyes glitter, the lower lids smudged in black. Slashes of gills pulsate in a succession of vindictive fits from the Fae's throat. The merman seethes at me, a swamp of hair agitating around his head.

Scorpio.

I remember Elixir lashing him while dragging me across The Twisted Canals. Elixir, choking him for trying to pounce on me in The Mer Cascades. Elixir, poisoning him later for that same incident.

The Fae wears every single grudge on his countenance. I see him relish this stroke of luck, his vice grip hooking onto me. I lurch away, but he seizes my elbows.

His expression asks, *Where do you think you're going?*

Scorpio can't kill me before the game is over. But he can make sure this moment hurts.

Yet more than horror, a turbulent madness builds in my fists, in the soles of my feet, and in my molars. Elixir could be harmed or trapped.

Maybe this fiend had done it, or maybe I'm finished tolerating these beings, because maybe I've had enough of them and enough of this hatred.

I fight back, scraping my fingernails across the Fae's cheeks as his webbed hands lug me down. I might as well be brawling with iron shackles. Against his immortal strength and ability to draw breath down here, I'm waging a losing war.

But there's one thing that always works, no matter the creature. Also, I've learned from making love to Elixir that mermen have all the necessary parts. I grab my assailant by the shoulders, use them for leverage, and ram my knee into his groin.

The merman howls, frothing at the mouth and keeling forward. He releases me into the tumult. As he does, a streak of light gleams from his chest, where a small vial hangs like a charm from a neck strap. I recognize the salted contents but can't fathom why Scorpio has the vial or how he'd managed to obtain it from Elixir's den.

Either way, my left hand takes advantage and swipes the vial from around the merman's throat, the way I used to pickpocket baubles from nobles. Then I thumb open the stopper and fling the contents into Scorpio's eyes. A dust cloud of sparkling granules detonates into his pupils. The Fae's howls amplify as he wedges his palms into his eye sockets.

I release the vial, pump away from the merman, and twist to flee when my gaze stumbles into two asterisks of light. Gilded irises cut through the void, the rings kindling with fury.

Gold. So much gold.

Elixir's body slices through the water like a blade, his viper tail whipping the rabid current out of the way. He lances straight for the merman, whose own tail has shifted into legs.

Remnant flecks of salt bleed into the river and sting my eyes, as if the pool has turned into the ocean. I recall Elixir saying the vial would salt any body of water. My eyes blink against the sensation, struggling to remain open.

In a fit of violence, Scorpio recovers. Webbed hands capture my knees, intent of finishing what they'd started.

I thrash, squint into the tempest, and locate Elixir's murderous profile as he propels toward the merman—then drives a forked dagger into the

Fae's thigh. My attacker releases me, and a scream knots in my throat as shawls of blood pool into the river.

Elixir balances the merman like a speared fish. At which point, the water lord's eyes flash, two beams of gold stabbing through the water and incinerating the merman's orbs.

As his victim flounders, Elixir yanks the weapon from the Fae's body. Then it happens in a single heartbeat. Amidst his hysteria, the merman's fingers sweep across my hips, and in a final bout of outrage, Scorpio clamps on and hurtles me toward a spinning funnel, the eddies certain to suffocate me.

Just before the whirlwind devours me, another pair of arms intercepts. Muscled limbs catch me, scoop up my form, and send me gliding into a pocket of freshwater.

My eyes flutter open, but the merman is gone. For a moment, so is Elixir.

Then I spot him just outside the vortex, his body suspended in saltwater. Like the merman, his tail has shuddered and split into naked limbs. Yet unlike the merman, he's sinking.

My heart stalls. I charge forth, putting every ounce I have left into the swim, but now Elixir appears so far away, too far away. Across the distance, his body convulses. His limbs paddle like those of a youth, clumsy and wayward, toiling to stay afloat.

It comes to me, rising from a dormant place, a memory cracking open like a clamshell. The way he's struggling. The way he's sinking. It harkens to nine years ago in that stream, when I tried to stop him from escaping.

It had been the only saltwater route in my village. Finally, I remember a detail that had been too fuzzy to recall. When I'd crashed with him into that stream, his tail hadn't materialized—because it hadn't been able to. Instead, he'd still had his legs.

That's why Scorpio's tail had shifted. That's why Elixir's own tail has done the same. Saltwater makes them sprout limbs.

In his den, he'd been so apprehensive, so cautious about handling the vial, as if it might shatter in his hand. That's because he had feared it.

Elixir had nearly sunk that fateful night for the same reason he's sinking now. He can't inhale saltwater, and he doesn't know how to use his limbs down here, because he's never needed to.

Without freshwater, the river ruler can't breathe under the surface.

And without his viper tail, the river ruler doesn't know how to swim.
He's drowning.

33

He's too weak, I realize. He's far too weak to try.

My pulse escalates to a frantic drum, and my lungs disappear so I can't feel them working, and there are only my limbs pumping. I stroke fast and fierce while the maddened flood wallops around me, the water lunging to and fro.

I push through, push around, push under and over.

Elixir writhes against the current. He thrashes and twists, to no avail. His glazed eyes jump left and right, searching but not seeing. He'd known. He had known he was swimming into a deathtrap, that saving me would damn him.

With his connection to nature, why can't he swim instinctively? Why isn't he beseeching the river to help him? Had Scorpio taken the mixture from Elixir's den for this purpose?

I pitch myself down, down, down. All the while, I think about enchanted souls and cursed souls. The seelie Fae's counter spell ripples in my head.

Change comes only from the bewitcher, who must see, feel, enact the opposite of old truths and past deeds.

Years ago, I stared into golden eyes and saw evil. Because I saw evil, I felt hatred. Because I felt hatred, I sought to drown that evil, to save my people.

I will drown you.

Not if I drown you first!

Here and now, I see him once again beneath the surface. Here and now, I see layers and hidden crevices, a multitude of levels burrowing deeper, like the underground itself. And within those layers, I see goodness. And amidst that goodness, I feel something greater, eternal, and unconditional.

I feel love. I love this viper, this monster, this Fae.

I love him.

The emotion inundates my being, inflating from a droplet to a fathomless sea, from tranquil to turbulent. I see goodness and feel love.

And finally, I must *enact the opposite of old truths and past deeds*. Many times, Elixir has told me to make my choice. In this moment, I do so with every thump of my pulse.

I'd once wanted to drown him. Now I'll do the reverse.

I will save you.

My body shoots from one pocket of water to the next, from freshwater to saltwater. The brine prickles my eyes like a hundred needles. And still, I launch toward his descending form, all glittering scales and piercing orbs and a pool of black hair. Elixir's chest spasms. His eyelids twitch and flap shut, his frame slumping as though cut from its strings.

My lips want to scream, because I can't lose him, won't lose him. Instead, my body protests, shoving its way through and defying the weight of a rampant river.

I blink against the salt. I do my utmost to focus, to extinguish the bite of it, to stamp out the pain.

At last, my fingers graze his limp ones. Instantly, his digits trace mine, recognize mine—and grasp. We thread together, holding tightly. The flood has stolen his bronze fingercaps, but that's all right, because I've got him, and I'll cover those scars for him.

I kick, but he's so large, so heavy, and the river's pressing on us. My temperature drops with cold fear, my bloodstream jets through me with exertion, and my oxygen is depleting.

Help me, I beg fate. Please, help me.

Elixir's head ticks. Then he sways his feeble digits, and a tiny socket of water swoops beneath my heels, and it nudges me upward, and upward, and upward. Eventually, it peters out as Elixir slumps once more.

By then, the surface lashes into view, and I do the rest. I heave us toward the crusted extension where four figures wait, then catapult through the expanse and into blessed air.

A groaning, suctioning sound erupts from my mouth as I inhale and sling my arm atop the mantel. A host of voices overlap, colliding with the sound of splashing water. A bunch of hands seize my arms and heft me to safety, and the weight of Elixir vanishes as more hands tug him onto the precipice.

We flop on the bracket. My eyes gawk at the dome of teal specks above. Two heads leap into view, one framed in green, the other in white.

"Cove!" Juniper yells. "That was three hundred and *six* seconds!"

"Dammit, Cove!" Lark chokes. "You scared the shit out of us!"

Elixir. I vault upright and swerve toward where he lies motionless and flanked by Cerulean and Puck, who hunker over him with bowed heads and grim expressions. Emitting a cracked noise, I crawl over to Elixir's naked form. His head sags to the side, his profile slack. All that warm, olive color has leached from his body.

Wedging myself between Cerulean and Puck, I grasp Elixir's face and wheel it toward me. "Elixir!" I plead, my lips wobbling. "Elixir, wake up! Please, please!" My voice splinters, and tears spring, and I taste salt.

I press my ear to his chest and hear...nothing.

"No," I sob, hovering over him. "No, no, no, pl-please. Elixir, please!"

I shake him, slap him, and I don't know if it's the right way with Faeries, but as a swimmer, I've been taught how to revive a drowned victim. I perform the steps, alternating between his chest and mouth, but nothing happens, nothing happens, and still nothing happens.

Puck swears under his breath, and Cerulean utters something in Faeish. I hear their grief, their shock. The texture is uneven, the intonation slippery. They're not used to death, yet they accept it so quickly.

But I won't. I won't let him go.

I frame his exquisitely brutal face. "I've done it, haven't I? I won the game. I broke the curse. I see goodness, and I feel love, and I saved you. I know what you've done, I know who you are, and I want all of it. I want the darkness. You feel this?" I take his fingers and run them over my features, sketching every detail, every nuance. "This is what love looks like. Let me love you. Wake up and love me back. Wake up, you asshole!"

I lean over to resume working on his chest and lips—but his body jolts, as if lanced by a thunderbolt. Elixir's back arches, then drops. I pause, wait, and hold my breath for as long as it takes.

With the speed of a viper, his eyes lash open. Those golden irises flare with life, and they strike out—and find me.

34

Confusion pierces across those orbs, the rings bright and unsteady. They reflect a montage of images—the domed ceiling, the river flood, and my own eyes fixed on him. I see myself in his thunderstruck gaze, my features blurry at first, then solid. Clarity rinses away his bafflement, replaced by disbelief, then fear, then doubt. Each emotion is a wave rushing to the forefront before ebbing.

At last, those eyes steady. They anchor themselves to me, becoming as lucid as water, until all that's left is awe.

We move like the tide, fluid and synchronized. He inhales, and I exhale. His fingers steal out to graze my lips, and mine brush the damp strands of hair from his face. Like this, we explore one another, learning how to see each other.

I hover over Elixir while his touch travels from my mouth. Overwhelmed with uncertainty, his eyes close in concentration, and he resumes the usual manner of feeling me. As if making sure this is real, this is to be trusted, this is happening. He etches his way across my lips and traces my skin, my outtakes, and a single tear leaking down my cheek. Finally, Elixir peers at me, grasps my face, and pins our foreheads to one another.

"My light," he rasps.

"My dark," I whisper.

"You're here."

"I'm here."

"And I see you."

He does. He sees me the way he did years ago, except my body's older, and my heart is changed.

Elixir's eyes jump all over me, consuming each crevice, drinking in every detail the way I do him. As his complexion resurfaces, I feel the riveted brush of his gaze and the rapt heat of his attention. It's new yet the same, like a resurrected memory.

As the billows swarm around us, there's only me and him locked, our bodies trembling and tangled. I did it. I broke the curse, and I've survived, and I've won. And he's still here with me. Who knows how long we have, but in this moment, we're alive and together.

"I was drowning," Elixir recalls, his bare chest heaving for air. "The saltwater."

"But why?" I splutter. "How?"

"Because I'm of the river, not the ocean." Shame cinches his features. "I never taught myself to swim with legs, much less to hold my breath for long spells in saltwater. After the Trapping, I was…I was too scared."

Too scared. For all his magic, this viper can't survive in saltwater. For all his experience with brews and the depths, this ruler had never learned to swim with his limbs or trained his lungs to endure. For all his knowledge, he'd never taken those precautions. For such a powerful being, fear had impaired him.

How very human. How very Fae.

"You saved me," Elixir says.

"You saved me first," I remind him, thinking of Scorpio. "How did you know where to swim?"

"I felt your temperature. I sensed your blood. I heard your pulse." He wavers, marveling. "I could follow them again."

The signs of my fear, my exhaustion, and my love.

Elixir felt those things. But he could only do that if…

He studies my expression and interprets my silence, the very sensation of it clogging my throat. "Could it be? Have I made you speechless?"

I half-laugh, half-sob. "Fables forgive you, but I think so."

"And I think…I think I know what it's like." He seizes my hand and rests it on his heart, the pulse heavy and rapid, the tempo escalating when he looks at me. "This is love?"

I nod and choke out, "Yes."

"Then it's yours. Forever, it shall be yours," Elixir hisses, barely finishing the sentence as his lips snatch mine. Our mouths part and slant. My whimper matches his growl, both thick and desperate as the kiss sweeps us under.

His tongue delves, flexing against me. I split my lips against his, catching the salted taste of him. Our mouths fuse, undulating in tandem. The kiss is hectic and deep and over too soon.

At the lash of a wave against the rocks, Elixir pries his lips from mine. His head snaps in the flood's direction, his brows furrowing, his eyes once again unfocused. He squints, that gaze unable to land on any specific location.

My intuition surfaces, bringing with it all the adaptations that come with magic and spells. "Elixir?" I press.

When he swings back to me, his pupils sharpen. "I see you, but…" As he turns to survey the figures hunkering behind us, I realize my sisters and his brothers have been quietly watching us.

Puck holds Juniper from behind, walling her in from the deluge. Cerulean's on bended knee, his splayed wings shrouding Lark from the billows. They fixate on us, waiting with mixtures of elation, amazement, and concern.

I alternate between our weathered group, with our torn clothes and bruised bodies, and Elixir's distant gaze. One by one, he drifts over the faces. Just like that, I know before my sister draws her conclusion.

"You can't see us," Juniper says.

"I cannot," Elixir confirms, peering toward the small gathering marooned on this platform, then swerving to me. "Yet I see light."

My heart swells with joy. The river ruler sees his bewitcher. He sees me, and it's new, and it's the same, and it's beautiful. Because he has always seen me. In a thousand different ways, he feels me, and he touches me, and he knows me.

Elixir sits up and cups my face. He stares as if he's reached his safe harbor, a place he already knows well, already knows the path to, only now he treasures it from a different angle. "I see you," he whispers. "That is all I desire."

I smile tearily into his hands. "I see you, too."

When we drag ourselves apart, my sisters crush themselves to me on either side. Cerulean hands Lark my necklace, and she drapes it over my throat while Juniper holds my hair.

I want to cover Elixir's nudity, not out of shame but privacy. However, there's nothing we can do about that, and he's hardly concerned about who sees him.

Quickly, I explain about Scorpio, the saltwater, Elixir's near-drowning, and the spell. Despite this shock of information and the calamity surrounding us, Elixir's brothers regard him with dark smirks that fail to conceal their shaken relief.

Puck shakes his head. "You fucker," he mutters.

"I'm pleased to see you in one piece as well," Elixir grunts.

"Now who said anything about one piece?" To illustrate, the satyr indicates a split in one of his antlers. "Don't suppose you know a way off this rock before I lose another part of my crown?"

Still too weak to move swiftly, Elixir says, "This flood is beyond me. I lack the strength." He glances across the gulch. "However…"

He draws his fingers over the thrashing river, sending ripples across the gulch. Seconds later, the water agitates from where the rapids usually run. Several waves break from the depth and roll toward us, the water shaping itself into the graceful bodies of six horses with glistening scales and finned manes.

The sight robs me of breath. Of course! I recall his tales about this place and how these water horses once rushed through this realm, chiseling out the secret passages and subterranean channels of The Deep. If they did that once, they can do it again.

The Kelpies gallop our way. They whinny, the sound infinite and vibrating through the expanse. As they race through the flood, the river splits and bleeds back into the recesses and tunnels. The animals drive off the flood, pushing the water back to where it came from. In their wake, the gulch drains, and the cave reappears from beneath the swells.

Half of the team speeds off, clearing the flood as they pass into farther areas of The Deep. The other half offers each pair a ride. Elixir slumps behind me, securing my midriff with his arms and draping his legs over one side as the kelpie dashes ahead, its liquid limbs pounding across the river. As we race through the arteries, the stampede snuffs out the last vestiges of chaos, and the water calms.

We emerge into The Twisted Canals, the devastation unhinging my mouth. Chunks of buildings and bridges have collapsed, waterfalls are overflowing, and puddles of foliage crowd the currents. A host of water dwellers swarm the river proper, from distressed dolphins to sharks and crocodiles, along with legions of other fish and reptiles, some floating lifeless.

Merfolk, undines, and water sprites drift about in a hollow daze, either bobbing in the ripples, collecting dead sea creatures or fallen Fae, salvaging boats and weapons, nursing contusions and bloody lacerations, or trying to scrape the debris from pathways.

My sisters and I take in the carnage of Faeries and fauna who didn't survive, their bodies amassing beside one of the few bridges left intact. There are visions one wishes they could unsee. For me, the suffering of innocent beings is one of those visions. I cover my mouth and catch Lark and Juniper doing the same, their eyes welling.

Cold terror grips me as I think of my chamber and how far the flood might have reached. My eyes dart about, scouring the environment for a snake with brown-marble scales. The longer this goes on, the worse my heart cracks.

Please! Please not him!

Puck and Cerulean wear agonized expressions. I turn to see Elixir's face twisting with grief. He glimpses the signs across my countenance, and beyond that, he senses them.

He smells the fallen. He hears the echoes of bereavement from his kin as they growl and weep and sing laments.

"I'm here," I tell him, caressing his jaw. "I'm right here."

"As am I," he says gruffly, covering my hand with his own. "We will find him."

Lotus. My eyes sting because of how much I want to believe Elixir.

The Folk stop to observe our approach, their murderous glares slackening as they watch us mounted on the majestic horses—The Three and their mortal sacrifices united atop the kelpies. Many of the wrathful expressions give way to widespread shock, while others seethe with bitterness. This is too monumental, too blatant a reality, too brutal an example of this world fading for them to weather any semblance of compassion or tolerance.

Only Elixir's presence pacifies them, along with the warning scowls of Puck and Cerulean. The kelpies slow to a trot, then stall before a walkway. We dismount to a strained audience, tension escalating by the second. Once the kelpies depart, that pressure intensifies. Already, we're forming a weaponless ring to guard one another.

Yet again, I want to preserve Elixir's modesty, though his subjects show no sign of caring about his state of undress. By now, I've seen enough of their unclad forms roaming about this domain to know better.

Thankfully, a figure with silvery blue hair hastens past the throng. Coral must have seen us coming because she's carrying a pair of leggings. And coiled safely around her arm is a loving sight.

"Lotus!" I dash from the huddle and meet the guard halfway. "Lotus!"

The reptile scrolls from the female's arm to mine, and I cradle my friend to my chest while gasping, "You're all right."

After accepting and donning the leggings, Elixir moves to stand behind me, visibly pleased to hear my relief. Coral inclines her head, her crystalline eyes having lost their luster. Blood has dried on her temple, her bronze skin is wan, and her billowing pants are shredded.

"The wee one must have sensed the incoming flood, because he was searching for you," she tells me. "The splashing was unmistakable. I found him cutting through The Sunken Isle just before the water gushed in."

She glances at Elixir. "Sire, I sought to alarm you, but The Pit of Vipers was empty apart for that coward, Scorpio, raiding your supplies. I tried to..." She huffs, clears her throat. "He fled before I could apprehend him, but I suspect he meant to impair you—" she slides her head toward me, "—or sabotage her. Be assured, I won't let him get away the next time."

"Never mind Scorpio," Elixir grates. "He is taken care of, for the time being."

The river Faeries watch us, pensive and alert. One false move, and the tension will snap. One false word, and this could turn into a bloodbath. Cerulean and Puck yield to their brother, waiting for him to take the initiative, all the while both Faeries shift in front of my sisters.

But this is one juncture where actions speak louder than words. Elixir is the epitome of this, so I know he'll understand.

I set my fingers on his arm. "If I may."

His eyes warm on me. "Always."

With Lotus strapped to my arm, I swap covert glances with my sisters, who break from their lovers. Without delay, our trio steps across the walkway and does as our village did after The Trapping.

The Faeries gawk as the three of us begin to help clear the wreckage. In my periphery, I catch pride slanting across Elixir's countenance, which transfers to Puck and Cerulean as they join us. Coral looks impressed, then falls in line and inspires handfuls of others to follow suit.

Soon enough, the entirety of The Twisted Canals is laboring in unison, gathering the detritus and the fallen, then bidding farewell to the latter as the water buries the lost beneath the ripples. For this brief time, an unspoken truce forms. Silence engulfs The Deep as Faeries and humans work together to pick up the pieces.

We do what we can until the surviving crickets cease chirping, and dawn falls over the land. Cascades tumble down loose mantles. The river has preserved its aquamarine glow, and orbs wink from the canopy like celestials.

According to Coral, the flood had reached The Pit of Vipers shortly after Scorpio exited there. Coral and the resident vipers had escaped, but Elixir's inventory didn't last. With a grisly snarl, Elixir orders everyone away from that immediate area and charges in its direction to evaluate the damage. He's gone for longer than I care to think about, and when he returns, a terrible weight drags down his features.

Elixir has managed to recover a handful of restoratives for the wounded, but he could have done a great deal more with his territory intact. Unfortunately, the majority of his mixtures had shattered, infesting the den with free-floating dark magic. For the foreseeable future, none are permitted to enter but Elixir, who will need weeks, if not months, to purge and rebuild the vicinity.

In the meantime, we bathe our injuries in the cleanest parts of the river and dress our wounds. Cerulean and Puck offer whatever reserves they can spare from the mountain and forest, including any natural textiles, elements, and ingredients that will help. It's a start, at least.

Ultimately, we've made a small dent in progress. In addition to healing, it will take a long time to restore what's left of this realm and the fauna territories. Although my sisters and I have endured plenty of setbacks while rescuing mortal animals, this amount of desolation exceeds what we've ever experienced. Our hearts bear too many emotional fractures at once, so I pause regularly to wrap Lark and Juniper in my arms, hugging them until they're ready to continue.

By now, the river Faeries are either too sedated, too traumatized, or too fatigued to grieve or seek vengeance. At one point, I catch sight of a mer child sniffling in a cattail pool. I kneel beside him and ask, "Would you like to hear a story?"

The Fae gawks through wide-set lavender eyes but nods timidly. With a grin, I settle my legs into the water and begin the first lines of *The Viper in the Waterfall*, a comforting tale and one of the more humorous stories about food. I soften my tone, and within seconds, the child sighs in delight and shyly pets Lotus, who's now hanging off my neck like a sling.

While narrating, I feel golden eyes lingering on me, warming my back like a beacon.

A few Faeries who eavesdrop cast me furtive glances. After the child swims off, I migrate to several other figures in need of comfort and offer words of encouragement. For the ones who respond favorably, their shoulders unwind, and their jaws relax.

Once the colony has retired to their broken homes, tunnel recesses, and underwater lairs, Coral departs with Lotus. The guard knows of a nearby pool where she assures me the wearied snake will be safe and contented to rest.

Cerulean flies off with Puck harnessed to his chest. Elixir follows via the water.

Despite my objections that Elixir's too drained for the excursion, and despite Lark's protests that Cerulean's wings are too tattered to make the journey, the males had insisted on searching for our weapons in The Kelpie Rapids.

They return with Lark's whip, plus Puck and Juniper's archery, and my spear. But they've yet to locate Cerulean's javelin and Elixir's forked daggers.

I've lost the map I'd drawn for them. Likely, the original sketch has also been vanquished, but I can make another version later.

All in good time. What matters is that we're alive.

We move from The Twisted Canals to the same walkway where I'd once trailed Elixir in The Fauna Tides. The extension is remote enough for us to speak freely. A draft rustles the remaining bulrushes lining the planks. Banked in lantern light, we stand together, worn but unwilling to forfeit our plans.

Puck folds his arms over his torn leather vest and regards me. "You know, I admire you, to the point of jealousy."

"This should be interesting," Cerulean says with his profile casually propped between his thumb and index finger.

"And educational," Juniper adds blandly.

"The way you wooed this fucker." The satyr clicks his head toward Elixir, and the pair of leaf earrings looped through Puck's earlobes jingle. "Killing the water lord with kindness, so he never saw it coming. Your knack for altruism even lured some of the river Fae to your side. That's a whole new level of badassery."

While Elixir glowers toward his brother, I laugh. "Thank you."

"A merry pleasure."

"Where do we go from here?" Lark asks while combing her fingers through her matted white hair. "If this happened to the river, there's no telling what'll happen next in the mountain or forest."

"We continue to repair The Deep while monitoring our own terrains," Cerulean provides, his voice as swift as a breeze. "In addition to a dozen other crucial, considerable, confounding tasks."

"Such as potential war," Puck drawls in his Fae accent. "Saving our world, that sort of shit."

"But first we recruit allies," Juniper lists while counting off her fingers. "All the while, researching how to end mortal sacrifices, in addition to the historic strife between humans and Faeries."

"Finding this 'second way' you spoke of," Elixir interprets. "The alternative you discovered in a Fable."

Juniper gives a brisk nod. "Restoration, recruits, and research. And if necessary, self-defense. In that order."

"We'll need a middle ground," I say. "A safe place to rendezvous, possibly a stronghold."

"We've been meeting at my home in The Fauna Tower," Cerulean says. "The elevation and panoramic view give us an advantage against invasion. Though, there's always The Congress of Ravens."

"What the fuck?" Lark blurts out, amazed. "There's a Congress of Ravens?"

Cerulean smirks, his blue eyes glinting. "The sky is infinite, and The Solitary Mountain is vast, with ranges unfrequented and peaks not yet explored. It's close to The Flight of Kestrels."

"There's a Flight of Kestrels?!"

A teasing grin slants his dark lips. "Oops. Dear me, did I also forget to mention The Crown of Kingfishers?"

Lark smacks his arm. "You are sooooo taking me to these places. Are there hidden corners to get frisky, too?"

"Does it need to be designated?" Cerulean's voice dips to a hum. "Rest assured, I can fuck you anywhere."

I force out a cough and peek at Elixir, my cheeks blazing. We haven't spoken since I broke the curse. "Are there more caverns in The Deep we haven't reached?"

He turns my way, his irises liquid gold—molten and piercing. "The underground is nearly as infinite as the sky. The places we sought are only the beginning."

"Ah, ah, ah," Puck says, breaking our trance by wagging his finger at Juniper, who's scowling at him in silent accusation. "Trust me, I've taken you to every damn location in the woodland. My domain is sandwiched between these two pricks." He gestures between Cerulean and Elixir while enduring my know-it-all sister's scrutiny. "The forest is smaller, easier to cover ground, and because I know you, I get shit done with spare time to fry you pancakes. You've seen everything."

"I'd better have," she declares.

"Pancakes?" Lark parrots. "You mean, she actually lets you control the stove?"

Puck shrugs. "I know it's hard to believe, but I'm not just a roguish face."

"You cook?"

"I dabble."

Pride lifts Juniper's chin. "His dishes could bring kings and queens to their knees."

Lark leans into Cerulean while reexamining the satyr. "You know, I thought I'd hate you less once you proved yourself worthy of Juniper, but I was wrong. I hate you more."

"Jealous?" Puck taunts with a mischievous grin.

"You know it. But don't get used to that. I'm the sister. I've got dibs." Lark points at me. "That goes for you, too, missy."

I blow her a kiss. "You'll always have me."

Elixir grunts. "I would not compare the woodland to the inside of a sandwich. It is degrading."

"Ah, but that's where the meat is," Puck replies. "That's where you find the good stuff, and it's the midpoint, which is why I nominate my turf as the new meeting point. I'm tired of risking a nosebleed in The Fauna Tower, and there's no way in hell I'm wearing these leathers down in your muggy snake pit."

"So, take 'em off." Lark quirks a brow. "I dare you."

Puck swings his gaze her way. "Luv, you don't want to get into a stripping contest with me. You'll lose."

"Reckon I won't, but I've had enough games to last me a lifetime."

"For Cerulean's sake, I hope you mean outside of bed."

Lark's mate sniggers while I interject, "What about allies?"

"We have a few," Lark says. "A cantankerous moth, a jumbo centaur, and a handful of other accomplices, plus a menagerie of fauna."

"What about Foxglove?" Juniper adds, then notices her lover's sudden, deadly glare. "Give her a chance, Puck."

"For you, and only for you," he concedes, all traces of mischief gone from his expression. "But it's really Cypress who needs to give the nymph a chance. He's the one that bitch shot."

"Is Cypress a forgiving soul?" I ask.

"Guess we'll see," Puck answers.

After that, there's not much else to discuss without fainting from exhaustion and hunger. Elixir designates the nearest safe landscapes and vacant chambers for everyone to claim, most of them close to The Drift of Swans and The Mer Cascades.

Before disbanding, Elixir squints toward Juniper, his pensive gaze straying over her. Thankfully, neither she nor Puck notice. When Elixir catches me watching him in confusion, he clears his throat. "For the eternal wild."

The saying is a balm to my soul. We repeat the farewell to one another, then split apart. As we do, my sisters corral me to the sidelines flanked by bulrushes.

"What—," I begin.

"We know that look," Lark interrupts, planting her fists on her curvy hips. "Don't do it, Cove."

"Don't what?"

"Don't give him up," Juniper clarifies in her smoky voice. "Your love broke that spell. And the way you two looked at each other during the flood? It was like…"

"Like you wanted to rip each other's clothes off and swear eternal devotion," Lark says flatly. "That is, if Elixir *had* been wearing clothes at the time. Anyway, you've barely spoken since then, despite all the fuck-me looks you've been tossing each other."

"We have not—"

"Yes," Juniper states. "You have. And for once in my life, I insist you disregard practicality. If you're in love, be in love. Period."

A lump forms in my throat. "It's not that simple."

They know why. Lark and Cerulean are mated, and Juniper has a chunk of Puck's immortality, but the curse prevents Elixir and me from having any such fortune. Eventually, our ages will show, and he'll outlive me.

Besides, if Lark and Juniper stay here, someone needs to be with Papa. I won't leave him alone.

"Hon." Lark tucks a strand of teal behind my ear. "Papa would want you to be happy. And you can visit him with us whenever you want. As for the rest, who gives a shit? Reckon there are no guarantees in either world. Might as well grab your sexy Fae—the bloke's got one hell of a naked body, by the way—and keep 'im for as long as you can."

Juniper straightens, her spruce-green eyes vivid in the shadows. "You've always been the one who sees the best in all people, no matter who they are. If he's worth it, then be stubborn. Choose who deserves you, who matches you, not who makes sense."

"A few questions," Lark adds. "How's the fucking?"

My face suffuses with warmth. "It's…it's…."

Deep and dark and dangerous. That's how it is.

"Uh-huh." She gives me a saucy look. "Based on the sight of his bare ass and other certain parts, I can guess. Lots of muscle there. But can you talk to each other?"

"About anything."

"Do you laugh?"

"In our own way."

"Do you understand one another?"

"Every time."

"Does he make you feel safe?"

"Yes."

"Are you still enemies?"

"No."

Lark gestures, as if the rest speaks for itself, while Juniper concludes, "Then what's the problem?"

In the cast of lantern light, I take in my sisters' faces. Their features are stronger, happier. All the while, that same bond we've shared since childhood is still there, as if we've never left home. I snatch them and crush us together, our trio exchanging embraces and kisses.

"Hot damn." Lark appraises Cerulean, who's speaking in Faeish with his brothers, the draft tousling his blue-black hair. "Don't think I'll be sleeping just yet."

"To this day, your smutty train of thought astounds me," Juniper says.

"Whatever. Based on your radiant complexion lately, I'd say you have no right to judge. I know about the kinks of a satyr, and I know what you two were doing right before Cerulean and I stopped at your cabin on the way here. It took forever for anyone to answer the door, and you were both dewy and breathless. Not to mention, Puck was wearing low-slung breeches and grinning like an asshole, and your blouse was on backward, and your reading spectacles were askew. What was he doing to you this time?"

Juniper's face bloats with crimson as she peeks at the satyr, who tosses her a devoted and rather wicked smirk. "It's always new," she confides in wonder. "How many ways can one possibly have sex?"

"A lot more in Faerie," Lark declares.

We chuckle, then sober quickly as Juniper frets, "It's wrong to think this way, with everything in ruins."

I give her a consoling smile and wind my arm around her shoulders. "Lovemaking in a time of strife isn't something to feel guilty about. We're alive, and why not express our gratitude for that? Take Cerulean and Puck into your arms. Relish every second with them. Loving is living, and isn't that what we're fighting for?"

Juniper pulls me into a hug. Lark joins in, and we stay like that for a while, soaking in one another's presence.

Moments later, Cerulean is airborne with Lark, who's already toying with his loose shirt. Puck's tone smolders as he mutters something in my sister's ear that causes her breath to hitch, and he leads her to one of the remaining boats.

Then they're gone, leaving me and Elixir behind. In the quiet darkness, I feel his sideways glance like a thrust of water—powerful and penetrating. We're alone, standing on opposite ends of the walkway.

As the river licks the banks, we turn to face each other.

35

The distance seems short, yet it stretches before me like a chasm, as if I'll never reach him quick enough, soon enough. I'd heard my sisters' words loud and clear, but I need to hear his. I need to know what he's thinking and if it's the same thing floating through me. But he's never been a creature of many words, so I settle for the expression on his face.

Elixir gazes at me through panels of long, black hair. He stares as if having found shelter, a tranquil port in which to dwell, to anchor himself. Those burnished irises punch through the dark, striking true and swift. They swarm me like golden pools, seeping into my veins. It's a newfound sensation, but already it rocks me to the core.

Water laps against the platform. Eddies pass through the bulrushes with a soft swish, as if whispering, *Hush, it's all right.*

Everything will be all right. This is okay, it's real, and it's safe.

My bare feet shuffle in place. Elixir observes this, his visage riveted with affection. In the past, he's heard and sensed me making such gestures, however this is the first time he's witnessing them. The hate and vengeance of years before have vanished, swept away with the tide and the passage of time. Now there's only raw longing and sudden uncertainty.

He opens his mouth. "You—"

I open mine. "We—"

We stagger into another awkward pause. This is the part where we would laugh sheepishly, but none of this is funny, because too much of this matters.

Elixir waits for me to continue, but my tongue freezes, caught in a net of fear and desire, hope and doubt, dismay and comfort. I can't say which emotions are more potent, more promising.

The water lord hisses in Faeish and stalks forward. The planks rattle under his weight, and the leggings cling to him like film, and his skin permeates the air with the intoxicating scents of bergamot and black pepper—its own breed of dark, sinful magic. Plates of olive muscle shift with his movements, his bare torso flexing as though every part of him is fighting to hold itself together.

He pauses to loom before me, a tremulous edge to his voice, his accent more pronounced. "If you will not speak, I shall. I must deserve this moment with you."

"Elixir—," I start, wanting to assure him that he's already earned this moment, however tongue-tied I appear to be.

Regardless, his fingers land on my lips. The pad of his thumb rides across the seam. "Let me," he implores. "Please."

His digit tingles my flesh, traveling down the center of me, to the cleft between my thighs. I find the wits to nod. We stand there, suspended over the river, at the hub of this world, where anyone who's still awake can see us.

Yet neither of us hides nor shrinks from view. Instead, we move closer until his chest grazes my breasts.

The way Elixir physically buoys himself for a speech is utterly endearing. The vision clamps onto my heart. "In The Fauna Tides, and later in The Fountain of Tears, you asked me questions I would not answer. I will do so now."

Elixir fastens his gaze to mine. "You asked what I desired above all else for myself. The answer is you. It has always been you. It was you in every form, in every guise. I wanted your pain, your guilt, and your punishment. I wanted to make you pay for what happened to my kin, for what the curse did to my mothers. I blamed you to hell.

"But damnation, I also wanted to cure your pain, erase that guilt, and free you from that punishment. I wanted to protect you from suffering. I wanted to forgive you. More than that, I wanted you to have that which you desired most—for you to forgive yourself. It was not your fault. If you cursed me, it was my doing. Do not protest," he demands when I shake my head.

We were only children. I've forgiven myself and him, and I know he's forgiven me. But I do as he bids and stay quiet.

"You asked why I'd chosen Elixir as my name. You asked what I was trying to heal," he murmurs. "To the latter, the answer is my grief. For nearly a decade, I have been seeking an antidote to the pain of losing my mothers, the anguish of knowing what my power did to them, and the agony of losing my kin. I saved some, but I failed to save them all. Despite the games and sacrifices, I swore to myself I would brew a restorative for this pain. To the former question, that is why I call myself Elixir.

"While I kept failing to devise a cure, I grew more bitter, angrier. Thus, I brewed what I knew would at least work. Remedies for my kin and poisons for my enemies—for humans.

"You asked what gave me comfort. The answer used to be revenge. Now the answer is this moment. It is here with you." He coasts his knuckles over my cheek, then runs them down my bobbing throat, and down still to my ramming heart. "In my den, you asked where I live, sleep, and take refuge. My answer is with you. Where you are is my refuge. Where you live and breathe is my home. Your ceaseless chatter is my home. Your kindness is my home. Your merciful smile is my home. Your selflessness is my home."

Elixir's orbs brim. "Your light is my home."

He drags his fingers away and strides backward, providing me the space to exhale and give my verdict. If I was speechless before, my vocal cords are drained now. I have no words left, because nothing I feel for him would fit in my mouth. It scarcely fits inside my body.

My eyes water. Being with him was always a risk, yet that risk always had a time limit.

Has that changed? How much farther am I willing to take this gamble?

A question forms in the shadows of Elixir's face, tinged with confusion as he beholds my paralysis. Whatever he sees unsettles him, the foundation sinking beneath.

"Er...I'm done now," he announces. "You were saying? Before I began?"

"Was I going to say something?" I utter. "I'm not sure."

"That is not like you."

"People change."

He peers at me. "Do they?"

After that speech, how can he ask that?

Oh. He isn't talking about himself.

I remember the words I'd spoken during our first clash in The Shiver of Sharks. *You haven't changed.* That couldn't be further from the truth now.

What I feel for him had guided me through a raging flood. What I feel for him cracked a Fae witch's spell wide open. What I feel for him defied this world and won my freedom.

If this unconditional emotion can accomplish all that, what else can it do? Where else can it take us? Instead of reasoning what's feasible if we're apart, I want to know what's possible if we stay together.

I saunter his way, my answer spilling forth with the resonance of a siren. "You must know that I've changed," I say while coiling a lock of his hair around my finger. "Otherwise, I wouldn't be touching you like this."

"But what is this expression on your face? It is strange." Frustration tenses his jaw, despite the way he leans into my touch, his baritone gruff. "It does not match the tone of your voice. How your forehead crinkles. The inward slope of your brows. I cannot recognize the shape of these things. I've never..."

Seen them before. That's what he means. He's never physically seen them on me before, apart from tracing them while in darkness.

"My expression is made of many emotions," I intone. "It's yearning and desperation and faith and happiness and terror. It's everything."

His frown deepens. "Terror."

"I'm not afraid of you. I'm afraid of hurting you." I gulp. "I won't live forever."

Comprehension spreads across his features. If he outlives me, it will cause him anguish. I can't do that to him.

"It's true, isn't it?" I ask. "That line from the Fable? About the curse preventing any other magic from affecting us?"

"It is true," he murmurs, sadness clashing with determination. "But I do not give a shit about that. I never have. I would choose a moment with you over an eternity with anyone else."

The surety of our fate drills its fangs into me, yet his words buoy me like a raft. "It appears we're in accord. I still can't let this go, not if it's worth the risk, because what if the pleasures of this life outweigh the grief? I could be with a human, and it would be the same gamble. But I don't want a mortal man or woman. I want the uncertainty and poignancy. I want the danger and passion. I want the darkness and lightness. I want to go deep with you. I want only you."

Elixir swallows. "Is there…any other emotion on your face?"

"Let me show you." I take his fingers and drape them over my mouth, then along my chin, over my nose, under my eyelids, and up to my temple. I stand on my tiptoes for better access, and my mouth braces against him as I whisper, "This is what love looks like."

His eyes shutter, seeing my features in his mind. "I see it."

"And do you feel it?"

Those eyes whip open and peer at me, the orbs mesmerized and ravenous. "Yes," he hisses. "Fuck, yes."

My arms sling around his neck, my fingers dive into the black pool of his hair, and my voice cracks like a whip. "Then tell me."

He grabs my face, his lips sizzling against mine. "I love you."

"Say it again."

"I love you."

"Again."

"I want you," he says desperately. "I crave you. I desire you. I do not want you to leave. If need be, I shall tie you to this fucking platform. Or I shall toss you over my shoulder."

"Why?" I demand. "Tell me again."

"Because I love you!" he growls.

I nod vehemently, our mouths a brushfire about to ignite. "I love you, too."

"Then show mercy. Or tempt me, and I might poison the universe. Or disarm me, and I might brew a weapon to taint the world outside this walkway, so there is no one left but us."

"Don't you dare," I warn, but I know he's only partly serious.

"For you, I would drown the world," he swears, his arms banding around me. "I would flood these lands, so I'm the only one left to hear you moan while I fuck you. I would give you the space to climax as loudly as you need, as deeply as you can go, for as long as you are capable. I would make any corner of this world your home—our home. Or if it does not yet exist, I would tear a hole in these walls and claim that territory for you."

"Monster," I scold while chuckling. "Savage."

"Temptress," he grits out. "Salvation."

"You would never do those things, even for me."

A ruthless divot burrows into his cheek, tempting me to sketch it with my thumb, my lips, my tongue. "Do not challenge what I would forsake for you, for my restraint knows no bounds where you are concerned. You have only to say the word, my light. I'm at your behest. I'm yours to command. I'm yours to defy." He pulls back, those eyes blazing. "Make your choice."

I curl myself against Elixir, every soft part of me compressing with every hard part of him. "I already have."

Elixir's face darkens with ambition, his solid body and possessive gaze and hot timbre scorching me beneath the flimsy clothing. "Cove?"

"Elixir?" I gasp, heady and hungry.

"For what I intend to do to you, we need to get much closer."

Much closer, I agree. And far more private.

36

The instant I tell him yes, Elixir has never moved faster. With a fiendish growl, he jerks me into him, snatches the backs of my thighs, and hoists me off the ground. I chortle and hook my legs around his waist, the caftan riding high to my pelvis. With the speed of a viper, he secures me to his frame, charges across the walkway, and hurtles us off the edge.

I half-scream, half-laugh just before we crash under. The tepid water swallows us, scattering a troop of catfish and a few straggling stingrays. The river bathes us in glittering aquamarine, vermillion moss clings to the rocks, and stalks of foliage sway. We're down for mere seconds before Elixir's momentum shoves us back to the surface.

We break through, droplets splintering like broken crystals. I feel the lower portion of Elixir's body shift, his limbs fusing into a black and gold viper's tail that tears through the leggings he'd received from Coral. Bracing me to his chest, my dark Fae surges forth and slices like an arrow across the river. Scrolls of water pitch out of the way as he shears through, producing small billows over the expanse. His gaze clings to mine, our noses tapping, our lips rubbing.

I can't tell where we're going or how long it will take to get there, but our bodies have other ideas. My groin abrades the stiff ridge protruding from his waist, the friction so torturous it should be outlawed. My teeth sink into my lower lip to blot out a whimper, the sound curling up my throat. My blood changes temperature, and the space between my legs pools with fluid.

Elixir sees, hears, and feels my arousal. He narrows his eyes. "Oh, fuck waiting."

He clamps onto the back of my neck, hauls me forward, and snatches my mouth with his. A startled moan lurches from my lips, which yield and soften. The moment they do, Elixir groans and dives in for the kill. Slanting his head, he flexes his tongue along the seam of my lips, teasing them open. I split my mouth and melt as his tongue flexes into me, swatting me into a frenzy.

The wet, hot cave of his mouth dissolves me from the inside. The taste of freshwater and wine drugs my senses. The strength of his jaw pushes the kiss deeper, harsher.

I splay my lips wide and roll them with his, every lick sending embers up my limbs. We heave ourselves into it, our nostrils flaring, the kiss on the brink of going wild as he accelerates through the river. We've scarcely begun when Elixir pries himself away, both of us fighting to preserve oxygen. Fables forgive me, I don't think I'll last at this rate.

In that instant, I catch Elixir struggling to tamp down a heady grin. He glowers to conceal it, but his swollen lips keep twitching, creating a divot in his cheek that I want to sketch with my tongue.

I tap his lips. "What's that?"

"Nothing," he grunts, the sound gravely with lust.

"It looks like something to me. Can I guess? Is it a smile?"

"No and no."

"Um, yes and yes. I know what I see."

Sinful inspiration alights his face, making it clear he's aware of something I'm not. We vault into a tunnel, into a shawl of blackness. I jolt in surprise, when truly I should have expected this. Shadows ripple through the area; otherwise, the faint gleam of Elixir's eyes is the only source of light.

In the mouth of the passage, he slows and breathes thickly against my mouth, the sensation heightened in the darkness. "What you see is one thing. What you feel is another."

Some type of vicious intent oozes from his voice. He lets the reply hang in the air, a second before my back hits a wall draped in hanging foliage. The plants cushion the impact. Even so, I gasp. Excitement and desire knot in my core as Elixir traps me against the foundation, his solid muscles fencing me in and spreading me around him.

Those irises crackle. With that, he slithers down my body. His pectorals run down my breasts, which quiver and toughen through the caftan.

Elixir sinks under the surface. One hand fastens to my hip, keeping me afloat as I gawk ahead, realizing what he's about to do. My eyelids flutter at the sensation of his palm gliding over my naked legs. He bunches the caftan higher until it's a mess of drenched fabric around my waist, then he hitches my knees over his shoulders and spreads me wide. I suck in a breath, the noise skittering down the tunnel.

But the inhalation quickly turns into a stuttered moan the instant his head ducks between my thighs. His hair brushes my skin. Both hands splay under my buttocks, fixing me in place so that I can't move.

My core pulses, the inner flesh exposed—then inundated as the soft tip of his tongue flicks at the slit. I cry out, the sound fragmenting. A flurry of sensation erupts in the place where his mouth makes contact. With agonized slowness, Elixir samples the tender folds, the flat of his tongue sketching them, then nudging them farther apart, then dipping into them. He starts a rhythm, probing through my walls, in and out.

My muscles liquefy. My thighs quaver.

I squirm, my fingers dunking under the water and skewering into the roots of his hair. Using that for leverage, I grind my hips against his face, keening aloud with every lashing pump of his tongue.

Elixir licks into me, lapping at the wetness that leaks from my body, as if he wants to drink me dry. He does this until I'm inconsolable, my moans tight and needy, the water splashing around me.

He withdraws, rides his tongue along the seam, and finds the ridge of nerves within the thatch of curls. First, that tongue dabs at my clit, etching the ruched skin over and over. The feather-light touch ignites a thousand prickles and turns my cries into sobs. And when his mouth seals around the bud and tugs with force, white spots burst through the darkness.

He sucks and sucks and sucks me deeply.

The pleasure rises and rises and rises.

I feel the texture of his hum, satiny against the kernel of nerves. He alternates between pulling on the apex, lunging his tongue into my slickness, and urging more fluid from my body. The darkness swirls around us, blinding me to our surroundings, fixating me to his ministrations.

Everything heightens, magnifies, and amplifies.

My hips gyrate astride his mouth and ride that silken, sinful tongue. The precipice edges nearer yet farther. Tremors wrack me, the spasm close, so very close. Elixir inches back and brings his full attention back to my nub, patting it rhythmically, laving that crest until it swells...throbs... and ruptures.

My digits yank on his mane, and my back arches, and dots explode in my vision. Heat bursts from my core. I shatter into the passage, weeping with pleasure while he gives me several more passes of his tongue, draining every forsaken drop, every streak of rapture from me.

I slump against the wall as Elixir sloshes up from the below, those eyes smoldering. He catches me in his arms, and his mouth brushes my slack lips, and he husks, "Does your cunt want more?"

"Yes," I breathe.

My voice flutters, spent yet not entirely satiated. Elixir nods, his gaze brimming. He scoops me up and coasts across the tunnel while I hang on to him, limp as a blanket.

The pitch black evaporates behind us, replaced by a teal-spangled ceiling and a nearby waterslide. I recognize the passage now. Of course. I'd ventured through here on my way to the Middle Moon Sail, and I'd sat in a boat here with his brothers and my sisters. It's the shortcut to the network of subterranean corridors that connects some of my favorite spots in this world, the places also accessible from the secret tunnel of The Sunken Isle.

Until now, I hadn't realized how shallow the water becomes here. It would be effortless to stand upright. In fact, that would make it easy to do other things.

When Elixir reaches the landing where I've met him numerous times, the sight of that ledge restores my energy. He pauses and frames my waist, about to heft me onto the platform.

But I have another idea. And I move quicker.

I wiggle from his grasp, seize his shoulders, whirl him around, and push him against the landing. Elixir makes a gruff sound of surprise. His eyes stagger across mine. "What—"

"Sit on the ledge," I order, then bat my lashes coyly. "Please, Sire?"

Because when I'd said I wanted more, I hadn't meant for just myself.

Elixir hears the polite dominance in my tone. His visage creases, amorous and carnal.

Obediently, he tows himself onto the landing, the brackets of his arms bunching as they bear his weight. His viper tail shudders into limbs. I brace my fingers on the rim while watching the profile of his backside contract. In one glorious, dripping sprawl, the viper sits there with his smooth calves dangling over the sides.

He looks down, awaiting my intentions. I think he's expecting me to mount the landing and straddle his waist.

A decadent thrill eddies through me, rinsing away the remnant shyness. Elixir gazes with interest, but it isn't until I sidle between his knees that his face slackens, and he speaks through his teeth. "Cove."

"Shh," I beseech, placing a finger against my puckered lips. "This is only fair."

He'd tasted me first, after all. His throat pumps, and his chest siphons air, but he doesn't speak.

Just how speechless can I render him?

I slip into the vent of his legs, where his cock rises like a mast from his waist. It's long, flushed dark, and swollen for me.

All for me.

My mouth tingles. I slide my fingers over Elixir's thighs and clutch his hips. Above me, his exhalations turn gritty and uneven. That's the final encouragement as I dip my head.

My tongue comes out and drags up his cock in a single, prolonged lick. An inarticulate noise grates from Elixir's mouth. Around me, his body tenses, then melts as my tongue climbs to the underside, then repeats the motion, then rolls over the head.

The apex of my tongue traces the slit, and salt dissolves on my palate, and a moan skitters from his mouth. I tease him like this repeatedly, swirling his crown until he's panting, his groans as rough as sand.

I glimpse him clutching the rim with one hand, the veins popping in his wrist. His spine is bowed, and his head lulls back, and his free hand descends into my hair. He cups my head but lets me explore, lets me sample every inch of his hard flesh.

His moans wet me anew. I need more of him, so much more. The second my lips strap around his length, Elixir's body jolts.

"For fuck's sake, Cove," he gushes.

My name is a plea, a surrender. Spurred on, my mouth rushes over him. I exert pressure and suck in his entire length, suctioning around his cock and stroking it to the brink. My head bobs, guided by the speed and depth of his moans while the ruler of this river, the lord of water Fae, my captor, my friend, my lover, shakes like a droplet, yielding his power and growling into the caverns.

He arches forward, holds my scalp with his free hand, and juts his hips, his cock meeting my open lips. We work together, sinking him deeper. Each wild howl into the void motivates me to do irreparable damage, to empty him of any other sensation but this.

Elixir watches, groaning as my tongue alternates between gliding up his length and etching that sensual incision across the engorged head. His body tightens, almost there, almost there. His moans of pleasure become fractured, unwieldy, and helpless.

That's it. Lose it like a villain.

So, he does. Elixir goes still, then convulses with a final shout.

His joints contract, his body quaking. I moan with him, consuming his release, a stream of heat pouring down my throat. Like he'd drained me, I drain him back.

The water lord buckles onto the landing, but only for a second. I've barely lifted my head when a pair of hands catches and wrenches me out of the river.

I yelp. Elixir stands while planting me on the landing, water spilling around our feet. He mutters something in Faeish, then claims my mouth while ushering me into the corridor. With our lips welded together, we stumble through the passages, occasionally plastering ourselves against the walls to feast on one another.

"In the water." He nips my throat. "On the grass."

"In the tunnels." I lick the peak of his ear. "In bed."

"Against the wall." He snags on my caftan and yanks it down my body. "Atop a table."

"Everywhere," I agree, my breasts mashing against his chest. "Every way."

"Never fucking enough," he vows.

We flounder naked down the halls, finally making it past a cave entrance bordered in reeds. The pond glistens with its blue sheen, and the pearlescent lilies glow from their floating pads. We hadn't known, but it appears the flood has spared this place, apart from the cave's sodden state and a few chunks of uprooted shrubs.

Elixir presses his forehead to mine and walks me backward. He flicks his wrist, inciting a swifter cascade from the pond's rear foundation. The deluge tumbles from the same overhang beneath which I'd found Elixir stroking himself, where I'd touched him, where I had finished what he'd started.

My heart beats a hectic percussion in my chest. My core is drenched and yearning to be filled.

Elixir must know, because he maneuvers me quicker. He steers me under the waterfall, which splatters over us. I move in sync with him, pressing my back flush against the spongy facade, where a portion of the torrent races down.

Our pace is feverish and impatient. Panting, I clamp onto Elixir's shoulders as he hoists me off the ground. My thighs spread around his waist, my ankles linking beneath his solid buttocks. My nipples pit into his chest, my knees steeple high, and my entrance pulsates with want.

His prick nudges between mine, and he slants my hips, the angle a prelude to how deeply he plans to reach. I whine as his cock poises at my opening, the scantest of touches sending blasts of heat to that place. My cleft throbs like a pulse point.

Suddenly, Elixir gives me a tender kiss, light and brief. His lips pause there, rest there—and his hips vault upward. His cock pitches high and hot into me. I cry out, the impact jostling me upward, the force of it sprawling me wider.

Elixir keeps his mouth on mine and withdraws, then slams in again. I whimper louder, the wet clutch of my body fastening around him, sucking him in.

Without making a sound, Elixir braces our parted lips together and whips into me again, and again, and again. With controlled motions, his waist undulates between my thighs, my walls drenching him to the hilt.

Desperate moans vault from my throat. Other than a twitch of his face, his expression remains fixed, concentrating on my reactions, on the noises I make, on the way I cling to him, maneuver with him.

Elixir veers back to watch, which tilts me at a greater angle. I cling to his nape as his cock pitches into me, fucks steadily into me. His hips circle, grinding me into the mossy walls and hitting an unbearable spot. The tip of his shaft probes there, and his waist shoves between my thighs, which begin to shake.

My mouth falls open. "Oh."

"Feel it," he urges. "Take it."

I do continuously, tirelessly, thoroughly. We stare at one another while our pelvises thrust, catching a tempo and whisking in tandem. Yet he isn't nearly close enough, so I roll my hips sensually into his, causing his jaw to unhinge, a haggard groan toppling out of him.

"Cove," he rasps.

"Elixir," I keen, then echo similar words he'd offered me earlier. "Does your cock want more?"

"Shit," he entreats. "Yes."

I jerk him forward, pinning our eyes together. "Then fuck me more."

Gold flares in his eyes. A vehement sort of desire scrunches his features. He collides against me, the span of his waist splitting me open, our naked bodies plastered like film.

We charge at one another, the wet slap of skin resounding in my ears. Elixir pounds into me, his length striking into my slickness. Everything is sodden and seamless, hard and hot. My palm spans his buttocks, the dimples contracting, his lower body pumping with abandon.

My cries echo the pace of his cock, the beat of his hips. Elixir bows his head to scrape his teeth over one nipple until it peaks like a stone, and I chant so loudly it echoes through the cave.

He moves to the other nipple, teasing it while his waist pistons upward, slinging into me. Then he sucks on the crook of my neck, and I can't, I just can't anymore. I flatten my palm on the mossy mantel above us and use it for balance to swat his firm length.

Elixir hollers into my neck. He grapples an overhead ledge with his free hand and pivots high, meeting me halfway. Like this, I look down at him, he twists his face up to me, and we ride each other.

Everything converges. The waterfall dousing us. The torrent spraying mist at our flesh. The fluid sensation of him stretching me. The pressure building and the bliss escalating.

The rampant sounds of our moans smash together. We crash against the wall and wind ourselves tightly, my breasts squashed to his chest, his abdomen rippling. I take the brunt of his thrusts. The pleasure is so good, and his momentum is so wild, that my legs fall apart.

Elixir won't have that. He hooks my thighs under his arms and drives into me, his Fae stamina renewed. I sob for him to go faster, harder, deeper. He heeds my request, his cock whipping through my folds in quick, shallow strikes. The result is nothing short of excruciating and spine-tingling, locating an erotic spot that sends me into a tailspin.

"There," I gasp. "Fuck me there."

"Yes," he implores. "Come hard and sweet."

"Oh…"

"Come with me."

"I'm…"

"Come now."

My moans toughen into cries. I shout in tempo with his body, my folds coiling with tension. Elixir growls, and I feel the crown of his prick twitching on the verge of release.

Our mouths fuse. Our tongues tangle. Our breaths merge.

We stall, his cock lodged within me. We teeter, then dash off the edge. We come long and loud, our roars mingling, our walls constricting in a rush of liquid heat.

Regardless, Elixir doesn't stop. He surges his cock in tune to our climax, the cadence swift and then slowing to a gentle rock. When the tremors subside, his backside ebbs to a halt.

We sink into the wall and heave for air, sweat and mist dripping down our skin. Elixir's face presses to mine. He's still hard, and I still want him. But first I need to savor his thumping heartbeat, the heady sound of his rapture, and the gilded caress of his gaze.

We stare at one another, sweeping each other's hair from our faces and then threading our fingers. Elixir's brows crinkle in wonder. "Is love always like this? This craving to have you every time I touch you? The touch itself, so euphoric it becomes painful? Both a drug and a cure?"

My heart compresses into a fist, then softens and relaxes. "I don't know." I wring my arms around his shoulders. "But I hope so. We'll find out."

At last, that smile tugs on his lips. "We shall. Starting now," he vows right before slanting his hot mouth over mine.

He takes me again, making love to me slower this time. Yet there's still a tinge of savagery to it, barely contained restraint on our parts.

I love it. And I love how we're part of this wild world.

We swim in the lily pond afterward, prowling after each other, our fingers restless to grab. At last, we snatch. My curves mold to him, and my body straps around his torso, and his mouth sketches my collarbones.

The Fae layers his lips over mine, plying me with his tongue. In between kisses, I ask, "What is this place called?"

"The Lily Pond," Elixir says, his reply muffled against the crook of my mouth.

"Why?"

"Because it's a fucking lily pond," he husks, and I chuckle, and he devours the sound.

I hug him to me and sigh, "I would make a home in this place. I mean, I have a home with my family, and I know we haven't talked about where I'll live in The Deep, but if I could pick anywhere down here, it would be this pond. No predators. The blue water is cooler than others. Though, the lighting would have to be brighter, otherwise I'll turn into a nocturnal creature. I…ah," a gasp trips from my mouth as he sucks on the dip between my clavicles.

"I…uhh…Fables, you're good at that." Winded, I lick my lips. "You know, I…I once camped for fun beside the creek near my house, but I was nervous the whole time because I…insisted on being…alone. Ohh." His open-mouthed kisses ascend beneath my earlobe, where he draws the rounded top between his teeth. "I usually don't like being alone…but that time, I was. Ahh." I crush myself against him, my limbs tight around his waist while his tail swirls beneath us. "It's not like the caravan my sisters and I huddle inside for stories. My tent was exposed. Though, I suppose camping isn't the same as a home. I...what was I...what was I saying?"

Elixir's masculine chuckle rumbles into my skin. He twists to meet my gaze and speaks hoarsely, repeating everything I'd said before admitting, "Forgive me. I need to sample your tongue while it slips like that. I want to know the taste of every sound you make."

He means my lisp, so I nod. "Okay."

And after that, we withdraw from the water. Glazed in the pond's blue sheen, we crawl to the patch of grass where we'd first made love and collapse into the downy green. Resting on our sides, Elixir tucks me against him, kisses my shoulder, and settles his chin there.

Is it always like this? I think about his question, my lips tilting upward in response. Truly, I don't think it is, because it's different for every pair, even the ones who were enemies, then became lovers, then found happiness. It's always unique.

That's its own strength. That's what makes it real.

I nestle into Elixir's warmth, the world blurring as if we're underwater. At last, we do something we've never been able to do together, without it being forbidden.

Finally, we sleep.

Epilogue

Elixir

The vipers are restless tonight. I listen to them slinking through the den, the corded slide of their bodies rattling the vegetation. It is a far cry from their customary dormancy. Usually they idle beneath the shrubbery, twine into corkscrews, and content themselves to watch me work.

On this eventide, they break from routine. While kneeling beside the brewing vat, my ears detect nearby slopes of movement—a cobra slicing through underbrush and a python weaving between stalks. These serpents have an exceptional ability to change pace. At once, they are gradual. The next instant, predatory. It is a beautiful progression to hear, akin to the lash of a whip. Rarely do they require a shift in size, for they strike faster just as they are.

At the moment, they harbor no interest in hunting prey. So instead of retiring to the terrarium pit, the vipers have migrated to the den, the motions slow despite their attentiveness to my every step.

They are in a curious mood. Perhaps they suspect my intentions.

The corners of my lips curl. A certain mortal would call it a grin. In which case, it is fortunate she's not here to witness it. For the lady loves to tease me, and I lack the strength to deny her the diversion. She has always been impossible to resist.

She is also the reason I'm here. I could have remained in bed with her, soaking in the cadence of her breath while she dreamed. I could have listened to her pulse tap against her flesh, like a current lulling across a shoreline. I could have let her temperature seep into me. I could have watched her sleep, for I can do that now.

I could have awakened Cove, then fucked her deeply into the mattress. The memory of her wetness clenching around my cock mere hours ago sets my blood aflame. Desire floods my appendage. It is tempting to storm out of here. It would be a fierce pleasure to manifest into our bedroom, rip off the sheets, and strike hard and long until she comes. Though if we continue at this momentum, Cove will not be able to walk or swim straight.

I clench the vial in my fist. The pressure reminds me of the task at hand.

Instead of sinking between Cove's legs, I have pried myself from the lady's naked curves and materialized here. It was no trifling feat to leave her. However, a small globe of perspiration trailing down Cove's neck while she rested had imbued me with a sudden thought. An inspiration, of sorts.

As my blood cools, I fixate on the sounds frothing from the vat. My palm levels over the steam. If a human were to do this, the act would blister them to the point of agony.

It has no such effect on a Fae. I tilt my head to assess the signs. Vapors lick my skin, the texture slick. Bubbles multiply in droves. Once the mixture has reached the appropriate degree, a sweet incense rises from the surface.

My nostrils flare in recognition. "Jasmine," I murmur.

That is what the vipers smell. It is the scent of her.

From the moment Cove had brandished her spear against me in The Shiver of Sharks, the fragrance wafting off her damp skin had infused my senses. Even then, the potency of it nearly sunk me. From that moment on, the aroma became an intoxicant, of which there existed no antidote.

Now I welcome the intrusion. For it is my addiction and redemption. I take a heady draught and let it fill me to the fucking brim.

Even her sweat carries that scent. The serpents' attention makes sense. This is hardly a typical aroma in my den, in spite of the lustier, more advantageous concoctions divided amongst my cache.

While I have used a droplet from Cove before, to create a remedy for the wounds she suffered while battling the crocodiles, the ingredients that had percolated with the bead must have staunched the scent. By comparison, this particular blend enhances the floral whiff, the essence of petals mulled with several other components. An extract of lily pads. Rainwater from The Solitary Mountain, provided by Cerulean. Macerated pome fruit from The Solitary Forest, which Puck had collected. Lastly, a distillation of river water from The Solitary Deep. I'd harvested a spoonful from The Grotto That Whispers, the oldest well in this realm.

I graze my hand through the brew. Prickles across my knuckles signal a translucent appearance, at least from the onset. When one upends the contents, that will change.

I feel my eyes warm. The solution is ready.

It must be right. For I have been laboring on this for seven weeks since the flood, since the moment my den was restored and the most vital ingredients supplanted.

There is more to be done. There are tools and containers to replace. There are ingredients to harvest.

But for now, this is enough. I submerge the glass vial into the mixture and test the liquid by dripping a globule onto a leaf I'd plucked from the shrubbery. Hope surges through my veins when my fingers trace a bud that sprouts from the stem. Until tonight, the mixture had been incomplete. No matter how much I'd shredded myself in the past weeks, the answer had eluded me.

Finally, I'd realized what was missing. Finally, it is done.

Satisfied, I stopper the vessel, then stash it in my robe pocket and gain my feet. Twisting my head in the serpents' direction, I arch an eyebrow. "Wish me luck."

Turning on my heel, I stride from The Pit of Vipers. I have changed my mind about manifesting, for it takes a surplus of energy. I would rather preserve my strength for when I see Cove. In her presence, I shall need it. Otherwise, her smile alone will slay the eternal shit out of me.

I charge through the tunnels, shoot through the river, and stalk down another set of corridors. As I move, my fingers steal out to trace the walls, though I know the way. I have made this trek countless times, and the route to her is embedded into my mind.

But as the wild continues to fade, there is never a guarantee anything will stay the same. From one night to the next, a mountain might crumble, a forest might quake, or a raging river might swallow these passages.

After the flood, I leave nothing to chance.

The grave thought accelerates my pace. At last, the hushing sway of reeds fills my ears. I push through the fence of stalks and halt.

My heart pounds like a battering ram. Fables be damned, she is a vision.

From across The Lily Pond, Cove stands beneath the bleary margins and echoing splash of the waterfall overhang. Unaware of my arrival, she faces away from me and runs her fingers through a curtain of teal locks. Brilliant tresses fall down her back, where the waterdrop pendant dangles and winks between the strands.

Her glistening skin is a lodestar. Her hair is a wave of bright blue ripples. Her necklace is a golden flame, like the burning wick of a candle.

I may not see anything else in this world, not the way others do. But I see her.

I see my light.

Damnation. She is more stunning than I had fantasized. Visions of Cove had plagued me long before I ever touched her. Like a fever dream, the images had twisted my thoughts into knots whenever and wherever I slept, be it on a riverbank or a suite in The Twisted Canals.

How I'd hated this female for that. How I'd wanted her.

Oftentimes, I had caught myself reaching out when I sensed Cove was not looking. I had yearned to feel her, to grab her in my arms, to take her swiftly and tirelessly.

Under the moss overhang, a smaller flux pours from a crack. It races down her arms, charges across the hourglass of her hips, and showers over the swells of her beautiful ass. My throat dries, a rare occurrence for me. This mortal has no idea what she does to my sanity, for the bewitchment has never ceased.

Fuck, I cannot look away. From the beginning, I have never been able to tear myself away. Not from her scent or the blood coursing through her. Not from her ramblings or her voice. Not from the bittersweet sound of her laugh or the hot intake of her breath. Not from her compassion or kindness.

Against those weapons, I have never stood a chance. They are my undoing and my lifelines.

Cove lathers her tresses, suds frothing from the crown of her head. She's using the serum I brewed for her. The perfume of it travels across the grass to me, pulling a groan from my chest.

My eyes narrow on the half-moon glimpse of a breast. There and then, I lose all respect for the concept of patience.

I dig into my robe pocket and toss the vial into the pond. Then I strip off my leggings, shrug off the robe, and let it fall as my unshod feet prowl across the lawn. Descending to my calves, I step under the barrage and through a screen of mist. Installing myself behind Cove, I loom inches from her drenched body, a tail of water separating us.

Before I can seize her, Cove leans backward and settles her plush body against my torso. "Vicious creature," she quips as the slender torrent quivers down her front. "Were you trying to slither up on me?"

I relax against her softness and settle my palms on her waist. My voice lowers, on the feral side of guttural. "How did you know?"

"I'm learning," Cove answers.

Yes, she is. This bewitcher is growing increasingly attuned to the signs of my approach, a thought that dabs the crook of my lips.

"Oh," she teases. "Do I detect a smile?"

I smother the instinct with a grunt. "Hold still."

Cove is about to ask why, but my fingers winding through her hair stifle the impulse. I massage the roots to produce more foam. She sighs in appreciation as I knead the layers. While the cascade falls around us, I wash and rinse her hair until she melts fully into me, the press of her ass into my cock threatening my self-control.

Her knowing chuckle filters through the air. At which point, I'm done with this.

With a growl, I spin her around. She smiles at me, her eyes luminescent rings of teal that rob me of oxygen and restraint. I haul her into my arms, forcing her limbs to link around my waist.

With her astride me, I maneuver us into the pond, where my legs shift into a viper's tail. Cove stares at me while fondling my mane. The endearing contact temporarily mellows my appetite for her. Inspired, I circle the pond, coasting us through the lily pads.

"You didn't wake me," she says.

"You needed sleep," I tell her.

"I could say the same."

"I had a good reason."

"You had better. How long ago did you get home?"

Home. The word chips at a spot inside my chest, a fortification that was once impenetrable. At the north end of the bank stands a large hut wrought of stone and glass, with a dock jutting from the front steps. I cannot see it, but I know its shape, hear its subtle creaks, and smell its newness in this cave. Several times, Cove has also described it to me.

My brothers, Cove's sisters, and the river Faeries who haven't isolated themselves from us helped with the construction. We finished erecting the house several days ago, though it would have taken longer if Faeries lacked speed.

Likewise, this accounts for why my den has been refurbished so swift-ly. As for the rest of The Deep, the restoration is vaster and has been less expedient.

I fail to detect Lotus in the vicinity. Not only does the snake reside with us, but he shadows Cove everywhere. If the creature is not swim-ming in this pond, he must be nesting inside.

I tuck a lock of teal beneath Cove's rounded ear. "I only just arrived."

She winds her arms around my neck. "Wonderful. Then you're not going anywhere for the rest of the night. From this second forth, I'm claiming you all to myself. Not that I haven't claimed you officially, but I mean, especially for what's left of this evening. As it is, we haven't been keeping to the normal dawn and dusk routines, which makes sense with everything that needs to be done, but still, we've been making progress. This is all to say, it's going to be fine. Between reinforcing The Deep and meeting with your brothers, my sisters, and our allies, a respite is over-due for whatever lies ahead. I have demands, and this is one of them. That's the rule."

"Is that so?"

Cove nods. "If we want to do right by our worlds, we need a break, if only for a few days."

The canals are functioning again—somewhat.

The fauna habitats are being revived—slowly.

We found Cerulean's javelin, my daggers, and my harp—all mangled and being painstakingly repaired.

Cove has redrawn The Deep's map. This time, she has pressed points into the lines, enabling my fingers to trace the geography.

Though, regions that were once whole are now broken into segments, due to the environment's destruction. We are rebuilding, yet I have doubts whether this land or its inhabitants will ever be the same. The thought forces my knuckles to clench, fury stinging the tips of my fingers. However often Cove tamps down the reflex, anger still lives and breathes within me, eager to be unleashed on the next enemy that comes our way.

Fables help any fucking idiot who dares come near my light.

Scorpio, for one. He is blind but still out there, as are other enraged Faeries.

I seek out Cove's face, which staunches the urge to pulverize something. "A break," I recap with a smirk. "Tell that to your sister."

Cove sighs. "Juniper is an overachiever who hates loose ends, but I know how to calm her down, and Puck knows how to distract her."

"I bet the little shit does," I remark.

"Little isn't a word I'd associate with that bulky satyr," she jokes.

It has taken a while to grow accustomed to Cove's facial expressions, to interpret their meanings without shutting my eyes and tracing them. From what I can deduce, an inquisitive thought slants her expression. "This is overdue, but I've been meaning to ask. What did you hear when you shook hands with Juniper?"

I must seem flummoxed, because she explains. "In The Kelpie Rapids, just before the flood. You agreed to join the campaign and sealed Juniper's terms with a handshake, but right after that, you gave her this puzzled look, or maybe it was a startled look. Then on reflex, you nearly blinded her. It was as if you'd heard something inside Juniper, in her blood or temperature. I know that look, and whenever we see her, you do the same thing." Cove looks worried. "Is something wrong? Is she ill?"

Shit. Realization dawns.

Cove is right. I had heard a noise—something floating through her sister's womb, as tiny as a seed. The sound had unfurled, though it had taken me a bit longer to speculate on what it was. For it is a rare occurrence in Faerie and a phenomenon in Juniper's case, with her being human.

That I see what others cannot is true. Call it instinct. But from the shape, size, and sound of what I'd detected, it can be only one possibility.

However, this secret belongs to Juniper. It belongs to her and Puck.

They might already know. Or they might not, as such conditions take longer to develop and become recognizable in a world of immortals.

Either way, I cannot speak unless they do first. Or unless it becomes crucial. But fuck, I must tell Cove something.

I maneuver my words into position, reshaping the truth without betraying her. "Juniper is well," I assure Cove. "I heard something potent within her, a sort of newfound strength burgeoning from her union with Puck. You have no cause to be alarmed."

At least, I hope not.

Cove scans my face, her eyes slitting. "You promise?"

I brush her lips with my own. "I promise you should not worry."

At least, not yet.

At present, I sense no harm. Whether it stays that way is another matter.

The pond douses this cave in blue. The floating lilies pulse with white.

I nestle Cove closer, her enticing breasts rubbing against my flesh. "During this respite, whatever shall we do with each other?"

A grin wreathes across her face. "Show me again what darkness is like."

Oh, with relish. I swat my fingers through the ripples, and the pond answers my request. Thereupon, I sense when the watery sheen and glowing lilies snuff out like candles.

As it should be, Cove becomes the only thing brightening this cave.

While cloaked in the murk, my rasp tracks across her mouth. "Darkness comes in many shapes and colors, like a moving spectrum of blacks." I nibble on her lower lip. "Swatches of ebony. Puddles of oil black." I sweep beneath her jaw and nip the skin. "Spider-black streaks. Raven shades. Sooty shadows."

My blood hums as I ascend to her earlobe and snatch the flesh between my teeth. Cove's moan skitters through the air. She clutches me tighter, the abrasion of her cunt against my cock sending a bolt of need through me.

Not yet, I warn myself. For the vial is still bobbing somewhere across the surface. With a dash of my fingers, I draw the container in our direction.

Meanwhile, I hiss against her skin, "And sometimes, the darkness comes in the shape of a bottle." The vial slides into my waiting grip, and I pull back to watch her face in the shadows, the sight quickening my pulse. "And in that bottle is an even deeper hue."

Cove blinks as I set the glass container in her palm. "What's this?" she asks.

"Happy birthday," I murmur.

Her face transforms, teal eyes shimmering with surprise and amusement. "But you already gave me—"

"Several times, hours ago. Yes, I remember."

Despite the murk, pink drenches her cheeks. "I meant the spear case."

To celebrate her twentieth year, I had gifted Cove with a case for her weapon, as well as a rapid succession of orgasms.

I wheel my arms backward, ferrying us to the dock fronting the hut. At the ledge, I hoist her onto the planks, then haul myself out of the water, my tail shifting into legs. I settle behind Cove, tucking her against my chest. Naked, I beseech the pond to illuminate itself once more, then perch my chin on her shoulder and whisper from behind, "This gift took longer."

"So, that's what you were doing in the den," she concludes while gazing at the vial. "You know, the Fables warn humans about accepting presents from Faeries."

"My price will be pleasurable."

At the husk in my tone, her flesh prickles. "You were mentioning the color black, but the liquid is clear."

"Turn it upside down."

Cove does as bid and gasps. I hear swirls of black and pearlescent white curling through the fluid, the colors saturating the contents with lightness and darkness.

"It's beautiful," she says.

I clear my swollen throat. "It is an elixir."

"For what?"

I make no reply, letting the silence fill this void until she goes rigid, then whips toward me. Her head snaps over her shoulder, and her eyes sting. "Oh…oh, my Fables. Elixir, did you…"

My hands cradle her face. "I mentioned once being the ancestor of an unseelie witch and the son of two mermaids who loved to brew. One instilled the art in my blood. The others taught me everything I know."

The vial's contents will keep Cove alive and ageless for as long as she wishes. One drop on the tongue shall yield an extra hundred years. Should she require more, I will brew more.

I tell Cove how the final necessary ingredient had become clear: I'd needed a piece of her. The bead of perspiration had completed the mixture to create an elixir for an extended life.

We cannot be mated through fate. I cannot give her half of my immortality. But I can give her this.

The curse separates us. But potions can cure that.

If one is clever, there are methods to skirt the rules. As a Fae, I know this.

Cove's face twitches in ways that escape me. Is she happy? Is she furious?

She has chosen this life. Yet I cannot be certain if she'll want it forever, if given the opportunity.

I might suffocate from her response. She might drown me, as she had sworn to do long ago.

Cove's chin trembles. "Truly?"

"Truly," I say. "If you want this, it is yours."

If you want me eternally, I am yours.

Make your choice.

Please.

My muscles tense. I steel myself, awaiting her decision.

Her eyes simmer, kindling with blue flames. "Yes."

I blink. It takes a moment—one fraction of a moment—for the reply to soak in and reach my lungs. When it does, my chest hitches as though a chink has broken loose. A humid gust of air blows from my mouth.

"Yes?" I ask. "That is your choice?"

"That's my choice." Her teary laugh rings through the cave. "Can't you tell?"

Her joy ripples through my ears like a spring, her blood flows through her veins, and her body warms against mine. Cove perches sideways on my lap. Together, we uncap the vial. Whiffs of jasmine saturate the air as she extends her tongue.

My retinas spark. With our gazes pinned, I overturn the bottle. A droplet falls on her palate.

"Swallow," I rasp.

As she does, her slender throat contorts. I imagine the elixir dissolving inside her. Instantly, those teal eyes flash, and her complexion flushes.

It is done.

But no, we are far from done. And she knows it.

We stare at one another. Voracious. Possessive. Her fingers climb my abdomen, the nails digging into the flesh of my shoulders.

"Kiss me," she whispers.

I obey. Cupping the back of her head, I sink my mouth into hers. We fuse into one, tilting and burrowing deeply. I lick the seam of her lips until they split, my tongue striking into her. Fables help me, even her moan tastes sweet. The effect oozes like nectar and pools into my cock. And when she curls that little tongue with mine, my blood surges.

We move at the same time. Hectic, she scrambles astride my waist as I yank her into me. Our mouths slant, lock, and undulate. My tongue flexes with hers, the pace frantic. She writhes atop my prick, grinding her folds and ass on me, to the point of pain. Between her quavering thighs, the molten humidity radiating from her cunt drives me to madness.

"Fuck," I seethe.

"Now," she answers.

Yes. I'm going to feast on her. I'm going to fill her so thoroughly with my cock, she will have no room left inside. I'm going to drain her of every last moan.

On a growl, I yank her so close, her legs splay wide around my waist. The viper in me takes over. Trapping her like this, with her body at my disposal, I arch her backward. Her breasts swell into the air, her nipples toughening into shells.

Leaning over, I seize the first nipple between my teeth. A broken cry vaults from her mouth. The whimpering sounds multiply as I swathe my tongue over the erect peak, tracing until it's crimson and ruched to my satisfaction. With a hum, my mouth fastens around the second puckered nipple, then sucks.

I repeat the motions, exerting pressure. All the while, my tongue flicks at the crest, lapping the morsel into a tight bud. I feed on it the way I have devoured the dainty protrusion of skin between her legs.

Cove's mouth falls open, plaintive whines leaping from her lips. She clutches my skull and gyrates into me, her hips rolling. Wetness leaks from the cleft of her thighs and coats the distended head of my cock.

My length stands high, the stiff flesh aching for her. Good, for I want this to hurt. I want this to be excruciating, so that when I sink into her, it is earned.

I draw on her nipples, then nip them, then suck her into another stupor. But when the folds of her body part around my crown, we rock into motion.

I haul Cove upright just as she vaults toward me. Rather than facing one another, she wheels toward the pond, aligning her back with my torso. The maneuver is equally bashful and ambitious.

My mouth ticks. So, that is what she wants.

Cove raises her arms behind her and latches onto my nape. The instant she wiggles her ass into my prick, I hiss and catch her hips. I reach around to spread her thighs over mine, positioning her damp slot above my shaft. The area drenches with heat and a pulsating tension.

My canines grind. Fables almighty, she's dripping on me.

I bite the top of her ear, then murmur, "Breathe for me."

And my hips pitch upward. Cove gives a hard cry as my cock lunges into her dark, sweet core. Her frame bows, her head lolling on my shoulder.

My forehead lands on her temple. I groan with her, the hot slickness of her walls sealing around me. We pause on the brink, drag air into our lungs, and savor the feeling.

Then we throw ourselves into it.

With measured thrusts, I pump my length into her. Cove angles her hips and catches every rotation of my waist. Our moans converge, in cadence with our heaving movements.

Cove's walls clamp around me. They wet me from stem to crown.

With one hand, I grab her hip. With the other, I palm a jostling breast.

Pinning her to me like this, I snap my waist, widening the clutch, opening her. She takes it so exquisitely. My stomach bunches with each swipe of my cock. I tug her into it, and she rides my lap, straddling me broader.

That's it, my light. Let me in. Make that choice.

Cove chants my name. "Elixir."

I groan her name. "Cove."

My lips part on a silent "Ah." I accelerate, fucking into her with quick lurches of my cock. All the while, I twist and watch her profile.

I see her jut from the impact. I see her face crease with ecstasy. I see what I do to her.

I see it.

The vision sets me ablaze. I bury myself deeper, faster, rougher.

Using all my strength, I heft myself into the effort. Cove sobs, high. I grunt, low. We crash helplessly against one another, lost to the swift rhythm. We chase the depth, driving deeply. Our waists beat, my cock and her cunt slamming hard.

The head of my prick throbs. Her soaked body cinches around it, welcoming the onslaught.

Our groans amplify into hollers. The noises quake through the cave.

Cove turns, her mouth straining. My lips claim hers while our lower bodies swivel, my hardness probing her wetness. Her tongue wraps around mine, the contact shattering my heart to pieces.

The kiss explodes. She keens into my mouth, our tongues whisking.

My hand falls from her breast to land on her other hip, securing her as I ply my length in and out. The torturous climax veers out of reach. We hurl ourselves toward that precipice, jutting our bodies toward the release.

It heightens, turning our moans into gravel. The sounds fray, tearing at the seams.

Cove's walls tense. She grips me, her arousal running free from between her legs. At last, I find the liquid spot inside her and charge forth. My cock propels through, slinging deep, deeper, deeper still—until the convulsion hits.

She cries out, her body coming in a sequence of quivering jolts. Her inner muscles contort around my cock, squeezing me to the hilt. I double my efforts, launching into her, ripping every last moan from her tongue.

Again. Again. Again.

With a final shuddering thrust, the spasms unleash. My frame racks, a burst of fluid heat rushing from my cock. A roar catapults from my lips and shoots to the rafters, where it collides with her moan.

We slump in a boneless heap. Cove lands against me. I ring my arms around her, pressing her nearer.

For a while, we recover our breathing. Our feet sway through the water, rustling the surface. From nearby, I hear the curtains shifting in the windows of our home.

Cove rests her head beneath my jaw. "What's your true name?"

It is a bold question. To bestow that knowledge would grant the listener power over me, which is how Juniper was able to share Puck's immortality. Notwithstanding, because the curse ensures no other magic exists between Cove and me, there is no such advantage or risk.

Though, that is not why I haven't told her my true name. The reason is simple.

"I have none," I tell her. "None but the one I gave myself."

My mothers called me their son, nothing more until I grew old enough to decide what to call myself. They did not live long enough to hear the name, yet I know they would have favored it.

Cove twists to look at me, her face flushed and happy. "I love your name."

My forehead rests against hers. "I love yours, too."

She brushes my eyelashes. My mouth lifts at the corners, for her eyes only.

I could love her like this for an immortal lifetime. I *will* love her like this.

That's my choice.

I have shown her the darkness. Now she has shown me the light.

Continue with the heart-stopping series conclusion in book 4!

Vicious Faeries #4

Never Miss a Release!
Get new release alerts, exclusive content, and wicked details about my
books by subscribing to my newsletter at:
www.nataliajaster.com/newsletter

Author's Note

Oh, Elixir and Cove. How this couple lured me in.

Their romance was a beautiful mixture of quiet strength and dark vulnerability. I love how deeply they went together, how Cove's kindness became its own empowering force, and how Elixir slowly opened himself to emotions he'd never felt before. As the most fragile relationship of the three, theirs was a unique story.

For this one, I took another step out of my comfort zone. And I'm so grateful I did. In the end, the emotional reward was so very worth it.

I hope you adore these two as much as I do.

And I hope you're excited for the fourth and final book! This wasn't planned, but partway through writing *Curse the Fae*, I realized I wouldn't have room to continue the battle between Faeries and humans, much less wrap up the subplots and give these couples the conclusion they deserve. So yes, one more spicy installment is coming, where all the characters from the last three books will join together. Get ready for all the feels!

As always, I've got one hell of a magical ensemble to thank.

Hugs to my unicorn-shaped constellation of friends and betas: Michelle, Jessa, and Candace.

To my family, for your unconditional support.

To Roman, my beloved (and wicked) mate.

And to my incredible readers. To my ARC team, the Myths & Tricksters FB group, the Vicious Faeries spoiler group, and everyone who has opened my books. Thank you, eternally.

See you in the Solitary wild for the epic series conclusion! I can't freakin' wait. And neither can Cerulean, Puck, and Elixir…

About Natalia

Natalia Jaster is a fantasy romance author who routinely swoons for the villain.

She lives in a dark forest, where she writes steamy New Adult tales about rakish jesters, immortal deities, and vicious fae. Wicked heroes are her weakness, and rebellious heroines are her best friends.

When she's not writing, you'll probably find her perched atop a castle tower, guzzling caramel apple tea, and counting the stars.

⸙

Come say hi!

Bookbub: www.bookbub.com/authors/natalia-jaster
Facebook: www.facebook.com/NataliaJasterAuthor
Instagram: www.instagram.com/nataliajaster
TikTok: www.tiktok.com/@nataliajasterauthor
Website: https://www.nataliajaster.com

See the boards for Natalia's novels on
Pinterest: www.pinterest.com/andshewaits

Printed in the USA
CPSIA information can be obtained
at www.ICGtesting.com
LVHW040756250124
769463LV00005B/585